NORA ROBERTS

ANGELS
FALL

THORNDIKE
WINDSOR
PARAGON

This Large Print edition is published by Thorndike Press®, Waterville, Maine USA and by BBC Audiobooks Ltd, Bath, England.

Published in 2006 in the U.S. by arrangement with G. P. Putnam's Sons, a division of Penguin Group (USA) Inc.

Published in 2006 in the U.K. by arrangement with Judy Piatkus (Publishers) Ltd.

U.S. Hardcover   0-7862-8829-9   (Basic)
U.K. Hardcover 10: 1 4056 1506 0   (Windsor Large Print)
U.K. Hardcover 13: 978 1 405 61506 8
U.K. Softcover 10: 1 4056 1507 9   (Paragon Large Print)
U.K. Softcover 13: 978 1 405 61507 5

While the author has made every effort to provide accurate telephone numbers and Internet addresses at the time of publication, neither the publisher nor the author assumes any responsibility for errors, or for changes that occur after publication. Further, the publisher does not have any control over and does not assume any responsibility for author or third-party websites or their content.

The text of this Large Print edition is unabridged. Other aspects of the book may vary from the original edition.

Set in 16 pt. Plantin.

Printed in the United States on permanent paper.

British Library Cataloguing-in-Publication Data available

Library of Congress Cataloging-in-Publication Data

Roberts, Nora.
    Angels fall / by Nora Roberts. — Large print ed.
      p. cm.
    "Thorndike Press Large Print Basic" — T.p. verso.
    ISBN 0-7862-8829-9 (lg. print : hc : alk. paper)
    1. Large type books.   2. Wyoming — Fiction.
  I. Title.
  PS3568.O243A84 2006b
   813′.54—dc22   2006018098

For Mom

SIGNPOSTS

Everywhere is nowhere.

— SENECA

1

Reece Gilmore smoked through the tough knuckles of Angel's Fist in an overheating Chevy Cavalier. She had two hundred forty-three dollars and change in her pocket, which might be enough to cure the Chevy, fuel it and herself. If luck was on her side, and the car wasn't seriously ill, she'd have enough to pay for a room for the night.

Then, even by the most optimistic calculations, she'd be broke.

She took the plumes of steam puffing out of the hood as a sign it was time to stop traveling for a while and find a job.

No worries, no problem, she told herself. The little Wyoming town huddled around the cold blue waters of a lake was as good as anywhere else. Maybe better. It had the openness she needed — all that sky with the snow-dipped peaks of the Tetons rising into it like sober, and somehow aloof, gods.

She'd been meandering her way toward them, through the Ansel Adams photograph of peaks and plains for hours. She hadn't had a clue where she'd end up when she started out that day before dawn, but she'd bypassed Cody, zipped through Dubois, and though she'd toyed with veering into Jackson, she dipped south instead.

So something must have been pulling her to this spot.

Over the past eight months, she'd developed a strong belief in following signs and impulses. Dangerous Curves, Slippery When Wet. It was nice that someone took the time and effort to post those kinds of warnings. Other signs might be a peculiar slant of sunlight aimed down a back road, or a weather vane pointing south.

If she liked the look of the light or the weather vane, she'd follow, until she found what seemed like the right place at the right time. She might settle in for a few weeks, or, like she had in South Dakota, a few months. Pick up some work, scout the area, then move on when those signs, those impulses, pointed in a new direction.

There was a freedom in the system she'd developed, and often — more often now — a lessening of the constant hum of anxiety in the back of her mind. These past months of living with herself, essentially by herself, had done more to smooth her out than the full year of therapy.

To be fair, she supposed the therapy had given her the base to face herself every single day. Every night. And all the hours between.

And here was another fresh start, another blank slate in the bunched fingers of Angel's Fist.

If nothing else, she'd take a few days to enjoy the lake, the mountains, and pick up enough money to get back on the road again. A place like this — the signpost had said the population was 623 — probably ran to tourism, exploiting the scenery and the proximity to the national park.

There'd be at least one hotel, likely a couple of B and B's, maybe a dude ranch within a few miles. It might be fun to work at a dude ranch. All those places would need someone to fetch and carry and clean, especially now that the spring thaw was dulling the sharpest edge of winter.

But since her car was now sending out thicker, more desperate smoke signals, the first priority was a mechanic.

She eased her way along the road that ribboned around the long, wide lake. Patches of snow made dull white pools in the shade. The trees were still their wintering brown, but there were a few boats on the water. She could see a couple guys in windbreakers and caps in a white canoe, rowing right through the reflection of the mountains.

Across from the lake was what she decided was the business district. Gift shop, a little gallery. Bank, post office, she noted. Sheriff's office.

She angled away from the lake to pull the laboring car up to what looked like a big barn of a general store. There were a couple men in flannel shirts sitting out front in stout chairs that gave them a good view of the lake.

They nodded to her as she cut the engine and stepped out, then the one on the right tapped the brim of his blue cap that bore the name of the store — Mac's Mercantile and Grocery — across the crown.

"Looks like you got some trouble there, young lady."

"Sure does. Do you know anyone who can give me a hand with it?"

He laid his hands on his thighs and pushed out of the chair. He was burly in build, ruddy in face, with lines fanning out from the corners of friendly brown eyes. When he spoke, his voice was a slow, meandering drawl.

"Why don't we just pop the hood and take a look-see?"

"Appreciate it." When she released the latch, he tossed the hood up and stepped back from the clouds of smoke. For reasons she couldn't name, the plumes and the fuss caused Reece more embarrassment than anxiety. "It started up on me about ten miles east, I guess. I wasn't paying enough attention. Got caught up in the scenery."

"Easy to do. You heading into the park?"

"I was. More or less." Not sure, never sure, she thought and tried to concentrate on the moment rather than the before or after. "I think the car had other ideas."

His companion came over to join them, and both men looked under the hood the way Reece knew men did. With sober eyes and knowing frowns. She looked with them, though she accepted that she was as much of a cliché. The female to whom what lurked under the hood of a car was as foreign as the terrain of Pluto.

"Got yourself a split radiator hose," he told her. "Gonna need to replace that."

Didn't sound so bad, not too bad. Not too expensive. "Anywhere in town I can make that happen?"

"Lynt's Garage'll fix you up. Why don't I give him a call for you?"

"Lifesaver." She offered a smile and her hand, a gesture that had come to be much easier for her with strangers. "I'm Reece, Reece Gilmore."

"Mac Drubber. This here's Carl Sampson."

"Back East, aren't you?" Carl asked. He looked a fit fifty-something to Reece, and with some Native American blood mixed in once upon a time.

"Yeah. Way back. Boston area. I really appreciate the help."

"Nothing but a phone call," Mac said.

"You can come on in out of the breeze if you want, or take a walk around. Might take Lynt a few to get here."

"I wouldn't mind a walk, if that's okay. Maybe you could tell me a good place to stay in town. Nothing fancy."

"Got the Lakeview Hotel just down a ways. The Teton House, other side of the lake's some homier. More a B and B. Some cabins along the lake, and others outside of town rent by the week or the month."

She didn't think in months any longer. A day was enough of a challenge. And *homier* sounded too intimate. "Maybe I'll walk down and take a look at the hotel."

"It's a long walk. Could give you a ride on down."

"I've been driving all day. I could use the stretch. But thanks, Mr. Drubber."

"No problem." He stood another moment as she wandered down the wooden sidewalk. "Pretty thing," he commented.

"No meat on her." Carl shook his head. "Women today starve off all the curves."

She hadn't starved them off, and was, in fact, making a concerted effort to gain back the weight that had fallen off in the past couple of years. She'd gone from health club fit to scrawny and had worked her way back to what she thought of as gawky. Too many angles and points, too many bones. Every time she undressed, her body was like that of a stranger to her.

She wouldn't have agreed with Mac's *pretty thing.* Not anymore. Once she'd thought of herself that way, as a pretty woman — stylish, sexy when she wanted to be. But her face seemed too hard now, the cheekbones too prominent, the hollows too deep. The restless nights were fewer, but when they came, they left her dark eyes heavily shadowed, and cast a pallor, pasty and gray, over her skin.

She wanted to recognize herself again.

She let herself stroll, her worn-out Keds nearly soundless on the sidewalk. She'd learned not to hurry — had taught herself not to push, not to rush, but to take things as they came. And in a very real way to embrace every single moment.

The cool breeze blew across her face, wound through the long brown hair she'd tied back in a tail. She liked the feel of it, the smell of it, clean and fresh, and the hard light that poured over the Tetons and sparked on the water.

She could see some of the cabins Mac had spoken of, through the bare branches of the willows and the cottonwoods. They squatted behind the trees, log and glass, wide porches — and, she assumed, stunning views.

It might be nice to sit on one of those

porches and study the lake or the mountains, to watch whatever visited the marsh where cattails speared up out of the bog. To have that room around, and the quiet.

One day maybe, she thought. But not today.

She spotted green spears of daffodils in a half whiskey barrel next to the entrance to a restaurant. They might have trembled a bit in the chilly breeze, but they made her think spring. Everything was new in spring. Maybe this spring, she'd be new, too.

She stopped to admire the tender sprouts. It was comforting to see spring making its way back after the long winter. There would be other signs of it soon. Her guidebook boasted of miles of wildflowers on the sage flats, and more along the area's lakes and ponds.

She was ready for flowering, Reece thought. Ready for blooming.

Then she shifted her eyes up to the wide front window of the restaurant. More diner than restaurant, she corrected. Counter service, two- and four-tops, booths, all in faded red and white. Pies and cakes on display, and the kitchen open to the counter. A couple waitresses bustled around with trays and coffeepots.

Lunch crowd, she realized. She'd forgotten lunch. As soon as she'd taken a look at the hotel, she'd . . .

Then she saw it in the window, the sign, hand-lettered.

COOK WANTED
INQUIRE WITHIN

Signs, she thought again, though she'd taken a step back before she caught herself. She stood where she was, making a careful study of the setup from outside the glass. Open kitchen, she reminded herself, that was key. Diner food, she could handle that in her sleep. Or would have been able to, once.

Maybe it was time to find out, time to take another step forward. If she couldn't handle it, she'd know, and wouldn't be any worse off than she was now.

The hotel was probably hiring, in anticipation of the summer season. Or Mr. Drubber might need another clerk at his store.

But the sign was right there, and her car had aimed toward this town, and her steps had brought her to this spot, where daffodil shoots pushed out of the dirt into the first hesitant breaths of spring.

She backtracked to the door, took a long, long breath in, then opened it.

Fried onions, grilling meat — on the gamey side — strong coffee, a jukebox on country and a buzz of table chatter.

Clean red floors, she noted, scrubbed white counter. The few empty tables had their lunch setups. There were photographs on the walls — good ones to her eye. Black-and-whites of the lake, of white water, of the mountains in every season.

She was still getting her bearings, gathering her courage, when one of the waitresses swung by her. "Afternoon. You're looking for lunch you've got your choice of a table or the counter."

"Actually, I'm looking for the manager. Or owner. Ah, about the sign in the window. The position of cook."

The waitress stopped, still balancing a tray. "You're a cook?"

There'd been a time Reece would have sniffed at the term good-naturedly, but she'd have sniffed nonetheless. "Yes."

"That's handy, 'cause Joanie fired one a couple of days ago." The waitress curled her free hand, brought it up to her lips in the mime for drinking.

"Oh."

"Gave him the job in February when he came through town looking for work. Said he'd found Jesus and was spreading his word across the land."

She cocked her head and her hip and gave Reece a sunny smile out of a pretty face. "He preached the Word, all right, like a disciple on crack, so you wanted to stuff

18

a rag in his mouth. Then I guess he found the bottle, and that was that. So. Why don't you go right on and sit up at the counter. I'll see if Joanie can get out of the kitchen for a minute. How about some coffee?"

"Tea, if you don't mind."

"Coming up."

Didn't have to take the job, Reece reminded herself as she slid onto a chrome-and-leather stool and rubbed her damp palms dry on the thighs of her jeans. Even if it was offered, she didn't have to take it. She could stick with cleaning hotel rooms, or head out and find that dude ranch.

The juke switched numbers, and Shania Twain announced joyfully she felt like a woman.

The waitress walked back to the grill and tapped a short sturdy woman on the shoulder, leaned in. After a moment, the woman shot a glance over her shoulder, met Reece's eyes, then nodded. The waitress came back to the counter with a white cup of hot water, with a Lipton tea bag in the saucer.

"Joanie'll be right along. You want to order some lunch? Meatloaf's house special today. Comes with mashed potatoes and green beans and a biscuit."

"No, thanks, no, tea's fine." She'd never be able to hold anything more down, not with the nerves bouncing around in her belly. The panic wanted to come with it, that smothering wet weight in the chest.

She should just go, Reece thought. Go right now and walk back to her car. Get the hose fixed and head out. Signs be damned.

Joanie had a fluff of blond hair on her head, a white butcher's apron splattered with grease stains tied around her middle and high-topped red Converse sneakers on her feet. She walked out from the kitchen wiping her hands on a dishcloth.

And she measured Reece out of steely eyes that were more gray than blue.

"You cook?" A smoker's rasp made the brisk question oddly sensual.

"Yes."

"For a living, or just to put something in your mouth?"

"It's what I did back in Boston — for a living." Fighting nerves, Reece ripped open the cover on the tea bag.

Joanie had a soft mouth, almost a Cupid's bow, in contrast to those hard eyes. And an old, faded scar, Reece noted, that ran along her jawline from her left ear nearly to her chin.

"Boston." In an absent move, Joanie tucked the dishrag in the belt of her apron. "Long ways."

"Yes."

"I don't know as I want some East Coast cook who can't keep her mouth shut for five minutes."

Reece's opened in surprise, then closed again on the barest curve of a smile. "I'm an awful chatterbox when I'm nervous."

"What're you doing around here?"

"Traveling. My car broke down. I need a job."

"Got references?"

Her heart tightened, a sweaty fist of silent pain. "I can get them."

Joanie sniffed, frowned back toward the kitchen. "Go on back, put on an apron. Next order up's a steak sandwich, med-well, onion roll, fried onions and mush-rooms, fries and slaw. Dick don't drop dead after eating what you cook, you probably got the job."

"All right." Reece pushed off the stool and, keeping her breath slow and even, went through the swinging door at the far end of the counter.

She didn't notice, but Joanie did, that she'd torn the tea bag cover into tiny pieces.

It was a simple setup, she decided, and efficient enough. Large grill, restaurant-style stove, refrigerator, freezer. Holding bins, sinks, work counters, double fryer, heat suppression system. As she tied on an apron, Joanie set out the ingredients she'd need.

"Thanks." Reece scrubbed her hands, then got to work.

Don't think, she told herself. Just let it come. She set the steak sizzling on the grill while she chopped onions and mushrooms. She put the precut potatoes in the fry basket, set the timer.

Her hands didn't shake, and though her chest stayed tight, she didn't allow herself to dart glances over her shoulder to make sure a wall hadn't appeared to close her in.

She listened to the music, from the juke, from the grill, from the fryer.

Joanie tugged the next order from the clip on the round and slapped it down. "Bowl of three-bean soup — that kettle there — goes with crackers."

Reece simply nodded, tossed the mushrooms and onions on the grill, then filled the second order while they fried.

"Order up!" Joanie called out, and yanked another ticket. "Reuben, club san, two side salads."

Reece moved from order to order, and just let it happen. The atmosphere, the orders might be different, but the rhythm was the same. Keep working, keep moving.

She plated the original order, turned to hand it to Joanie for inspection.

"Put it in line," she was told. "Start the next ticket. We don't call the doctor in the next thirty minutes, you're hired.

We'll talk money and hours later."

"I need to —"

"Get that next ticket," Joanie finished. "I'm going to go have a smoke."

She worked another ninety minutes before it slowed enough for Reece to step back from the heat and guzzle down a bottle of water. When she turned, Joanie was sitting at the counter, drinking coffee.

"Nobody died," she said.

"Whew. Is it always that busy?"

"Saturday lunch crowd. We do okay. You get eight dollars an hour to start. You still look good in two weeks, I bump in another buck an hour. That's you and me and a part-timer on the grill, seven days a week. You get two days, or the best part of two off during that week. I do the schedule a week in advance. We open at six-thirty, so that means first shift is here at six. You can order breakfast all day, lunch menu from eleven to closing, dinner, five to ten. You want forty hours a week, I can work you that. I don't pay any overtime, so you get stuck behind the grill and go over, we'll take it off your next week's hours. Any problem with that?"

"No."

"You drink on the job, you're fired on the spot."

"Understood."

"You get all the coffee, water or tea you

want. You hit the soft drinks, you pay for them. Same with the food. Around here, there ain't no free lunch. Not that it looks like you'll be packing it away while my back's turned. You're skinny as a stick."

"I guess I am."

"Last shift cook cleans the grill, the stove, does the lock down."

"I can't do that," Reece interrupted. "I can't close for you. I can open, I can work any shift you want me to work. I'll work doubles when you need it, split shifts. I can flex time when you need me over forty. But I can't close for you. I'm sorry."

Joanie raised her eyebrows, sipped down the last of her coffee. "Afraid of the dark, little girl?"

"Yes, I am. If closing's part of the job description, I'll have to find another job."

"We'll work that out. We've got forms to fill out for the government. It can wait. Your car's fixed, sitting up at Mac's." Joanie smiled. "Word travels, and I've got my ear to the ground. You're looking for a place, there's a room over the diner I can rent you. Not much, but it's got a good view and it's clean."

"Thanks, but I think I'm going to try the hotel for now. We'll both give it a couple of weeks, see how it goes."

"Itchy feet."

"Itchy something."

"Your choice." With a shrug, Joanie got up, headed to the swinging door with her coffee cup. "You go on, get your car, get settled. Be back at four."

A little dazed, Reece walked out. She was back in a kitchen, and it had been all right. She'd been okay. Now that she'd gotten through it, she felt a little light-headed, but that was normal, wasn't it? A normal reaction to snagging a job, straight off the mark, doing what she was trained to do again. Doing what she hadn't been able to do for nearly two years.

She took her time walking back to her car, letting it all sink in.

When she walked into the mercantile, Mac was ringing up a sale at a short counter opposite the door. The place was what she'd expected: a little bit of every-thing — coolers for produce and meat, shelves of dry goods, a section for hard-ware, for housewares, fishing gear, ammo.

Need a gallon of milk and a box of bullets? This was the spot.

When Mac finished the transaction, she approached the counter.

"Car should run for you now," Mac told her.

"So I hear, and thanks. How do I pay?"

"Lynt left a bill here for you. You can run on by the garage if you're going to charge it. Paying cash, you can just leave it here. I'll be seeing him later."

"Cash is good." She took the bill, noted with relief it was less than she'd expected. She could hear someone chatting in the rear of the store, and the beep of another cash register. "I got a job."

He cocked his head as she pulled out her wallet. "That so? Quick work."

"At the diner. I don't even know the name of it," she realized.

"That'd be Angel Food. Locals just call it Joanie's."

"Joanie's then. I hope you come in sometime. I'm a good cook."

"I bet you are. Here's your change."

"Thanks. Thanks for everything. I guess I'll go get myself a room, then go back to work."

"If you're still looking at the hotel, you tell Brenda on the desk you want the monthly rate. You tell her you're working at Joanie's."

"I will. I'll tell her." She wanted to take out an ad announcing it in the local paper. "Thanks, Mr. Drubber."

The hotel was five stories of pale yellow stucco that boasted views of the lake. It harbored a minute sundry shop, a tiny coffee and muffin stand and an intimate linen tablecloth dining room.

There was, she was told, high-speed Internet connection for a small daily fee, room service from seven a.m. to eleven p.m. and a self-service laundry in the basement.

Reece negotiated a weekly rate on a single — a week was long enough — on the third floor. Anything below the third was too accessible for her peace of mind, and anything above the third made her feel trapped.

With her wallet now effectively empty, she carted her duffel and laptop up three flights rather than use the elevator.

The view lived up to its billing, and she immediately opened the windows, then just stood looking at the sparkle of the water, the glide of boats, and the rise of the mountains that cupped this little section of valley.

This was her place today, she thought. She'd find out if it was her place tomorrow. Turning back to the room, she noted the door that adjoined the neighboring guest room. She checked the locks, then pushed, shoved, dragged the single dresser in front of it.

That was better.

She wouldn't unpack, not exactly, but take the essentials and set them out. The travel candle, some toiletries, the cell phone charger. Since the bathroom was hardly bigger than the closet, she left the door open while she took a quick shower.

While the water ran, she did the multiplication tables out loud to keep herself steady. She changed into fresh clothes, moving quickly.

New job, she reminded herself and took the time and effort to dry her hair, to put on a little makeup. Not so pale today, she decided, not so hollow-eyed.

After checking her watch, she set up her laptop, opened her daily journal and wrote a quick entry.

Angel's Fist, Wyoming
April 15
I cooked today. I took a job as a cook in a little diner-style restaurant in this pretty valley town with its big, blue lake. I'm popping champagne in my mind, and there are streamers and balloons.

I feel like I've climbed a mountain, like I've been scaling the tough peaks that ring this place. I'm not at the top yet; I'm still on a ledge. But it's sturdy and wide, and I can rest here a little while before I start to climb again.

I'm working for a woman named Joanie. She's short, sturdy and oddly pretty. She's tough, too, and that's good. I don't want to be coddled. I think I'd smother to death that way, just run out of air the way I feel when

I wake up from one of the dreams. I can breathe here, and I can be here until it's time to move on.

I've got less than ten dollars left, but whose fault is that? It's okay. I've got a room for a week with a view of the lake and the Tetons, a job and a new radiator hose.

I missed lunch, and that's a step back there. That's okay, too. I was too busy cooking to eat, and I'll make up for it.

It's a good day, April fifteenth. I'm going to work.

She shut down, then tucked her phone, her keys, driver's license and three dollars of what she had left in her pockets. Grabbing a jacket, she headed for the door.

Before she opened it, Reece checked the peep, scanned the empty hall. She checked her locks twice, cursed herself and checked a third time before she went back to her kit to tear a piece of Scotch tape off her roll. She pressed it over the door, well below eye level, before she walked to the door for the stairs.

She jogged down, counting as she went. After a quick debate, she left her car parked. Walking would save her gas money, even though it would be dark when she finished her shift.

Couple of blocks, that was all. Still, she fingered her key chain, and the panic button on it.

Maybe she should go back and get the car, just in case. Stupid, she told herself. She was nearly there. Think about now, not about later. When nerves began to bubble, she pictured herself at the grill. Good strong kitchen light, music from the jukebox, voices from the tables. Familiar sounds, smells, motion.

Maybe her palm was clammy when she reached for the door of Joanie's, but she opened it. And she went inside.

The same waitress she'd spoken to during the lunch shift spotted her, wiggled her fingers in a come-over motion. Reece stopped by the booth where the woman was refilling the condiment caddy.

"Joanie's back in the storeroom. She said I should give you a quick orientation when you came in. We got a lull, then the early birds will start coming in soon. I'm Linda-gail."

"Reece."

"First warning. Joanie doesn't tolerate idle hands. She catches you loitering, she'll jump straight down your back and bite your ass." She grinned when she said it in a way that made her bright blue eyes twinkle, deepened dimples in her cheeks. She had doll-baby blond hair to go with it, worn in smooth French braids.

She had on jeans, a red shirt with white piping. Silver and turquoise earrings dangled from her ears. She looked, Reece thought, like a western milkmaid.

"I like to work."

"You will, believe me. This being Saturday night, we'll be busy. You'll have two other wait staff working — Bebe and Juanita. Matt'll bus, and Pete's the dishwasher. You and Joanie'll be manning the kitchen, and she'll have a hawk eye on you. You need a break, you tell her, and you take it. There's a place in the back for your coat and purse. No purse?"

"No, I didn't bring it."

"God, I can't step a foot outside the house without mine. Come on then, I'll show you around. She's got the forms you need to fill out in the back. I guess you've done this kind of work before, the way you jumped in with both feet today."

"Yeah, I have."

"Restrooms. We clean the bathrooms on rotation. You've got a couple of weeks before you have that pleasure."

"Can't wait."

Linda-gail grinned. "You got family around here?"

"No. I'm from back East." Didn't want to talk about that, didn't want to think about that. "Who handles the fountain drinks?"

"Wait staff. We get crunched, you can fill drink orders. We serve wine and beer, too. But mostly people want to drink, they do it over at Clancy's. That's about it. Anything else you want to know, just give me a holler. I've got to finish the setups or Joanie'll squawk. Welcome aboard."

"Thanks."

Reece moved into the kitchen, took an apron.

A good, wide solid ledge, she told herself. A good place to stand until it was time to move again.

2

Linda-gail was right, they were busy. Locals, tourists, hikers, a scatter of people from a nearby campground who wanted an indoor meal. She and Joanie worked with little conversation while the fryers pumped out steam and the grill spewed heat.

At some point, Joanie stuck a bowl under Reece's nose. "Eat."

"Oh, thanks, but —"

"You got something against my soup?"

"No."

"Sit down at the counter and eat. It's slowed down some and you've got a break coming. I'll put it on your tab."

"Okay, thanks." The fact was, now that she thought about eating food instead of just preparing it, she realized she was starving. A good sign, Reece decided as she took a seat at the end of the counter.

It gave her a view of the diner, and the door.

Linda-gail slid a plate over to her with a sourdough roll and two pats of butter on it. "Joanie said you need the carbs. Want some tea with that?"

"Perfect. I can get it."

"I'm in the mode. You're quick," she

added as she brought over a cup. After a glance over her shoulder, she leaned closer and grinned. "Quicker than Joanie. And you plate food pretty. Some of the customers commented on it."

"Oh." She wasn't looking for comments or attention. Just a paycheck. "I didn't mean to change anything."

"Nobody's complaining." Linda-gail tilted her head with a smile that showed off her dimples. "Kind of jumpy, aren't you?"

"I guess I am." Reece sampled the soup, pleased that the broth had a subtle bite. "No wonder this place stays busy. This soup's as good as anything you'd get in a five-star."

Linda-gail glanced back toward the kitchen, assured herself Joanie was occupied. "Some of us have a bet going. Bebe thinks you're in trouble with the law. She watches a lot of TV, that one. Juanita thinks you're running from an abusive husband. Matthew, being seventeen, just thinks about sex. Me, I think you just got your heart broken back East. Any of us hit?"

"No, sorry." There was a little twinge of anxiety at the idea the others were speculating, but she reminded herself that restaurants were full of little dramas and a lot of gossip. "I'm just at loose ends, just traveling."

"Something in there," Linda-gail said with a shake of her head. "To my eye you got heartbreak written all over you. And speaking of heartbreakers, here comes Long, Dark and Handsome now."

He was long, Reece thought as she followed the direction of Linda-gail's gaze. A couple inches or so over six feet. She'd give him dark, too, with the shaggy jet hair and olive complexion. But she wasn't sold on handsome.

It was a word that meant slick and classy to her mind, and this man was neither. Instead, there was a rough, rugged look about him with a scruff of beard over rawboned features. Something rougher yet, to her mind, about the hard line of his mouth and the way his eyes tracked around the room. There was nothing slick about the battered leather jacket, faded jeans or worn-down boots.

Not the cowboy type, she decided, but one who looked like he could handle himself outdoors. He looked strong, and maybe just a little mean.

"Name's Brody," Linda-gail said in undertones. "He's a writer."

"Oh?" She relaxed a little. Something in his stance, his absolute awareness of the room, had said cop to her. Writer was better. Easier. "What kind?"

"He does magazine articles and like that,

and he's had *three* books published. Mysteries. Fits, too, because that's what he is. A mystery."

She flipped her hair back, shifted her angle so she could watch out of the corner of her eye as Brody strode to an empty booth. "Word is he used to work for a big newspaper in Chicago and got fired. He rents a cabin on the other side of the lake, keeps to himself, mostly. But he comes in here three times a week for dinner. Tips twenty percent."

She turned back to Reece as Brody sat. "How do I look?"

"Terrific."

"One of these days I'm going to figure out how to get him to hit on me, just to satisfy my curiosity. But for now, I'll take the twenty percent."

Linda-gail wandered toward the booth, drawing her pad out of her pocket. From where she sat, Reece could hear her cheerful greeting.

"How you doing, Brody? What do you have in mind for tonight?"

While she ate, Reece watched the waitress flirt, and the man Brody order without consulting the menu. When she turned away, Linda-gail shot Reece an exaggeratedly dreamy look. Even as Reece's lips quivered in response, Brody shifted his gaze, locked in on her face.

The full-on stare made her stomach jump. Even when she quickly averted her eyes she could feel his on her, rudely, deliberately probing. For the first time since she'd begun her shift, she felt exposed and vulnerable.

She pushed off the stool, stacked her dishes. Fighting the urge to look over her shoulder, she carried them back into the kitchen.

He ordered the elk chops and whiled away the wait time with a bottle of Coors and a paperback. Someone had paid for Emmylou Harris on the jukebox, and Brody let the music hum in the back of his mind.

He wondered about the brunette and that look in her eye. Richard Adams had coined the word *tharn* in *Watership Down*. Good word, he thought, and one that suited the new cook with her sudden, frozen stillness.

From what he knew of Joanie Parks, the brunette wouldn't have a job if she wasn't competent. He suspected Joanie had a soft heart under the shell, but that shell was thick and prickly, and didn't suffer fools.

Of course, he had only to ask the little blonde and he'd get chapter and verse on the newcomer. But then it would circle around that he'd asked, then others would ask him what he thought, what he knew. He knew how places like Angel's Fist worked, and the fuel of talk they ran on.

It would take a little longer to find out about her without asking, but there would be murmurs and comments, rumors and speculation. He had a good ear for that sort of thing when he was in the mood for it.

She had a fragile look about her, the sort that could turn on a dime to brittle. He wondered why.

Still, from his vantage point he could see he'd been right about competency. She worked steadily, in that professional cook's way that made it seem to him she had an extra pair of hands tucked away somewhere.

It might have been her first day on the job here, but he'd lay odds it wasn't her first in a restaurant kitchen. Since — at least for now — she was more interesting than his book, he continued to watch her work while he nursed his beer.

Not attached to anyone from town, he decided. He'd lived there the best part of a year and if anyone's long-lost daughter, sister, niece, third cousin twice removed was due to breeze in, he'd have gotten wind. She didn't look like a drifter to him. More like a runner, he mused. That was what he'd seen in her eyes, the wariness, the readiness to leap and dash at a moment's notice.

And when she moved to set a finished order in line, those eyes flicked in his direction — just a flick, then away again. Before she turned back to the grill, the door opened, and her gaze shifted there. The smile flashed onto her face so quickly, so unexpectedly, Brody actually blinked. Everything about her changed, went lighter, softer, so that he saw there was more — at least the potential for more — than fragile beauty tucked away in there.

When he looked over to see what had caused that mile-wide smile, he saw Mac Drubber shooting her a grin and a wave.

Maybe he'd been wrong about that local connection.

Mac slid into the booth across from him. "How's it going?"

"Can't complain."

"Got a hankering to eat something I don't have to fry up myself. What looks good tonight?" He waited a beat, wiggled his eyebrows. "Besides the new cook?"

"I ordered the chops. Don't see you in here on Saturday nights, Mac. You're a creature of habit, and that's Wednesdays, spaghetti special."

"Didn't feel like opening a can, and I wanted to see how the girl was doing.

Limped into town today with a broken radiator hose."

All you had to do was wait five minutes or so, Brody thought, and information fell into your lap. "Is that so?"

"Next thing you know, she's working here. You'd've thought she'd won the lottery by the look on her face. Comes from back East. Boston. Got herself a room at the hotel. Name's Reece Gilmore."

He stopped when Linda-gail brought Brody's plate to the table.

"Hi there, Mr. Drubber, how's it going? What can I get you tonight?"

Mac leaned over to take a closer look at Brody's plate. "That looks pretty damn good."

"The new cook's a real hand. You let me know how you like those chops, Brody. Get you anything else?"

"Take another beer."

"Coming right up. Mr. Drubber?"

"I'll take a Coke, honey, and the same thing my friend here's having. Those chops look good enough to eat."

They did, Brody thought, and were presented with a generous portion of scalloped potatoes and lima beans. The food was artistically arranged on the plain white plate, unlike the haphazard mounds Joanie normally served up.

"Saw you out in the boat the other day,"

Mac commented. "Catch anything?"

"Wasn't fishing." He cut into one of the chops, sampled.

"That's one of the things about you, Brody. You go on out on the lake now and then but you don't fish. Go out in the woods now and then but you don't hunt."

"If I caught anything or shot anything, I'd have to cook it."

"There's that. Well?"

"It's good." Brody cut another bite. "Pretty damn good."

Since Mac Drubber was one of the few people Brody would voluntarily spend an evening with, he loitered over his coffee while Mac finished plowing through his own meal. "Beans taste different. Fancier. Got to say better, too, but you repeat that where Joanie gets wind, I'll call you a stinking liar."

"She's putting up at the hotel, she may not be planning on staying long."

"Booked a week." Mac liked knowing what went on, and who it went on about, in his town. He not only ran the mercantile, he was mayor. Gossip, he liked to think, was part of his duties. "Truth is, Brody, I don't think the girl has much money." He wagged his fork at Brody before stabbing the last of the beans. "Paid cash for the radiator hose, and the hotel, I hear."

No credit cards, Brody mused, and wondered if the mystery woman was running under the radar. "Could be she doesn't want to leave a trail for someone, or something, to follow."

"You got a suspicious mind." Mac worked off the last sliver of elk from the bone. "And if she doesn't, she'll have a reason for it. She's got an honest face."

"And you have a romantic bent. Speaking of romance." Brody cocked his head toward the door.

The man who came in wore Levi's and a chambray shirt under a black barn coat. He accented it with snakeskin boots, a Sam Brown belt and a stone-gray Stetson in a way that screamed cowboy.

Sandy, sun-streaked hair curled under his hat. He had a smooth, even-featured face set off by a shallowly clefted chin and light blue eyes that, everyone knew, he used as often as possible to charm the ladies.

He swaggered — there was no other way to describe the deliberate, rolling gait — to the counter and perched on a stool.

"Lo's coming 'round to see if the new girl's worth his time." Mac shook his head, scooped up the last of his potatoes. "You can't help but like Lo. He's an affable sort, but I hope she's got more sense."

Part of the entertainment Brody had enjoyed in and around the Fist the past year was watching Lo knock over women like tenpins. "Ten bucks says he sweet-talks her, and she adds a notch to his bedpost before the end of the week."

Mac's brows knit in disapproval. "That's no way to talk about a nice girl like that."

"You haven't known her long enough to be so sure she's a nice girl."

"I say she is. So I'm going to take that bet, just so it costs you."

Brody gave a half laugh. Mac didn't drink, he didn't smoke, and if he chased women he didn't do it where anyone noticed. And Brody found his slightly puritanical bent part of his charm. "It's just sex, Mac." Then he let out a full grin when the tips of Mac's ears went red. "You remember sex, don't you?"

"I got a vague recollection of the process."

In the kitchen, Joanie set a piece of apple pie on the work counter. "Take a break," she ordered Reece. "Eat the pie."

"I'm not really hungry, and I need to —"

"Didn't ask if you were hungry, did I? Eat the pie. No charge on it. It's the last of the dish, and it won't be any good tomorrow anyway. You see the one just sat down at the counter?"

"The one who looks like he just rode in off the trail?"

"That would be William Butler. Goes by Lo. That's short for Lothario, which he got

43

labeled with when he was a teenager and proceeded in making it his life's work to bed every female within a hundred miles."

"Okay."

"Now on most Saturday nights, Lo would have himself a hot date, or he'd be hanging out down at Clancy's with his pals, trying to decide which heifer to cut out of that particular herd. He's come in here to get a look at you."

Because she didn't see she had any real choice, Reece began to eat the pie. "I don't imagine there's much to see at this point."

"Regardless, you're new, you're female, young and, as far as it goes, unattached. To give him his due, Lo doesn't poach on married women. You see he's flirting with Juanita now, who he was banging like a drum over a few weeks last winter, until he shifted his sights to some snow bunnies who came around to ski."

Joanie grabbed the huge mug of coffee that was always close at hand. "Boy's got charm to spare. I've never known any woman he's rolled off of to hold it against him when he buttons his jeans and strolls off."

"And you're telling me this because you assume he'll be rolling off me some night?"

"Just letting you know how it is."

"Got it. And don't worry, I'm not looking for a man — temporarily or permanently. Especially one who uses his penis as a divining rod."

Joanie let out a bark of laughter. "How's the pie?"

"It's good. Really good. I never asked about the baking. Is that done on the premises, or do you buy from a local bakery?"

"I do the baking."

"Really?"

"Now you're thinking I'm better at that than the grill. And you'd be right. How about you?"

"Not my strong suit, but I can give you a hand when you need it."

"I'll let you know." She flipped a pair of burgers, then dumped fries and beans on the plates with them. Joanie was tossing the pickles and tomatoes on the plates when Lo sauntered back into the kitchen.

"William."

"Ma." He bent, kissed the top of her head while Reece's stomach sank.

Ma, she thought, and she'd made a crack about his penis.

"Heard you were classing up the place." He sent Reece a slow, easy smile before he tipped back the beer he'd carried back with him. "Friends call me Lo."

"Reece. Nice to meet you. I'll take those, Joanie." Reece grabbed the plates, took them to the line. And noted with annoyance that for the first time all night, there were no tickets waiting to be filled.

"Shutting down the kitchen shortly," Joanie told her. "You go ahead and clock out, head out. I got you on first shift tomorrow, so you be here by six, sharp."

"All right. Sure." She started to untie her apron.

"I'll drive you down to the hotel." Lo set his half-full beer aside. "Make sure you get there safe."

"Oh, no, don't bother." Reece glanced toward his mother, hoping for some help in that quarter, but Joanie had already turned away to shut down the fryers. "It's not far. I'm fine, and I'd like a walk anyway."

"Fine, I'll walk you. Got a coat?"

Argue, she decided, and it was rude. Don't argue, and tread on thin ice. She'd have to tread. Without a word, she got her jean jacket. "I'll be here at six."

She mumbled her goodbyes, started toward the door. She could feel the writer — Brody — staring holes in her back. Why was he still here anyway?

Lo opened the door for her, then stepped out after her.

"Cool tonight. Sure you're going to be warm enough?"

"I'm fine. It feels good after the heat in the kitchen."

"I bet it does. You're not letting my ma work you too hard now, are you?"

"I like to work."

"I bet you were busy tonight. Why don't I buy you a drink so you can unwind a little. And you can tell me the story of your life."

"Thanks, but the story's not worth the price of a drink, and I've got the early shift tomorrow."

"Supposed to be a pretty day." His voice was as lazy as his gait. "Why don't I pick you up when you get off? I'll show you around. No better guide in Angel's Fist, I can promise you. And I can bring references documenting I'm a gentleman."

He had a great smile, she had to admit it, and a look in his eyes that was as seductive as a hand stroking along the skin.

And he was the boss's son.

"That's awfully nice of you, but since I only know a handful of people — and those less than a day — you could forge those references. I'd better pass, and take tomorrow to settle in a little."

"Rain check, then."

When he took her arm, she jumped, and his voice lowered to soothe as if she were a spooked horse. "Easy now, I'm just slowing you down. Can tell by the way you walk like you're late for an appointment you're from back East. Take a minute,

47

look up there. That's a sight, isn't it?"

Her heart was still beating too fast for comfort, but she looked up. And there, above the ragged shadows of the mountains, hung a full, white moon.

Stars exploded around it, as if someone had loaded a shotgun with diamonds and blasted away. Their light turned the icing of snow on the peaks an eerie blue, and dashed the crevices and gullies into deep, rich shadow.

This, she thought, was what she missed when she allowed nerves to hunch her over, to force her gaze to the ground. And though she might have wished she'd had this moment alone, she had to give credit to Lo for making her stop, making her look.

"It's beautiful. The guidebook I bought called the mountains majestic, and I thought no. When I saw them before, I thought not majestic but tough and rugged. But that's how they look now. Majestic."

"There are spots up there that you have to see to believe, and they change, even while you're looking. This time of year, if you go up, stand by the river, you can hear the rocks clack in the spring runoff. Take you on a ride up. Nothing better than seeing the Tetons on horseback."

"I don't ride."

"I can teach you."

She began to walk again. "Scenic guide, riding instructor."

"That's what I do, mostly, out of the Circle K. Guest ranch about twenty miles out. I can get the cook there to pack up a nice picnic, get you a gentle mount. Can promise you a day you'll write home about."

"I'm sure you would." She'd like to hear the rocks clack, and see the moraines and meadows. And right now, with that spectacular moonlight, it was almost tempting to let him show her. "I'll think about it. Here's my stop."

"I'll walk you up."

"You don't have to do that. I'm —"

"My mother taught me to walk a lady right to her door."

He took her arm again, casually, and opened the door to the hotel. He smelled, she noticed, appealingly of leather and pine.

"Evening, Tom," he called out to the clerk on night duty.

"Lo. Ma'am."

And Reece saw the ghost of a smirk in the clerk's eyes.

When Lo turned toward the elevator, Reece pulled back. "I'm just on the third floor. I'm going to walk up."

"One of those exercise nuts, are you? Must be why you stay so slim." But he changed direction smoothly, then pulled open the door to the stairs.

"I appreciate you going to all this trouble." She ordered herself not to panic because the stairwell seemed so much smaller with him beside her. "I certainly dropped into a friendly town."

"Wyoming's a friendly state. May not be many of us here, but we're congenial. I heard you were from Boston."

"Yes."

"First time out this way?"

"That's right." One more flight, then the door would open.

"Taking some time off to see the country?"

"Yes. Yes, that's exactly right."

"Brave thing to do, all by yourself."

"Is it?"

"Shows a sense of adventure."

She would have laughed, but she was too relieved when he held the door open for her and she stepped out into the hall on three. "I'm right here." She dug out her key card, automatically glancing down to make sure the tape across the door was secured.

Before she could slide the key card into the slot, he took it from her, did the small chore himself. He opened the door, then handed the key back to her. "Left all your lights on," he commented. "TV running."

"Oh, I guess I did. Overanxious to start work. Thanks, Lo, for the escort."

"My pleasure. We're going to get you up on a horse right soon. You'll see."

She managed a smile. "I'll think about it. Thanks again. Good night."

She eased through the doorway, shut the door. Flipped the dead bolt, then hooked the safety chain. Moving to the far side of the bed, she sat where she could look out the window, at all that open space, until she no longer had to work to keep her breath even.

Steadier, she went back to check the peep to make sure the hallway was clear before she pushed a chair against the door. Once she'd checked the locks again, and the sturdiness of the dresser blocking the door to the adjoining room, she got ready for bed. She set the alarm on the clock radio for five, then used her own travel alarm as a backup.

She updated her journal, then bargained with herself over how many lights she could leave burning through the night. It was her first night in a new place; she was entitled to leave the light on the desk burning, and the one in the bathroom. The bathroom didn't really count anyway. That was just for safety and convenience. She might have to get up in the middle of the night to pee.

She took her flashlight out of her knapsack, set it by the bed. There could be a power failure, caused by a fire. She wasn't the only one in the hotel, after all. Someone could fall asleep smoking in bed, or some kid could be playing with matches.

God knew.

The whole building could go up in flames at three a.m. for all she knew. Then she'd have to get out quickly. Having the flashlight close was just being prepared.

The little tickle in her chest made her think longingly of the sleeping pills in her bathroom kit. Those and the antidepressants, the antianxiety medications were just a security blanket, she reminded herself. It had been months since she'd taken a sleeping pill, and she was tired enough tonight to sleep without help. Besides, if there *was* a fire and power failure, she'd be groggy and slow. End up burning to death or dying of smoke inhalation.

And the idea of that had her sitting on the side of the bed with her head in her hands cursing herself for having an overactive and foolish imagination.

"Just stop it, Reece. Stop it now and go to bed. You've got to get up early and perform basic functions like a normal human being."

She made one more round with the locks before getting into bed. She lay very still, listening to her heart thud, listening for sounds from the next room, from the hallway, from outside the window.

Safe, she told herself. She was perfectly safe. There wasn't going to be a fire. A bomb wasn't going to explode. No one was going to break into her room to murder her in her sleep.

The sky was not going to fall.

But she kept the TV on low and used the old black-and-white melodrama to lull her to sleep.

The pain was so shocking, so vicious, she couldn't scream over it. The black, the anvil of black plummeted onto her chest to trap her. It crushed her lungs so she couldn't breathe, couldn't move. The hammer beat on that anvil, pounding her head, her chest, slamming, slamming down on her. She tried to gasp for air, but the pain was too much, and the fear was beyond even the pain.

They were out there, outside in the dark. She could hear them, hear the glass shattering, the explosions. And worse, the screaming.

Worse than the screaming, the laughing.

Ginny? Ginny?

No, no, don't cry out, don't make a sound. Better to die here in the dark than for them to find her. But they were coming, they were coming for her, and she couldn't hold back the whimpers, couldn't stop her teeth from chattering.

The sudden light was blinding, and the wild screams that burst in her head came out as feral growls.

"We've got a live one."

And she slapped and kicked weakly at hands that reached for her.

Woke in a sweat, with those growls in her throat as she grabbed for the flashlight and gripped it like a weapon.

Was someone there? Someone at the door? At the window?

She sat shivering, shaking, ears straining for any sound.

An hour later, when her alarms beeped, she was sitting up in bed, the flashlight still in her hand, and every light in the room burning.

3

After the gut-shot of panic, it was hard to face the kitchen, the people, the pretense of being normal. But not only was she essentially broke, she'd given her word. Six o'clock sharp.

Her only other choice was to go back, retreat, and all the months she'd been inching forward would be wiped away. One phone call, she knew, and she'd be rescued.

And she'd be done.

She took it a step at a time. Getting dressed was a victory, leaving the room another. Stepping outside and aiming her feet toward the diner was a small personal triumph. The air was cold — winter still had a few bites left — so her breath puffed out visibly in the shimmer of predawn. The mountains were dark and sturdy silhouettes against the sky now that the night's fat moon had sunk below the peaks. And she could see a long, low blanket of fog spread out at their feet. Fingers of mist rose from the lake and whisked around the leafless trees, thin as fairy wings.

In the chilly dark, it all looked so fanciful, so still, so perfectly balanced. Her heart jumped once as something slid out of those mists. Then settled again as she saw it was just an animal.

Moose, elk, deer, she couldn't be sure at this distance. But whatever it was seemed to glide, and the mists tattered around it as it moved closer to the lake.

As it bent its head to drink, Reece heard the first chorus of birdsong. Part of her wanted to just sit down, right on the sidewalk, and be quietly alone to watch the sun rise.

Soothed, she began to walk again. She'd have to face the kitchen, the people, the questions that always circled around the new face in any job. She couldn't afford to be late, to be nervous, and God knew she didn't want to draw any more attention to herself than absolutely necessary.

Stay calm, she ordered herself. Stay focused. To help her do just that she recited snatches of poetry in her head, concentrating on the rhythm of the words until she realized she was murmuring them out loud, and cringed. No one around to hear, she reminded herself, and the distraction got her to the door of Angel Food.

The lights burned bright inside, easing some of the tension in her shoulders. She could see movement inside — Joanie, already in the kitchen. Did the woman ever sleep?

She had to knock on the door, Reece told herself. Knock, put a smile on her face, wave. Once she took this next step, once she pushed herself inside, she'd drown this anxiety in the work.

But her arm felt like lead and refused to move. Her fingers were too stiff, too cold to curl themselves into a fist. She stood where she was, feeling stupid, useless, helpless.

"Problem with the door?"

She jolted, swung around. And there was Linda-gail slamming the driver's door of a sturdy little compact.

"No. No. I was just —"

"Zoning? You don't look as if you got much sleep last night."

"I guess I was. I guess I didn't."

The already cold air chilled with every step Linda-gail took toward her. The bright blue eyes, so friendly the day before, were aloof, dismissive. "Am I late?"

"Surprised you showed up at all with the night you must've put in."

Reece thought of huddling in bed, gripping the flashlight, listening. Listening. "How do you —"

"Lo's got a reputation for endurance."

"Lo? I don't — Oh!" Surprise laced with amusement jumped right over the nerves. "No, we didn't — *I* didn't. God, Linda-gail, I met him for like ten minutes. I have to know a guy at least an hour before I test his endurance."

Linda-gail lowered the hand she'd lifted to the door, narrowed her eyes at Reece. "You didn't go to bed with Lo?"

"No." This, at least, she could handle. "Did I break some secret town tradition? Am I going to be fired? Arrested? If being a skank is part of the job requirement, it should've been made clear up front and I should be making more than eight an hour."

"That clause is voluntary. Sorry." Through a flush, the dimples winked. "Really sorry. I shouldn't have assumed and jumped on you just because you left together."

"He walked me back to the hotel, suggested a drink, which I didn't want, and shifted to showing me the area, which I can see for myself, then maybe a trail ride. I don't ride, but I may give that part a try. He gets a ten on the cute-factor scale, and another ten on behavior and manners. I didn't realize you two had a thing."

"A thing? Me and Lo?" Linda-gail made a dismissive blowing sound. "We don't. I'm probably the only single female under fifty in a hundred miles who hasn't slept with him. A slut's a slut in my book, whether they're a man or a woman."

She shrugged, then once again studied

Reece's face. "Anyway, you really do look worn out."

"Didn't sleep well, that's all. First night in a new place, new job. Nerves."

"Put them away," Linda-gail ordered as she opened the door, and the warmth was back in her eyes. "We're not scary around here."

"Wondered if you two were going to stand out there and gab all day. I'm not paying you to gossip."

"It's five after six, for God's sake, Joanie. Dock me. Oh, speaking of pay, here's your share of last night's tips, Reece."

"My share? I didn't wait any tables."

Linda-gail pushed the envelope into Reece's hands. "Shop policy, the cook gets ten percent of the tips. We get tipped for service, but if the food's crap, we're not going to make as much."

"Thanks." Not completely broke, Reece thought as she stuffed the envelope in her pocket.

"Don't spend it all in one place."

"If you're finished passing the time now?" Joanie folded her arms at the counter. "Get those breakfast setups going, Linda-gail. Reece, you think you're ready to get your skinny ass back here and work?"

"Yes, ma'am. Oh, and just to clear the air," she added as she rounded the counter for an apron, "your son's very charming, but I slept alone last night."

"Boy must be slipping."

"I couldn't say. I intend to continue to sleep alone while I'm in Angel's Fist."

Joanie set aside a bowl of pancake batter. "Don't like sex?"

"I like it fine." Reece moved to the sink to wash her hands. "It's just not on my to-do list at the moment."

"Must be a pretty sad, short list then. Can you make huevos rancheros?"

"I can."

"They're popular on Sundays. So are flapjacks. You go on, start frying up bacon and sausage. Early crowd'll be right along."

Shortly before noon, Joanie pushed a plate holding a short stack, a scoop of scrambled eggs and a side of bacon into Reece's hand. "Go on, take this into the back room. Sit down and eat."

"There's enough for two people here."

"Yeah, if both of them are anorexic."

"I'm not." She forked up a bite of the eggs as if to prove it.

"Go take it back in my office and sit. You got twenty."

She'd seen the office, and *room* was a very generous term. "Listen, I've got a problem with small spaces."

"Afraid of the dark, and claustrophobic.

60

You're a bundle of phobias. Sit out at the counter, then. You've still got twenty."

She did what she was told, sitting at the end of the counter. A moment later, Linda-gail put a cup of tea beside her, gave her a wink.

"Hey, Doc." Linda-gail gave the counter a swipe, sent a good-morning smile to the man who slid onto the stool beside Reece. "Usual?"

"Sunday cholesterol special, Linda-gail. My day to walk on the wild side."

"You got it. Joanie," she called back without bothering with a ticket. "Doc's here. Doc, this is Reece, our new cook. Reece, meet Doc Wallace. He'll treat anything that ails you. But don't let him pull you into a poker game. He's a slick one."

"Now, now, how am I going to fleece the newcomers if you talk like that?" He shifted on his stool, gave Reece a nod. "Heard Joanie got herself somebody knew what they were doing in the kitchen. How's it going for you?"

"So far, so good." She had to make an effort and remind herself it wasn't as if he was wearing a lab coat and coming at her with needles. "I like the work."

"Best Sunday breakfast in Wyoming at Joanie's. Now the hotel, they put on a big buffet for the tourists, but the smart money's right here." He settled back with the coffee Linda-gail put in front of him. "You go right on and eat that while it's hot."

Instead of looking at it, he thought, like the food on the plate was a puzzle to be solved. He'd been the town doctor for nearly thirty years, and so he told her. He'd come as a young man, answering an ad the town council had placed in the Laramie paper. And so he told Reece as she played with her food.

"Looking for adventure," he said in a voice with the barest hint of rural western twang. "Fell in love with the place, and a pretty brown-eyed girl named Susan. Raised three kids here. Oldest is a doctor himself — first-year intern — in Cheyenne. Middle one, our Annie, married a fella takes pictures for the *National Geographic* magazine. They moved all the way out to Washington, D.C. Got a grandson there, too. Youngest is in California, working on a degree in philosophy. Don't know what the hell he's going to philosophize about, but there you go. Lost my Susan two years back to breast cancer."

"I'm so sorry."

"It's a hard, hard thing." He glanced down at his wedding ring. "Still look for her beside me when I wake up in the morning. Expect I always will."

"Here you go, Doc." Linda-gail set a

plate in front of him, and both of them laughed when Reece goggled at it. "He'll eat every bite, too," Linda-gail said before she headed off.

There was a stack of pancakes, an omelet, a thick slice of ham, a generous portion of home fries and a trio of link sausages.

"You really can't eat all that."

"Watch and learn, little girl. Watch and learn."

He looked fit, Reece thought, in his plaid shirt and sensible cardigan. Like someone who ate healthy meals and got a reasonable amount of exercise. His face was ruddy and lean, with a pair of clear hazel eyes behind wire-rimmed glasses.

Yet he tucked into the enormous breakfast like a long-haul trucker.

"You got family back East?" he asked her.

"Yes, my grandmother in Boston."

"That where you learned to cook?"

She couldn't take her eyes off the way the food was disappearing. "Yes, where I started. I went to the New England Culinary Institute in Vermont, then a year in Paris at the Cordon Bleu."

"Culinary Institute." Doc wiggled his eyebrows. "And Paris. Fancy."

"Sorry?" She realized abruptly she had said more about her background in two minutes than she normally did to anyone in two weeks. "More intense, actually. I'd better get back to work. It was nice meeting you."

Reece worked through the lunch shift, and with the rest of the afternoon and evening stretched out in front of her decided to take a long walk. She could circle the lake, maybe explore some of the forests and streams. She could take pictures and e-mail them to her grandmother and, between the fresh air, the exercise, tire herself out.

She changed into her hiking boots, outfitted her backpack precisely as her guidebook recommended for hikes under ten miles. Outside again, she found a spot near the lake to sit and read over the handout brochures she'd gotten from the hotel.

She'd take time every day she could manage it, she decided, fanning out from the town, into the park, maybe dip just a little into the backcountry. She was better outdoors, always better in the open.

When she had her first full day off, she'd take one of the easier trails and hike up to see the river. But for now she'd better get started doing what her guide suggested and break in the hiking boots.

She set out at an easy pace. That, at least, was one of the advantages of her life now. There was rarely any hurry. She could do what she chose to do in her own time, at her own speed. She'd never really given herself this in the time before. In the past eight months, she'd seen and done more than she had in the previous twenty-eight years. Maybe she was a little bit crazy, and she was certainly neurotic, phobic and slightly paranoid, but there were pockets of herself she'd managed to fill again, and pieces of herself she'd worked back into place.

She'd never be again what she'd once been — the bustling, ambitious urbanite. But she'd discovered she liked whatever she was forming into. Now, she paid more attention to details that had once blurred by. The play of light and shadows, the lap of water, the sensation of the spongy, thawing ground under her feet.

She could stop where she was, right now, and watch a heron rise, silent as a cloud, from the lake. She could watch the ripples fan out over the surface, wider, wider, until they reached the tip of the paddles plied by a young boy in a red kayak.

She remembered her camera too late to capture the heron, but she captured the boy and his red boat, and the blue water, and the dazzling reflection of the mountains that spanned its surface.

She'd attach little notes to each photo, she thought as she started to walk again. In that way, her grandmother would feel part of the journey. Reece knew she'd left worry behind in Boston, but all she could do was send chatty e-mails, make a phone call now and then to let her grandmother know where and how she was.

Though she wasn't always perfectly truthful on the how.

There were houses and cabins scattered around the lake, and someone, she noted, was having a Sunday barbecue. It was a good day for it — grilled chicken, potato salad, skewers of marinated vegetables, gallons of iced tea, cold beer.

A dog paddled out into the water after a blue ball, while a girl stood on the banks laughing and calling encouragement. When he retrieved it and paddled back to shore, he shook like a mad thing, showering the girl with water that caught the sunlight and fired like diamonds.

His bark was full of insane joy when she threw the ball again, and he leaped back into the water to repeat the cycle.

Reece took out her bottle of water, sipping as she veered away from the lakefront and strolled into the evergreens.

She might see deer, or a moose, even elk — maybe the same one she'd spied that morning — if she was quiet enough. She could do without the bear the brochures and guides said lived in the forests of the area, even if the guidebook claimed most bears would leave if they sensed a human nearby.

For all she knew the bear would be in a pissy mood that day and decide to take it out on her.

So she'd be careful, she wouldn't go far, and though she had her compass, she'd stick to the trail.

Cooler here, she thought. The sun couldn't get to the pools and pockets of snow, and the water of the little stream she came across had to force itself through and over the chunks of ice.

She followed the stream, listening to the hiss and plop of the ice as it slowly thawed. When she found tracks and scat, she was thrilled. What sort of tracks? What sort of poop? she wondered. Wanting to know, she started to dig her guidebook out of her pack.

The rustle had her freezing, cautiously looking over. It was a toss-up who was more taken by surprise, Reece or the mule deer, but they stood staring at each other in mutual shock for one breathless moment.

I must be upwind, she thought. Or was it downwind? As she reached slowly for her camera, she made a mental note to look that up again. She managed a full-on shot, then made the mistake of laughing in delight. The sound had the deer bounding away.

"I know what that's like," she murmured as she watched it race away from human contact. "The world's just full of scary stuff."

She tucked the little camera back in her pocket, realizing she couldn't hear the dog barking any longer, or any rumble from cars driving on the main road of town. Just the breeze moving through the trees like a quiet surf, and that hissing bubble and plop from the stream.

"Maybe I should live in a forest. Find myself a little isolated cabin, grow some vegetables. I could be a vegetarian," she considered as she took a running leap across the narrow stream. "Okay, probably not. I could probably learn to fish. I'd buy a pickup and go into town once a month for supplies."

She began to imagine it, painting the image in her head. Not too far from the water, not too deep in the mountains. Lots and lots of windows so it would be almost like living outside.

"I could start my own business. Little cottage industry. Cook all day, sell the products. Do it all over the Internet, maybe. Never leave the house. And end up adding agoraphobia to my list."

No, she'd live in the forest — that part

was good — but she'd work in town. It could even be here, and she'd keep working for Joanie.

"Give it a few weeks, that's the best thing. See how it goes. Get out of that hotel, that's for damn sure. That's not going to work for very long. Where else though, that's a problem. Maybe I'll see about —"

She let out a yelp, stumbled back and nearly landed on her ass.

It was one thing to run into a mule deer and another entirely to come across a man lying in a hammock with a paperback splayed over his chest.

He'd heard her coming — hard not to, he thought, when she was holding a verbal debate with herself. He'd assumed she'd turn off toward the lake, but instead she veered straight toward his hammock, eyes on the toes of her barely scuffed hiking boots. So he set his book down to watch her.

Urban female picking her way through the wilderness, he mused. L.L. Bean backpack and boots, Levi's that at least showed some wear, water bottle.

Was that her cell phone sticking out of her pocket? Who the hell was she going to call?

She'd scooped her hair back, looping the tail of it through the back opening in the black cap she wore. Her face was pale, the eyes huge and startled, and a deep, rich Spanish brown.

"Lost?"

"No. Yes. No." She looked around as if she'd just dropped in from another planet. "I was just taking a walk, I didn't realize. I must be trespassing."

"You must be. You want to wait here a minute, while I go get my gun?"

"Not really. Um. That's your cabin, I guess."

"That gives you two for two."

"It's nice." She studied it for a moment, the simple log structure, the long sweep of the covered porch with its single chair, single table. It was a lovely thing, she decided. A single chair, a single table.

"Private," she added. "I'm sorry."

"I'm not. I like it private."

"I meant . . . well, you know what I meant." She took a deep breath, twisting and untwisting the cap on her bottle of water. It was easier for her with strangers. It had come to be the pitying, the concerned glances of those she knew she'd been unable to bear.

"You're doing it again. Staring at me. It's rude."

He lifted an eyebrow. She'd always admired people who could do that, as if that single brow had an independent set of

70

muscles. Then he reached down, unerringly hooked a bottle of beer. "Who decides that kind of thing? What's rude in any given culture?"

"The PRS."

It only took him a moment. "The Prevention of Rudeness Society? I thought they disbanded."

"No, they continue their good work, in secret locations."

"My great-grandfather was a member of the PRS, but we don't talk about it much seeing as he was a complete asshole."

"Well, you'll have this in any family or group. I'll let you get back to your reading."

She took a step back, and he debated whether to ask her if she wanted a beer. Since it would have been an almost unprecedented gesture, he'd already decided against it when a sharp sound blasted the air.

She hit the dirt, throwing her arms up to cover her head like a soldier in a trench.

His first reaction was amusement. *City girl.* But he saw, when she neither moved nor made a sound, it was more than that. He swung his legs off the hammock, then crouched down.

"Backfire," he said easily. "Carl Sampson's truck. It's a wreck on wheels."

"Backfire."

He could hear her murmur it over and over as she trembled.

"Yeah, that's right." He put a hand on her arm to steady her, and she tightened up.

"Don't. Don't touch me. Don't touch me. Don't. I just need a minute."

"Okay." He got up to retrieve the water bottle that had gone flying when she dropped to the ground. "You want this? Your water?"

"Yes. Thanks." She took the bottle, but her shaking fingers couldn't manage the cap. Saying nothing, Brody took it from her, unscrewed the cap, handed it back.

"I'm fine. Just startled me."

Startled, my ass, he thought.

"I thought it was a gunshot."

"You'll hear that kind of thing, too. Nothing in season — hunting, that is — but people around here target shoot. It's the wild, wild West, Slim."

"Of course. Of course they do; it is. I'll get used to it."

"You go walking in the woods, the hills, you're going to want to wear something bright. Red, orange."

"That's right. Of course, that's right. I'll make sure I do next time."

Some color had come back into her face, but in Brody's judgment, it was pure embarrassment. Even when she pushed herself to her feet, her breath remained choppy. She made a halfhearted attempt to brush herself off.

"That completes the entertainment portion of our program. Enjoy the rest of your day."

"Plan to." A nicer guy, he thought, would probably insist she sit down, or offer to walk her back to town. He just wasn't a nicer guy.

She kept walking, then slowed to glance over her shoulder. "I'm Reece, by the way."

"I know."

"Oh. Well. See you around."

Hard to avoid it, Brody thought, even when she walked fast and with her eyes on the ground. Spooky woman with those big, doe-in-the-thicket eyes. Pretty though, and she'd probably edge up to sexy with another ten pounds on her.

But it was the spooky that intrigued him. He could never resist trying to figure out what made people tick. And in Reece Gilmore's case, he figured whatever ticked inside her had a lot of very short fuses.

Reece kept her eyes on the lake — the ripples, the swans, the boats. It would be a long walk around the curve of it, but that would give her time to settle down again, and for the burn of embarrassment to cool. It was already transforming into a migraine, but that was all right, that was okay. If it didn't ease back, she'd take something for it when she got back to the hotel.

Maybe her stomach was twisted up, but it wasn't that bad. She hadn't gotten sick and completely capped off the mortification.

Why couldn't she have been alone in the woods when the stupid truck backfired? Of course, if she had been, she might still be curled up there, whimpering.

At least Brody had been matter-of-fact about it. Here's your water, pull yourself together. It was so much easier to handle that than the strokes and pats and there-theres.

Because the sun hurt her eyes now, she dug into her backpack for her sunglasses. Ordered herself to keep her head up, to walk at a normal pace. She even managed to smile at a couple who strolled along the lake as she did, and lift her hand in a wave in answer to the salute from a driver in a passing car when she finally, *finally* reached the main road.

The girl — Reece couldn't pull her name out of her pounding head — was on the desk again at the hotel. She shot Reece a smile, asked how she was, how she had enjoyed her hike. Reece knew she answered, but all the words seemed tinny and false.

She wanted her room.

She got up the stairs, found her key, then just leaned back against the door when she was inside.

Once she'd checked the locks — twice — taken her medication, she curled on the bed, fully dressed, still wearing her boots and sunglasses.

And closing her eyes, she gave in to the exhaustion of pretending to be normal.

4

A spring storm dropped eight inches of wet, heavy snow, and turned the lake into a frothy gray disk. Some of the locals plowed through it on snowmobiles while kids, bundled into shapeless stumps in their winter gear, entertained themselves building snow people around the verge of the lake.

Lynt, with his wide shoulders and weather-scored face, took breaks from his snowplowing duties to refill his thermos with Joanie's coffee and complain about the wind.

Reece had experienced it herself on her walk to work that morning. It blew like wrath down the canyon, across the lake, sparking fresh snow as it burned ice through the bone.

It beat at the windows, howled like a man bent on murder. When the power died, Joanie herself yanked on coat and boots to trudge outside and fire up her generator.

The roar of it competed with the scream of the wind and the thunder of Lynt's snowplow, until Reece wondered why every mother's son and daughter didn't go raving mad from the unrelenting noise.

It didn't stop people from coming in. Lynt turned off his plow to settle in with an enormous bowl of buffalo stew. Carl Sampson, with his cheeks red from the wind, puffed in to sit with Lynt and chow down on meatloaf, and stayed to eat two pieces of huckleberry pie.

Others came and went. Others came and lingered. They all wanted food and company, she understood. Human contact and something warm in the belly to remind them they weren't alone. While she grilled, fried, boiled and chopped, she, too, felt steadier for the hum of voices.

But there wouldn't be voices and contact once she finished her shift. Thinking of her hotel room, she fought her way down to the mercantile on her break for spare batteries for her flashlight. Just in case.

"Winter's got to take her last slap," Mac told her as he rang up her batteries. "Going to have to reorder these. Had a run on them. Close to running out of bread, eggs and milk, too. Why is it people always load up on bread, eggs and milk in a storm?"

"I guess they want to be able to make French toast."

He gave a quick, wheezing laugh. "Might be they do. How you doing down at Joanie's? Haven't made it down there since this hit. I like to get by all the businesses that're open when we get socked. Being mayor, it just seems the thing to do."

"Generator's going, so we're still in business. You, too."

"Yeah, don't like to close the doors. Lynt's got the roads clear enough, and the power should be back up in a couple hours. I checked on that. And she's already passing. The storm."

Reece glanced toward the windows. "It is?"

"Time the power's back, she'll be done. You'll see. Only real trouble we've had from this is the roof of Clancy's storage shed caving in. His own fault anyway. It was due for repair, and he didn't get it shoveled off. Tell Joanie I'll be down to check on things first chance."

In just over an hour, Mac's predictions proved on target. The wind tapered down to an irritable mutter. Before another hour had passed, the juke — which Joanie refused to run on her generator — whined back on, hiccuped, then offered up Dolly Parton.

And long after the heavy fall of snow and brutal wind left town, Reece could see it raging in bruised clouds in the mountains. It added, she thought, to their fierceness, gave them a cold, aloof power.

It made her grateful she could stand in the warmth of her hotel room and look out at them.

She mixed up vats of stew according to Joanie's recipes, grilled pounds and pounds of meat and poultry and fish. At the end of every shift, she counted up her tip money, then tucked it in an envelope she kept zipped in her duffel bag.

Sometime during the day or evening, Joanie would stick a plate of food under Reece's nose. She'd eat in a corner of the kitchen while meat smoked on the grill, the jukebox played and people sat at the counter and gossiped.

Three days after the storm, she was ladling up stew when Lo strolled back. He made a small production out of sniffing the air. "Something sure smells good."

"Tortilla soup." She had finally convinced Joanie to let her prepare one of her own recipes. "And it is good. Do you want a bowl?"

"I was talking about you, but I wouldn't turn down a bowl of that."

She handed him the one she'd just prepared, then reached up for another bowl. He slid up behind her, reaching up as she did. A classic move, Reece thought, as was her easy side step. "I've got it. Your mother's back in her office if you want to see her."

"I'll catch her before I head out. Came in to see you."

"Oh?" She filled the next bowl, sprinkled on the cheese she'd grated for it, the tortilla strips she'd fried. She thought wistfully how much better it would have been with fresh cilantro as she set it on a plate with a hard roll and two pats of butter. Shifting around, she put it in line. "Order up," she called out, then took the next ticket.

Maybe she could talk Joanie into adding cilantro, and a few other fresh herbs, to the produce order. Some sun-dried tomatoes and arugula. If she could just —

"Hey, where'd you go?" Lo demanded. "Can I come, too?"

"What? Sorry, did you say something?"

He looked a little put out, and surprised with it. She imagined he wasn't used to having a woman forget he was there. Boss's son, she reminded herself, and offered a quick smile. "I get caught up when I'm cooking."

"Guess you do. Still, business is pretty light today."

"Steady though." She got out the makings for a bacon cheeseburger and a chicken sandwich, kept moving to set up the two orders of fries.

"Damn! This *is* good." He spooned up more of the soup.

"Thanks. Make sure to tell the boss."

"I'll do that. So, Reece, I checked the schedule. You're off tonight."

"Mmm-hmm." She nodded at Pete when the bantamweight dishwasher came in from his break.

"Thought you might want to take in a movie."

"I didn't know there was a movie theater in town."

"There isn't. I've got the best DVD collection in western Wyoming. Make a hell of a bowl of popcorn, too."

"I wouldn't be surprised." Boss's son, Reece reminded herself again. Tread carefully between friendly and dismissive. "That's a nice offer, Lo, but I've got a lot of things to catch up on tonight. You want a roll with that soup?"

"Maybe." He edged a little closer, not quite crowding her at the grill. "You know, honey, you're going to break my heart if you keep turning me down."

"I doubt that." She kept it light as she flipped the grill orders, then got him a roll and a plate. "You don't want to get too close to the grill," she warned. "You may get splattered."

Instead of taking the soup out to the restaurant as she'd hoped, he just leaned back against the work counter. "I've got an awful tender heart."

"Then you want to steer clear of me,"

she told him. "I stomp all over them. I left a trail of bleeding and bruised hearts all the way from Boston. It's a sickness."

"I might be the cure."

She glanced at him then. Too good-looking, too full of charm. Once upon a time she might have enjoyed being pursued by him, even caught for a while. But she just didn't have the energy for games. "You want the truth?"

"Is it going to hurt?"

It made her laugh. "I like you. I'd prefer to keep liking you. You're my boss's son, and that makes you the next thing to the boss in my lineup. I don't sleep with the boss, so I'm not going to sleep with you. But I appreciate the offer."

"Didn't ask you to sleep with me yet," he pointed out.

"Just saving us both time."

He spooned up soup, ate in a slow and thoughtful way. His smile was the same — slow and thoughtful. "Bet I could change your mind, you give me half a chance."

"That's why you're not getting one."

"Maybe you'll get fired, or my ma'll disown me."

When the fryer buzzed, she let the potatoes drain in the baskets while she finished the sandwiches. "I can't afford to get fired, and your mother loves you."

She finished the orders, put them up.

"Now go on out, sit at the counter and finish your soup. You're in the way."

He grinned at her. "Bossy women are a weakness of mine."

But he strolled out when she started on the next ticket.

"He'll try again," Pete told her from the sink in a voice that still said Bronx even after eight years in Wyoming. "He can't help himself."

She felt a little harried, a little hot. "Maybe I should've told him I was married, or a lesbian."

"Too late for that now. Better tell him you've fallen wild in love with me." Pete sent her a grin, showing the wide gap between his two front teeth.

She chuckled again. "Why didn't I think of that?"

"Nobody does. That's why it'd work."

Joanie came in, stuck a check in the pocket of Pete's apron, handed another to Reece. "Payday."

"Thanks." And Reece made a decision on the spot. "I wonder if when you have a chance you could show me the apartment upstairs. If it's still available."

"Haven't seen anybody move in, have you? In my office."

"I need to —"

"Do what you're told," Joanie finished and headed out.

Left without a choice, Reece followed. Inside, Joanie opened a shallow wall cabinet emblazoned with a cowboy riding a bucking horse. There was an army of labeled keys on hooks. She took one out, passed it to Reece. "Go on up, take a look."

"It's not time for my break."

Joanie cocked a hip, fisted a hand on it. "Girl, it's time if I say it's time. Go on. Stairs out the back."

"All right. I'll be back in ten."

It was cold enough even with the snow rapidly going to slush that she needed her coat. She was grateful for it once she'd climbed the rickety open stairs and unlocked the door. Joanie was obviously frugal enough to keep the heat off upstairs.

She saw it was essentially one room with an alcove where an iron daybed was nestled, and a short counter on the street side that separated a little kitchen. The floors were random-length oak that showed some scars, while the walls were an industrial pasty-flesh beige.

There was a bath that was actually slightly larger than the one in her hotel room with a white pedestal sink and an old cast-iron claw-foot tub. Rust stains bloomed around their drains. The mirror over the sink was spotted, the tiles a stark white with black borders.

The main room held a sagging plaid sofa, a single faded blue armchair and a couple tables holding lamps that had obviously been flea market bargains.

She was smiling even before she turned to walk to the windows. A trio of them faced the mountains, and seemed to open up the world. She could see the sky where the blue streaks were fighting to overtake the dull white, and the lake where that blue was shimmering against the gray.

The snow people were melting into deformed hobbits that spread low over the winter-brown grasses. The willows were shabby bent sticks, and the cottonwoods shivered. Shadows shifted over the snow-laced peaks as the clouds gathered and parted, and she thought she saw a faint glimmer that might have been an alpine lake.

The town with its slushy streets, its cheerful white gazebo, its rustic cabins spread out below her. Standing where she was she felt a part of it, yet still safe and separate.

"I could be happy here," she murmured. "I could be okay here."

She'd have to buy some things. Towels, sheets, kitchen supplies, cleaning supplies. She thought of the paycheck in her pocket, the tip money squirreled away. She could manage the essentials. And it could be fun.

The first time she'd bought her own things in nearly a year.

Big step, she thought, then immediately began to second-guess herself. Was it too big a step, too soon? Renting an apartment, buying sheets. What if she had to leave? What if she got fired? What if —

"God, I annoy myself," she muttered. "What-ifs are for tomorrow. The moment's what matters. And at this moment, I want to live here."

As she thought it, clouds parted and a beam of fragile sunlight arrowed through them.

That, she decided, was enough of a sign. She'd make a try here, for as long as it lasted.

She heard footsteps on the stairs outside, and the bubble of fear opened in her chest. Groping in her pocket, she closed her hand around her panic button, gripped one of the tacky table lamps with the other.

When Joanie opened the door, Reece set the lamp down as if she'd been examining it.

"Ugly, but it gives decent light," Joanie said, and left it at that.

"Sorry, I took longer than I meant to. I'll go right down."

"No rush. We're slow, and Beck's on the grill. Long as it's nothing too complicated, he can handle things. You want the place or not?"

"Yes, if I can manage the rent. You never said what —"

In shirtsleeves, her stained apron and her thick-soled shoes, Joanie took a quick pass around the room. Then she named a monthly figure that was slightly less than the hotel rate.

"That's including your heat and lights, unless I find you've gone crazy there. You want a phone, that's on you. Same thing if you get it into your head you want to paint the walls. I don't want a bunch of noise up here during business hours."

"I'm pretty quiet. I'd rather we do it by the week. I like to pay as I go."

"Doesn't matter to me as long as the rent's on time. You can move in today if you want."

"Tomorrow. I need to get some things."

"Suits me. Pretty sparse in here." Joanie's eagle eyes tracked around the room. "I probably have a few things sitting around I can bring up. You need help moving your stuff, Pete and Beck'll give you a hand with it."

"I appreciate it. All of it."

"You're paying your way. You got that raise coming."

"Thanks."

"No need for gratitude on something that was agreed on from the get-go. You do the job and you don't cause trouble.

Don't ask questions, either. Now I figure that's either because you were absent the day they handed out your portion of curiosity, or you don't want questions asked back."

"Is that a question or a statement?"

"But you're not stupid." Joanie's hand patted her apron pocket where Reece knew she kept a pack of cigarettes. "Let's get this said. You got trouble. Anybody with two licks of sense can see it just by looking at you. I guess you've got what they like to call *issues*."

"Is that what they call them?" Reece murmured.

"The way I see it, if you're working through them or just standing still, it's your business. But you don't let it get in the way of your job, so that's mine. You're a good worker, and you're a better cook than I ever had behind the grill. I figure on making use of that, especially if I figure you're not going to go rabbiting off some night and leave me flat. I don't like to depend on anybody. You just get disappointed that way. But I'm going to make use of you, and you'll get your pay on time, and a reasonable rent on this place. You'll get your time off, and if you're still here in another couple months, you'll get another raise."

"I won't leave you flat. If I need to go, I'll tell you beforehand."

"Fair enough. Now I'm going to ask you straight out, and I'll know if you're lying. You got the law after you?"

"No." Reece combed her fingers through her hair and let out a weak laugh. "God, no."

"Didn't figure you did, but you might as well know some folks around here are speculating on that. People in the Fist like to speculate, passes the time." She waited a beat. "You don't want to say what it is behind you, that's your business, too. But it might help if someone comes looking for you, you tell me whether you want them to find you, or be pointed in another direction."

"No one's going to come looking for me. There's only my grandmother, and she knows where I am. I'm not running from anyone." Except maybe herself, she thought.

"All right, then. You've got the key. I got a duplicate in my office. You don't have to worry about me coming up and poking around once you move in. But you're late with the rent, I'll take it out of your pay. No excuses. I've already heard them all."

"If you can cash my paycheck, I'll give you the first week now."

"I guess we can work it that way. Another thing, I could use some help with the baking now and again. May tap you for that, have you give me a hand. I use my own kitchen for the baked goods."

"I can do that."

"I'll work it into the schedule. Well, let's get back before Beck poisons somebody."

With the rest of her pay and a portion of her tip money, Reece headed to the mercantile. Basics, she reminded herself. Essentials and no more. This wasn't Newberry Street and she couldn't afford indulgences.

But God, it was a kick to be going shopping for more than new socks or a pair of jeans. The idea of it lightened her steps until she could actually *feel* good, healthy color in her cheeks.

She breezed in with a quick jingle of the bell that hung over the door. There were other shoppers, and some she recognized from the diner. Steak san, extra onions for the man in the plaid jacket in the hardware section. The woman and the little boy browsing in dry goods — fried chicken for him, Cobb salad for her.

She made a group of four as campers, loading up on supplies they had stacked in one of the rolling grocery carts.

She lifted a hand at Mac Drubber, and found a comfort in his acknowledging nod. It was nice to recognize and be recognized.

All so casual and normal. And here she was looking at packaged sheet sets. She rejected the plain white immediately. Too reminiscent of hospitals. Maybe the pale blue, with its pattern of tiny violets, and the dark blue blanket. And for towels the buttery yellow for some sunshine in the bath.

She took the first haul to the counter.

"Got yourself a place, did you?"

"Yes. The apartment over Joanie's," she told Mac.

"That's fine. You want me to start an account for you?"

In her current mood it was tempting. She could get everything she needed, and a few things she only wanted, and pay for it later. But that would be breaking the hard-and-fast rule she'd lived by for more than eight months.

"That's all right. It's payday. I just need to get a few things for the kitchen, and I'm set for now."

She did the math in her head as she scanned, debated, deleted or selected what was absolutely necessary over what could be done without. A good cast-iron skillet, a decent pot. She couldn't afford the kind of cookware she'd once owned, or good knives, but she could make do.

Even as she calculated, adjusted her list, she glanced up and over each time the little bell jingled.

So she saw Brody come in. Same battered leather jacket, she noted, same down-at-the-heels boots. He looked like he might have shaved in the last couple of days. But that look in his eyes, something that said he'd seen it all already and didn't miss it, was still there as his gaze passed over her before he headed to the grocery section.

Thankfully, she'd already hit that area for what she considered pantry and refrigerator staples.

She pushed her cart to the counter. "That should do it, Mr. Drubber."

"I'll ring you up. No charge on the teakettle. It's a housewarming gift."

"Oh, you don't have to do that."

"My store, my rules." He wagged a finger at her. "Be a minute here, Brody."

"No problem." Brody set a quart of milk, a box of cornflakes and a pound of coffee on the counter. Nodded to Reece. "How's it going?"

"Fine, thanks."

"Reece is moving into the apartment over Joanie's."

"That so?"

"I get this rung and boxed, you give her a hand hauling it over there, Brody."

"Oh, no. No, that's okay. I can manage."

"You can't cart all this stuff on your own," Mac insisted. "Got your car outside, don't you, Brody?"

There was a ghost of a smile around his mouth as if he found the whole situation amusing. "Sure."

"Heading on down to Joanie's for dinner anyway, right?"

"That's the plan."

"See that, no trouble at all. This cash or charge, honey?"

"Cash. It's cash." And, deducting the teakettle, nearly to the dollar of what she'd brought with her.

"Just put my stuff on my account, Mac." Brody stacked his purchases on top of one of the boxes Mac had already packed, hefted it. Before the rest was finished, Brody was back for box number two.

Trapped, Reece lifted the last one. "Thanks, Mr. Drubber."

"You enjoy your new place," he called out as she followed Brody to the door.

"You don't have to do this. Seriously," she began the minute they were outside. "He put you on the spot."

"Yeah, he did." Brody loaded the second box into the bed of a black Yukon, then turned and reached for the one Reece carried. She wrapped her arms more tightly around it.

"I said you didn't have to do this. I can do it myself."

"No, I don't, and no, you can't. So let's do ourselves a favor and get it done while we're young." He simply yanked the box out of her arms, loaded it. "Get in."

"I don't want —"

"You're being an idiot. I've got your stuff," he continued as he rounded the hood. "You can get in and ride with it, or you can walk."

She'd have preferred the second option, but that would make her a moron as well as an idiot. She got in, gave the door an irritated slam shut. And not caring, particularly, about his comfort, opened the window so she didn't feel closed in.

He said nothing, and since the radio was blasting out Red Hot Chili Peppers, she didn't have to pretend to make polite conversation on the short drive.

He parked on the street, then got out to drag a box out one side of the car while she pulled one from the other. "The entrance is around back." Her voice was clipped, surprising her. She couldn't remember the last time she'd been seriously annoyed with anyone other than herself.

She had to lengthen her stride so she didn't trail behind him, and though she breezed by him on the stairs, she fumbled when she had to prop the box against the wall in order to deal with the key.

Brody simply shifted the box he held to one arm, took the key, unlocked the door.

A fresh wave of resentment washed

through her. This was *her* place now. She should be able to invite in whom she liked, and keep out whom she didn't. And here he was striding across the floor to dump her box of precious new possessions on the counter.

Then he was striding out again, without one comment. On a huff of breath, Reece set her box down. She dashed to the door and out, hoping to catch him and take the last load herself.

But he was already starting back.

"I'll take it from here." The breeze blew her hair across her face. She gave it an annoyed swipe back. "Thanks."

"I've got it. What the hell's in here? Bricks?"

"It's probably the cast-iron skillet, and the cleaning supplies. I can get it, really."

He simply ignored her and climbed the steps. "Why the hell did you lock the door when we were coming right back?"

"Habit." She turned the key, but before she could shift to reach for the box, he'd pushed by to take it in himself.

"Well, thanks." She stood beside the open door, knowing it was not only rude, but that she was letting in cold air. "Sorry for the imposition."

"Uh-huh." He turned a circle, hands in his pockets now. Small, depressing space, he thought, until you took in the view. It

95

was all about the view. And it was clean, that would be Joanie's doing. Empty or not, she'd have banished any dust or cobwebs regularly.

"Could use some fresh paint," he commented.

"I suppose."

"And some frigging heat. You'll freeze those bird bones of yours in here."

"No point in turning up the heat until I move in tomorrow. I don't want to hold you up."

He turned back, aimed those eyes at her. "You're not worried about holding me up, you just want me out."

"Okay. Bye."

For the first time, he gave her a quick, genuine smile. "You're more interesting when you've got a little bite to you. What's the special tonight?"

"Fried chicken, parsley potatoes, peas and carrots."

"Sounds good." He strolled to the door, stopped directly in front of her. He swore he could almost hear her body brace. "See you around."

The door closed quietly behind him, and the lock snicked before he'd gone down the first step. He circled the building and, to satisfy his curiosity, looked up when he reached the front.

She was standing at the center window,

staring out at the lake. Slim as a willow stem, he thought, with windblown hair and deep, secret eyes. He thought she looked more like a portrait in a frame than flesh and blood. And he wondered just where she'd left the rest of herself. And why.

Spring thaw meant mud. Trails and paths went soft and thick with it, and caked boots left it streaked over the streets and sidewalks. At Joanie's, the locals who knew her wrath scraped off the worst of it before coming in. Tourists, who would flock to the parks and campgrounds and cabins in another month, were in short supply. But there were those who came for the lake, and for the river, paddling their canoes and kayaks over the cold water, and through the echoing canyons.

Angel's Fist settled down to the quiet interlude between its winter and summer booms.

At just past sunrise, when the sky was blooming with pinks, Reece navigated one of the narrow, bumpy roads on the other side of the lake. More a trail than a road, she thought as she twisted the wheel and slowed to avoid a dip in the hard-packed dirt.

When a moose wandered across the track, she not only gasped out loud in surprised delight, but sent up a little prayer of gratitude that she'd been going about ten miles an hour.

Now, she'd sing hosannas if she wasn't lost.

Joanie wanted her there at seven, and though she'd given herself twice the time needed, she feared she'd be late. Or end up driving to Utah.

Since she'd been looking forward to spending the morning baking, she didn't want to end up in Utah.

She passed the stand of red willows, as advertised. At least she thought they were red willows. Then caught the glimmer of a light.

"Round the willows, bear left and then . . . Yes!"

She saw Joanie's ancient Ford pickup, mentally pumped her fist in the air. And then just stopped the car.

She didn't know what she'd been expecting. A rustic little cabin, maybe. A small western bungalow. Either would have suited her image of where her sharp-tongued, impatient boss might live.

But she hadn't been expecting the style and space she saw in the log-and-glass house, the long sweep of porches, of decks that butted out to rise over marsh and into glade.

Nor had she expected a small flood of winter pansies, all cheery and purple, spilling out of window boxes. She thought: Gingerbread house, though it had straight, practical lines rather than curlicues. But there was something about the way it was tucked into the woods, like a secret, that made it fanciful.

Charmed, she followed the orders she'd been given and parked, then climbed out to walk around to the back.

Windows in every direction, Reece noted. Generous ones that would offer views of mountain, of marsh, of lake and of the town. More pots of pansies, others that held spears that would bloom with daffodils and tulips and hyacinths once the weather warmed.

Light beamed against the glass. She could see Joanie through one of the kitchen windows, wearing a sweatshirt with its sleeves shoved up to her elbows, already mixing something in a bowl.

Reece made her way around to a door, knocked.

"It's open!"

The fact that it wasn't locked made Reece wince. What if she were a madman with a club? Shouldn't a woman, especially one living alone, consider such possibilities and take basic precautions? But she stepped into a tidy mud/laundry room where an old flannel jacket and a shapeless brown hat hung on hooks, and a pair of ancient work boots stood handily by the door.

"You got any mud on your shoes, you take them off before you come into my kitchen."

Reece checked, hunched her shoulders guiltily, then took off her shoes.

If the exterior of the house had been a revelation, the kitchen was the answer to every prayer.

Spacious, well lit, with an acre of solid-surface counter in gorgeous tones of bronzes and coppers. Double ovens — oh God, she thought, a convection oven. Sub-Zero fridge, she noted, almost quivering with pleasure as a woman would before sex with an Adonis. She nearly salivated at the sight of a Vulcan range, and oh sweet Jesus, a Berkel mixer.

She literally felt tears burn the back of her eyes.

And with the high-end efficiency was charm. Forced spring bulbs bloomed in little glass bottles in the windowsill, interesting twigs and grasses lanced out of a burl-wood vase. There was a little hearth with a fire simmering. And the air was redolent with the perfumes of fresh bread and cinnamon.

"Well?" Joanie set the bowl she held on a counter. "Are you just going to stand there gawking, or are you going to get an apron and get to work?"

"I want to genuflect first."

Joanie's pretty mouth twitched. She obviously gave up, and she grinned. "Kicks ass, doesn't it?"

"It's fabulous. My heart sings. I figured we'd be . . ." She broke off, cleared her throat.

"Baking in some broken-down oven and working at a spit length of counter?" Joanie snorted, walked over to a stainless steel coffeemaker. "This is where I live, and where I live I like some comfort, and a little style."

"I'll say. Will you be my mommy?"

Joanie snorted again. "And I like my privacy. I'm the last place on this side of town. There's a good quarter mile between here and the Mardson place. Rick and Debbie, their kids. You see their youngest girl out with her dog by the lake every chance she gets."

"Yes." Reece thought of the little girl, throwing the ball in the water for the dog to fetch. "I've seen her a few times."

"Nice kids. Other side of them — with space between — is Dick's place. The one I let you practice on when you first came in. Old coot," she said with some affection. "Likes to pretend he's a mountain man, when what he is, is gay as the daisies in May. In case you haven't noticed."

"I guess I did."

"Then just beyond that is the cabin Boyd's using. Couple others planted here and there, but most of them're rentals. So it's a nice quiet spot."

"It's a beautiful spot. I ran into a moose. I mean, I saw one. We didn't make actual contact."

"Get so they'll come up and all but knock on my door. I don't mind them, or any of the other wildlife comes around. Except when they start in on my flowers."

Studying Reece, Joanie picked up a dishcloth, wiped her hands. "I'm going to have coffee and a smoke. Water's on simmer there in the kettle. Go ahead, make yourself some tea. We're going to be working for the next three hours or so, and once we get down to it, I don't like idle conversation. We're going to get that out of the way first."

"Sure."

Joanie took out a cigarette, lit it. Leaning back against the counter, she blew out a stream. "You're wondering what I'm doing, living in a place like this."

"It's beautiful."

"Had it nearly twenty years now. Over those two decades, I've added on, fiddled and fooled when I had a mind to." She paused to sip her coffee, crossed ankles covered in gray, woolly socks. "It's about what I had in mind now."

Reece took the kettle off the burner. "Your mind has really good taste."

"And you're wondering, since it does and I do, why my place isn't spiffier. I'll tell you," she said before Reece could comment. "People come into Angel Food because they want to be comfortable. They want good food, and they want it fast and at a good value. I had that in mind when I opened it, almost twenty years ago."

"You do a good business."

"Bet your skinny ass, I do. I came here because I wanted my own, and I wanted to give my boy a good, solid life. Made a mistake once upon a time and married a man who wasn't good for anything at all except looking handsome. While he was damn good at that, he sure wasn't good for me or my boy."

Cautious now, Reece picked up the tea she'd made. "You've done well without him."

"If I'd stayed with him, one of us would be dead." Joanie shrugged, took another drag. "Better all around that I kicked his ass out, pulled up stakes. Had some money, a nice nest egg." Her lips quirked into something between a smile and a sneer. "I may have been stupid enough to marry him, but I was smart enough to keep my own bank account and not tell him about it. I worked my butt off from the time I was sixteen. Waitressing, doing short-order work, fry cook. Went to night school and studied restaurant management."

"Smart. All around."

"When I got rid of that weight around my neck, I decided if I was going to work my butt off, I'd work it off for me and my boy. Nobody else. So I landed here. Got a job as cook in what was, back then, The Chuckwagon."

"Your place? Joanie's was The Chuckwagon?"

"Greasy burgers and overfried steak. But I made it mine within four months. Owner was an idiot, and was losing his shirt. He sold me the place for a song, seeing as he was about to go under. And when I was done wheedling him down, it was a damn short song at that." Satisfaction over the memory showed on her face. "I lived up above, me and William, we lived up above where you do now, for the first year."

Reece tried to imagine a woman and a small boy sharing that space. "Hard," she murmured, with her eyes on Joanie. "Very hard for you to start a business, raise a son, make a life on your own."

"Hard isn't hard if you've got a strong back and a purpose. I had both. I bought this land, had a little house put up. Two-bedroom, single bath, kitchen about half the size this one is now. And it was like a palace after being cooped up with an eight-year-old in that apartment. I got what I wanted because I'm a stubborn bitch when I need to be. That's most of the time, to my way of thinking. But I remember, I damn well remember what it was like to pick up and go, leave what I knew — no matter how bad it was — and try to find my place."

Joanie gave a half shrug as she drank more coffee. "I see what I remember when I look at you."

Maybe she did, Reece thought. Maybe she saw something of what it was that made a woman wake at three in the morning and worry, second-guess. Pray. "How did you know it was yours? Your place."

"I didn't." With quick jabs, Joanie stubbed out her cigarette, then drank the last swallow of her coffee. "It was just someplace else, and better than where I'd been. Then, I woke up one morning and it was mine. That's when I stopped looking behind me."

Reece set her mug down again. "You're wondering why someone with my training is on your grill. Wondering why I picked up stakes and landed here."

"I've given it more than a passing thought."

This was the woman who'd given her a job, Reece thought. Who'd helped her with a place to live. Who was offering her, in Joanie's no-nonsense way, a sounding board. "I don't mean to make a mystery of it, it's just that I can't talk about the details. They're still painful. But it wasn't a person — not like a husband — that had me pulling up stakes. It was . . . an event. I had an experience, and it damaged me, physically, emotionally. You could say it damaged me in every way there is."

She looked into Joanie's eyes. Strong eyes, steely. Not eyes full of pity. It was impossible to explain, even to herself, how much easier that made it to go on.

"And when I realized I wasn't going to heal, not really, if I stayed where I was, I left. My grandmother had already put her life on hold to take care of me. I couldn't stand it anymore. I got in my car one day, and I drove off. I called her, my grandmother, and tried to convince her I was fine. I was better, and I wanted some time alone."

"Did you? Convince her."

"Not really, but she couldn't stop me. Over the last few months, she's relaxed with it. She's started to think of it as Reece's Adventure. It's easy for me to color it that way when it's e-mail and

106

phone calls. And sometimes it's true. It's an adventure."

She turned to take an apron off the hook by the mudroom. "Anyway, I'm better than I was. I like where I am now, for now. That's enough for me."

"Then we'll leave it at that. For now. I want you to make up some piecrusts. If I see you've got a decent hand with that, we'll move on from there."

5

With only a scattering of customers, Linda-gail took counter duty. She dumped a piece of apple pie in front of Lo, topped off his coffee. "We've sure been seeing a lot of you in here the last couple of weeks."

"Coffee's good, pie's better." He forked up a huge bite, then grinned. "View's not bad."

Linda-gail glanced over her shoulder to where Reece worked the grill. "Heard you struck out there, slugger."

"Early innings yet." He sampled the pie. Nobody baked a pie like his ma. "Got any more of the story on her?"

"Her story, I figure. Her business."

He snorted over his pie. "Come on, Linda-gail."

She struggled to stay aloof, but damn it, she and Lo had loved talking the talk since they were kids. When it came down to it, there was no one she liked dishing with more than Lo.

"Keeps to herself, doesn't shirk the work, comes in on time, and stays till it's done or Joanie shoos her along." With a shrug Linda-gail leaned on the counter.

"Doesn't get any mail, from what I'm told. But she did get a phone for upstairs. And . . ."

He leaned in so their faces were close. "Keep going."

"Well, Brenda over at the hotel told me while Reece was staying there she moved the dresser over in front of the door to the next room. If you ask me, she's afraid of something, or someone. Hasn't used a credit card, not one time, and she never used the phone in the hotel except for the dial-up, once a day for her computer. Room had high-speed access, but that cost ten dollars per day, so dial-up's cheaper. That's it."

"Sounds like she could use a distraction."

"That's some euphemism, Lo," Linda-gail said in disgust. She pulled back, annoyed with herself that she'd gotten drawn back into an old habit. "I tell you what she doesn't need. She doesn't need some horny guy sniffing at her heels hoping to score. What she could use is a friend."

"I can be a friend. You and me, we're friends."

"Is that what we are?"

Something shifted in his eyes, over his face. He slid his hand over the counter toward hers. "Linda-gail —"

But she looked away from him, drew

back and put on her waitress smile. "Hey, Sheriff."

"Linda-gail. Lo." Sheriff Richard Mardson slid onto a stool. He was a big man with a long reach, who walked with an easy gait and kept the peace by reason and compromise when he could, by steely-eyed force when he couldn't.

He liked his coffee sweet and light, and was already reaching for the sugar when Linda-gail poured him out a cup. "You two wrangling again?"

"Just talking," Lo told him. "About Ma's newest cook."

"She sure can work that grill. Linda-gail, why don't you have her do me a chicken-fried steak." He dumped half-and-half in his coffee. He had clear blue eyes to go with blond hair he wore in a brush cut. His strong jaw was clean-shaven since his wife of fourteen years had nagged him brainless to get rid of the beard he'd let grow over the winter.

"You after that skinny girl, Lo?"

"Made a few tentative moves in that direction."

Rick shook his head. "You need to settle down with the love of a good woman."

"I do. Every chance I get. The new cook's got an air of mystery." He swiveled around, settled in for a talk. "Some people think maybe she's on the run."

"If she is, it isn't from the law. I do my job," Rick said when Lo raised his eyebrows. "No criminal on her, no outstanding warrants. And she cooks a hell of a steak."

"I guess you know she's living upstairs now. Linda-gail just told me she heard from Brenda at the hotel Reece kept the dresser pulled across the door to the next room while she stayed there. Sounds to me like the woman's spooked."

"Maybe she's got reason." His level blue gaze shifted toward the kitchen. "Most likely took off from her husband, boyfriend, who tuned her up regular."

"I don't get that kind of thing, never did. A man who hits a woman isn't a man."

Rick drank his coffee. "There are all kinds of men in the world."

Once she finished her shift, Reece settled in upstairs with her journal. She had the heat set at a conservative sixty-five and wore a sweater and two pairs of socks. She calculated the savings there would offset the fact that she left lights burning day and night.

She was tired, but it was a pleasant sensation. The apartment felt good to her, safe and spare and tidy. Safer yet as she braced one of the two stools Joanie had given her for the counter under the doorknob whenever she was in the room.

Slow again today. Nearly everyone who came in was a local. It's too late to ski or snowboard, though I hear some of the mountain passes won't be open for another few weeks. It's strange to think there must be feet of snow above us, while down here it's all mud and brown grass.

People are so odd. I wonder if they really don't know I can tell when they're talking about me, or if they think it's just natural. I suppose it is natural, especially in such a small town. I can stand at the grill or the stove and feel the words pressing against the back of my neck.

They're all so curious, but they don't come right out and ask. I guess that wouldn't be polite, so they hedge around.

I have tomorrow off. A full day off. I was so busy cleaning in here, setting things up on my last day off, I barely noticed. But this time when I first saw the schedule I nearly panicked. What would I do, how would I get through a full day and night without a job to do?

Then I decided I'd hike up the canyon as I'd planned when I first got here. I'll take one of the easy trails, go as far as I can, watch the river. Maybe the rocks are still clacking, the way Lo said they did. I want to see the white water, the moraines, the meadows and marshes. Maybe someone will be rafting on the river. I'll pack a little lunch and take my time.

It's a long way from the Back Bay to the Snake River.

The kitchen was brightly lit, and Reece hummed along with Sheryl Crow as she scrubbed down the stove. The kitchen, she thought, was officially closed.

It was her last night at Maneo's — the end of an era for her — so she intended to leave her work space sparkling.

She had the entire week off, and then — *then* — she'd start Dream Job as head chef for Oasis. Head chef, she thought, doing a little dance as she worked, for one of the hottest, trendiest restaurants in Boston. She'd supervise a staff of fifteen, design her own signature dishes, and put her work up against the very best in the business.

The hours would be vicious, the pressure insane.

She couldn't wait.

She'd helped train Marco herself, and between him and Tony Maneo, they'd do fine. She knew Tony and his wife, Lisa, were happy for her. In fact, she had good reason to know — since her prep cook, Donna, couldn't keep a secret — that there

was a party being set up right now to cele-
brate her new position, and to say
goodbye.

She imagined Tony had waved the last
customers away by now, except for a
handful of regulars who'd have been invited to her goodbye party.

She was going to miss this place, miss
the people, but it was time for this next
step. She'd worked for it, studied for it,
planned for it, and now it was about to
happen.

Stepping back from the stove, she
nodded in approval, then carried the
cleaning supplies to the little utility closet
to put them away.

The crash from outside the kitchen had
her rolling her eyes. But the screams that
followed it spun her around. When gunfire
exploded, she froze. Even as she fumbled
her cell phone out of her pocket, the
swinging door slammed open. There was a
blur of movement, and an instant of fear.
She saw the gun, saw nothing but the gun.
So black, so big.

Then she was flung backward into the
closet, punched by a hot, unspeakable pain
in her chest.

The scream she'd never loosed ripped
out of Reece now as she lurched up in bed,
pressing a hand high on her chest. She

114

could feel it, that pain, where the bullet had struck. The fire of it, the shock of it. But when she looked at her hand, there was no blood; when she rubbed her skin, there was only the scar.

"It's all right. I'm all right. Just a dream. Dreaming, that's all." But she trembled all over as she grabbed her flashlight and got up to check the door, the windows.

No one was there, not a soul moved on the street below, on the lake. The cabins and houses were dark. No one was coming to finish what they'd begun two years before. They didn't care that she lived, didn't know where she was if they did.

She was alive — just an accident of fate, just the luck of the draw, she thought as she rubbed her fingertips over the scar the bullet had left behind.

She was alive, and it was almost dawn of another day. And look, look there, it's . . . it's a moose coming down to the lake to drink.

"Now there's something you don't see every day," she said aloud. "Not in Boston. Not if you spend every minute pushing to move up, move forward. You don't see the light softening in the east and a knobby-kneed moose clopping out of the woods to drink."

Mists flowed along the ground, she noted, thin as tissue paper, and the lake still as glass. And there, the light came on in Brody's cabin. Maybe he can't sleep, either. Maybe he gets up early to write so he can lie in the hammock in the afternoon and read.

Seeing the light, knowing someone was awake as she was, was oddly comforting.

She'd had the dream — or most of it — but she hadn't fallen apart. That was progress, wasn't it? And someone turned a light on across the lake. Maybe he'd look out his window as she was looking out hers, and see the glow in her window, too. In that strange way, they'd share the dawn.

She stood, watching the light in the east streak the sky with pink and gold, then spread over the glass of the lake until the water glowed like a quiet fire.

By the time she'd stocked her backpack according to the recommended list for a trail hike, it felt like it weighed fifty pounds. It was only about eight miles, up and back, but she thought it was better to be cautious and use the list for hikes over ten miles.

She might decide to go farther, or she might take a detour. Or . . . whatever, she'd packed it now and wasn't unpacking it again. She reminded herself she could stop whenever she wanted, as often as she wanted, set the pack down and rest. It was a good, clear day — a free day — and she was going to take every advantage of it.

She'd barely gotten ten feet when she was hailed.

"Doing a little exploring this morning?" Mac asked her. He wore one of his favored flannel shirts tucked into jeans, and a watch cap pulled over his head.

"I thought I'd hike a little bit of Little Angel Trail."

His brows came together. "Going on your own?"

"It's an easy trail, according to the guidebook. It's a nice day, and I want to see the river. I've got a map," she continued. "A compass, water, everything I need, according to the guide," she repeated with a smile. "Really, more than I could possibly need."

"Trail's going to be muddy yet. And I bet that guide tells you it's better to hike in pairs — better yet, in groups."

It did, true enough, but she wasn't good in groups. Alone was always better. "I'm not going very far. I've hiked a little bit in the Smokies, in the Black Hills. Don't worry about me, Mr. Drubber."

"I'm taking some time off myself today — got young Leon at the mercantile counter, and the grocery's covered, too. I could hike with you for an hour."

"I'm fine, and that's not what you wanted to do with your day off. Really, don't worry. I won't be going far."

"You're not back by six, I'm sending out a search party."

"By six, I'll not only be back, I'll be soaking my tired feet. That's a promise."

She shifted her pack, then set out to skirt the lake and take the trail through the woods toward the wall of the canyon.

She kept her stride slow and easy, and enjoyed the dappled light through the canopy of trees. With the cool air on her face, the scent of pine and awakening earth, the dregs of the dream faded away.

She'd do this more often, she promised herself. Choose a different trail and explore on her day off — or at least every other day off. At some point, she'd drive into the park and do the same, before the summer people flooded in and crowded it all. Good, healthy exercise would hone her appetite, and she'd get in shape again.

And for mental health, she'd learn to identify the wildflowers the guide spoke of that would blanket forest and trailside, the sage flats and alpine meadows in the summer. It would be a good incentive to stay put, to see the blooming.

When the trail forked, she rolled her shoulders to adjust her pack, and took the fork marked for Little Angel Canyon. The incline was slow, but it was steady through the damp air sheltered by the conifers where she saw nests high up in the trees.

Huge boulders sat among the pools of melting snow and rivers of mud where her guidebook claimed an abundance of wild-flowers would thrive in a few more weeks.

But for now, Reece thought it was almost like another planet, all faded green and brown and silent.

The trail rose, gently at first, up the moraine, tracking the slope through a stand of firs and dropping over the side to a deep, unexpected gulch. The mountains speared up, snow-breasted pinnacles shining in the strong sunlight, and as the trail angled up, more steeply now, she remembered to try to use the lock step, and briefly locked her knee with each step. Small steps, she remembered.

No rush, no hurry.

When she'd hiked the first mile, she stopped to rest, to drink and to absorb.

She could still see the glint of Angel Lake to the southeast. There were no mists now as the strong sun in a clear sky had burned it away. The breakfast shift would be peaking now, she thought, with the diner full of clatter and conversation, the kitchen ripe with the smell of bacon and coffee. But here it was quiet and stunningly open with the air stinging with pine.

And she was alone, completely, with no sound but the light wind swimming through the trees, carving through the grasses of a marsh where ducks minded their own business. And that, the distant and insistent drumming of a woodpecker having his own breakfast in the woods.

She continued on, with the climb steep enough to have her quads complaining. Before she'd been hurt, Reece thought in disgust, she could have taken this trail at a jog.

Not that she'd ever hiked, but how different was it from setting the elliptical at the health club to a five-mile hill climb?

"Worlds," she muttered. "Worlds different. But I can do this."

The trail cut through the still sleeping meadows, switchbacked over the steeps. Along the sun-drenched slope where she paused again to catch her breath, she could see a small, marshy pond where out of the cattails a heron rose with a flopping fish in its beak.

Though she cursed herself for reaching for her camera too late, she continued to huff her way along the switchback until she heard the first rumble that was the river. When the muddy trail forked again, she looked wistfully at the little signpost for Big Angel Trail. It would wind high up the canyon, and require not only endurance but some basic climbing skills.

She didn't have either, and had to admit her leg muscles were in shock, and her feet were annoyed. She had to stop again, drink again, and debated whether she should simply content herself with the views of marshes and meadows on this first outing. She could sit on a rock here, soak in the sun, perhaps be lucky enough to see some wildlife. But that rumble called to her. She'd set out to hike Little Angel, and hiking it was what she would do.

Her shoulders ached. Okay, she'd probably gone seriously overboard with the supplies in her backpack. But she reminded herself she'd made it halfway, and even at her meandering pace, she could make her goal before noon.

She cut through the meadow, then up the muddy slope. When she made it up and around the next switchback, she had her first look at the long, brilliant ribbon of the river.

It carved through the canyon with a steady murmur of power. Here and there huddles of rock and boulders were stacked on its verge as if the river had simply flung them out. Still it was nearly placid here, almost dreamy curling through the steep, sheer walls on its way west.

She got out her camera, already knowing a snapshot wouldn't capture the scope. A picture couldn't give her the sounds, the feel of the air, the staggering drops and wild rises of the rock.

Then she saw a pair of bright blue kayaks, and delighted, framed them in to use for scale. She watched the kayakers paddle, circle, heard the dim sound of voices that must have been raised to shouts.

Someone was getting a lesson, she decided, then pulled out her binoculars to get a closer look. A man and a boy — young teens, she decided. The boy's face was a study in concentration and excitement. She saw him grin, nod, and his mouth moved as he called out something to his companion. Teacher?

They continued to paddle, moving side by side, heading west down the river.

On the trail above, Reece hung her binoculars around her neck and followed.

The height was enthralling. As her body pushed itself forward she felt the burn of muscles, the giddiness of adventure, and no tingle of worry or anxiety. What she felt, she realized, was utterly human. Small and mortal and full of wonder. She had only to tip back her head, and the whole of the sky belonged to her. To her, she thought, and those mountains that shone blue in the sunlight.

Even with the chill on her face, the sweat of effort dampened her back. Next stop, she told herself, she was taking off her jacket and drinking a pint of water.

She trudged up and up, panting.

And stopped short, skidding a little, when she saw Brody perched on a wide, rocky ledge.

He barely spared her a glance. "Should've known it was you. You make enough noise to start an avalanche." When she glanced up, warily, he shook his head. "Maybe not quite that much. Still, making noise on the trail usually wards off the predators. The four-legged ones, anyway."

If she'd forgotten about the possibility of bear — and she had — she sure as hell had forgotten the possibility of human. "What are you doing up here?"

"Minding my own business." He took a slug out of his water bottle. "You? Other than tromping along singing 'Ain't No Mountain High Enough.' "

"I was not." Oh, please, she was not.

"Okay, you weren't singing it. It was more gasping it."

"I'm hiking the trail. It's my day off."

"Yippee." He picked up the notebook sitting on his lap.

Since she'd stopped, she needed a minute to catch her breath before she started climbing again. She could cover the fact that she needed a minute or two to rest with conversation. "You're writing? Up here?"

"Researching. I'm killing someone up

here later. Fictionally," he added with some relish when the color the exertion had put in her cheeks drained away. "Good spot for it, especially this time of year. Nobody on the trails this early in the spring — or nearly nobody. He lures her up, shoves her over."

Brody leaned out a little, looking down. He'd already taken off his jacket, as she longed to do. "Long, nasty drop. Terrible accident, terrible tragedy."

Despite herself, she was intrigued. "Why does he do it?"

He only shrugged, broad shoulders in a denim shirt. "Mostly because he can."

"There were kayakers on the river. They might see."

"That's why they call it fiction. Kayakers," he mumbled and scribbled something on his pad. "Maybe. Maybe better if there were. What would they see? Body dropping. Scream echoes. Splat."

"Oh, well. I'll leave you to it."

Since his response was nothing but an absent grunt, she continued on. It was a little irritating, really, she thought. He had a good spot to rest and to take in the view. Which would've been *her* spot if he hadn't been there. But she'd find another, she'd find her own. Just a little higher up.

Still, she kept well away from the edge as she hiked, and tried to erase the image of a body flying off the end of the world, down to the rocks and water below.

She knew she was hitting the wall of her endurance when she heard the thunder again. Stopping, she braced her hands on her thighs and caught her breath. Before she could decide if this was the spot, she heard the long, fiercesome cry of a hawk. Looking up, she saw it sweep west.

She wanted to follow the hawk, like a sign. One more switchback, she decided, just one more, then she'd sit in splendid solitude, unpack her lunch and enjoy an hour with the river.

She was rewarded for that last struggle of effort with a view of white water. It churned and slapped at the fists and knuckles of rock, spewed up against towers of them, then spilled down on itself in a short, foaming waterfall. The roar of it filled the canyon, and rolled over her own laugh of delight.

She'd made it after all.

With relief she unshouldered her pack before sinking down to sit on a pocked boulder. She unpacked her lunch, and pleased herself by eating ravenously.

Top of the world, that's how she felt. Calm and energized at once, and absolutely happy. She bit into an apple so crisp it shocked her senses as the hawk cried out again and soared overhead.

It was perfect, she thought. Absolutely perfect.

She lifted her binoculars to follow the hawk's flight, then skimmed them down to track the powerful surge of the river. With hope, she began to scout the rocks, the stands of willow and cottonwood, back into the pines for wildlife. A bear might come fishing, or she might spot another moose, an elk who came to drink.

She wanted to see beaver and watch otters play. She wanted to simply be exactly where she was, with the peaks rising up, the sun shining and the water a constant rumble below.

If she hadn't been searching the rough shoreline, she would have missed them.

They stood between the trees and the rocks. The man — at least she thought it was a man — had his back to her, with the woman facing the river, hands on her hips.

Even with her binoculars, the height and the distance made it impossible to see them clearly, but she saw the spill of dark hair over a red jacket, under a red cap.

Reece wondered what they were doing. Debating a camping spot, she mused, or a place to put into the river. But she skimmed the glasses along and didn't see a sign of a canoe or kayak. Camping, then, though she couldn't spot any gear.

With a shrug, she went back to watching

them. It seemed intrusive, but she had to admit there was a little thrill in that. They couldn't know she was there, high up on the other side of the river, studying them as she might have a couple of bear cubs or a herd of deer.

"Having an argument," she mumbled. "That's what it looks like to me."

There was something aggressive and angry in the woman's stance, and when she jabbed her finger at the man, Reece let out a low whistle.

"Oh yeah, you're pissed off. Bet you wanted to stay at a nice hotel with indoor plumbing and room service, and he dragged you out to pitch a tent."

The man made a gesture like an umpire calling a batter safe at the plate, and this time the woman slapped him. "Ouch." Reece winced, and ordered herself to lower the binoculars. It wasn't right to spy on them. But she couldn't resist the private little drama, and kept her glasses trained.

The woman shoved both hands against the man's chest, then slapped him again. Reece started to lower the glasses now as the nasty violence made her a little sick.

But her hand froze, and her heart jolted when she saw the man's arm rear back. She couldn't tell if it was a punch, a slap or a backhand, but the woman went sprawling.

"No, no, don't," she murmured. "Don't. You both have to stop now. Just stop it."

Instead, the woman leaped up, charged. Before she could land whatever blow she'd intended, she was thrust back again, slipping on the muddy ground and landing hard.

The man walked over, stood over her while Reece's heart thumped against her ribs. He seemed to reach down as if to offer her a hand up, and the woman braced herself on her elbows. Her mouth was bleeding, maybe her nose, but her lips were working fast. Screaming at him, Reece thought. Stop screaming at him, you'll only make it worse.

It got worse, horribly worse when he straddled the woman, when he jerked her head up by the hair and slammed it to the ground. Not aware that she'd leaped to her own feet, that her lungs were burning with her own screams, Reece stared through the glasses when the man's hands closed over the woman's throat.

Boots beat against the ground; the body bucked and arched. And when it went still, there was the roar of the river and the harsh sobs ripping out of Reece's chest.

She turned, stumbling, slipping and going down hard on both knees. Then she shoved herself to her feet, and she ran.

It was a blur with her boots slithering on

the path as she took the downhill slope at a crazed speed. Her heart rammed into her throat, a spiny ball of terror while she stumbled and slid around the sharp switch-backs. The face of the woman in the red coat became another face, one with staring, baby-doll blue eyes.

Ginny. It wasn't Ginny. It wasn't Boston. It wasn't a dream.

Still it all mixed and merged in her mind until she heard the screams and the laughter, the gunshots. Until her chest began to throb, and the world began to spin.

She slammed hard into Brody, struggled wildly against his hold.

"Stop it. What are you, crazy? Suicidal?" Voice sharp, he shoved her back against the rock face, bracing her when her knees gave way. "Shut it down, now! Hysteria doesn't help. What was it? Bear?"

"He killed her, he killed her. I saw, I saw it." Because he was there, she threw herself against him, buried her face against his shoulder. "I saw it. It wasn't Ginny. It wasn't a dream. He killed her, across the river."

"Breathe." He drew back, gripped her shoulders. He angled his head down until her eyes met his. "I said breathe. Okay, again. One more time."

"Okay, okay. I'm okay." She sucked air

in, pushed it out. "Please help me. Please. They were across the river, and I saw them, with these." She lifted her binoculars with a hand that simply wouldn't steady. "He killed her, and I saw it."

"Show me."

She closed her eyes. Not alone this time, she thought. Someone was here, someone could help. "Up the trail. I don't know how far I ran back, but it's up the trail."

She didn't want to go back, didn't want to see it again, but he had her arm and was leading her.

"I stopped to eat," she said more calmly. "To watch the water, and the little falls. There was a hawk."

"Yeah, I saw it."

"It was beautiful. I got my binoculars. I thought I might see a bear or a moose. I saw a moose this morning at the lake. I thought . . ." She knew she was babbling, tried to draw it back inside. "I was scanning the trees, the rocks, and I saw two people."

"What did they look like?"

"I . . . I couldn't see very well." She folded her arms over her chest. She'd taken off her jacket, spread it on the rock where she'd had lunch. To soak up the sun.

Now she was so cold. Into-the-bone cold.

"But she had long hair. Dark hair, and

she had a red coat and cap. She had sunglasses on. His back was to me."

"What was he wearing?"

"Um. A dark jacket, and an orange cap. Like hunters wear. He . . . I think . . . Yes, I think he had sunglasses, too. I didn't see his face. There, there's my pack. I left everything and ran. Over there, it was over there." She pointed, and quickened her pace. "They were over there, in front of the trees. They're gone now, but they were there, down there. I saw them. I have to sit down."

When she lowered herself to the rock, he said nothing, but took the binoculars from around her neck. He trained them below. He saw no one, no sign of anyone.

"What exactly did you see?"

"They were arguing. I could tell she was pissed off by the way she was standing. Hands on her hips. Aggressive." She had to swallow, focus, because her stomach was starting to roil. And shivering, she picked up her jacket and put it on. Wrapped it tight around her. "She slapped him, then she shoved him back and slapped him again. He hit her, knocked her down, but she got up and went after him. That's when he hit her again. I saw blood on her face. I think I saw blood on her face. Oh God, oh God."

Brody did no more than flick a glance in

Reece's direction. "You're not going to get hysterical again. You're going to finish telling me what you saw."

"He got down, and he grabbed her by the hair and he slammed her head down, I think. It looked like . . . he strangled her." Replaying it, Reece rubbed the back of her hand over her mouth, prayed she wouldn't be sick. "He strangled her, and her feet were beating the ground, and then they weren't. I ran. I screamed, I think, but it's so loud with the rapids, it's loud."

"It's a long distance, even with the glasses. You're sure about this?"

She looked up then, her eyes swollen and exhausted. "Have you ever seen someone killed?"

"No."

She pushed herself up, reached for her pack. "I have. He took her somewhere, carried her body away. Dragged her away. I don't know. But he killed her and he's getting away. We have to get help."

"Give me your pack."

"I can carry my own pack."

He pulled it away from her, sent her a pitying look. "Carry mine, it's lighter." He shrugged out of it, held it out to her. "We can stand here and argue about it. I'll still win, but we'll waste time."

She put on his pack, and of course he was right. It was considerably lighter.

132

She'd brought too much, but she'd just wanted to be sure . . .

"Cell phone! I'm an idiot."

"That may be," he said as she dug into her pocket. "But the cell phone won't do you any good here. No signal."

Though she kept walking, she tried it anyway. "Maybe we'll hit a spot where it'll get through. It's going to take so long to get back. You'd make it faster alone. You should go ahead."

"No."

"But —"

"Who'd you see killed before?"

"I can't talk about it. How long will it take to get back?"

"Until we get there. And don't start that are-we-there-yet crap."

She nearly smiled. He was so brusque, so brisk, he pushed her fear away. He was right. They'd get there when they got there. And they'd do what they needed to do when they did.

And the way his stride ate up the ground, they'd be there in half the time it had taken her to do the trail in the first place. If she managed to keep up with him.

"Talk to me, will you? About something else? Anything else. About your book."

"No. I don't talk about works in progress."

"Artistic temperament."

"No, it's boring."

"I wouldn't be bored."

He shot her a look. "For me."

"Oh." She wanted words, his, her own. Any words at all. "Okay, why Angel's Fist?"

"Probably for the same reason as you. I wanted a change of scene."

"Because you got fired in Chicago."

"I didn't get fired."

"You didn't punch your boss and get fired from the *Tribune*? That's what I heard."

"I punched what could loosely be called a colleague for cribbing my notes on a story, and since the editor — who happened to be the asshole's uncle — took his word over mine, I quit."

"To write books. Is it fun?"

"I guess it is."

"I bet you killed the asshole in the first one you wrote."

He glanced at her again, and there was a hint of amusement in his eyes. Eyes of such an interesting green. "You'd be right. Beat him to death with a shovel. Very satisfying."

"I used to like to read thrillers and mysteries. I haven't been able to . . . for a while." She ignored the protesting muscles in her legs as they continued the descent.

She was supposed to walk differently now, going down inclines. Keeping the weight forward, stepping onto her toes rather than her heels. As Brody was.

"Maybe I'll try one of yours."

He gave that disinterested shrug again. "You could do worse."

6

They walked awhile in silence, across the meadow, around the marshy pond. She'd seen ducks, she remembered, and the heron. And the poor, doomed fish. Her body felt numb, her mind hazed.

"Brody?"

"Still right here."

"Will you go with me to the police?"

He stopped to drink, then offered her the water bottle. His eyes were cool and calm on hers. Green eyes. Dark, like the leaves in late summer.

"We'll call from my place. It's closer than going all the way around the lake into town."

"Thanks."

Relieved, grateful, Reece continued to put one foot in front of the other in the direction of Angel's Fist.

To keep centered, she ran through recipes in her head, visualizing herself measuring, preparing.

"Sounds pretty good," Brody commented, and jerked her out of the visual.

"What?"

"Whatever you're making in there." He tapped a finger to his temple. "Grilled shrimp?"

No point, she decided, absolutely no point in being embarrassed. She was way beyond that. "Brined grilled shrimp. I didn't know I was talking to myself." She kept her gaze straight ahead. "It's a problem I have."

"I don't see a problem, except now I'm hungry, and shrimp's not in big supply around here."

"I just need to think about something else. About anything else. I just need — oh boy, oh crap." Her chest went tight and her breath short. The anxiety attack simply whipped out a hand to squeeze her throat. As her head went light with it, she bent from the waist, gasping. "Can't breathe. Can't."

"Yes, you can. You are. But if you keep breathing like that you're going to hyperventilate and pass out on me. No way I'm carrying you back, so cut it out." His tone was flat and matter-of-fact as he hauled her up straight. Their eyes locked. "Cut it out."

"Okay." There were gold rims around his pupils, around the outer verge of his irises. It must be what made his eyes so intense.

"Finish cooking the shrimp."

"The what?"

"Finish cooking the shrimp."

"Ah, um. Add half the garlic oil to the

bowl of grilled shrimp, toss. Transfer to a platter, garnish with lemon wedges and divided bay leaves, and serve with grilled ciabatta bread and the rest of the garlic oil."

"If I get my hands on some shrimp, you can pay me back for this and make me a plate of that."

"Sure."

"What the hell is ciabatta bread?"

She couldn't have said why that made her laugh, but her head cleared while they walked. "Also called Italian slipper bread. It's good. You'll like it."

"Probably. You planning on fancying up Joanie's?"

"No. It's not my place."

"Did you have one? Your own place? Restaurant? The way you handle the kitchen, it's obvious you've handled one before," he added when she said nothing.

"I worked in one. I never had my own. I never wanted my own."

"Because? Isn't that the American dream? Having your own?"

"Cooking's art. Owning the place adds business. I just wanted to . . ." She'd nearly said create, but decided it sounded too pompous. "To cook."

"Wanted?"

"Want. Maybe. I don't know what I want." But she did, and as they walked through the cool forest, she decided just to say it. "I want to be normal again, to stop being afraid. I want to be who I was two years ago, and I never will be. So I'm trying to find out who I'm going to be for the rest of my life."

"The rest is a long time. Maybe you should figure out who you're going to be for the next couple weeks."

She glanced up at him, then away. "I might have to start with the next couple of hours."

He only shrugged as he dug for his cell phone. The woman was a bundle of mystery wrapped in nerves. It might be interesting to peel off some of the layers and get to the center of it. He didn't think she was as fragile as she believed herself to be. A lot of people wouldn't have managed the long hike back without breaking down after seeing what she'd seen.

"Should get a signal from here," he said and punched in some numbers. "It's Brody. I need the sheriff. No. Now."

She wouldn't have argued with him, Reece decided. There was steely authority in his tone simply because it held no urgency or desperation. She wondered if she'd ever regain even a portion of that kind of control and confidence.

"Rick, I'm with Reece Gilmore, just about a quarter mile from my place on

Little Angel Trail. I need you to meet us at my cabin. Yeah, there's trouble. She witnessed a murder. That's what I said. She can fill you in on that. We're nearly there."

He closed the phone, shoved it back in his pocket. "I'm going to give you some advice. I fucking hate advice — giving or getting."

"But."

"But. You're going to need to stay calm. You want to get hysterical again, cry, scream, faint, wait until after he's finished taking your statement. Better, wait till you're out of my cabin altogether because I don't want to handle it. Be thorough, be clear and get it done."

"If I start to lose it, will you stop me?" She actually felt his scowl before she glanced up to see it. "I mean interrupt me, or knock over a lamp. Don't worry, I'll pay for it. Anything to give me a minute to pull myself back?"

"Maybe."

"I can smell the lake. You can just see it through the trees. I feel better when I see water. Maybe I should live on an island, except I think that might be too much water. I have to babble for a minute. You don't have to listen."

"I've got ears," he reminded her, then veered off to take the easiest route to his cabin.

He approached it from the rear where it was tucked in the trees and sagebrush. She imagined he could see the ring of mountains from any window.

"It's a nice spot. You have a nice spot." But her mouth went dry as he opened the back door. He hadn't locked it. Anyone could come in through an unlocked door.

When she didn't follow him in, he turned. "You want to stand outside and talk to Rick? The sheriff?"

"No." Screwing up her courage, she stepped through the doorway behind him.

Into the kitchen. It was small, she noted, but laid out well enough. He cleaned like a man. A terrible generalization, she thought, but most of the men she knew who weren't in the business cleaned kitchen surfaces only. Do the dishes — maybe — swipe the counters and you're done.

There were a couple apples and an overripe banana in a white mixing bowl on the stone gray counter, a coffeemaker, a toaster that looked older than she was and a notepad.

Brody went immediately to the coffeemaker, filling the tank, measuring the grounds before he'd taken off his jacket. Reece continued to stand just inside the door as he flipped it onto brew, then reached in a cupboard for a trio of white stoneware mugs.

"Um, do you have any tea?"

He shot a drily amused glance over his shoulder. "Oh sure. Let me just find my tea cozy."

"I'll take that as a no. I don't drink coffee; it makes me jittery. More jittery," she amended when he cocked a brow at her. "Water. Water'd be fine. Do you leave the front door unlocked, too?"

"No point in locks out here. If somebody wanted in, they'd just kick the door down or break a window." When she actually paled, he angled his head. "What? You want me to go check the closet, look under the bed?"

She simply turned away from him to un-shoulder his backpack. "I bet you've never been afraid a day in your life."

Got a rise out of her, he thought, and preferred the edge of insult and anger in her tone to the shakes and quivers. "Michael Myers."

Confused, she turned back. "Who? Shrek?"

"Jesus, Slim, that's Mike Myers. Michael Myers. The creepy guy in the mask. *Halloween*? I saw it on tape when I was about ten. Scared the living shit out of me. Michael Myers lived in my bedroom closet for years after that."

Her shoulders relaxed a little as she pulled off her jacket. "How'd you get rid of him? Didn't he keep coming back in the movies?"

"I snuck a girl into my room when I was sixteen. Jennifer Ridgeway. Pretty little red-head with a lot of . . . energy. After a couple hours in the dark with her, I never gave Michael Myers another thought."

"Sex as exorcism?"

"Worked for me." He moved to the re-frigerator, got her out a bottle of water. "Let me know if you want to try it."

"I'll do that." Sheer reflex had her catching the bottle he lobbed lightly to her. But she nearly bobbled it, and her shoulders went to stone again with the brisk knock on the front door.

"That'll be the sheriff. Michael Myers doesn't knock. Want to do this in here?"

She looked at the manhole cover–sized kitchen table. "Here's good."

"Hang on a minute."

When he went to answer, she twisted the top off the bottle and gulped down cold, cold water. She heard the low murmurs, the heavy tread of men's boots. Calm, she reminded herself. Calm, concise and clear.

Rick came in, nodded at her with his eyes level and unreadable. "Reece. Got some trouble, I hear."

"Yes."

"Let's sit down here, so you can tell me about it."

She sat, and she began, struggling to relay the details without bogging it down, without skimming over anything relevant. In silence, Brody poured coffee, set a mug in front of Rick.

As she spoke she ran a hand up and down the bottle of water, up and down, while the sheriff took notes, watched her. And Brody leaned back against the gray counter, drinking coffee, saying nothing.

"Okay, tell me, you think you could identify either one of them?"

"Her, maybe. Maybe. But I didn't see him. His face, I mean. His back was to me, and he had a hat. I think they both had on sunglasses. She did, at first. She had brown hair, or black. But brown, I think. Long brown hair. Wavy. And she had on a red jacket and a hat. Cap."

Rick swiveled to look back at Brody. "What did you see?"

"Reece." Brody moved back to the pot, topped off his mug. "She was about a quarter mile up the trail from me when she stopped. Couldn't have seen the spot where this happened from where I was sitting if I'd been looking that way."

Mardson pulled on his lower lip. "You weren't together."

"No. Like Reece said, she went by where I was working, we had a couple of words, and she kept going. I headed up maybe

144

close to an hour after, ran into her running back. She told me what happened, and I hiked back up to where she'd been."

"You see anything then?"

"No. You want to know the spot, I'll get a map, show you where."

"Appreciate that, Brody. Reece," Rick continued when Brody walked out, "did you see any boat, car, truck? Anything like that?"

"I didn't. I guess I looked for a boat, sort of, but I didn't see one. I thought they must've been camping, but I didn't see any equipment or a tent. I just saw them. I just saw him choking her."

"Tell me everything you can about him. Just whatever comes to your mind," he prompted. "You never know what you're going to pick up, what you're going to remember."

"I wasn't paying attention, not really. He was white — I'm pretty sure. I saw his hands, but he had gloves on. Black or brown. But his profile . . . I'm sure he was white. I suppose he might've been Hispanic, or Native American. It was so far away, even with the binoculars, and at first I was just passing the time. Then she slapped him. Slapped him twice. The second time she did, he shoved her, or hit her. She went down. It all happened so fast. He had a black jacket. A dark jacket and one of those orange, reddish-orangeish hunting caps."

"Okay, that's a good start. How about his hair?"

"I don't think I noticed." She wanted to shiver. It had been like this before. The questions she simply couldn't answer. "The hat would've covered it, I guess, and his coat. I don't think it was long. I yelled, screamed maybe. But they couldn't hear. I had my camera, right in my pack, but I never thought of it. I just froze, then I just ran."

"I guess you could've jumped into the river, tried to swim across it, then dragged him off to the authorities with the power of your will." Brody's comment was careless as he came back in with a map of the area. Brody laid the map on the table, pointed with his finger. "Here."

"You sure about that?"

"I am."

"Okay, then." Rick nodded, pushed to his feet. "I'm going out there right now, see what there is to see. Don't you worry, Reece, we're going to take care of this. I'll get back to you. Meanwhile, I want you to think back through it. Anything comes to you, anything at all, even if it doesn't seem important, I want to hear about it. Okay now?"

"Yes. Yes, okay. Thanks."

After nodding to Brody, Rick picked up his hat and headed out.

"Well." Reece let out a long sigh. "Do you think he can . . . Is he capable?"

"I haven't seen anything to make me think otherwise. It's mostly drunk and disorderlies around here, a few domestic disputes, kids shoplifting, scuffles. But he handles them. And there's lost or injured hikers or boaters, rock climbers, traffic crap and so on when the tourists come in. He seems to do the job. He's . . . dedicated, would be the term."

"But murder. Murder's different."

"Maybe, but he's the guy in charge here. And since it happened outside town limits, he'll have to call in the county or state. You saw what you saw, you reported it, gave your statement. Nothing else for you to do."

"No, nothing else." Like before, she thought, nothing else to do. "I guess I'll go. Thanks for . . . all of it," she said as she got up from the table.

"Nothing else for me to do, either. I'll drive you home."

"You don't have to bother. I can walk."

"Don't be stupid." He hauled up her backpack and headed out of the kitchen toward the front.

Because she felt stupid, Reece dragged on her jacket and followed. He strode

147

straight out, not giving her the time she might have liked to study and gauge his home. She had a quick impression of simplicity, casual disorder and what she thought of as the habitat of the single male.

No flowers, tchotchkes, throw pillows or softening touches in the living area she passed through. A couch, a single chair, a couple tables and what she saw was a cozy stone-faced fireplace dominating the far wall.

There was an impression of earthy tones, straight lines and no nonsense before she was out the door.

"I've put you to a lot of trouble today," she began.

"Damn right you have. Get in."

She stopped, and gratitude warred with insult, outrage and exhaustion. Gratitude lost. "You're a rude, insensitive, insulting son of a bitch."

He leaned back on his car. "And your point is?"

"A woman was murdered today. Strangled to death. Do you *get* that? She was alive, now she's dead, and no one could help her. I couldn't help her. I just had to stand there and watch. Do nothing, just like before. I watched him kill her, and you were the only one I could tell. Instead of being outraged and upset and sympathetic, you've been short and snippy and dismissive. So go to hell. I'd rather walk back up that trail for six miles than ride two miles with you in your stupid, macho SUV. Give me my goddamn backpack."

He stayed just as he was, but he no longer looked bored. "About time. I wondered if you had anything approaching a normal temper in there. Feel better?"

She hated that she did. Was infuriated that his carelessness had revved her up until she'd spewed out a great deal of her anxiety and dread. "You can still go to hell."

"I'm hoping for a reserved seat. But meanwhile, get in. You've had a crappy day." He pulled the door open. "And, just FYI. Guys can't be snippy. We're physiologically incapable of snippiness. Next time use *callous*. That works."

"You're an irritating, confusing man." But she climbed into the car.

"That works, too."

He slammed the door, then strode around to the driver's side. After tossing her pack in the backseat, he got behind the wheel. "Did you have any friends in Chicago?" she asked him. "Or just people who found you irritating, confusing and callous?"

"Some of both, I guess."

"Aren't reporters supposed to be sort of

personable, so they can get people to tell them things?"

"Couldn't say, but then I'm not a re-porter anymore."

"And fiction writers are allowed to be surly and solitary and eccentric."

"Maybe. Suits me anyway."

"To the ground," she replied, and made him laugh.

The sound surprised her enough to have her look over. He was still grinning as they rounded the lake. "There you go, Slim. Already know you've got spine. Nice to know you've got teeth to go with it."

But when he pulled up in front of Angel Food, and she glanced up at her own window, she felt her spine loosen, and her teeth wanted to chatter. Still, she got out, and would have reached for her backpack if he hadn't pulled it out from his side first.

So she stood on the sidewalk wavering between pride and panic.

"Problem?"

"No. Yes. Goddamn it. Look, you've come this far. Could you just walk up with me, for a minute?"

"To make sure Michael Myers isn't waiting for you?"

"Close enough. Feel free to take back the compliment — if that's what it was — about me having a spine."

He only tossed the backpack over his

shoulder and started around the building to her steps. Once she'd dug out her key and unlocked the door, he opened it himself to walk in ahead of her.

She lowered his insensitivity quotient. He hadn't sneered, he hadn't spoken, he'd just gone in first.

"What the hell do you do in here?"

"What? Excuse me?"

"No TV," he pointed out, "no stereo."

"I just moved in, really. I don't spend a lot of time here."

He poked around, and she didn't stop him. There wasn't that much to see.

The neatly made daybed, the couch, the bar stools. But it smelled, female, he noticed. But he didn't see any sign of the nest building he expected from a woman. No pretty and useless things sitting around, no mementos from home or from her travels.

"Nice laptop." He tapped a finger on it.

"You said you were hungry."

He glanced up from her computer, and it struck him how the nearly empty room made her seem so alone. "Did I?"

"Before. If you are, I could make you a meal. Payback. We could call it payback for today, and be even."

She said it lightly, but he was good at reading people and this one wasn't ready to be alone. Anyway, he was hungry, and

151

had firsthand knowledge she could cook.

"What kind of meal?"

"Ah." She pushed a hand through her hair, glanced toward the kitchen. He could almost see her doing a mental inventory of her stock. "I could do some chicken and rice quickly. Twenty minutes?"

"Fine. Got beer?"

"No. Sorry. I have wine." She turned toward the kitchen. "A nice white. It's chilled."

"Good enough. Are you cold?"

"Cold?"

"If you're not, take off your coat."

She got out the wine first, and a corkscrew. Then took a pack of two skinless chicken breasts out of the tiny freezer. She'd have to thaw them, at least partially, in the equally tiny microwave, but it couldn't be helped.

While she took her coat, and the one he'd tossed over a stool, to lay on the daybed, Brody opened the wine.

"I only have regular tumblers." She crossed back to open a cupboard. "Actually, the wine was mostly for cooking."

"You're serving me cooking wine. Well, *sláinte.*"

"It's a good wine," she said with some aggravation. "I wouldn't cook with anything I wouldn't drink. It's a very nice

Pinot Grigio. So *salute* is more appropriate."

He poured some into the tumbler he gave her, then reached over her head for a second one and added wine to it. He sampled, nodded. "Okay, we'll add you know wine to your résumé. Where'd you study cooking?"

She turned away and got to work. "A couple of places."

"One being Paris."

She took out garlic, green onion. "Why ask if Doc Wallace already told you?"

"Actually, it was Mac, who got it from Doc. You haven't picked up the small-town rhythm yet."

"I guess not." She took out a pot to boil water for the rice.

Brody took his wine, settled on a stool and watched her.

Competence, he thought. Control with a dash of poetry. The nerves that seemed to hum around her otherwise didn't sound or show when she was in this element.

What she needed was to eat more of what she prepared until she put on a solid ten pounds, minimum. Pounds he was speculating she lost after whatever had sent her running from Boston.

Again, he wondered who she'd seen killed. And why. And how.

She did something, quick and easy, with

some crackers, cream cheese and olives, and a sprinkle of what he thought might be paprika. Then arranged them on a saucer in front of him.

"First course." She offered him a hint of a smile before she started slicing chicken, mincing garlic.

He'd polished off half the crackers — nice bite to them — by the time she had the rice going. The air was pungent with garlic.

While he sat, quiet, she handled three pans — the chicken deal, the rice and another in which she stir-fried slices of peppers and mushrooms, small trees of broccoli.

"How do you know how to cook it all and have it ready at the same time?"

She glanced back, and her face was relaxed, a little rosy from the heat. "How do you know when to end a chapter and go on to the next?"

"Good point. You look good when you cook."

"I cook better than I look." She gave the vegetables a toss, shook the skillet holding the chicken.

As if to prove it, she shut down the heat, then began to plate the meal. She set his in front of him, had him lifting a brow. "Twenty minutes. And it smells a hell of a lot better than the can of soup I'd figured to open tonight."

"You earned it." She fixed her own plate — with considerably smaller portions than his — before she came around the counter to sit beside him. And for the first time, picked up her wine.

She half toasted him, sipped. "Well? How is it?"

He took his first bite, sat back as if to consider. "You've got a face on you," he began. "Fascinating in its way, and a lot of it's about those big, dark eyes. Suck a man right in and drown him if he isn't careful. But," he continued as she seemed to draw back from him, just a little, "maybe you do cook better than you look."

The way her grin flashed in appreciation made him think otherwise, but he continued to eat and to enjoy the meal, and her company more than he'd expected.

"So, you know what's buzzing around downstairs about now?" he asked her.

"In Joanie's?"

"That's right. People see my car out front, don't see me in there. Somebody says something, somebody else says, 'I saw him go up with Reece' — or Joanie's new cook. 'Been up there some time now.' "

"Oh." She blew out a breath. "Oh well, it doesn't matter." Then she sat up a little straighter. "Does it? Does it matter to you what they say?"

"Couldn't care less. You don't care what

people think or say about you?"

"Sometimes I do, too much. Sometimes I don't care at all. I sure as hell don't care that you lost a bet with Mac Drubber over me diving into bed with Lo."

His eyes lit with amusement as he continued to eat. "Overestimated Lo, underestimated you."

"Apparently. And maybe if people think we're having something going for a while, Lo will stop trying to charm me into going out with him."

"He hassling you?"

"No, not like that. And it's been better since I made myself clear. But this won't hurt. So I guess I owe you another one."

"I guess you do. Do I get another dinner out of it?"

"I . . . well, I suppose." Her brows drew together in confusion. "If you want."

"When's your next night off?"

"Ah . . ." God, how'd she managed to box herself in so neatly? "Tuesday. I have the early shift, off at three."

"Great. I'll come by at seven. That work for you?"

"Seven. Sure. Sure. Well, is there anything you don't eat, don't like, have an allergy to?"

"Don't fix up internal organs and expect me to chow down."

"Nix the sweetbreads, got it."

Now what? she wondered. She just couldn't think of any small talk, conversational gambits. Once she'd been good at this, she thought. She'd enjoyed dating, liked sitting with a man over a meal talking, laughing. But her brain just wouldn't walk down that road.

"He'll be here when he gets here."

She met Brody's eyes. "If I'm that transparent, I'm going to have to install some shades."

"It's only natural to have it stuck in your head. You let it go some while you were cooking."

"He must've found her by now. Whoever did it couldn't have taken her far, and if he buried her . . ."

"Easier to weigh her down with rocks, throw her in the river."

"Oh God! Thanks very much for that image, sure to dance in my head later."

"Of course, the body probably wouldn't stay down, not with the current. It'd end up surfacing downriver somewhere. Some guy going down to fish is going to stumble over her, or some hiker, paddler, tourist from Omaha, whatever you like. Someone's going to get a big surprise when they find her."

"Would you *stop* that." But she frowned. "Even if he did something like that, there'd be some sign, some evidence of what happened. Blood. He rapped her head pretty hard, or where the brush got trampled, or . . . footprints. Wouldn't there?"

"Probably. He didn't know anyone saw him, so why bother to cover tracks at that spot? Seems to me he'd be most concerned about getting rid of the body and getting away."

"Yes. So the sheriff will find something."

She jumped at the sound of footsteps outside.

"Probably him now," Brody said easily and slid off the stool to answer the door himself.

7

"Brody." Rick removed his hat as he stepped inside. "Reece." His gaze skimmed over the counter. "Sorry to interrupt your dinner."

"We're finished. It's not important." Though her knees shook, Reece slid off the stool to stand. "Did you find her?"

"Mind if we have a seat?"

How could she have forgotten the ritual when cops came to call? Ask them to come in, to sit down, offer them coffee. She'd stocked coffee in those days, for friends. For police.

"Sorry." Reece gestured to the sofa. "Please. Can I get you something?"

"I'm just fine, thanks." After settling on the sofa, Rick set his hat on his lap and waited for Reece to sit. As he had earlier in his own cabin, Brody remained leaning against the counter.

She knew before he spoke, saw it in his face. She'd learned to read the carefully neutral expression police wore.

"I didn't find anything."

And still, she shook her head. "But —"

"Let's just take it slow," Rick interrupted. "Why don't you go over what you saw for me again?"

"Oh God." Reece rubbed her hands hard over her face, pressed her fingers to her eyes, then dropped her hands in her lap. Yes, of course. Go over it again. Another part of the ritual. "All right."

She recited it all, everything she remembered. "He must have thrown the body in the river, or buried it, or —"

"We'll look into that. Are you sure about the location?" He glanced at Brody as he asked.

"I showed you the place on the map where Reece told me she saw it happen. Right near the little rapids."

"Other side of the river," Rick said to Reece, with his tone as neutral as his face. "That kind of distance, you could've been off. Considerably off."

"No. The trees, the rocks, the white water. I wasn't off."

"There wasn't any sign of struggle in that area. There wasn't any I could find when I branched out from there."

"He must've covered it up."

"Could be." But she heard the doubt in his tone, a slight slip out of neutral. "I'm going back in the morning, once we've got some light. Brody? Maybe you want to go on out there with me, make sure I've got the right area. Meanwhile, I'm going to make some calls, see if any female tourists or residents are missing."

"There are some cabins scattered around that area." Brody picked up the wine he'd left on the counter.

"I went by a couple of the closest ones. Got my own, Joanie's got a couple. Rental places out there, and this time of year, they don't get much business. Didn't see anyone, or any sign they were being used. I'm checking on that, too. We'll get to the bottom of this, Reece. I don't want you to worry. Brody? You want to take a ride out there with me in the morning?"

"Sure, I can do that."

"I can go downstairs now, ask Joanie for the morning off and go with you," Reece began.

"Brody was right there. I think one of you's enough. And I'd appreciate it if you wouldn't say anything about this to anyone else. For the time being. Let's get this checked out before the word spreads." Rick pushed to his feet, nodded at Brody. "How about I come by your place and pick you up about seven-thirty?"

"I'll be there."

"You try to enjoy the rest of your evening. Reece, put this out of your mind for a while. Nothing more you can do."

"No. No, nothing I can do." Reece stayed seated as Rick settled his hat on his head and went out.

"He doesn't believe me."

"I didn't hear him say that."

"Yes, you did." Helpless anger bubbled up. "We both did, under it."

Brody set his wine down again, crossed to her. "Why wouldn't he believe you?"

"Because he didn't find anything. Because no one else saw it. Because I've only been in town a couple of weeks. Because, because."

"I've got all that same information and I believe you."

Her eyes stung. The urge to pop up, press her face to his chest and just let the tears roll was overwhelming. Instead, she stayed seated, gripping her hands together hard in her lap. "Thanks."

"I'm going to head home. You might try to take the sheriff's advice and put this out of your head for a while. Take a pill, go to bed."

"How do you know I have any pills to take?"

His lips curved, just a little. "Take an Ambien and tune out. I'll tell you what's what — one way or another — tomorrow."

"Fine. Thanks." She got up to walk over and open the door herself. "Good night."

Satisfied he'd left her annoyed rather than depressed, he strolled out without another word.

She locked the door, checked it, checked the windows. Habit made her start toward the kitchen first to clean up the dishes and pots, but she turned instead and booted up her laptop.

She would write it all out, everything, in her journal.

As Reece sat down at her keyboard, Rick let himself into the sheriff's office, switched on the lights. He hung up his hat, his coat, then went back to the small break room to brew a short pot of coffee.

While it brewed, he called home. As he expected, his oldest girl answered on the first ring. "Hey, Daddy! Can I wear mascara to the Spring Fling? Just a little, *everybody* else does. Please?"

He pressed his fingers to his eyes. Not yet thirteen and already it was mascara and school dances. "What did your mother say?"

"She said she'd think about it. Daddy —"

"Then I'll think about it, too. Put your mama on, baby."

"Can't you come home? We could *discuss* this."

God save him. "I have to work late tonight, but we'll discuss it tomorrow. Put your mama on now."

"*Mom!* Daddy's on the phone. He has to work late, and we're going to talk about me wearing mascara like a *normal* person tomorrow."

"Thanks for the bulletin." Sounding

163

more amused than harassed — how did she manage it? Rick wondered — Debbie Mardson chuckled into the receiver. "I was hoping you were on your way home."

"Stuck here at the office for a while. Can't say how long. Why the hell does that girl have to wear mascara? She's got your eyes, longest lashes in Wyoming." He could see them, that long sweep, the bluebonnet eyes under it.

"Same reasons I do — light lashes. And it's a basic female tool."

"You're going to let her?"

"I'm considering."

Now he rubbed the back of his neck. He was a man woefully outnumbered by females. "First it was lipstick."

"Gloss," Debbie corrected. "Lip gloss."

"Whatever the hell. Now it's mascara. Next thing she'll be wanting a tattoo. It's the end of the world."

"I think we can hold back the tattoo awhile yet. You want to call before you leave? I could have your dinner warmed up."

"May be late. I picked up a meatloaf sandwich at Joanie's. Don't worry about it. Kiss the girls for me."

"I will. Don't wear yourself out, so you can come home and kiss me."

"I'll be sure to do that. Deb? Love you."

"Love you back. Bye."

He sat for a time in the quiet, drinking his coffee, eating his sandwich, thinking of his wife and three daughters. He didn't want his baby wearing makeup. But she'd wear him down on it, he already knew. His oldest had his mother's tenacity.

With a sigh, he stuffed the paper napkin in the take-out bag, tossed it away. And pouring a second cup of coffee, he went over Reece's statement in his head, winding his way — again — through the details, the timing. With a shake of his head, he added powdered creamer to his coffee, carried it back to his office.

He, too, booted up his computer. It was time to find out more about Reece Gilmore than she had no criminal record and came from Boston.

He spent several hours searching, reading, making calls and taking notes. When it was done, he had a file and, after some internal debate, stored it in the bottom drawer of his desk.

It was late when he left the office for home, wondering if his wife had waited up.

And when he drove by Angel Food, he noted that the light still burned in the apartment upstairs.

At seven-thirty in the morning while Reece was struggling to concentrate on buttermilk pancakes and eggs over easy,

Brody armed himself with a thermos of coffee and climbed into Rick's car.

"Morning. Appreciate you going out with me, Brody."

"No problem. I'll think of it as research."

Rick's smile came and went. "Guess you could say we've got a mystery on our hands. How long again did you say it was from the time Reece said she saw this happen until you got back there with her?"

"I don't know how long it took her to get down to me. She was running, and I was already heading up the trail. No more than ten minutes, at a guess. Five minutes, I'd say, before we headed back, maybe another ten, fifteen to get to where she'd stopped."

"And her state of mind when you saw her?"

Irritation crackled. "Like you'd expect it to be when a woman sees another woman strangled to death."

"All right now, Brody, don't go thinking I don't understand the situation. The thing is, I have to look at this differently. I want to know if she was coherent, if she was clear."

"After the first couple minutes, yeah. You take into consideration that she was miles from help, from any way to get help — other than me — that it was her first

166

time on that particular trail. That she was alone, shocked, scared and helpless while she watched it happen."

"Through binoculars, across the Snake River." Rick held up a hand. "Might've happened just the way she said, but I have to factor in the circumstances, and the lack of evidence. Can you tell me you're sure, without a doubt, she wasn't mistaken? Maybe saw a couple of people having an argument, even saw this man she says she saw hit this woman."

He'd given it a lot of thought the night before. Gone over the details himself, point by point. And he remembered her face — clammy and pale, her eyes huge, glassy and deep.

A woman didn't wear abject terror when she witnessed an argument between strangers. "I believe she saw exactly what she said she did. What she told me on the trail, and what she's told you three times in her statements. She hasn't veered off the details, not once."

Rick puffed out his cheeks. "You're right about that. Are you two involved?"

"In what?"

Rick snorted out a laugh. "I gotta like you, Brody. You're a smart son of a bitch. Are you two personally involved with each other?"

"What difference does it make?"

"Information always makes a difference in an investigation."

"Then why don't you just ask me if I'm sleeping with her?"

"Well now, that was an attempt to be sensitive and subtle," Rick said with the faintest of smirks. "But all right, then. Are you sleeping with her?"

"No."

"All right, then," he repeated.

"What if I said yes?"

"Then I'd factor that information in, like a good law-enforcement official. Your business is your business, Brody. Except, of course, that sort of business gets around town quick as a cat pouncing on a mouse. Nothing so interesting as sex, whether you're having it, or talking about someone else doing it."

"I'd rather have sex than talk about it."

"That'd be you." The smile came and went once more. "And me, come to that."

They drove awhile in silence until Rick pulled off the road.

"Easiest spot to cut through and reach the place by the river you showed me on the map."

Brody slung a small pack over his shoulder. Even for such a short hike, it wasn't wise to set out without the essentials. They moved through sagebrush and forest, where the soft dirt held tracks

Brody recognized as deer, bear — and, he assumed, Rick's boots from the day before.

"No human tracks leading to the river," Rick pointed out. "Mine from yesterday. 'Course they could've come in from another angle, but I took a good look around. You got a body to deal with, you have to get rid of it. Throw it into the river, might be first instinct, first panic reaction."

He kept his gait slow, kept his gaze tracking ground and trees. "Or you'd bury it. There'd damn well be signs of that, Brody. No point dragging a dead body far, and it's a hell of a lot harder to dig a grave than you might think."

He set his hands on his hips, the heel of one hand resting idly on the butt of his service weapon. "It'd show, and the wildlife around here would find it pretty quick. You can see for yourself now, there's no sign anybody came in or out of this area yesterday. I'm going to ask you again, could you have given me the wrong location?"

"No."

Through the lodgepole pines, the huckleberry, the elderberry bushes, they hiked northwest toward the river. The ground was moist from the thaw, Brody noted. And should've held human tracks as well as it did the tracks of deer and moose. Though he saw signs animals had passed this way, there were no human tracks. They skirted a thicket, and as Brody paused to look, crouched down to look for any signs it had been disturbed, Rick waited.

"I guess you did this yesterday."

"Did," Rick agreed. "Get some nice berries around here in season," he said conversationally. "Got your huckleberries, your bearberries." He paused, then looked toward where he could scent the river now. "Brody, if a man tried to hide a body in there, there'd be signs of it. And by this time, I expect, animals would have caught the scent and come exploring."

"Yeah." Brody pushed back to his feet. "Yeah, you're right. Even a city slicker like me knows that much."

Despite the circumstances, Rick flashed a grin. "You handle yourself pretty well in the backcountry for a slicker."

"How long do I have to live around here before I lose the slicker label?"

"Might wear off some after you've been dead ten, fifteen years."

"That's what I figured," Brody said as they began to walk again. "You weren't born here, either," he remembered. "Army brat."

"Being as my mother settled in Cheyenne before my twelfth birthday, I got a big leg up on you. Local-wise. Hear the rapids now."

The low rumble came through the quaking aspens, the cottonwoods and red willows. The sunlight grew stronger until Brody could see it reflected off the water. Beyond was the canyon, and the spot high up on the other side where he'd stood with Reece.

"That's where she was sitting when she saw it happen." Shielding his eyes with the flat of his hand, Brody pointed out and over to the rocks.

Cooler here, Brody thought, cooler beside the water, with the wind sighing through the trees. But it was bright enough that he pulled his sunglasses out of his pack.

"I've got to say, Brody, that's a fucking long way." Rick took out his field glasses and followed the direction Brody had indicated. "A fucking long way," he repeated. "Get some glare, too, that time of day. Bouncing off the water."

"Rick, we've had a friendly relationship the past year."

"We have."

"So I'm going to ask you straight out. Why don't you believe her?"

"Let's just take it a step at a time, first. She's up there, sees this happening down here, runs back down the trail, where she runs into you. Meanwhile, what's this guy doing with the dead woman? Throws her

171

in, she's going to wash up. And she'd have been spotted by now, more than likely. Not much right around here to weigh the body down, and by your timing, only about a half an hour to do it. That was the plan, it would've taken time — more, in my opinion, than it took the pair of you to get back within sight of this spot."

"He could've dragged her behind those rocks there, or into the trees. We wouldn't have seen her from across the river. Maybe he went to get a shovel, or rope. Christ knows."

Rick bit off a sigh. "You seen any signs anyone's been tromping in and out of here, dragging off a body, burying one?"

"No, I haven't. Not yet."

"Now you and me, we'll take a walk around, like I already did yesterday. There's not one sign of a fresh grave. That leaves dragging or carrying her out of here, to a car, to a cabin. Long way hauling dead weight, long way not to leave a single sign either one of us could see."

He turned back to Brody. "You're telling me you're sure this is where she saw it, and I'm telling you I can't see anything to indicate there was anyone here passing the time of day, much less knocking a woman to the ground and strangling her."

The logic of it was indisputable. And still. "He covered his tracks."

"Maybe, maybe. But when the hell did he do that? He carted her off, dragged her out of sight, came back, covered up his tracks here — and that's not knowing anyone saw him kill anyone."

"Or assuming he didn't see Reece up there."

Now Rick took out his own sunglasses and through them looked over the water, up to the trail. "All right then, change that around and say he did. He still managed to clear out in the thirty minutes you say passed. Give it forty, and it still doesn't hold for me."

"You think she's lying? Made it up? What's the point?"

"I don't think she's lying." Rick shoved back his hat, gave his brow a troubled rub. "There's more to this, Brody. Seeing you two together yesterday — first at your place, then at hers — I figured you had something going. That maybe you knew more about her."

"More of what?"

"Let's do that walk around, and I'm going to tell you. I expect you can keep what I tell you to yourself. I figure you're one of the few people in the Fist who can do that."

As they walked, Brody kept his eyes on the ground, or studied the brush. He wanted, more than he'd realized, to find something to prove Rick wrong.

Which meant, he realized, he was trying harder to prove some woman was dead instead of another woman was mistaken.

But he remembered how she'd looked, how she'd struggled to keep herself from dissolving on the long hike back. And how alone she'd looked standing in her nearly empty apartment.

"I did some checking up on her." When Brody stopped, narrowed his eyes, Rick shook his head. "I consider that part of my job. Somebody new comes around, settles in, I want to know they're clean. Did the same with you."

"And did I pass the audition?"

"You and I haven't had any words otherwise, have we?" He paused, lifted his chin to the left. "That's the back of one of Joanie's cabins. That one's the closest, and it took us about ten minutes to walk it. Setting a good pace, and not carrying dead weight. Couldn't've gotten any sort of vehicle closer than this. Either way, there'd be tire tracks."

"Did you go inside? The cabin?"

"Having a badge doesn't mean I can go inside somebody's property. But I looked around, looked in the windows. Doors are locked. Went to the two others that are closest, which includes my own. And there I did go in. Nothing there."

Still they continued on, reaching the cabin, circling it.

"Reece is clean, if you're interested," Rick continued when Brody peered through the cabin windows. "But she was involved with something a few years ago."

Brody stepped back, spoke carefully. "Involved with what?"

"Spree killing at the restaurant where she worked in Boston. She was the only survivor. She was shot twice."

"Jesus Christ."

"Yeah. Left for dead in some kind of closet, storage closet. I got details from a Boston cop who worked the case. She was in the kitchen, everyone else was in the dining room — after hours. She heard screams, gunshots, remembers, or thinks she remembers, grabbing for her cell phone. One of the men came in, shot her. She doesn't remember much more — or didn't. Didn't get a good look at him. Got knocked back in the closet and left there until the cops found her a couple hours later. Cop I talked to said she damn near didn't make it. Coma after surgery for best part of a week, and her memory was patchy after. And her mental state wasn't much better than her physical."

Nothing, nothing he'd imagined came close. "How could it have been?"

"What I'm saying is she had a breakdown. Did some months in a psychiatric hospital. She was never able to give the cops enough details or description. They never caught who killed all those people, then she dropped off the map. The lead investigator got in touch with her off and on during that first year or so. Last time he tried, she'd moved, left no forwarding. She got family — a grandmother — but all she could tell him was Reece was gone, and wasn't planning to come back."

Rick stopped, gave a long, slow scan, then changed directions and backtracked. A warbler began to call out in its quick, high-pitched song. "I recollect bits of it myself. The killing made the national news. I thought, as I remember, thank God we live out here, not in the city."

"Yeah, no guns out here."

Rick's jaw firmed. "People around here value their constitutional right to bear arms. And they respect it. City slicker."

"You forgot the pinko liberal part."

"I was being polite."

"Sure you were," Brody said mildly. "You right-wing lunatic."

Rick let out a rumble of laughter. "Don't know how I got to be friends with some urban elitist." He angled his head. "I'm surprised you didn't hear about this business, Brody. Being a big-city reporter."

Brody calculated the timing. If it happened right after he quit the paper, he would have been baking out his bitterness in the sun and surf of Aruba. He hadn't read a paper for nearly eight weeks, and had boycotted CNN. Just on principle.

"I took what we'll call a moratorium from the news for a couple of months after I left the *Trib*."

"Well, I guess the media business of it would have petered out in that length of time. Always something else to bombard the public with."

"Constitutionally, the First Amendment comes before the Second."

"And it's a damn shame about that. But to get back to it, I gotta say, what happened to Reece? That's a goddamn hell of a thing for anyone to come back from, and it could be she's not all the way back."

"So she, what, hallucinated a murder? Screw that, Rick."

"Might've fallen asleep, just nodded off for a few minutes and had a bad dream. Cop who worked the case told me she was prone to them. It's a long way up that trail for a novice, and she'd have been tired by the time she got all the way up to where she stopped. Could've been light-headed on top of it. Joanie says the girl hardly eats unless she shoves a plate at her. Got some nerves, too. Dragged the dresser in front of the door of the adjoining room in her hotel, kept it like that the whole time she was there. Never unpacked."

"Overly cautious isn't crazy."

"Now, Brody, I never said *crazy*. But I think it's likely she's still emotionally disturbed." He shot up both hands immediately. "Let me take back *disturbed* and say *fragile*. That's how I'm seeing it because, when it comes down to it, that's all I have to see. Not that I'm not going to keep looking into this, but I'm not calling in State at this point. Nothing for them to do here. I'll make inquiries into missing persons, see if I find anyone matches what description she could give me of the woman she saw. Can't do more than that."

"Is that what you're going to tell her? You can't do any more?"

Rick took off his hat, raked fingers through his hair. "You seeing what I'm seeing here? Which is nothing? If you've got the time I'd like you to go with me while I check out the other cabins in the vicinity."

"I've got the time. But why me instead of one of the deputies?"

"You were with her." Face set, Rick settled his hat back on his head. "We'll call you a secondary witness."

"Covering your ass, Rick?"

"You want to call it that," Rick said without rancor. "Look here, I believe she thinks she saw something. But there's no evidence to support it. What I think is she fell asleep, had a bad dream, and you've got to at least entertain the possibility that's just what happened. I don't want to add to her troubles, whatever they may be, and I've got to work with facts. The fact is, there's no sign of foul play here. No sign anyone's been here at all, come to that, certainly not in the last twenty-four hours. We'll do another sweep on the way back and check out the cabins in this section. We find anything — hell, we come across a ball of fucking lint — I'll call up State and pursue this. Otherwise all I can do is check with Missing Persons off and on."

"You just don't believe her."

"At this point, Brody?" Rick looked across the river, up to the rocks. "No, I surely don't."

When the breakfast rush was over, Reece dove straight into the prep for the soup of the day. She simmered beans, cubed left-over ham, diced onions. Joanie's didn't run to fresh herbs, so she made do with dried.

Better with fresh basil and rosemary. And coarsely ground black pepper would be an improvement over the damn gray powder in a can on the shelf. And for Christ's sake, how was she supposed to cook with garlic powder? She wished she had some sea salt. And wasn't there any-where around here that had tomatoes this time of year with some *taste?*

"Sure are full of complaints." Joanie walked over to the pot, sniffed. "Looks good enough to me."

Talking to myself again, Reece realized. "Sorry. It's fine; it'll be fine. I'm just in a mood."

"I could see that for myself all morning. Hearing it now, too. This ain't no cordon bleu establishment. You want fancy, you should've aimed your car toward Jackson Hole."

"It's fine. I'm sorry."

"Didn't ask for the first apology, and the second's just annoying. Haven't you got any backbone in there?"

"I used to. It's still in the shop for re-pair."

Whatever had caused the mood, the look in Reece's eye and the jerky way she'd been moving, was worrying. "Told you to make up what you liked for today's soup, didn't I?" Joanie kept her voice brisk. "You want something we don't have in here, you make a list. I'll think about ordering it. Maybe. If you don't have enough gump-tion to ask, don't stand around muttering and bitching about it later."

"Okay."

"Sea salt." With a derisive snort, Joanie

strode over to pour herself a cup of coffee. From that angle, she could give Reece a good study without being obvious about it. The girl was on the pale side, she noted, with shadows under her eyes. "Doesn't look to me as if a day off did you much good."

"No, it didn't."

"Mac said you hiked up Little Angel Trail."

"Yes."

"Saw you come back with Brody."

"We . . . we ran into each other on the trail."

Joanie took a slow sip of coffee. "The way your hands are shaking you're going to end up slicing your hand instead of those carrots."

Reece set the knife down, turned. "Joanie, I saw —" She broke off when Brody came into the diner. "Can I take my break?"

Something's up, Joanie thought, as she watched the way Brody paused and waited. Something's off. "Go ahead."

Reece didn't run around the counter but she moved fast, and she kept her eyes locked on Brody's face. Her heart slammed against her ribs. And her hand reached out for his while she was still two paces away.

"Did you find —"

"Let's go outside."

She only nodded, which was just as well since he was already pulling her to the door. "Did you find her?" Reece repeated. "Tell me. Do we know who she is?"

He kept walking, his hand firm on her arm, until they were around the side of the building at the base of the steps to Reece's apartment.

"We didn't find anything."

"But . . . He must have thrown her into the river." She'd visualized that countless times through the night. "Oh God, he threw her body in the river."

"I didn't say anyone, Reece. I said anything."

"He must have . . ." She caught herself, sucked in a hard breath. Then she spoke very carefully. "I don't understand."

"We went to the place where you said you'd seen them. We covered the ground from there to the road and back from different directions. We went to the five cabins closest to the area. They're empty, and there's no sign they've been otherwise."

The sick dread started in the center of her belly. "They didn't have to be staying in a cabin."

"No. But they had to get where you saw them from somewhere. There weren't any tracks, there weren't any signs."

"You went to the wrong place."

"No. We didn't."

She hugged her arms now, but it wasn't the sharp spring breeze that chilled her. "That's just not possible. They were there. They argued, they fought, he killed her. I *saw* it."

"Didn't say otherwise. I'm telling you there's nothing out there to support that."

"He'll get away with it. He'll just walk away and live his life." Reece sat down heavily on the steps. "Because I'm the only one who saw, and I didn't see enough, couldn't do anything."

"Does the world always revolve around you?"

She looked up then, torn between shock and misery. "And how the hell would you feel? I guess you'd just shrug it off. Gee, I did what I could, better go have a beer and stretch out in the hammock."

"Little early yet for a beer. Sheriff's going to check on missing persons. He's going out to the guest ranch, the B and B's, hitting some of the outlying places and campgrounds. Have you got a better way to handle it?"

"It's not my *job* to handle it."

"Mine either."

She shoved to her feet. "Why didn't he come back to talk to me? Because he doesn't think I saw anything," she said before he could answer. "He thinks I made it up."

"If you want to know what he thinks, ask him. I'm telling you what I know."

"I want to go out there, see for myself."

"Up to you."

"I don't know how to get there. And maybe you're the last person I want to ask for a goddamn favor, but you know what? You're also the only person I'm absolutely sure didn't kill that woman. Unless, among your other talents, you can sprout wings and fly. I'm off at three. You can pick me up here."

"Can I?"

"Yeah, you can. And you will. Because you wonder about this just as much as I do." She dug into her pocket, pulled out a faded and wrinkled ten-dollar bill. Slapped it into his hand. "There. That should cover the gas."

She strode off, leaving him staring at the ten with a mixture of amusement and annoyance.

8

Reece turned the soup to simmer, and since her blood was up, started a list of what she considered essential items for any kitchen.

Five-star restaurant, small-town diner, personal kitchen. What the hell did it matter? Food was food, and why the hell shouldn't it be perfectly prepared?

She handled a few orders for people who, for reasons that escaped her, wanted a buffalo burger before noon. Between orders, she set to work scrubbing down the kitchen, from the inside of the cabinets out.

She was on her knees washing out the area under the sink when Linda-gail crouched beside her. "Are you trying to make the rest of us look bad?"

"No. I'm keeping busy."

"When you're done keeping busy here, you can go over to my house and keep busy there. Are you mad at Joanie?"

"No. I'm mad at the world. The whole stinking, fucked-up world."

Linda-gail glanced over her shoulder, lowered her voice. "Got your period?"

"No."

"It's just that one or two days a month, I usually get mad at the whole stinking, fucked-up world. Anything I can do?"

"Can you wipe out the last twenty-four hours with the power of your mind?"

"Probably not." She laid a hand on the small of Reece's back, gave it a rub. "But I've got chocolate in my purse."

Reece let out a sigh, dropped her rag back in the bucket of soapy water. "What kind of chocolate?"

"The little pads in the gold foil the hotel puts on pillows at night. Maria in housekeeping's my pusher."

The smile felt so foreign on Reece's face it almost hurt. "They're not bad. Thanks, maybe —"

"Reece." Joanie's voice, clipped and cool, brought Reece's head out from under the sink. "My office a minute."

Reece and Linda-gail exchanged a look — and Linda-gail's was ripe with pity — before Reece got up and followed Joanie into the little office.

"Close that door. I just got a call from my boy. Seems the sheriff's been out to the ranch asking questions. Appears he's looking for some people, most especially a woman who might've gone missing. Lo didn't get much out of him, but I didn't raise any fools, so he got enough."

Turning to her tiny office window, she

186

shoved it open before yanking her cigarettes out of her pocket. "Rick says maybe somebody saw something happen to this woman, maybe that person was up on Little Angel and thought something happened across the river. Not being a fool, either, I figure somebody who maybe saw something would be you."

"The sheriff asked me not to say anything until he'd investigated, but since he's not finding anything . . . I saw a man kill a woman. I saw him strangle her, and I was too far away to help. I was too far away to do anything. And now they can't find anything. It's like it never happened."

Joanie blew out a quick stream of smoke. "What woman?"

"I don't know. I didn't recognize her; I didn't see her that well. Her face. Or his. But I saw . . . I saw . . ."

"Don't you go hysterical on me." Joanie kept her voice cool and firm. "You sit down if you need to, but you don't get hysterical."

"Okay. All right." Reece didn't sit, but rubbed away the tears with the heels of her hands. "I saw them. I saw what he did to her. I was the only one who saw anything."

Her boots drumming into the ground.

High-topped black Nikes with silver swatches outside the storeroom door.

His black jacket and orange hunter's cap.

Dark gray hoodie, big, black gun.

"I was the only one who saw anything," she repeated. "And I didn't see enough."

"You said you and Brody were on the trail."

"He was farther down. He didn't see. He went back up with me, but there was nothing to see." Because she couldn't get enough air in the room, the tiny box of a room, Reece moved to the window. "I didn't imagine it."

"Why would I think you had? If you were upset about this, you could've had today off."

"I had yesterday off, and look what happened. Did Lo say . . . was there a woman staying at the ranch?"

"Everyone booked there, working there, is accounted for."

"Of course." Unsure if she should be relieved or terrified, Reece closed her eyes. "Of course they are."

After a brief knock, Linda-gail stuck her head in. "Sorry. But we're starting to back up out here."

"Tell them to hold their water," Joanie ordered, then waited for the door to close again. "You okay to finish out your shift?"

"Yes. I'd rather have something to do."

"Then go cook. Meanwhile, if you've got something eating at your belly, screw what

188

Rick Mardson tells you. You can come to me."

"Thanks. My insides feel like they've been wrung out like a dishrag."

"I'm not surprised. It should feel better, spitting it out."

"It does. If I were to ask you — I asked Brody, but he and Sheriff Mardson are friends — so if I asked you, would you tell me what you think of him? As the sheriff."

"Highly enough to have voted for him both times he's run. I've known him and Debbie a dozen years, since they moved here from Cheyenne."

"Yes, but . . ." Reece moistened her lips. "As far as police work."

"As far as that, he does what needs doing, and doesn't make a fuss about it. You may not think there's much needs doing in a town this size. But I guarantee you, every mother's son, and daughter, in Angel's Fist has a gun. Most more than one. Rick makes sure people use them for hunting and target practice. He keeps things as peaceable as you can expect when this town bulges at the seams with tourists. He does his job."

It didn't take a hawk eye to see Reece wasn't convinced. "Let me ask you this," Joanie continued. "Anything else you can do about this business but what you did?"

"I don't know."

"Then leave it to Rick, and go on back in the kitchen and do your job."

"All right. I guess you're right. Um, Joanie? I'm making that list, and I just wanted to mention that buying bulbs of garlic would be cheaper and more practical in the long run than buying garlic powder."

"I'll keep that in mind."

The soup was a hit, so there was no point thinking it would've been better if she'd had everything she wanted at hand.

That was past — that constant striving for better, for best, for perfection. Hadn't she learned by now it was fine to get by? Nobody here cared if the oregano was fresh or had been sitting in plastic jars for six months.

Why should she?

She only had to cook, serve and pick up her check.

She had no investment here. In fact, she'd probably made a mistake taking the apartment upstairs. It was too close to settling in. She should move back to the hotel.

Better, she should just toss her things into her car and move on.

Nothing to keep her here. Nothing to keep her anywhere.

"Brody's here," Linda-gail called out. "Ticket up, he and the doc are going for the soup."

"Brody and the doctor," Reece mumbled. "Isn't that perfect?"

She'd fix them soup, all right. No problem at all.

With rage just beginning to bubble, she ladled up two bowls, plated them with rolls and butter. And as the bubbling went to steam, she personally carried them out to the booth where the men sat.

"Here's your soup. And for a side dish, let me make this clear. I don't need or want a medical examination. I'm not sick. There's nothing wrong with my eyesight. I didn't fall asleep on the trail and dream I saw a woman being strangled to death."

She spoke clearly enough, and with the outrage of her words stinging the air, conversations stopped at the tables near the booth. For a moment, the only sound was Garth Brooks on the juke.

"Enjoy your lunch," Reece finished and strode back to the kitchen.

She yanked off her apron, grabbed her jacket. "My shift's over. I'm going upstairs."

"Go right ahead." Joanie placidly flipped a burger on the grill. "You're on eleven to eight tomorrow."

"I know my schedule." She walked out the back, round the side, and stomped up the steps.

Inside the apartment, she went directly

to her maps and guides and took out the ones that applied. She'd find her way to the spot by herself. She didn't need an escort; she didn't need some man tagging along to placate and patronize her.

She pulled open the map, then watched it flutter to the floor from her limp fingers.

It was covered with jagged red lines and loops and splotches. The area across from the trail where she'd stood the day before was heavily circled, dozens of times.

She hadn't done that, she hadn't. Still, she looked at her fingers as if expecting to see red smears on the tips. The map had been pristine only the day before, and now it looked as if it had been folded and refolded again and again, drawn and scribbled on in some crazy code.

She hadn't done it. She couldn't have done it.

Breath wheezing, she dashed to the kitchen drawer, dragged it open. There, just where she'd put it, was her red marker. With trembling fingers, she pulled off the top, and saw the tip was dull and flattened.

But it hadn't been. She'd bought it only a few days before from Mr. Drubber.

With great care she replaced the top, laid the marker back in the drawer. Closed the drawer. Then she turned, keeping her back to the wall, and scanned the apartment.

There was nothing out of place. She'd know. She'd know if a book had been moved an inch out of position. But everything was precisely how she'd left it that morning. When she'd locked the door behind her.

Checked the lock twice. Maybe three times.

She looked down at the map on the floor again. Had she done that? Sometime during the night, between the bad dreams and the shakes, had she gotten up and taken the marker out of the drawer?

Then why couldn't she remember?

It didn't matter, she told herself, and walked back to pick up the map. She'd been upset, that was natural. She'd been very upset and she'd gotten the marker to be certain she didn't forget the exact spot where she'd seen the murder.

It didn't make her crazy.

She refolded the map. She'd buy a new one, she decided. She'd throw this one away — bury it in Joanie's trash — and buy a new one. It was only a map. Nothing to worry about.

But when she heard footsteps on the stairs, she stuffed it hastily — guiltily — in her back pocket.

The knock was brisk and, if she could interpret the sound of knuckles on wood — irritated. It made her certain it was Brody on the other side of the door.

She took a moment to be sure she was calm enough, then walked to the door to unlock and open it.

"You ready?"

"I changed my mind. I'll go by myself."

"Fine. Do that." But he nudged her back a step, then slammed the door behind him. "I don't know why I bother. I didn't drag Doc downstairs to take a look at you. Why the hell would I? It happens he comes in for lunch a few times a week — which, unless you're blind and stupid, you've seen for yourself by now. It also happens that if we happen to be in there at the same time, we sometimes sit down together. It's called being sociable. Happy now?"

"No. Not especially."

"Good because this is bound to get you going again anyway. Rick's made some inquiries — which would be his job, by my description of it — so word's getting around. Doc asked me if I knew anything about it. Whether I'd have told him or not was up for debate until you served the soup. Damn good soup, by the way. You maniac."

"I was in a psych ward for three months. Being called a maniac doesn't hurt my feelings."

"Maybe you should've given it a few more weeks."

She opened her mouth, shut it. Then walked to the daybed, sat. And laughed. Kept laughing as she pulled the tie out of her hair so it fell free down her back. "Why is that comforting? Why the hell is that sort of rude, inappropriate response easier to hear than all the 'you poor things,' the 'there, there, it's all right nows.' Maybe I am a maniac. Maybe I am just out of my mind."

"Maybe you should stop feeling sorry for yourself."

"I thought I had. I guess not. Well-meaning people, people who care about me, lined up doctors or therapists every time I blinked."

"I'm not well meaning. I don't love you."

"I'll remember that next time." She set the tie on the little table by the daybed. "Are you still willing to take me out there?"

"My day's shot to hell anyway."

"Okay then." She rose to retrieve her pack.

He stood by the door and watched her check the contents. Zip the pack. Unzip it, check inside again. Unless he missed his guess, when she zipped it shut a second time, she struggled for a moment not to open it yet again.

When he opened the door, she went out,

locked it. Then simply stood for a moment staring at the door.

"Go ahead. Check the lock. No point worrying and obsessing over it after we leave."

"Thanks." She checked it, sent him a brief, apologetic look, then checked it again before she made herself start down the stairs.

"It's an improvement," she told him. "It used to take me twenty minutes to get out of a room. And that was with a Xanax to take the edge off."

"Better living through chemistry."

"Not so much. Pills make me . . . off. More off than I might seem to be to you." Before she got into his car, she checked the backseat. "I didn't care about feeling off for a while, but I'd rather just take the time to make sure about things than take a pill and not care about them."

She secured her seat belt, tested it. "Don't you care why I was in a psych ward?"

"Are you going to tell me your life story now?"

"No. But I figure since I've pulled you in this far, you should know part of it."

He pulled away from the curve to start the drive around the lake and out of town. "I already know part of it. The sheriff did a background check on you."

"He —" She broke off, made herself think it through. "I guess that would be a logical step. Nobody knows me, and suddenly I'm yelling murder."

"Did they ever catch the guy who shot you?"

"No." Automatically her hand came up to rub absently on her chest. "At least, they think they identified one of them, but he OD'd before they could bring him in and question him. There was more than one. I don't know how many, but more than one. There had to be."

"Okay."

"Twelve people. People I worked with or cooked for and cared about. All dead. I should've been dead, too. It's one of the things I think about. Why I lived and they didn't. What's the meaning of that?"

"Luck of the draw."

"Maybe. Maybe it's just that cold." Was there comfort in the cold? she wondered. "They didn't get but a couple thousand. Most people use credit cards when they go out to dinner. A couple thousand, and whatever was in wallets, purses. Some jewelry — nothing special. Wine and beer. We kept a good wine cellar. But that wasn't why they died. Nobody would have stopped them, nobody would have put up a fight. Not over some money, some wine, some watches."

"Why did they die?"

She stared at the mountains, so powerful, so wild against the milky blue of the sky. "Because the people who came in wanted it that way. For the fun of it. Thrill kills. I heard the cops say that. I'd worked there since I was sixteen. I grew up in Maneo's."

"You worked at sixteen. You must've been a wild child."

"I had my moments. But I wanted to work. I wanted restaurant work. I bused tables, did food prep on weekends, during the summer and holidays. I loved it. I loved them."

She could see it now, as it had been then. The bustle in the kitchen, the clatter outside the swinging door, the voices, the smells.

"It was my last night. They were giving me a little going-away party. It was supposed to be a surprise, so I was fooling around in the kitchen to give them time to set it up. There was screaming and gunfire and crashing. I think I went blank, just for a minute. You didn't hear screaming and gunfire in Maneo's. Not in a nice family restaurant. Sheryl Crow."

"What?"

"On the kitchen radio. It was Sheryl Crow. I grabbed for my cell phone — that's how I remember it, anyway. And the door swung open. I started to turn — or maybe I started to run. In my head, when I think about it, or dream about it, I see the gun, and the dark gray hooded sweatshirt. That's all. I see that and I'm falling, then the pain erupts. Twice, they said. Once in the chest, and the other bullet grazed my head. But I didn't die."

When she paused, he glanced toward her. "Keep going."

"I fell back into the closet. Cleaning supplies. I'd been putting away cleaning supplies in the closet, and I fell back inside. The cops told me that later. I didn't know where I was. I came out of it, a little. Felt numb and cold and confused."

She rubbed her hand between her breasts again. "I couldn't get my breath. This weight on my chest. This awful pain, and I couldn't breathe, couldn't get air. The door was still open, not all the way, just a few inches. I heard voices, and at first I tried to call out for help. But I couldn't. Lucky I couldn't. There was crying and screaming, and laughing."

She lowered her hand, very deliberately, into her lap. "Then I didn't think about calling for help. I only thought about being quiet, very quiet, so they wouldn't come and check. They wouldn't come kill me.

"Something crashed. My friend, my line cook, fell on the other side of the door.

Ginny. Ginny Shanks. She was twenty-four. She'd just gotten engaged the month before. Valentine's Day. They were getting married in October. I was going to be her maid of honor."

When Brody didn't speak, Reece closed her eyes and let the rest come. "Ginny fell; I could see her face through the crack of the door. Bruised and bloody where they must have hit her. She was crying, and she was begging. And our eyes met, just for a second. I think they did. Then I heard the gunshot, and she jerked. Just once, like a puppet on a string. Her eyes changed. A fingersnap, and the life was just gone. One of them must have kicked the door, because it shut. Everything was black. Ginny was just on the other side of the door, and there was nothing I could do for her. For any of them. I couldn't get out. I was in my coffin, buried alive, and we were all dead. That's what I thought.

"The police found me. And I lived."

"How long were you in the hospital?"

"Six weeks, but I don't remember the first two at all, and only patches of the next. But I didn't handle it very well."

"Handle what very well?"

"The incident, surviving it, being a victim."

"What would be the definition of handling well being shot, left for dead and seeing a friend killed?"

"Responding to therapy, accepting there was nothing I could have done to avoid or prevent any of it, eventually being grateful to have been spared. Finding Jesus or throwing myself into life's pleasures until I wrung them dry," she said impatiently. "I don't know. But I couldn't cope with it, or didn't cope with it. Flashbacks and night terrors. Sleepwalking, bouts of hysteria, then bouts of lethargy. I'd think I'd hear them coming for me, see that gray sweatshirt on strangers on the street. I had a breakdown, hence the psych ward."

"They put you in Psych?"

"I checked myself into a psychiatric hospital when I realized I wasn't getting better. I couldn't work, I couldn't eat. I couldn't anything." She rubbed her temple. "But I had to leave because I realized how easy it would be to stay in that controlled environment. I had to stop taking the pills because with them I pretty much stayed blank, and I'd been blank for large chunks of time too long already."

"So now you're just neurotic and anal."

"That would be about right. Claustrophobic, obsessive/compulsive, with some occasional paranoia and frequent panic attacks. Crappy dreams, and I do sometimes wake up thinking it's all happening again, or could happen again. But I saw those two people. I didn't project, I didn't imagine. I saw them."

"Okay." He veered off to the side of the road. "We'll walk from here."

She got out first and, bracing herself, pulled the map out of her pocket. "I went to get this when I was pissed, thinking you'd sicced the doctor on me. I went upstairs, got this out because I was going to come out here on my own."

She opened the map, handed it to him.

"I don't remember doing that, marking it up. I don't remember, but that doesn't mean I imagined what happened yesterday. I must've had a panic attack during the night, and I'm blocking it out."

"Then why are you showing it to me?"

"You ought to know what you're dealing with."

He studied the map briefly, then refolded it. "I saw your face yesterday when you came running down the trail. If you imagined seeing that woman killed, you're wasting your time in the kitchen. Anybody with that vivid an imagination should be in my line of work. You'd outsell J. K. Rowling."

"You really do believe me."

"Jesus. Listen up." He shoved the map back into her hands. "If I didn't I wouldn't be here. I've got my own life, my own work, my own time. You saw what you saw, and it's not fucking right. A woman's dead, and somebody ought to give a shit about it."

She closed her eyes a minute. "Don't take this the wrong way, okay?" So saying, she stepped up to him, wrapped her arms around him, pressed her lips lightly to his.

"What would be the wrong way to take that?"

"As anything other than sincere gratitude." She swung her pack over her shoulder. "Do you know the way?"

"Yeah, I know the way."

As they stepped off the road, she gave him a quick glance. "That's the first time I've kissed a man in two years."

"No wonder you're crazy. How was it?"

"Comforting."

He snorted. "Some other time, Slim, maybe we'll go for something a little more interesting than comforting."

"Maybe we will." Now think of something else, she ordered herself. "I ran down to the mercantile on one of my breaks this morning and bought your book, Jamison P. Brody."

"Which one?"

"*Down Low.* Mac said it was your first, so I wanted to start with that. And he said he really liked it."

"So did I."

She laughed. "I'll let you know if I do.

Does anyone call you by your first name?"

"No."

"What's the *P* stand for?"

"Perverse."

"Fits." Now she wet her lips. "They could have hiked through from any direction."

"You said you didn't see any packs, any gear."

"I didn't, but they could have left it farther back, out of my line of vision."

"There weren't any tracks, Reece, in any direction, but for Rick's going in and out. Look." He crouched. "See here? I'm no Natty Bumppo, but I can handle the basics. My tracks from this morning, and Rick's. Ground's pretty soft."

"Well, they didn't fly in on the wings of a damn dove."

"No. But if he knew anything about tracking, about hiking, he could've covered his tracks."

"Why? Who'd look here for a dead woman no one saw him kill?"

"You saw him. And maybe he saw you right back."

"He never looked around, never looked across."

"Not while you were looking across. You ran, didn't you? And left your stuff sitting on the rock. Maybe he caught a glimpse of you taking off, or just saw your pack on the rock. Two and two make four pretty quick. He covered up. It took us two hours to get back to my cabin. Another thirty minutes easy before Rick would've gotten out here. More like another hour because he talked to you first. Three hours? Hell, you could cover up an elephant march through here if you knew your ass from your elbow."

"He saw me." And her throat slapped shut on the idea of it.

"Maybe he did, maybe he didn't. Either way, he was careful. Smart and careful enough to take his time, cover up any sign he'd been here, or she had."

"He saw me. Why didn't I think of that before?" She passed a hand over her face. "He'd already dragged or carried her away, or weighed her down and tossed her in the water, by the time I got to you."

"I'd go for the first option. Takes time to weigh down a body."

"So he carried her away."

Reece stopped, because there was the river rushing by ahead of the line of trees, the tumble of rocks. The blade of it cut through the canyon so the walls seemed to fly straight up. As if we were in a box, she thought, with the lid off to the spread of sky.

"From here," she murmured. "It's all so . . . alone here. The river, the presence of it, cuts you off from everything. And it's all so beautiful, why would you care?"

"A good place to die."

"No place is. Once you've been close enough, you know no place is a good place to die. But this is so stunning — the trees, the rocks, the walls, the water. It would've been the last thing she saw, and she didn't see it at all. She was so angry. I think she didn't see anything but him and her own rage. Then there would've been the fear, and the pain."

"Can you see where you were from here?"

She walked out, closer to the river. Cooler today, she thought, and not as bright. The sun wasn't as strong and the clouds were thicker — streams and rolls of white over the blue.

"There." She pointed up, over. "I stopped there, sat there and ate a sandwich, drank some water. The sun felt good, and I liked hearing the water. I saw the hawk. Then I saw them, standing here."

She turned to Brody. "Like we are. She was facing him, like this, and he had his back to the water. I said before I didn't think she saw anything but him. I guess he was only seeing her, too. I watched her more, because she was more animated. A lot of movement."

Reece threw her arms out, demonstrating. "Drama. You could feel the heat of her across the river. She was steaming. But he seemed very controlled. Or his body language was. Am I making this up?" She pressed her fingers over her eyes. "Am I remembering what happened, or projecting?"

"You know what you saw."

The absolute calm in his tone had her dropping her hands, and quieted the flutters in her belly. "Yes. Yes, I do. She was winging her arms around, jabbing her finger at him. *I'm warning you.* It seemed like that. And she shoved him."

Reece planted her hands on Brody's chest, pushed. "I think he fell back a step," she said drily. "If you wouldn't mind getting into character."

"Okay." He obliged.

"He went like this." Reece crossed her hands, flung them out. "I thought, Safe! Like the umpire's signal."

"Baseball?" He felt a trickle of amusement. "You thought baseball?"

"For a second. But it was *That's it. I've had enough.* Then she slapped him."

When Reece swung her hand, Brody caught her wrist. "I get the picture."

"I wasn't going to hit you. He took it, the first time, then she hauled off and hit him again. That's when he pushed her down. Go ahead."

"Sure." Brody gave her a shove, and though it pushed her back a little, it didn't take her down.

"It must've been a lot harder than that. No." She lifted her hands when he smiled and feinted another shove. "I'll just go with it." She glanced back to gauge the distance to the rocks. Reenacting the crime didn't mean she had to knock herself silly. "Wait. She didn't have a pack on." Reece shrugged hers off, tossed it aside, then dropped to the ground.

"She must've fallen harder, and I think she hit her head — bumped it, anyway — on the ground, or maybe on the rocks here. She stayed down a minute. Her hat fell off. I forgot that. Her hat fell off, and when she shook her head — like she was a little dazed — there was a glint. Earrings. She must have been wearing earrings. I wasn't paying enough attention."

"I'd say you're wrong about that. What did he do? Move toward her?"

"No. No. She got up, fast, lunged at him. She wasn't afraid, she was pissed. Seriously pissed. She was screaming at him — I couldn't hear, but I could see. He tossed her down. Not a shove this time. And when she fell, he straddled her."

Reece got down, looked up at Brody. "Would you mind?"

"Sure. No problem." He planted a foot on either side of Reece.

"He held out a hand, I think, but she wouldn't let up. She propped up on her elbows and kept at him. Her mouth was moving, and I — in my head — heard her screaming and bitching. Then he got down.

"He more than sat on her, put his weight down to hold her," she said when Brody crouched. "Oh." She wheezed out a breath when Brody followed directions. "Yeah, like that. Nothing playful, nothing sexual — at least from my view. She was slapping out at him, and he held her arms down. No, don't!" Panic spurted into her when Brody clamped his hands over her wrists. "I can't. Don't."

"Take it easy." He kept his eyes on hers as he loosened his grip, shifted his weight. "I'm not going to hurt you. Tell me what happened next."

"She was struggling, twisting under him. But he was stronger. He yanked her head up by the hair, rapped it down hard. Then he . . . then he put his hands around her throat. She bucked, tried to throw him off, she grabbed his wrists, but I don't think she had much left in her. Wait . . . he pinned her arms down with his knees, to stop her from hitting out. I forgot that, too, damn it."

"You remembered it now."

"She kicked out, trying to get some leverage, I guess. Her feet hammered against the ground, and her fingers dug into the ground. Then they stopped. Everything stopped, but he kept his hands around her throat. He kept them there, and I ran. Get up, okay? Get up."

He merely shifted so he sat on the ground beside her. "Any chance she was still alive?"

"He kept his hands around her throat." Reece sat up, brought up her knees and pressed her face to them.

He said nothing for a few minutes, just let the river run beside them while clouds shifted shadows over rock and water. "I figure you're the glass-half-empty type."

"What?"

"Glass is probably more than half empty because it's cracked and what's in it's leaking out. So you see this happen and you think, Oh God, guilt, guilt, despair. I saw a woman murdered and couldn't do anything to stop it. Poor her, poor me," he continued. "Instead of thinking, I saw a woman murdered, and if I hadn't been where I was when I was, no one would have known what happened to her."

She'd propped her chin on her knees to study him while he spoke, and now cocked her head. "You're right. I know you're right, and I'm trying to look at it that way. Still, you don't strike me as the glass-is-half-full type."

"Half full, half empty, what the hell difference does it make? If there's something in the damn glass, drink it."

She laughed. Sitting where a woman had died only the day before, Reece felt the laugh rise in her chest and break free. "Good policy. Right now, I wish to God it held a nice chilly Pinot Grigio."

After pressing the heels of her hands to her eyes, she pushed to her feet. "Reenacting it left signs. Footprints," she said as he rose. "Dents in the ground from the heels of my boots, flattened dirt, handprints. You don't have to be Natty Bumppo to see a couple of people were here, fought here."

Brody walked off a few feet to break off a fanning branch of willow and began sweeping it over the disturbed ground. "He's smart," he said as he cleared off the tracks. "He drags or carries her off, out of sight of the river, the canyon, then he gets a branch like this from another area, comes back, makes sure neither of them dropped anything. Have to keep your cool."

He straightened, studied the ground. "Pretty clean. Natty might be able to see something, but I'm an amateur. Could be, maybe, you bring in a team of crime-scene experts, they'd find a stray hair, but what's that going to prove?"

He tossed the branch aside. "Nothing. All he has to do is cover the tracks leading out. Plenty of places to bury a body around here. Or, if it were me and I had a car, I'd toss it in the trunk and drive somewhere else. Somewhere I could take my time digging a hole deep enough the animals wouldn't uncover her."

"That's not cool. It's cold."

"Killing somebody takes ice or heat, depending. Getting away with it? Yeah, that takes cold blood. Seen enough?"

She nodded. "More than."

9

As they walked back, Reece uncapped her water bottle and drank. When Brody held out a hand, she passed it to him.

"They always say there's no such thing as a perfect murder."

He drank deep, handed her the bottle. "They say a lot of things, and they're wrong a good part of the time."

"They really are. But still, whoever she was, she belonged somewhere. She came from somewhere. Odds are she had a job, a home. She might have had a family."

"Might have, could have."

Annoyed, Reece jammed her hands in her pockets. "Well, she was connected to at least one person. And he killed her. They had something between them."

"Back to might have, could have. They could have met the day they ended up here, or been together for a decade. They could have come from anywhere. Traveling in from California, up from Texas, out from back East. Hell, they could've been French."

"French?"

"People kill in every language. The point is, the odds of them passing through are just as good as they are for them being from the area. Probably better. Fewer people live in Wyoming than live in Alaska."

"Is that why you moved here?"

"Part of it. Probably. You work for a newspaper, a big-city paper, you're in people up to your eyeballs. The point is, the odds are better that whoever these people were, they came from somewhere else."

"And they got into a fight to the death because they got lost and he wouldn't stop to ask for directions? It's a male plague worthy of some serious ass-kicking, I grant you. But I don't think so. They met there or went there because they had something to talk about. Or argue about."

He liked the way she talked, Brody decided. Rarely in a straight line. Like when she cooked, juggling any number of dishes at the same time. "Supposition, not fact."

"Fine, I'm supposing. And I'm supposing they weren't French."

"Possibly Italian. Lithuanian isn't out of the question."

"Fine, a Lithuanian couple gets lost because, like men across the globe, he values his penis — among other things — as a compass. So he's incapable of asking for directions and thereby disparaging the power of his penis."

He frowned at her. "This is a closely guarded male secret. How did you crack the code?"

"More of us know of this than you could possibly guess. In any case, they get out of their car, tromp through the trees toward the river, because sure, that's the way to figure out where they are. They argue, fight, he kills her. Then, being a Lithuanian mountain man, he expertly covers all tracks and takes the body back to their rented Taurus so he can bury her in their homeland."

"You ought to write that down."

"If that's the sort of ridiculous nonsense *you* write, I'm amazed you've been published."

"I might've stuck with the French, just for that international scope. But it goes back, Slim, to they could have been anyone from anywhere."

It helped to think of it as a puzzle. It gave it more distance somehow. "If he covered his trail the way he did, he knows something about hiking and tracking."

"A lot of people do. On the 'could be' side, they may have been here before."

Brody glanced around. He knew this type of terrain because he'd hiked in areas like it, and used areas like it in his work. There'd be columbine and money flowers spurting up before much longer. Honeysuckle blooming as it twined wherever it could reach. Shady spots, pretty spots.

It would show off better toward June.

"A little early in the season for tourists," he calculated, "but people come this time of year because they want to avoid the summer and winter crowds. Or they're heading somewhere else and stop for a short hike. Or the ones you saw live in the Fist and sampled your cooking."

"That's a really happy thought. Thanks."

"You saw what he was wearing. Would you recognize it again?"

"Orange hunter's cap, black all-weather jacket. Coat. No, jacket, I guess. I see that kind of thing every day. I just didn't get a good enough look at him. I could hand-feed him the soup du jour and not know the difference. I don't see how I'll ever . . . Oh my God."

He saw it, too. In fact, he saw the bear a good ten seconds before she noticed it lumbering along. "He's not interested in you."

"And you know that because you're a bear psychic?" It seemed so unreal she wasn't really scared. At least not actively. "God, he's really big."

"I've seen bigger."

"Good for you. Um, we're not supposed to run."

"No. That would just entertain him until

he caught up. Just keep talking, keep moving, just a little detour. Okay, he sees us."

All right, she thought, starting to get really scared. Hello, bear. "And that's good?"

She remembered the illustration in her guidebook of the suggested position for playing dead during a bear charge. It looked something like the child's pose in yoga.

She could do that, no problem. She could easily fall right down on the ground, because if it charged, her legs were going to buckle anyway.

Before she could test the guidebook's veracity, the bear gave them a long look, turned its tail and walked away.

"Mostly they're shy," Brody commented.

"Mostly. Excellent. I think I need to sit down."

"Just keep moving. Your first bear sighting?"

"That close up and personal, yeah. I forgot to think about them." She rubbed a hand between her breasts to make certain her abruptly drumming heart stayed where it belonged. "To be bear-aware, like it says in my guide. Kinda breathless," she said and tapped her fingers to her chest again. "I guess he was beautiful, in a terrifying sort of way."

"One thing. If there was a dead body

nearby that he could scent, he'd have been more aggressive. So that means it's either not around here, or buried deep enough."

Now she had to swallow, hard and deep. "More pleasant images for me. I'm definitely having that wine. A really big glass of wine."

She felt safer when she was back in the car. Safer, and ridiculously tired. She wanted a nap as much as she wanted the wine. A dim, quiet room, a soft blanket, locked doors. And oblivion.

When he started the car she closed her gritty eyes for just a moment. And slid off the edge of fatigue into sleep.

She slept quietly, Brody thought, not a sound, not a movement. Her head rested in that nook between the seat and the window, and her hands lay limp in her lap.

What the hell was he supposed to do with her now?

Since he wasn't entirely sure, he drove idly, taking impulsive detours to extend the trip back to town.

She handled herself better than she gave herself credit for. At least that was his opinion. A lot of people wouldn't have gone back through what she had. He figured most would consider their duty done and over by reporting the crime.

She didn't.

Maybe because of what she'd lived through before. Or maybe it was just the way she was built.

Checked herself into a psych hospital, he mused. And from the tone of her voice, he understood she thought of that as a kind of surrender.

He saw it as courage.

He also figured she considered her travels since Boston a kind of flight. He thought of it more as a voyage. Just as he considered his time since leaving Chicago. A flight was just fear and escape. A voyage? It was a passage, wasn't it? He'd needed that passage to dig in and do what he wanted, to live by his own terms, his own clock and calendar.

From his point of view, Reece Gilmore was doing pretty much the same thing. She just carried a lot more baggage with her on the trip.

He'd never been in fear for his life, but he could imagine it. Imagining was what he did. Just as he could imagine the panic of lying in pain and confusion in a hospital bed. The despair of doubting your own sanity. Add it all up, it was a lot for one person to handle.

And she'd roped him in, which wasn't easy to do. He wasn't the type to try to mend the broken wing of a baby bird. Nature took its course, and the less people interfered with it, the better.

But he was sucked in now, and not just because he was a degree of separation away from witnessing a murder. Though that would have been enough.

She pulled at him. Not her weaknesses, but the strength she struggled to find and use to fight them back. He had to respect that. Just as he had to acknowledge the low simmer of attraction.

He never would've said she was his type. The mending steel of spine under the fragile shell. It made her needy yet, and he had no patience for needy women. Usually.

He liked them smart and steady, and busy with their own lives. So they didn't take too much time out of his.

She'd probably been all of that before she was hurt, he decided. She might be that way again, but never exactly the same way. He thought it would be interesting to watch her finish putting herself back together, and get a good look at the results.

So he drove while she slept, across the yellow grasses and washed-out green of the ubiquitous sage. And he watched the Tetons spring up out of the plate of land. No gentle rise, no softening foothills to detract from that sudden and awesome power.

Snow still swirled on the peaks, and the slashes of white against the blue, the gray, added another layer of might as they knocked against the sky.

He could still remember his first sight of them, and how he, who'd never call himself a spiritual man, had been struck with their rough and terrible magic. The Rockies were grander, he supposed, and the mountains of the East more elegant. But these, the mountains that ringed what was, for now, his home, were primal.

Maybe he had come here because he didn't have to jam his elbows into people everywhere he went to get a little space. But those mountains were a hell of a bonus feature.

He drove fast along the empty road across the sage flats where a small herd of bison grazed. Lumbering along, he noted, coats shaggy, big heads lowered. A couple of calves, probably brand-new, stayed close to their mothers.

Though he imagined Reece would enjoy seeing them, he let her sleep.

He knew the flats would erupt into bloom under the summer sun, blaze with impossible color among the sage. And he imagined that with all those acres of open, a grave could go unnoticed by man or beast. If the man had the patience to dig, long and deep.

He wound toward Angel's Fist, and the stands of cottonwood and pine that bordered it. Reece moaned quietly in sleep. When Brody glanced at her, he saw she'd begun to quiver.

He stopped in the middle of the road, then turned to give her arm a quick shake. "Wake up."

"No!" She came out of sleep like a runner off the starting block. When her fist shot out, he blocked it with the flat of his hand.

"Hit me," he said mildly, "I'll hit back."

"What? What?" She stared blearily at her fist cupped firmly in his hand. "I fell asleep. Did I fall asleep?"

"If you didn't, you gave a good imitation of it for the past hour."

"Did I hit you?"

"You gave it a shot. Don't try it again."

"Check." She willed her heartbeat to steady. "Can I have my hand back?"

He opened his fingers so that she drew her fist back and let it fall into her lap. "You always wake up like you just heard the bell for Round Two?"

"I don't know. It's been a long time — I can't remember how long — since I slept when anyone's been around. I guess I feel comfortable around you."

"Comforting, comfortable." That eyebrow winged up. "You keep using words like that, I'm going to feel honor-bound to change your mind."

She smiled a little. "Your kind doesn't hurt women."

"Is that so?"

"Physically, I mean. You've probably shattered your share of hearts, but you don't rough the owner up first. You'd just stab her ego to death with words, which is — now that I think about it — just as bad as a pop on the jaw. Anyway, I appreciate you letting me sleep. I must've . . . Oh! Oh, just look at them."

She'd shifted away, and the view that filled the windshield blew everything else out of her mind. Struck, she unhooked her seat belt, pushed open her door. The wind streamed over her as she stepped out of the car.

"It's all so *raw,* so stunning and scary. All this open, and there they are, the — I don't know — fortress of them taking over everything. It's like they just shoved their way up, straight out of the ground. I love the suddenness of them."

She walked to the front of the car, to lean back against the hood. "I look at them every day, out my window, or when I'm walking to or from work. But it's not the same as being out here without buildings, without people."

"I'm people."

"You know what I mean. Out here, faced with them, you feel so utterly human."

She looked over, pleased he'd come around to join her. "I thought I'd pass through, pick up a little work, move on. And every morning I look out my window at the lake, and I see them mirrored in it, and I can't think of any reason to leave."

"Gotta land somewhere, eventually."

"That wasn't the plan. Well, I didn't really have a plan, so to speak. But I thought I'd end up winding my way back East sooner or later. Probably not Boston. Maybe Vermont. I went to school there, so it's familiar. I was sure I'd miss the green. That East Coast green."

"The meadows get green, and the flats bloom, the marshes. It's a picture."

"I bet it is, but so is this. Better than that glass of wine." She tipped her head back, closed her eyes and just breathed.

"You look like that sometimes when you're cooking."

She opened her eyes again, the deep Spanish brown. "I do? Like what?"

"Relaxed and calm. Happy."

"I guess that's where I'm confident, and being confident makes me relaxed and happy. And I've missed it. I couldn't make myself go into a kitchen after what happened. It stole that from me, or I let it be stolen from me. Whatever, I'm getting it back. Listen to the birds. I wonder what they are."

He hadn't noticed the birdsong until she mentioned it. Now she turned to look around, and her eyes went wide. She gripped his arm, pointed. "Look. Wow."

When he did, he saw the small herd of bison, munching their way over the sage flats. "First sighting there, too?"

"Like the bear, I've seen them. But I've never been standing out with them. It's more exciting. Oh look! Babies."

She'd softened on the word, drawing it out like it was melting.

"Why do women always say *babies* in just that tone?"

She merely batted the back of her hand at his arm. "They're so sweet, and then they get so big."

"Then you fry them up on the grill."

"Please, I'm having a really nice nature moment here. Seeing them makes me wish I was riding a horse instead of riding in an SUV. More, you know, home on the range on a horse. I want to see an antelope," she decided. "Well, first I'd have to know how to ride one."

"You want to ride an antelope?"

"No." She laughed again, low and easy. "Crossed my thoughts. I want to see an antelope while I'm riding a horse. But I don't know how to ride."

"Didn't Lo offer to teach you?"

She slid her hands into her pockets, still watching the herd. "That's not what he wanted me to ride. But I may take him up on it — the horseback riding lesson — when I'm sure he'll behave."

"You like your men to behave?"

"Not necessarily," she said absently. "But in his case."

The alarm bells didn't go off until after he'd turned, planted his hands on the hood on either side of her and caged her in.

"Brody."

"You're not stupid, and you're not slow. Jittery's different. Do you want to tell me you didn't figure this was coming?"

Her heart kicked, and maybe some of it was fear. But not all of it. "My mind hasn't been focused in this area for a long time. I guess it slipped by me. Mostly slipped by me," she corrected.

"If you're not interested, you'd better make it clear."

"Of course I'm interested, it's just — whoa."

The last word all but squeaked out as he took her arms, lifted her right up to her toes. "You'd better get your breath," he warned. "We're going for a dive."

She couldn't get her breath, or her brains, or her balance. The dive was steep and sudden so that the air that had been so fresh and cool went pumping hot. His mouth wasn't patient or kind, didn't persuade or seduce. It just took what it wanted. The sensation of being swept up, swept away, swept apart left her giddy and loose.

Hot, she thought. Hard, she thought. Hungry. She'd nearly forgotten what it was like to have a man hunger for the taste of her, then take his fill.

Even as she wondered if there'd be anything left of her when he was done, her arms locked around his neck. His hands gripped her hips and yanked her roughly against him.

Her heart pounded against his — beat after hard, fast beat. And she trembled. But her mouth was as avid as his; her arms twined firm around his neck. It wasn't fear he tasted as he ravaged her lips, but shock spearing through a sultry blast of need.

Because he wanted more, he simply hitched her up by the hips until she sat on the hood of his car. Then he moved in, and took more.

Maybe she lost her mind, and she'd worry about it later. But for now she gave in to the demands of her body and hooked her legs around his waist.

"Touch me." She nipped his bottom lip, his tongue. "Touch me somewhere. Anywhere."

His hands streaked under the soft cotton of her sweater, closed over her breasts. The moan broke from her as her body strained for more. More contact, more sensation, more everything. His hands were rough and hard, like the rest of him, rough and hard and direct. Strong, so that everywhere he touched she felt wonderfully swollen, tenderly bruised.

Her response, her demands, had the control he hadn't expected to need thinning to its last taut wire. He could see himself taking her right on the hood of the car, just ripping off whatever clothes were in the way and driving into her until this raw, ripe tension was released.

"Easy." His hands weren't completely steady this time as he took her arms. "Let's ease back a little."

She could barely hear him over the roaring in her head, so she let that head fall limply to his shoulder. "Okay. Okay. Wow. We can't — we shouldn't —"

"We did. We damn sure will again, but since we're not sixteen, it won't be in the middle of the road on the hood of a car."

"No. Right." Is that where they were? She managed to lift her head, focus. "Jesus. We're in the middle of the road. Move. You have to move."

She leaped down, dragged her hands

228

through her disordered hair, tugged at her sweater, her jacket.

"You look fine."

She didn't feel fine. She felt used — but not nearly used enough. "We can't . . . I'm not ready to . . . This isn't a good idea."

"I'm not asking you to marry me and bear my children, Slim. It was a kiss, and a damn good idea. Sleeping together's an even better one."

She pressed her hands to her temples. "I can't think. My head's going to explode."

"A few minutes ago, it felt like another part of you was going to explode."

"Stop. Would you just stop? Look at us, groping each other, talking about sex. A woman's dead."

"She's going to be dead whether or not we go to bed. If you need a little time to get your head around that, fine. Take a couple days. But if you think, after that, we're not going to have each other, then I was wrong. You are stupid."

"I'm not stupid."

"See. I was right." He turned to stroll around the car.

"Brody. Will you just wait a goddamn minute."

"For what?"

She stared at him, big and male and rugged, backed by the towering spread of

229

the dramatic Tetons. "I don't know. I absolutely don't know."

"Then let's get back. I want a beer."

"I don't sleep with every man I'm attracted to."

Now he leaned on the open car door. "According to you, you haven't slept with anybody in two years."

"That's right. If you think you're going to take advantage of my . . . dry spell —"

"Bet your skinny ass I am." And he grinned as he slid into the car.

She marched her skinny ass to the passenger door and huffed her way inside. "This is a ridiculous conversation."

"So shut up."

"I don't even know why I like you," she muttered. "Maybe I don't. I may have responded to you the way I did because it's been a long time since I had any . . . intimate personal contact."

"Why don't you just say you haven't gotten laid?"

"Obviously, I don't have your elegance with words. But my point is, just because I responded doesn't mean I'm going to let you dump me into bed."

"I don't plan to knock you on the head with my club and drag you off by the hair into my cave."

"Wouldn't surprise me." She fumbled out the shield of her sunglasses. "And while I'm grateful to you for believing me, for supporting me, I —"

He braked so hard she jerked against the seat belt. "One has nothing to do with the other." His voice was dangerously cold. "Don't go there."

"I . . ." She closed her mouth, took a breath when he began to drive again. "That was insulting, you're right. It was insulting to both of us. I told you I couldn't think. My body's all churned up, and my brain's inside out. I'm pissed off, I'm scared, and I'm horny. And I'm getting a headache."

"Take a couple of aspirin, lie down. And let me know when horny leads the pack."

Reece stared at the mountains. "This has been the strangest couple of days."

"Tell me about it."

"I want to talk to the sheriff. You could just drop me off there."

"Go home, take the aspirin, call him."

"I need to talk to him face-to-face. Drop me off," she repeated as they crossed the line into Angel's Fist. "Go have your beer." When Brody didn't respond, she shifted in her seat to face him. "I'm not asking you to go with me. I don't want you to. If Sheriff Mardson doesn't think I can stand up for myself, he has less reason to believe me."

"Suit yourself."

"I'm trying to."

When he pulled over in front of the sheriff's office, he sent her a curious look. "What's for dinner tomorrow?"

"What?"

"You're feeding me."

"Oh. I forgot. I don't know. I'll think of something."

"That sounds delicious. Go on, get this done. Then get some sleep. You look ready to drop."

"Please, no more flattery. You'll turn my head." She waited one beat, two, then grabbed her pack from the floor and fumbled for the door.

"Problem?"

"No. Well, I thought you'd kiss me goodbye."

His lips twitched as he cocked an eyebrow. "Gee, Slim, are we going steady?"

"You're such an asshole." But a laugh tickled her throat as she shoved open the door. "And when you ask me to go steady, make sure to bring a ring." She stuck her head in the door. "And tulips — they're my favorite." Then slammed it.

The baffled amusement carried her to the sheriff's door. Nerves didn't start to bump until she'd opened it, stepped inside.

It smelled of stale coffee and wet dog. She noted the location of the first on a short counter on the left side of the room where a nearly empty pot of what looked like black mud steamed away. And the source of the second lay snoring on the floor beside the two face-to-face metal desks where, she assumed, the deputies worked.

Only one was occupied. Mop of dark hair, little goatee, cheerful hazel eyes, slight, youthful build. Denny Darwin, Reece remembered, who liked his eggs over hard and his bacon next to burnt.

He glanced up as the door opened, flushed a little. The way his fingers hurriedly tapped keys on the computer led her to believe whatever he'd been doing on it wasn't official business.

"Hey, Ms. Gilmore."

"Reece." He wasn't that much younger than she was, she thought. Twenty-five, maybe, and with a fresh open face despite the goatee. "I was hoping to speak to the sheriff if he's in."

"Sure, he's back in his office. Just go ahead."

"Thanks. Nice dog." She paused, took a closer look. "I've seen that dog. It's the one who likes to swim in the lake."

"That'd be Moses. Abby Mardson's dog. Sheriff's middle girl?"

"Yes, of course. She tosses a ball in the lake for him so he can dive in and get it."

"He likes to keep us company when the kids're in school. Stayed over some today."

Moses rolled one eye open, gave Reece the once-over out of a brown furry face and stirred enough to thump his huge, hairy tail.

"We've usually got some soup bones over at Joanie's. Just let me know if Moses wants one."

"Appreciate that."

"Nice meeting you, Moses."

She walked through the outer office in the direction Denny had gestured. There was another desk for Dispatch, empty and quiet now, just before the hallway.

Down one end of the hall were two open cells, currently unoccupied, and down the other a door marked STORAGE, another marked LAVATORY. Across from the storeroom, Rick Mardson's office door stood open.

He sat behind an oak desk that looked as if it had been through several wars. He faced the door, with the window behind him high enough so that it gave him privacy while it let in light. Besides the expected computer and phone system, the desk held a couple of picture frames, file folders and a bright red mug as a nesting pot for various pens and pencils.

On the old coatrack in the corner hung his hat and a faded brown barn jacket. Movie posters cheered up the industrial beige walls with images of John Wayne,

Clint Eastwood, Paul Newman in their cowboy best.

He rose as she hesitated at the doorway. "Come on in, Reece. I just called your place again."

"I should get an answering machine. Have you got a minute?"

"Sure. Have a seat. Want some of the nastiest coffee in Wyoming?"

"I'll skip it, but thanks. I wondered if you had any news."

"Well, on the good-news front, everyone in Angel's Fist's accounted for. Same for any visitors we've had in and around last few days. No missing persons in the area matching the description of the woman you reported."

"No one's realized she's gone yet. It's only been a day."

"That may be, and I'll check on that periodically."

"You think I imagined it."

He walked over to the door, shut it, then came back to sit on the edge of his desk. There was nothing in his face but kindness and patience. "I can only tell you what I know. Right now, I know every female in my town is accounted for, and the visitors who're here, or were here as of yesterday, are alive and well. And I know, because part of my job is to check these things out, that you had a bad time a couple years back."

"That doesn't have any bearing on this."

"Maybe it does. Now I want you to take some time and think it all through. It could be you saw a couple of people, just as you said, having an argument. Maybe things even got physical. But you were some ways off, Reece, even with the field glasses. I want you to think if it's possible both those people walked away."

"She was dead."

"Now, seeing as you were across the river, up on the trail, you couldn't take her pulse, could you?"

"No, but —"

"I went over your statement a couple of times. You took off running, got Brody, went back. Got about thirty minutes there. Isn't it possible that woman got up and walked off? Maybe still mad, maybe with a few bruises, but alive and healthy?"

The glass wasn't half empty or half full, Reece thought. It was just a damn glass, and she'd seen it for herself. "She was dead. If she walked off, how do you explain the fact there were no tracks? No sign anyone had been there?"

He didn't speak for a moment, and when he did that same endless patience was in his tone. It was beginning to crawl up her spine like spiders. "You're not from around here, and it was your first time on the trail. You were shocked and upset. It's a long river, Reece. Easy for you to mistake the spot when you got back with Brody. Hell, it could've been a half a mile on up."

"I couldn't have been that far off."

"Well, I've looked the best I can, but it's a lot of ground to cover. I went ahead and contacted the closest hospitals. No woman was admitted or treated who matched your description with trauma to the neck or the head. I'll follow up on that again to-morrow."

She got to her feet. "You don't think I saw a thing."

"You're wrong. I think you saw something that scared and upset you. But I can't find a single thing to support you witnessed a homicide. My advice is to let me follow through on this, and you've got my word I will. And you put it aside for now. I'm about to head on home, see my wife and kids. I'll give you a lift."

"I'd rather walk, clear my head." She stepped to the door, turned. "That woman was dead, Sheriff. That's not something I can just put aside."

When she left, Mardson blew out a breath, shook his head. He'd do all he could do, he thought, and that was all that could be asked of a man.

Now he was going to take his dog and go home, and have dinner with his wife and kids.

10

Brody got his beer and tossed a frozen pizza in the oven. When he punched the button on his answering machine, it spit out a message from his agent. The book scheduled for early fall had snagged a very decent book-club deal. Which might call for a second beer with dinner.

Maybe, with a part of his take from it, he'd splurge on a new TV. Plasma. He could hang it over the fireplace. Could you hang plasma screens over a fireplace? Or would the heat screw it up?

Well, he'd find out, because it would be very sweet to stretch out on the couch and watch ESPN on one of those big-ass screens.

But for now, he stood in the open doorway of his kitchen, drinking the beer in his hand while he watched the light soften and the shadows deepen toward evening.

The quiet went down just as smoothly as that first cold beer.

He had work to make up — can't afford a big-ass plasma TV if you didn't put in the time at the keyboard. Which meant he'd likely put in a couple hours on his current work-in-progress before he called it a night. Besides, he was looking forward to digging into it.

He had a woman to kill.

Still, over a beer, waiting for his pizza, he could spare the time to think about another woman.

She didn't go down smooth. Reece Gilmore had too many jagged edges to slide easy into a man. Maybe that's what made her so intriguing when he hadn't had any intention of being intrigued. He liked the opposition of her — gutsy and fragile, cautious and rash. People who walked straight down one road got tedious after a while.

Added to it, he couldn't help but feel they were in this *situation* together.

Until they found their way through that situation, it would pay to find out more about her.

He glanced around. His laptop was on the table.

"No time like the present," he decided, and with another sip of his beer, closed the door.

He booted up, then got the pizza out of the oven. The cutting wheel was, like his coffeemaker, one of his few kitchen essentials. He put the entire pie, cut into four slices, onto a plate, grabbed a couple paper towels and, popping the top on a second beer, considered it dinner.

He doubted it took him any longer than it had taken the sheriff to access background data on Reece. Googling her, he got enough hits to keep him busy, and interested.

He dug up an old article on up-and-coming Boston chefs that featured the then twenty-four-year-old Reece. He was right, he noted as he scanned the photo. She looked better carrying another ten pounds or so. In fact, she looked pretty damn amazing.

Young, vibrant, *essential,* somehow, grinning into the camera while holding a big blue bowl and a shining silver whisk. The article gave her educational background — a year in Paris added a lot of polish — personalized it with an anecdote about how she'd prepared five-course dinners for her dolls when she was a child.

It quoted both Tony and Terry Maneo, the owners of the restaurant where she'd worked — a couple who'd be dead in a few years. They stated she was not only the jewel of their business but one of the family.

There were other bits and pieces in the article, and a smattering of others. He learned she was orphaned at fifteen, raised from that point by her maternal grandmother. She'd remained single, spoke fluent French and enjoyed entertaining friends, among whom she was apparently renowned for her Sunday brunches.

Adjectives used to describe her were *energetic, creative, adventurous* and, his own previous choice, *vibrant.*

How would he describe her now? Brody asked himself as he sat back, chewed on pizza. Anal, nervous, determined.

Hot.

There was a splashy *Boston Globe* feature about her taking the position as head chef for a "wildly popular hot spot known for its American fusion cuisine and convivial atmosphere."

The standard background/color data was included along with a photo of a more sophisticated-looking Reece wearing her hair up and back — nice neck — and posed in what he assumed would have been the stainless steel glory of her new kitchen in a sexy black suit and mile-high seductress-red heels.

"I'll always treasure my years at Maneo's, and everyone I've worked with or cooked for there. Tony and Terry Maneo not only gave me my first professional opportunities, but gave me an extended family. While I'll miss the comfort and familiarity of Maneo's, I'm thrilled and excited to

241

join the creative team of Oasis. I intend to uphold the restaurant's high standards — and add a few surprises."

"Look good enough to eat yourself there, Slim," he said aloud, scanning back from her quote to her photo.

He checked the date of the article, noted it had been published just about the time he told his editor at the *Trib* to kiss his ass. When he brought up the first report of the killings at Maneo's, he saw it was three days after the *Globe* feature.

Goddamn lousy deal, all around. Reece was listed as the only survivor, suffering from multiple gunshot wounds and in critical condition. Police were investigating and so on. It spoke of the owners, and the restaurant they'd run for more than a quarter of a century. There were quotes from family and friends — the shock, the tears, the outrage. The reporter used terms like *bloodbath, carnage, brutality.*

Subsequent articles reported the progress of the investigation — little to none — and Brody could read the frustration of the investigators in every clipped quote.

Funerals and memorial services were reported on for those who'd died. Reece's condition was moved up to serious. She was reported to be under police protection.

Then it petered out, little by little, the stories moving from front page, above the fold, to page three, and back. There was a small mention, almost an afterthought, when Reece was released from the hospital. There was no quote from her, no photo.

That's the way it went, Brody mused. News was only news until something else came along. It took juice to get the print, the airtime, and the juice had been wrung out of the Maneo Massacre, as the papers had dubbed it, in under three weeks.

The dead were buried, the killers unidentified, and the single survivor left to pick up what pieces she could from a shattered life.

While Brody finished his pizza and read about her, Reece filled her little bathtub with hot water and an indulgent squirt of drugstore bath foam. She'd taken the aspirin, forced herself to eat some cheese and crackers, with a sprig of grapes to balance it out.

Now she was going to soak, drink her wine and start Brody's book in the tub. She didn't want to think about reality, at least not for the next hour. She debated whether or not to close and lock the bathroom door. She'd have preferred to lock it, but the room was so small she'd never be able to handle being closed in that way.

She'd tried it locked a couple of times already and had ended up scrambling out of the tub, dripping and panting, to reopen the door.

The front door was locked, she reminded herself, and the back of a chair under the handle. She was perfectly safe. But after she slid into the tub she had to sit up twice, to strain her body to see around the doorway into the living area. In case. To cock her ears for any sounds.

Impatient with herself, she took two long, slow sips of wine.

"Just stop it. Just relax. You used to love to do this, remember? Sit and soak in a bubble bath with a glass of wine and a book. It's time to stop scrubbing yourself down in three minutes flat and scrambling out of the shower as if Norman Bates were waiting to hack you to death.

"And oh, for *God's* sake, shut up!"

She closed her eyes, took another sip of wine. Then opened the book.

The first line read:

Some said that Jack Brewster had been digging his own grave for years, but as the shovel bit through the hard winter earth he was a little pissed off to have that comment taken literally.

It made her smile, and hope that Jack wasn't going to end up in the ground anytime soon.

She read for fifteen minutes before nerves had her scooting up to peer into the living area again. And Reece marked it as a new record. Pleased with herself, she managed another ten before the growing jitters told her she'd had enough.

Next time, she promised herself as she pulled the plug, she'd try for longer.

She liked the book, and that was a relief, she decided. She set it down so she could slather the body cream that matched the bath foam on her skin. She'd get into bed with it, that's what she'd do. She'd use Brody's Jack Brewster to close out all the places her mind wanted to go.

She wouldn't write in her journal, not tonight.

Maybe she'd been upset with Sheriff Mardson when she left his office, but now that she was calmer she had to admit he was doing all he could possibly do.

Whether he believed her or not, he hadn't been dismissive. Exactly.

So, she was going to do her best to take at least one piece of his advice. She was going to put it aside, just for a few hours.

She pulled on the flannel pants and T-shirt she wanted to sleep in, yanked the pins out of her hair. A small pot of tea, she thought, and an evening with a book.

After putting the kettle on, she tried to drum up some enthusiasm for making a sandwich. Instead she toyed with a menu for the next night.

Red meat, naturally. Maybe a little pot roast with a red wine sauce. She'd have to zip to the market as soon as she could manage a break, slap some marinade together. Easy enough, she thought as she started a list. New potatoes and carrots, fresh green beans if she could find them. A manly meal. Fat buttermilk biscuits.

She could do some stuffed button mushrooms, if time allowed, for an appetizer. And polish it off with berries and cream. No, too girlie. Apple brown betty, maybe. Simple, traditional food.

Would she end up in bed with him after? It wasn't a good idea; in fact it was a terrible idea. But, damn it, he'd definitely gotten her juices flowing. There was relief in knowing they *could* flow, and frustration in not being sure what she should or could do about it.

She should wash her sheets, just in case. She only had the one set, so she wrote *Laundry* with a question mark on her list. She'd need to get a good red wine. Maybe brandy, too. And damn it, she not only didn't have any coffee, she had nothing to brew it in.

She stepped back, pressed fingers to the center of her forehead where the headache was sneaking back. She should cancel. Obviously she was going to make herself crazy trying to create the perfect meal when Brody would probably be fine with a couple of buffalo burgers and steak fries.

Smarter, better, she should cancel, pack her things, leave Joanie a note and get out of Angel's Fist. What reason was there to stay?

A woman had been murdered, which was a good reason to leave the area. By now, or certainly soon, everyone in town would know she claimed to have seen murder done, and there wasn't a shred of evidence to support that claim.

She didn't want people looking at her out of the corner of their eyes again. Like she was a bomb ticking toward the blast. Besides, she'd made progress here, and could leave without shame. She was back to cooking, she'd set up an apartment — such as it was. She'd lasted twenty-five minutes in the bathtub.

She could feel her sexuality starting to simmer.

Another session with Brody, she thought, that sexuality was going to boil over. Nothing wrong with that, not a thing wrong with it. They were both unattached adults. Sex was healthy; contemplating having sex with an attractive man was a normal female activity.

It was progress.

So she could take all that progress, all those steps, and use them in the next town.

She set her pencil down when the kettle began to sputter. It was whistling shrilly when she reached up for a cup and saucer. No teapot, she remembered. Maybe in the next place she stopped she'd treat herself to one.

She turned off the burner, moved the kettle to a cool one. As the whistle died, someone banged on the door.

She'd have shrieked if she'd had the breath left in her for it. As it was, she jerked back hard enough to rap her hip on the counter. Even as her hand closed around the handle of her chef's knife, Joanie's voice barked through the locked door.

"Open up, for chrissake. I haven't got all night."

On jellied knees Reece hurried across the room and, as quietly as she could manage, drew the chair away. "Sorry, just a second!"

She unlocked the door, unlatched the security chain. "I was in the kitchen," Reece said.

"Yeah, and this place is so spacious I'm surprised you heard me." Joanie trooped in smelling of spices and smoke. "Scraped together the last bowl of that soup — have to make more next time. You eat?"

"Well, I —"

"Never mind." Joanie set the covered hot take-away cup on the counter. "Eat now. Go on." She waved impatiently when Reece hesitated. "It's still hot. I'm taking my break."

So saying, she walked to the front window, opened it a few inches. Then she took out a lighter and a pack of Marlboro Lights. "You gonna piss me off and say I can't smoke in here?"

"No." Having nothing else suitable, Reece carried over the tea saucer to serve as an ashtray. "How's the crowd tonight?"

"Not bad. That soup was popular. You can do tomorrow's if you've got an idea for it."

"Sure, that's no problem."

"Sit down and eat."

"You don't have to stand by the window."

"Used to it." But Joanie planted a butt cheek on the sill. "Smells good in here."

"I just had a bath. Tropical Mango."

"Nice." Joanie took a contemplative drag. "You got company coming?"

"What? No, no, not tonight."

"Lo's downstairs." Absently, Joanie tapped ashes out the open window. "He wanted to bring that soup up. I don't think it was to hit on you, especially as he said he thought Linda-gail should come up with him. Still, give him an inch."

"That was nice of him."

"He's worried about you, figures you must be scared and upset."

"Used to it," Reece said with a half smile as she sat down to eat the soup. "But I'm doing all right."

"He's not the only one worried. Word's got around, as word does, about what you saw on the trail yesterday."

"Saw, or thought I saw?"

"Well, which is it?"

"I saw."

"Okay then. Linda-gail wanted me to tell you she'd come up and stay the night if you didn't want to be alone, or you could go to her place."

Reece paused with the spoon partway to her lips. "She did?"

"No, I just made that up so you could gawk at me."

"That's so sweet of her. But I'm all right."

"You look better than you did, I'll say that." Bracing her back against the window jamb, Joanie flicked more ashes. "Seeing as I'm your boss and your landlord, it's been my task today to field inquiries as to how you're doing, and to promise to give you people's good thoughts. Mac, Carl, Doc,

Bebe, Pete, Beck and so on. I won't say some of them didn't come by hoping to get a look at you, or a nugget of information from me, but most everyone was sincere in their concern. Thought you should know."

"I appreciate the inquiries, the good thoughts, the concern. Joanie, the sheriff can't find anything."

"Some things take longer to find than others. Rick'll keep looking."

"Yes, I suppose he will. But he doesn't really believe I saw what I said I saw. Why should he, really? Why should anyone? Or if they do now, they'll think about it differently once word gets around — as word does — about what happened back in Boston. And . . ." She trailed off, narrowing her eyes. "I guess it already has."

"Somebody murmured to somebody who murmured to somebody else. So, yeah, there's been some talk about what happened back there, and how you were hurt."

"Had to happen." She tried to shrug it off. "Now there will be more murmurs, more talk. Then it'll be, 'Oh, that poor thing, she had such a bad time and can't get past it. Imagining things.' "

"Damn, and me without my violin." With her habitual quick jabs, Joanie stubbed out the cigarette. "I'll make sure I have it next time you have a pity party."

"You're so mean." Reece spooned up

soup. "Why is it the two people who give me little to no sympathy in any area are the ones who help the most?"

"I figure you had a gutful of sympathy in Boston, and don't want a refill."

"Direct hit. Before you came up, I was talking myself into leaving. Nòw I'm sitting here eating soup — and it *would* be better with fresh herbs — and talking to you, and I know I'm not going anywhere. It feels better knowing that. Even though when you leave I'm going to check the lock on the windows, lock the door, check to make sure the phone's got a dial tone."

"You gonna put the chair under the doorknob again, too?"

"Nothing gets by you."

"Not a hell of a lot." Joanie carried the makeshift ashtray over to set down by the sink. "I've got sixty years under my belt, so —"

"You're sixty? Get out."

Unable to prevent a quick smile at Reece's obvious disbelief, Joanie shrugged. "I'll be sixty a year from next January, so I'm practicing. That way it won't be such a shock to my system. Now I've lost my train of thought."

"I'd've put you ten years under sixty."

Joanie gave her a long, cool look, but her lips twitched at a smile again. "You bucking for a raise before it's time for one?"

"If I can get it."

"I know good stock when I see it, that's what I was going to say. You're good stock, and you'll hold up. You held up to worse."

"I didn't."

"Don't tell me you didn't," Joanie snapped back. "I'm standing here looking at you, aren't I? You just remember, there may be big noses and big ears in the Fist, but there are good people in this town, else I'd've taken myself out of here long ago. Bad things happen everywhere; you've got cause to know that. People around here take care of themselves and each other when it's needed. You need a hand, you ask for it."

"I will."

"I have to get back down." As she stepped back, Joanie glanced around. "You want a TV up here? I've got an extra one I can spare for now."

Reece started to say no, don't bother, too much trouble. Tune those violins, she thought. "I'd really like to have one, if you've got one you can lend me."

"You can haul it up tomorrow." At the door, Joanie stopped, sniffed. "Rain's coming in again. Expect to see you at six, sharp."

Alone, Reece got up to close the windows, lock the door, but she deliberately took her time. Like any woman, she told herself, locking up for the night. And if she braced the chair under the knob, it didn't hurt anyone.

The rain came just after two a.m. and woke her. She'd fallen asleep with the lights on and Brody's book in her hand. There was a muffled roll of thunder under the slap of rain on the roof, against the windows. She liked the sound of it, the windy power of it that made her feel all the more cozy and snug in her little bed.

She snuggled down, rubbing the kink out of her neck. Yawned, tugged the covers up to her chin. And in her habitual scan of the room before closing her eyes again, she froze.

The front door was open. Just a crack.

Shuddering, she wrapped the blanket around her shoulders, then gripped the flashlight beside the bed like a club. She had to get up, she had to make her legs work. Her breath wheezed in and out as she quivered her way out of bed, then ran to the door.

She slammed it, locked it, turned the handle hard to be sure it didn't give. Her pulse continued to race as she dashed to the windows, assuring herself each one was securely locked as she took quick peeks through the glass.

There was no one out in the rain. The

lake was a black pool, the street slick and empty.

She tried to tell herself she'd left the door unlocked by mistake, or had managed to unlock it when she checked it that last time before she got into bed. The wind had blown it open a bit. The storm had come in, the wind had blown.

But she got down on her hands and knees by the door and saw the faint scratches where the chair had scraped.

The wind hadn't pushed the door open hard enough to shove the chair that inch.

She sat with her back to the wall by the door, the blanket wrapped around her shoulders.

She managed to doze, then managed to get dressed, to work. As soon as the mercantile opened for the day, she took her break and walked down to buy a dead bolt.

"You know how to install this thing?" Mac asked her.

"I thought I could figure it out."

He gave her a pat on the hand. "Why don't I do that for you? I thought I'd head up there for lunch today anyhow. Won't take me long."

Ask for help when you need it, Reece remembered. "I'd really appreciate that, Mr. Drubber."

"Next to done already. I don't blame

you for being a little bit nervous. A good strong lock'll make you feel better."

"I know it will." She looked around when the door opened. "Morning, Mr. Sampson," she said when Carl came in.

"Morning. How you doing?"

"I'm okay. Um, I guess the sheriff's already talked to you, but I just wonder if either of you has seen a woman with long dark hair and a red coat in town in the last few days."

"Had some hikers," Mac told her. "All of them male, though two of them wore earrings. One of 'em in his nose."

"Get lots of that in the winter with the snowboarders," Carl commented. "The boys got more hardware stuck to them than the girls. Had that retired couple from Minnesota come through here in an RV couple days ago," he reminded Mac.

"The woman's hair was stone gray, Carl, and he was carrying three hundred pounds if he was carrying an ounce. That's not the sort the sheriff asked about."

"Just saying." Carl glanced over at Reece. "Could be the people you saw were just wrestling. Playing around, like. People do the damnedest things."

"Yes, they do." Reece reached for her wallet. "Should I just leave the lock with you, Mr. Drubber?"

"That'll be fine, and put your money

away. I'll put this on Joanie's tab."

"Oh no, it's for me, so —"

"You planning on drilling it out of the door and taking it with you somewhere?"

"No, but —"

"I'll settle it up with Joanie. You got a soup special today?"

"Old-fashioned chicken noodle."

"That'll hit the spot. Anything else you need today?"

"Actually, I do, but I'll have to get it later. Break's over."

"Give me the list." He picked up a pencil, licked the tip. "I'll bring it up when I come for lunch."

"Some service. Ah, I need a small rump roast, a pound of new potatoes, a pound of carrots," she began.

When she'd run through it, Mac wiggled his eyebrows. "That sounds like company dinner."

"I guess it is." Where was the harm? "I'm cooking for Brody. He's helped me out with a few things recently."

"Bet he's getting the best end of that deal."

"Any leftovers, they're yours. For putting in the lock."

"There's a deal."

She headed back, drawing in air fresh and cool from the night's storm. She'd handled it. Done the sensible thing.

And when she went to bed that night — alone or otherwise — she'd have a strong new lock on the door.

Lo cruised into Angel's Fist in his Ford pickup with a Waylon Jennings CD wailing on the stereo. Outside of town he'd been listening to Faith Hill, whom he considered extreme on the hot-o-meter. But even with that, and her superior pipes, a guy just couldn't be riding around in town with a girl singing in his pickup.

Unless she was alive and kicking, anyway.

He had his mind on a girl now. Actually on a couple, but he had plenty of room in his mind for females. He saw one of them in skinny jeans and a red sweatshirt standing on a stepladder painting the shutters on the little dollhouse she rented a bright, sunny yellow.

He gunned the motor, waiting for her to turn and admire the way he looked in the muscular black truck. When she didn't, he rolled his eyes, pulled over.

God knew he'd always had to work harder with this female for crumbs than he ever did with others for the whole damn cake.

"Hey, Linda-gail!"

"Hey, yourself." She kept right on painting.

"What are you doing?"

"Having myself a facial and a pedicure. What does it look like I'm doing?"

He gave another eye roll and got out of the truck to saunter over. "Got the day off?" He'd already snuck a look at the schedule and knew she did.

"That's right. You?"

"Got some people in, but they're going on a paddling tour today. You seen Reece?"

"No." She slapped paint on wood hard enough to splatter it and make him jump out of range.

"Watch it."

"Move it."

Ornery woman, he thought. He didn't know why he kept coming back for more abuse. "Listen, I just wondered how she was, that's all."

"Your ma said to give her room, so I'm giving her room." Still she sighed, lowered the brush. "I wish I knew, though. It's an awful thing."

"Awful," he repeated and waited a moment. "Kind of exciting, though."

"It *is!*" She twisted around to look down at him. "We're sick, sick people, but God, murder and all. Bebe thinks it was a couple of people who robbed a bank or something, then had a falling-out, so he killed her and now he's got all the money."

"Good a theory as any."

Lowering her brush, she leaned on the ladder. "But *I* think they were having this adulterous fling and ran away together. Then she changed her mind and wanted to go back to her husband and kids, so he killed her in the heat of passion."

"Sounds good, too. Weighed the body down, then crammed it into an old beaver lodge."

"Oh, that's just *awful,* Lo. Worse than burying her out there."

"Probably didn't do that anyway." He leaned on the ladder as well. He could smell the paint, but standing this close, he could smell whatever she rubbed on her skin right along with it. "Have to know where to find an old beaver lodge, wouldn't he? And they couldn't have been from around here. Any way you slice it, he's long gone by now."

"I guess. Doesn't make it any better for Reece." She went back to painting, and the way he was standing, her cute butt was right at eye level.

A man only had to lean in a couple of inches to —

"I guess you're going to go by, see her."

"Who?" He blinked himself clear. "Oh, Reece. I don't know. I thought I might, if you wanted to go with me."

"Your ma told me not to pester Reece today. Besides, I've got this started. I need to finish it."

"Take you half the day the way you're going."

She looked over her shoulder. "I've got another brush, smart guy. You could do something useful instead of standing around posing."

"It's my day off."

"Mine, too."

"Shit." Damned if he wanted to paint stupid shutters. But he couldn't think of anywhere else to go, anything else to do. "Guess I could give you a hand." He reached down for a brush that still had the mercantile's price sticker on the handle. "Maybe, if we get this done before next Tuesday, we could drive out to the ranch. I could saddle us up a couple of horses. Nice day for a ride."

Linda-gail smiled to herself as she painted. "Maybe. It is a pretty nice day."

DETOURS

Pain has an element of blank;
It cannot recollect
When it begun, or if there were
A day when it was not —

— EMILY DICKINSON

11

Reece had to dash upstairs on her next break. Using the key Mac had dropped off at Joanie's, she unlocked the new, sturdy dead bolt.

Just hearing the sharp click made her feel better. She tested it a couple of times, then let out a sigh of relief.

But she had to hurry, she reminded herself, get the marinade made and the roast in it so she could zip back downstairs and finish her shift.

She found a note on her counter from Mac, written in his clear and careful hand, and held in place by the corner of the new roasting pan she'd had on her list.

Went ahead and put the groceries away for you, didn't want to leave the perishables out. Started a tab for you, so you can settle up with me at the end of the month. You enjoy your dinner. Me, I'm looking forward to those leftovers. M.D.

What a sweetie, she thought, and wondered idly why some smart woman hadn't snapped him up.

She got what she needed from the refrigerator, from the cupboard, then opened the cabinet below the counter for the mixing bowl.

It wasn't there. None of her bowls were there. In their place were her hiking boots and backpack.

She went down, slowly, to her knees.

She hadn't put them there, she hadn't. Her boots and the pack belonged in the little closet. Carefully, as if defusing a bomb, she drew them out, studied them. She unzipped the pack, found her spare water bottle, her compass, her penknife, the moleskin, the sunscreen. Everything just where it belonged.

Trembling a little, she carried them to the closet. And there were the mixing bowls, sitting on the shelf above the hangers.

It didn't mean anything, she told herself. A moment of absentmindedness, that was all. Anyone might make such a silly mistake. Anyone at all.

She set the boots on the floor, hung the pack on the hook she used for it. And could see herself doing exactly what she'd done when she returned from going out to the river with Brody: Even before she took the aspirin, before she ran her bath, she took off her boots, put them and her pack in the closet.

She would swear she did.

And the bowls. Why would she have moved them in the first place?

But she must have. The way she must have marked up the map. Just blanking it out. Lost time, she thought, resting her forehead on the closet door. She didn't want to believe she was losing time again, as she had during her breakdown. But the bowls were in the closet, weren't they?

Mac Drubber had hardly moved them around as a little joke. So that left her.

It was just stress, she assured herself. She'd had a trauma, and it plagued her mind, so she'd put a couple of things in the wrong place. It wasn't a problem, didn't have to be a problem if she recognized it for what it was.

She simply carried the bowls back, put the one she needed on the counter, set the rest where they belonged.

Refusing to think about it any further, she minced, measured and whisked.

When her shift was over, she unlocked the door again. This time she checked all her things. Cupboards, closet, medicine cabinet, dresser.

Everything was just where it should be. So she put the little incident aside, washed the new roasting pan Mac had delivered. And got down to doing what she loved.

It had been a long time since Reece had prepared a serious, intimate meal. And for her, it was like love rediscovered. The textures, the shapes, the scents, the selections were physical, emotional, even spiritual.

While the vegetables bubbled and browned in the roast's juices, she opened a bottle of Cabernet to let it breathe. It had probably been silly to buy the cloth napkins in their bright, paisley print, she thought as she arranged the place settings on the counter. But she couldn't bring herself to use paper for a company meal.

And they looked so pretty and festive tented on the simple white plates. And the candles were as practical as they were attractive. The power might go out sometime, and her flashlight batteries might die. Plus the little blue glass holders hadn't cost very much.

She'd decided to stay awhile, hadn't she? It didn't hurt to buy a few things to make the room more homey. More hers. It wasn't as if she was tearing through her paycheck on some spree buying rugs and curtains and artwork.

Though a bright colorful rug would look nice over the old, scarred floorboards. She could always sell it before she moved on. Something to think about anyway, she thought as she checked the time.

She caught herself humming as she

chopped and mixed the filling for the mushrooms. A good sign, she realized. A strong sign proving she was fine. Nothing to worry about here.

She'd always had music when she worked in the kitchen — rock, opera, New Age — whatever fit her mood and the meal.

Maybe she'd buy a little CD player for the counter, just for company. She glanced over at the reassuring glint of the new dead bolt against the faded paint of the door. She was safe here, so why not be happy and comfortable, as well?

She was going to hike again, too. And she might see about renting or borrowing a boat to take out on the lake. How hard could it be to row a boat? She'd like to find out.

That would be another step toward being normal instead of just pretending to be.

She had a date, didn't she? Sort of. And that was pretty damn normal. Just as Brody being ten minutes late was probably normal.

Unless he wasn't coming at all. Unless he'd rethought what had happened — or almost happened — between them and was opting out before things got complicated. Why would a man choose to get tangled up with someone who was emotionally screwed up? Someone who checked the door three times and still managed to leave it unlocked. Who couldn't remember writing all over a map with red marker. Who put her hiking boots in a kitchen cabinet.

Must be sleepwalking, Reece thought with a sigh. Regressing. Next thing she'd be wandering the street naked.

She stopped, closed her eyes and drew in a breath. She smelled the mushrooms, the peppers and onions, the roasting meat.

She was not only safe, and fairly sane, she was productive. She had nothing to worry about tonight but preparing a good meal. Even if she ended up eating it by herself. Even as she thought it, she heard footsteps on the stairs.

She let the initial panic come, let it go. By the time the knock sounded she was steady again. Wiping her hands on the dish towel hooked in her waistband, she crossed over to unlock the door.

Steady, she thought, but not stupid. "Brody?"

"You expecting someone else? What's for dinner?"

So she was smiling when she unlocked and opened the door. "Salmon croquettes and steamed asparagus with a side of polenta."

His eyes narrowed as he stepped in. Then he took a good sniff of the air and

270

gave a teeth-baring grin. "Meat. Looks like you might want to put this away for another time."

She took the wine he offered, noted it was a nice Pinot Grigio. He paid attention, she realized, even when he didn't seem to be.

"Thanks. I've got some Cabernet open, if you'd like a glass."

"Wouldn't turn it down." He took off his jacket, tossed it over the back of a chair. "New lock?"

Paid attention, she noted again.

"Mr. Drubber put it in for me. I guess it's overkill, but I'll sleep better."

"TV. You're coming up in the world."

"I decided to embrace technology." She poured him a glass of wine. Turning, she took the roast out of the oven, set it on the stovetop.

"Ah, just like Mom used to make."

"Really?"

"No. My mother could burn takeout."

Amused, Reece finished stuffing the mushrooms. "What does she do?"

"She's a psychiatrist. Private practice."

Trying to ignore the automatic bump in her belly, Reece concentrated on the mushroom caps. "Oh."

"And she macramés."

"She what?"

"Makes things by tying rope into knots. I

think she once macraméd a small studio apartment. Furnished. It's an obsession."

Reece slid the mushrooms into the oven, set the timer. "And your father?"

"My father likes to cook out on the grill, even in the winter. He's a college professor. Romance languages. Some people think they're an odd combo. She's intense and sociable, he's on the shy and dreamy side. But it works for them. You having any of this wine?"

"In a minute." She set out a dish of olives. "Any siblings?"

"Two, one of each."

"I always wanted a brother or sister. Someone to fight with, or to bond with against authority. I'm an only child, and both my parents were only children."

"More turkey at Thanksgiving that way."

"Always a bright side. One of the reasons I loved working at Maneo's was that it was so noisy and full and dramatic. We weren't noisy and dramatic at home. My grandmother's wonderful. Steady and loving and fair. So good to me." She raised her glass in a half toast, drank. "I've given her a lot to worry about the last couple of years."

"Does she know where you are?"

"Oh, sure. I call back home every couple weeks, e-mail regularly. My grandmother especially loves e-mail. She's a busy, modern woman, with a very full life of her own." She turned to check the mushrooms, flipped the gauge to broil. "She divorced my grandfather before I was born. I've never met him. She started her own decorating business."

Absently, Reece glanced around the tiny apartment. "She'd shudder to see what I haven't done with this place. Anyway, she loves to travel. Had to put a lot of that on hold when my parents were killed — car accident when I was fifteen, and Gram raised me from there. She didn't want me to leave Boston. And I couldn't stay."

"Steady and loving and fair. She probably wants you happy more than she wants you in Boston."

She mulled that over as she got out a plate. "You're right, but I've so enjoyed all my servings of guilt the last months. Anyway, I've got her mostly convinced I'm fine. So she's in Barcelona right now, on a buying trip."

She pulled out the mushrooms, sprinkled them with Parmesan. Set them under the broiler. "These would be better with fresh, but I couldn't find any."

"I'll probably be able to choke one or two down."

Once they were done to her specification, were arranged on a plate, she set them on the counter between them. "This is the first meal I've cooked for anyone in two years."

"You cook every day downstairs."

She shook her head. "That's work. I mean it's the first meal I've cooked for pleasure. The other night doesn't count. That was a throw-it-together deal. I've missed doing this, and didn't realize just how much until tonight."

"Glad to help." He picked up a mushroom, popped it in his mouth. "Good."

She took one herself, bit in. Smiled. "Yes, they are."

It wasn't so hard. Easier for her than going out, finding or going along with some activity designed to pass the time or create conversational gambits. She could relax here, enjoy making the final preparations for the meal. And oddly, she could relax with and enjoy him.

"It'll be easier with this setup if I plate the food. Is that all right with you?"

"Go ahead." He gestured toward his plate with his wineglass. "Don't be stingy."

While she served, he poured them both more wine. He'd noted the candles, the fancy napkins, the sturdy pepper grinder. All new, he thought, since his last visit.

And he'd noticed his book sitting on the tiny table by her daybed.

The woman was settling in, he decided, and fully expected to see a vase of flowers and a couple pictures on the wall before too much longer.

"I started your book." She lifted her gaze to his as she spoke, and his heart took one, quick lurch.

The woman had a pair of eyes on her.

"How's that going for you?"

"I like it." She came around the counter to sit beside him, spread her napkin on her lap. "It's scary, and that's good. It takes my mind off my own nerves. I like Jack — he's such a screwup. Hope he doesn't end up in that grave. Plus, I think Leah can straighten him out."

"Is that what women are supposed to do? Straighten men out?"

"People are supposed to straighten people out, when they can, and if they care enough. She cares for him. So I hope they end up together."

"Happily ever after?"

"If justice doesn't triumph and love doesn't make the circle in entertainment fiction, what's the point? Real life sucks too often."

"Happily ever after doesn't win Pulitzers."

She pursed her lips as she studied him. "Is that what you're after?"

"If it was, I'd still be working for the *Trib*. Cooking pot roast over a diner in Wyoming, or flipping buffalo burgers in that diner, isn't going to win you whatever the

275

epicurean equivalent of the Pulitzer might be."

"I thought I wanted that once, too. Important awards, acknowledgment. I'd rather cook pot roast." She paused a minute. "How's that going for you?"

"I'd give you an award." He cut another piece, then followed it up with part of the biscuit he'd generously buttered. "Where'd you get the biscuits?"

"I made them."

"Get out." His disbelief was instant and sincere. "Like with flour?"

"That would be one ingredient." She passed him the bowl so he could take another.

"A lot of happy steps up from the Doughboy and Hamburger Helper that ruled in my house."

"I should hope so. I'm a food snob," she said when he grinned at her. "Sue me. Let me guess what's in your larder. Frozen pizza, cans of soup and chili, cereal boxes, maybe some Eggos. Hot dogs, a couple of those Hungry-Man dinners."

"You forgot the mac and cheese."

"Ah yes, the single man's staple. Dried elbow pasta and cheese powder. Yum."

"Keeps body and soul together."

"Yes, like paste."

He speared one of the tiny roasted potatoes on his plate. "Going to straighten me out, Slim?"

"Well, I'll feed you now and then, which works for both of us. I can —" She broke off, dropping her fork when the quick blast sounded outside.

"Carl's truck," Brody said calmly.

"Carl's truck." She picked up her wine with both hands. "Gets me every time. I wish he'd get that damn thing fixed."

"You and everyone else in the Fist. Do you ever write any of this stuff down?"

"What stuff?"

"Recipes."

"Oh." She ordered herself to pick up her fork, to eat despite the fact that a fist was still kneading her stomach like a ball of dough. "Sure. I was organized and a little anal even before I went crazy. I've got recipes filed on my laptop with two thumb drive backups. Why? Are you planning on trying your hand at buttermilk biscuits?"

"No. I just wondered why you haven't done a cookbook."

"I used to think I might, eventually, when I got a prime slot on the Food Channel," she added with a quick smile. "Something hip and fun and skewed toward the young, urban dinner party and Sunday brunch crowd."

"Eventually's a myth. You want to do something, you do it."

"No Food Channel slot on my horizon. It's just not something I could handle."

"I meant the cookbook."

"Oh. I haven't given that any thought in . . . hmmm." Why couldn't she write a cookbook? She had hundreds of recipes in her files and had tested all of them.

"Maybe I'll play with it a little. Sometime or other."

"If you put a proposal together, I can send it to my agent if you want."

"Why would you do that?"

He ate the last bite of meat on his plate. "Damn good pot roast. Now if you'd written a manuscript for a novel, the only way I'd read it would be if you held a gun to my head or slept with me. Under those conditions, if it didn't completely suck, I might offer to have my agent give it a look. But since I've personally sampled your cooking, I can make the offer without the gun or the sex. Up to you."

"Seems reasonable," she replied. "Under those conditions, how many manuscripts have you sent to your agent?"

"That would be none. The subject's come up a few times, but I've managed to slip through loopholes."

"Do I have to sleep with you if I put a proposal together and your agent decides to represent me?"

"Well, yeah." He shook his head as if the question were ridiculous. "Obviously."

"Of course. I'll think about it." Relaxed

again, she sat back with her wine. "I'd offer you seconds, but, one, I promised Mr. Drubber some leftovers; two, there wouldn't be enough for me to send some of the roast home with you so you could make sandwiches; and three, you'll need to save room for dessert."

Brody latched on to point one. "How come Mac rates leftovers?"

"For installing my dead bolt. He wouldn't let me pay for it, either."

"He's a little sweet on you."

"I'm a little sweet on him. Why isn't he married?"

Brody gave a sad, sad sigh. "Typical female question. I had higher hopes for you."

"You're right, it is typical. But I wish he had someone making him pot roast and working with him in the store."

"He's got you making him pot roast, apparently. And he's got Leon and Old Frank working with him in the store. Beck fills in part-time when Mac wants him."

"Still, it's not like having someone who works with you and cares that you get a nice hot meal at the end of the day."

"Word is he had his heart broken about a quarter century ago. Was engaged, and she jilted him — if not at the altar, steps from it. Took off with his best friend."

"Not really. Really?"

"That's the word, which is probably duded up to make it more important. Some root of truth in it, I imagine."

"That bitch. She didn't deserve him."

"He probably doesn't even remember her name."

"Of course he does. I bet she's on her fourth husband by now, and has a raging prescription drug habit brought on by complications from her third face-lift."

"You're a little mean. I like it."

"When it comes down to someone hurting someone I care about, I'm vicious. So. Why don't you retire to the salon, enjoy your wine. I'm going to clear this up."

"Define *clear*."

"Watch and learn."

"Fine, but the view's better from here. I saw a picture of you from a few years back. Articles on the Internet, from papers, magazines," he explained when she only stared at him.

"Why were you looking at articles on the Internet?"

"About you specifically? Curiosity. Your hair was shorter."

Reece picked up the plates, took them to the sink. "Yes. I used to go to this upscale salon on Newberry. Pricey, but worth every penny. Or it was to me then. I haven't been able to handle a salon since . . ." She turned on the water, squirted in dish soap. "So I've let it grow."

"It's nice hair."

"I used to love going to the salon, having someone so focused on me, my appearance. Sitting there sipping the wine or tea or fizzy water they'd serve me, walking out feeling fresh and new. It was one of those areas of life where I loved being female."

She turned away from the sink to divide the leftovers into the two take-away boxes she'd gotten from Joanie's. "After I got out of the hospital, my grandmother treated me to a spa day at my salon. Booked hair, nails, a facial, a massage. Everyone was so solicitous, so gentle. I panicked in the dressing room. I couldn't even unbutton my shirt to put on the robe. Just had to get out."

She took the boxes to store in the refrigerator. "My stylist — I'd gone to him for years. He's a sweetheart. He offered to come to the house for me. But I just couldn't."

"Why not?"

"Mortification played a big role."

"That's just stupid."

"Maybe, but it was real. And it was easier to be embarrassed than afraid. In the big scheme, beauty-salon phobia isn't such a hardship. But they stack up."

"Maybe you should try it again."

From the sink, she shot him a look over her shoulder. "Do I look that bad?"

"You look good. You've got lucky genes. But it's stupid not to try to get back something you enjoy."

Lucky genes, she thought as she set dishes in the drainer. Not exactly a poetic compliment. Still, it made her feel better about her appearance than she had in a very long time.

"I'll put it on my list."

She turned, drying her hands on the cloth just as he pushed off the stool. She didn't take a step back — though she thought of it. Retreat wouldn't work with him. More to the point, she supposed, she wasn't sure if she wanted to step back or step toward him.

He took the cloth out of her hands, tossed it aside in a way that made her wince. It needed to be laid flat to dry so it wouldn't —

He laid his hands on the lip of the sink on either side of her, much as he'd done on the hood of his car. "What's for dessert?"

"Apple brown betty with vanilla bean ice cream. It's been warming in the oven while we . . ."

His mouth captured hers, firm and strong. She tasted the wine on his tongue, heady and tempting, and felt the testing graze of his teeth. Her blood flashed as it might with a lightning strike.

"Oh boy," she managed. "It's like having the circuits in my brain crossed. All sizzle and smoke."

"Maybe you need to lie down."

"I'd like to. Let me say first, I'd like that. I even washed the sheets, in case."

His lips quirked. "You washed the sheets."

"Seemed like the thing to do. But . . . Would you just take a step back? I can't breathe right."

He eased back. "Better?"

"Yes and no." He was so compelling, she thought. She stood by her initial impression of him. Not handsome, but so compellingly attractive. So absolutely male. Big hands, big feet, hard mouth, hard body.

"I want to go to bed with you; I want to have all those feelings again. But I think I need to wait until I'm a little more sure of myself."

"And of me."

"It's one of the things I like about you. You get the point of things. It would be normal for you — good, possibly great — but normal. For me, being intimate again would be — will be — monumental. I guess we'd both better be sure, because that's a big weight on you."

"Okay. You're not sleeping with me for my sake."

"In a manner of speaking."

"Damn considerate of you." He gave her a quick jerk, took her mouth again. This time his hands ran down her sides, shaping her breasts, waist, hips. And once more, he stepped back. "What the hell is apple brown betty?"

"Who? Oh. Wait." She took a moment, eyes closed, until her brain settled back down between her ears. "It's delicious, that's what the hell it is. Go sit down, give me a minute and I'll prove it. You want coffee?"

"You don't have coffee."

"Actually . . ." She sidestepped to avoid contact with him again, and picked up a thermos she had on the counter. "I got some from downstairs."

"You got coffee?"

She saw — for once — she'd surprised him. "Light, one sugar, right?"

"Yeah. Thanks."

She fixed the dessert, served it in the living area. "It's not sex," she said, "but it's a nice end to a meal."

He took the first spoonful. "Where has this been all my life?"

"I learned to make it for my father. It was a favorite of his."

"A man of good taste."

She smiled, toyed with her own. "You haven't said anything at all about . . . I'm not sure what to call it."

"I think the term's *murder*."

"Yeah, the term's *murder*. One of the sheriff's theories is that I mistook the spot, and she wasn't dead. Maybe I saw a couple of people in an altercation, but it wasn't murder. Which is why no one's reported anyone like her missing."

"And you disagree."

"On every point. I know what I saw and where I saw it. Maybe she hasn't been reported missing because she's not important to anyone. Or was, well, from France."

This time Brody smiled. "Wherever she was from, odds are someone saw her. Getting gas, buying supplies, in a campground, in a motel. How well can you describe her?"

"I've already told you."

"No, I mean, could you describe her to an artist?"

"Like a police artist?"

"Angel's Fist doesn't run to that, but we've got a couple of artists. I was thinking of Doc."

"Doc?"

"He does charcoal sketches. Sort of a hobby, but he's not bad."

"And I'd be describing a murder victim, not getting a medical evaluation?"

Brody shrugged. "If you don't trust Doc, we can get someone else."

"I trust you." She nodded when Brody

frowned. "See? I told you about the weight. I trust you," she repeated, "so I'm willing to try this with Dr. Wallace. If you come with me."

He'd already planned to go with her. There was no possible way he'd miss out on any angle of the situation. But he continued to frown as he spooned up more dessert. "You want me to go with you, what have you got to trade for my time? I'm thinking along the lines of something that goes with the bottle of white in your fridge."

"I've got Sunday off. I'll take care of the menu."

He polished off the last bite in his bowl. "I trust you. I'll talk to Doc."

12

"So how'd it go?" Linda-gail set the tub of cleared dishes on the counter for Pete, then gave Reece an elbow bump.

"How'd what go?"

"Your date with Brody last night."

Reece flipped the burgers she was grilling for a table of after-school teenagers. "I just fixed him dinner. A payback for a favor."

"Just dinner." Linda-gail rolled her eyes over at Pete. "And you're going to tell me you didn't make a move on that?"

"She's in love with me." Pete slid dishes into the sink. "She can't help herself."

"It's true. It's a constant battle of control back here, every shift."

"You bought candles," Linda-gail pointed out. "And cloth napkins. And fancy wine."

"Jesus." Reece didn't know whether to laugh or cringe. "Are there no secrets in the Fist?"

"None I can't unearth. Come on, give me some dish. My own love life's been as sparse as Pete's hairline lately."

"Hey! My hair's just taking a little rest between growing seasons." Pete slicked a hand over what hair he had left. "And can feel my scalp starting to tingle in anticipation of a new crop."

"Need some more fertilizer. Is he a good kisser?" Linda-gail demanded.

"Pete? Amazing. I'm a puddle at his feet. Order up," Reece said when she'd finished plating the burgers, fries, and the little tubs of coleslaw she already knew would go to waste on the high-school crowd.

"I'll get it out of you sooner or later." After gathering up the plates, Linda-gail sashayed out.

"I am an amazing kisser," Pete announced. "Just FYI."

"I never doubted it."

"Guys like me — you know, *compact* guys — pack a hell of a punch. We . . . fuck me."

"I really don't think I can take the time for that right at the moment." Amused, Reece glanced over.

Then everything inside her went woozy and sick. Blood dripped from the hands Pete gripped together and splattered on the floor at his feet.

"Teach me to pay attention to what's in the water, goddamn it. Sliced it good. Hey. Hey. Hey!"

She heard Pete shout as if he stood on a mountaintop and she in the valley below. Then the shouts went to buzzing, and the buzzing to silence.

The quick taps on her cheek brought her around. When Joanie's face swam into her vision, nausea rolled in Reece's belly. "There's blood."

"Is she all right? Christ, Joanie, she went down hard. I couldn't get to her. Is she all right?"

"Stop breathing down my throat, Pete. She's fine." But Joanie was already running a hand over the back of Reece's head, checking for bumps. "Go on down to Doc's. Get that hand stitched up."

"I just want to make sure she's okay. She might be concussed or something."

"How many fingers?" Joanie demanded of Reece.

"Two."

"There, she's fine. Now go get that hand tended to. Can you sit up, girl?"

"Yes. Pete." Fighting nausea and the shakes, Reece sat up on the kitchen floor. "Is it bad? Your hand."

"Aw, Doc'll sew it right up."

He had a cloth wrapped around it, but Reece could see the blood seeping through. "I'm sorry."

"My own fault. You just take it easy now." He patted Reece's shoulder with his good hand before he straightened up.

"Got a knot coming up on the back of your head here. I'll get you some ice."

"It's okay." Reece gripped Joanie's fingers. "I just need to get my breath back. Someone should go with Pete. That's a bad gash."

"Sit still a minute." Joanie got up. "You there, Tod! You drive Pete down to the doc's. Your burger'll wait five minutes, and it'll be free." She turned back. "Satisfied?"

"There's blood."

"I can see that. A man's bound to bleed when he slashes his hand with a knife. That's all there is to it. Accidents happen in kitchens all the time."

"I'll clean it up, Joanie." Linda-gail stepped in. "Juanita's covering my tables."

Saying nothing, Joanie got a small ice pack from the freezer, wrapped it in a thin cloth. "Hold that on the knot," she ordered Reece. "Once you get your feet back under you, you can go on upstairs. I'll take over here."

"No, I'm okay. I can work. I'd rather work."

"Fine. Get up then, and let's see how steady you are on your feet. Dead pale," Joanie pronounced when Reece gripped the counter to haul herself up. "Take a break, get some air. Drink some water." She pushed a bottle into Reece's hand. You get some color back, you can go on back to work."

"Air would be good. Thanks."

When Joanie jerked her head, Linda-gail

nodded and followed Reece out the back.

"You want to sit down?" she asked Reece.

"No, I'll just lean here for a minute. You don't have to watch me. I'm just feeling a little queasy and a lot stupid."

And shaky, Linda-gail thought as she took the bottle of water from Reece's unsteady hands and uncapped it herself. "Spiders do that to me. Not just the big fat ones — you know the ones that look like they could carry off a good-sized cat if they put their mind to it? But even the little bitty ones give me the serious creeps. I once ran straight into a door and knocked myself silly trying to get out of the room where I saw a spider.

"Put that ice pack on your head, like Joanie said to. Bet you've got yourself a big fat spider-sized headache."

"I guess I do. But Pete —"

"You fainting like that scared Pete so bad he forgot how bad his hand must've hurt. So that's something."

"A good deed."

"And Joanie's worried enough about both of you she hasn't gotten pissed yet that she's going to have to find somebody to fill in for him until the stitches are out. Two good deeds."

"I'm loaded with them."

"You want to go out for a beer later to toast your good deeds?"

Reece took another cool sip of water. "You know what, I would."

The bar food at Clancy's wasn't bad, at least not washed down with beer. But more important to Reece was she'd taken another step on her journey back.

She was sitting in a bar with a friend.

A very strange bar, to her East Coast sensibilities.

There were trophies hanging from the wall. Mounted heads of bear, elk, moose and mule deer adorned the knotty pine paneling, along with what Linda-gail identified for her as a couple of whopping cutthroat trout. They all stared out into the bar with what Reece thought of as a little shock, a little annoyance.

The paneling, with its lower section of logs, looked as if it had soaked up a generation of smoke and beer fumes.

The floors were scuffed and scarred and had probably been hit with kegs of spilled beer over time. Part of the area, just in front of a low stage, was sectioned off for dancing.

The bar itself was big and black, and lorded over by Michael Clancy, who'd come to Wyoming straight from County Cork some twelve years before. He'd married a woman who claimed to be a quarter Cherokee and called herself Rainy. Clancy looked like what he was, a big, bluff Irishman who ran a bar. Rainy tossed nachos and potato skins, and whatever else she might be in the mood for, in the kitchen.

The bar stools were worn down on the seat and shiny from a dozen years of asses. There was Bud and Guinness on draft, and in long-necks a few local brews including something called Buttface Amber, which Reece had declined. Other options were Harp by the bottle, or if you were female — or a pansy in Clancy's opinion — Bud Light. The crowded display of liquor behind the bar leaned heavily to whiskeys.

The wine Clancy poured from a box, Linda-gail had warned Reece, was cheap and tasted like warm piss.

There were a couple of pool tables in another section, and the sound of balls clacking carried through the music piped through speakers.

"How's the head?" Linda-gail asked her.

"Still on my shoulders, and probably feeling a lot better than Pete's hand."

"Seven stitches. Ouchie. But he loved how you fussed over him when he came back in. Making him sit down, serving him that fried trout yourself."

"He's a sweet guy."

"Yeah, he is. And speaking of guys, now

that I'm plying you with alcohol, spill. Just how hot is Brody?"

If she was going to have a girlfriend, Reece decided, she was going to act like one herself. She leaned in. "Combustible."

"I *knew* it!" Linda-gail banged a fist on the table. "You can just tell. The eyes, the mouth. I mean, there's the build and the rest of him, but the mouth especially. Biteable."

"It is, I must admit, it is."

"What other parts of him have you bitten?"

"That's it. I'm thinking about the rest."

Mouth open, eyes wide, Linda-gail sat back. "You have superhuman control. Is it learned or inherited?"

"It's what you call a by-product of abject fear. You've got the story on me by now."

To give them both a minute, Linda-gail sipped at her beer. "Does that bother you?"

"I don't know. Sometimes it does, and sometimes it's a relief."

"I didn't know whether to say anything about it or not. Especially after Joanie . . ." She trailed off and took a sudden, keen interest in her beer.

"Joanie what?"

"I wasn't supposed to say she'd said. But since I already have, sort of, she gave the bunch of us the what-for when Juanita started chattering about it. Juanita doesn't mean anything by it; she just can't keep her mouth shut. Or her skirt down, come to that."

Linda-gail took another sip of beer. "Anyway, Joanie pinned her ears back good about it. And she made it plain and clear that none of us were to poke at you about it. But since you kind of brought it up . . ."

"It's all right." And wasn't it, well, amazing, to have the inimitable Joanie Parks standing as her champion? "It's just not something I like to talk about."

"I don't blame you." Linda-gail reached out, squeezed a hand over Reece's. "Not one bit. If I'd been through something like that, I'd still be curled up in the corner crying for my mama."

"No, you wouldn't, but thanks."

"So, we'll just talk about men and sex and food and shoes. The usual."

"Works for me." Reece reached for another nacho. "As for food, you know what's gunked on here has absolutely no relationship with actual cheese."

"It's orange." Linda-gail dug in, scooped the loaded chip through something pretending to be guacamole. "Close enough. Just so we'll be on level ground, men-wise, I'm going to marry Lo."

"Oh, oh, my God!" Reece dropped the loaded chip on her plate with a plop. "This is great. I had no idea."

"Neither does he." Linda-gail crunched into her nacho. "And I figure it's going to take some more time and effort to refine him into anything worth marrying. But I'm really good at projects."

"Ah. Um, so you're in love with him."

Her pretty face softened, and the dimple deepened. "I've loved him all my life. Well, since I was ten, and that's a long time. He loves me, too, but his way of dealing with that is to run in the opposite direction and bang every female within reach so he won't think about me. I'm letting him get it out of his system — time's about up."

"Well, huh. That's a unique and broad-minded system you have there, Linda-gail."

"It's getting a little more narrow-minded these days."

"He and I never . . . in case you wonder."

"I know. I wouldn't hold it against you if you had. Or I wouldn't very much. Juanita and I get on fine, and he was lighting her up like Christmas a while back. Then again, who hasn't?" She chortled out a laugh. "But I probably wouldn't buy you a beer if he'd nailed you. We were together, Lo and me, when we were sixteen, but we weren't ready. Who is at sixteen?"

"Now you are."

"Yeah, now I am. He's just got to catch up. Brody hasn't dated anyone in the Fist, in case you wonder. Word was he was seeing some lawyer type in Jackson on and off for a while, and there's been a couple of suspected oners with tourist types, but nobody right local."

"I guess that's good to know. I'm not sure what's between us, really. Except some heat."

"Heat's a good place to start. Being a cook and all, you should know that."

"It's been a while." Idly Reece toyed with the ends of her hair as she studied Linda-gail's do. "Where do you get your hair done?"

"When I'm in a hurry or when I want to splurge?"

"I'm mulling the splurge."

"Reece, Reece, you can't mull the splurge. You just, by definition, take the splurge. I know just the place. We can finagle Joanie into giving us both the same day off next week and go for it."

"Okay, but I should tell you that the last time I tried to keep a salon date, I ran like a rabbit."

"No problem." Linda-gail sucked orange goo off her thumb and grinned. "I'll bring some rope."

As Reece broke into a grin, one of the local cowboys sauntered up toward the little stage. He was a lean six feet in cowhide boots, faded jeans. The white circle worn into the back pocket came, Reece had learned, from carrying a can of snuff.

"Live entertainment?" Reece asked as he picked up a microphone.

"Depends on how you measure entertainment. Karaoke." Linda-gail lifted her drink toward the stage. "Every night in Clancy's. That's Reuben Gates, works out at the Circle K with Lo."

"Coffee black, eggs up on toast, bacon and home fries, Sunday morning regular."

"You got it. He's pretty good."

He had a deep, strong baritone, and was an obvious favorite with the crowd that whistled and clapped as he broke into his rendition of "Ruby."

As she listened to him sing about a faithless woman, she tried to imagine him standing by the banks of the Snake River in a black jacket and orange hunter's cap.

It could be him, she thought. His hands would be strong, and there was a stillness about him now as he stood, as he sang.

It could be this one, a man she'd fried eggs and potatoes for on Sunday mornings. Or it could be any of the men hunched at the bar or scattered at the tables. Any one of them could be a killer. Any one, she thought again as panic tickled slyly at her throat.

Music tinkled out, and the deep baritone cruised through it. Conversations continued, muted now out of respect for the performance. Glasses clinked on wood, chairs scraped the floor.

And the tickling panic began to close into a fist to block her air.

She saw Linda-gail's face, saw her friend's mouth moving, but anxiety had stuffed cotton in her ears. She forced a breath out, forced another in. "What? Sorry, I didn't hear . . ."

"You okay? You've gone pretty pale. Does your head hurt?"

"No. No, I'm all right." Reece made herself look back at the stage. "I still have some trouble in crowds, I guess."

"You want to get out? We don't have to stay."

And every time she ran, it was a step back. Just one more retreat. "No, no, I'm okay. Um. Do you ever do that?"

Linda-gail skipped a glance toward the stage as Reuben ended to enthusiastic applause. "Sure. You want to?"

"Not for a million dollars. Well, a half a million." Another man headed for the stage, and since this one carried about two-sixty on a five-eight frame, Reece decided she could eliminate him from her list.

He surprised her with a sweet, if thready, tenor on a ballad. "I don't recognize him," Reece commented.

"T. B. Unger. Teaches in the high

school. T.B. for Teddy Bear. And that's his wife, Arlene, sitting there — the brunette in the white shirt? They don't come into Joanie's much, homebodies with two kids. But they come into Clancy's so he can sing, once a week. Arlene works at the school, too, in the cafeteria. They're sweethearts."

Literally, Reece thought as she watched the teddy bear sing his love song straight into his wife's eyes.

There was sweetness in the world, she reminded herself. And love, and kindness. It was good to be part of that again, to feel that again.

And to laugh when the next performer, a blonde with a tin ear and a lot of self-deprecating humor, butchered a Dolly Parton classic.

She made it a full hour, and considered the evening an enormous success.

Walking back to her apartment through the quiet streets, she felt almost safe, almost easy. As close to both, she concluded, as she had felt in a very long time.

And when she let herself in the door, she felt almost home.

After locking the door, checking the knob, bracing the back of a chair under it, she went to wash.

In the doorway of her little bathroom, she froze. None of her toiletries were on the narrow shelf by the sink. She squeezed her eyes shut, but when she reopened them, the shelf was still empty. She yanked open the mirrored medicine cabinet where she stored her medication, her toothpaste. It, too, was empty.

With a whimper of distress she spun around to scan the room. Her bed was neatly made, as she'd left it that morning. The kettle sat shining on the stove. But the hooded sweatshirt she *knew* she'd left hanging on the coatrack was missing.

And at the foot of the bed, rather than under it, sat her duffel.

Her legs trembled as she crossed to it, and the whimper became a muffled cry as she yanked the zipper and found her clothes neatly packed inside.

Everything she'd come with, she saw as she pawed through the bag. All her things, carefully folded and stored. Ready to go.

Who would do such a thing?

Giving in to her unsteady legs, she lowered herself to the side of the bed. And faced the truth. No one could. No one could, not with the new lock.

She'd done it herself. She must have done it. Some internal instinct, some remnants from the worst of her breakdown kicking in. Telling her to run, to go, to move on.

Why couldn't she remember?

Not the first time, she reminded herself, and dropped her head in her hands. Not nearly the first time she'd lost time, or couldn't quite recall doing something.

But it had been months since she'd had these kinds of episodes.

Almost home, she thought, fighting despair. She'd actually let herself believe she was almost home. When some deep-seated part of her knew she wasn't even close.

Maybe she should take a hint. Pick up the duffel and go down, toss it in her car and drive. To anywhere.

And if she did, *anywhere* would just be another place where she'd cease to be. She had a place here, if she dug in. She'd had a date, she'd had a beer with a friend. She had a job and an apartment. She had, if she held on to it, an identity here.

She put all her stuff away — the clothes, the toothbrush, the bottles, the shoes. Though her stomach was raw, she set up her laptop again. Wrapped in a blanket to try to battle a cold that came from inside, she sat down to write.

I didn't run. I cooked today, and earned my pay. Pete gashed his hand while washing dishes, and the blood shook me. I fainted, but I didn't run. After work, I went to Clancy's for a beer with Linda-gail. We talked about men, about hair, about normal things women talk about. There's karaoke at Clancy's, and the walls are crowded with the heads of dead animals. Elk and moose and deer, even bear. People sing, mostly country, with varying degrees of talent. There was the onset of a panic attack, but I didn't run, and it got better. I have a friend in the Fist. More than one, really, but there's nothing quite like a girlfriend.

Sometime today I must have packed my things, but I don't remember doing it. Maybe I did it on my break after Pete hurt himself. Maybe. The blood, seeing the blood shot me right back to Maneo's. So it was, for a minute, Ginny's blood, not Pete's.

But I've unpacked it all, and put everything away. Tomorrow I'm going to see Doc Wallace to describe, as best I can, the man and woman I saw along the river. Because I did see them. I saw what he did to her.

I didn't run today. And I'm not going to run tomorrow.

13

Doc Wallace set out tea and coffee, each in lovely old stoneware pots, and sugar cookies on a pale green Depression glass plate. He served it all among the framed family photographs and fussy throw pillows of his pretty parlor with the finesse of an elderly aunt entertaining her weekly book club.

If he'd troubled with the fussy touches to relax Reece, he'd succeeded. She found herself charmed instead of anxious while they sat in front of the low glow of the fire with the scent of gardenia potpourri scenting the air.

Her first impression was of comfort and ease, and her second: This was a man who'd been well trained.

No wall of animal heads here, she thought, no wagon wheel lights or thick, Indian-style blankets. Though she knew he fished, there was no stuffed trout over the mantel, but a lovely oval mirror in a cherrywood frame.

Her grandmother would have very much approved.

In fact, she thought the room could easily have been found in a home on

Boston's Beacon Hill, and said so.

"It was my Susan's favorite room in the house." Doc passed her the tea he'd poured himself. "She used to love to sit and read in here. She was a great reader. I've kept it as she liked it."

He smiled a little, handed Brody a cup of tea. "Figure she'd haunt me otherwise. And fact is . . ." He paused a moment, and behind the lenses of his glasses, his eyes were kind and shrewd. "I can sit down here after a long day and talk things over with her. Now, some people might think that's a little crazy, a man talking to his dead wife. I think it's just human. A lot of things some might think are a little crazy are just human."

"Being a little crazy's just human," Brody commented as he helped himself to a cookie.

"I'd be human then. And look," Reece began, "I appreciate you trying to put me at ease. I do, and you have. But I know I'm a simmering stew of neuroses with chunky bits of phobias, seasoned heavily with paranoia."

"It's good to know yourself." Brody bit into the cookie. "Most people don't know they're nuts, which is annoying to the rest of us."

She spared him a glance, then focused on Doc Wallace. "But I also know what I saw by the river was real. Not a dream, not a hallucination. Not figments of my fractured mind and hyper imagination. Whatever the sheriff thinks, whatever *anybody* thinks, I know what I saw."

"Don't get too worked up at Rick," Doc said mildly. "He's doing his job, best he can. And he does a good one for the Fist."

"So everybody says," Reece muttered.

"Still, it may be that we can help him along with it."

"Do you believe me?"

"Doesn't matter if I believe you or not. But I've got no reason not to take you at your word. Seems to me you've been doing everything you can to keep a low profile around here."

Doc doused his own coffee liberally with what Reece knew was half-and-half from the little glass creamer. After stretching out his legs, he crossed the ankles of feet clad in snazzy running shoes.

"I'm forced to report my attempts in this area have been a miserable failure."

"Well, reporting a murder tends to turn the spotlight on the messenger. Doesn't make much sense you'd make up a story like this and pull everybody's attention onto you." He nudged up his glasses, peered at her through sparkling clean lenses. "Besides, Brody appears to believe you, and I know him to be a tough sell. So . . ."

Doc set his coffee aside, picked up his sketch pad and a pencil. "I've got to admit, this is exciting for me. It's like being on *Law and Order*."

"Which version?"

Doc grinned. "I like the original myself. Now, Brody's told you I do a little sketching. Even got a couple of charcoals in The Gallery."

"I keep meaning to get in there."

"Ought to. They've got some nice work by local artists. Still and all, I've never done anything like this before, so I did a little research on the procedure. I'm going to ask you to think in shapes first, if you can. Think of the shape of her face to begin with. Square, round, triangular. Can you do that?"

"Yeah, I think I can."

"Close your eyes a minute, get the picture in your mind."

She did, and saw the woman. "Oval, I guess. But a long, narrow oval. Ellipse?"

"That's good. On the thin side, then?"

"Yes. She wore her hair long, and the cap — the red cap — was pulled down low on her forehead. But I got the sense of a long, narrow face. I couldn't see her eyes at first," Reece continued. "She wore sunglasses. Wraparounds, I think."

"How about her nose?"

"Her nose?" She drew a complete blank.

"God, I don't think I'm going to be very good at this."

"Do the best you can."

"I think . . . I think long and narrow, like her face. Not prominent. I noticed her mouth more because it was moving. She was talking — yelling I thought — a lot of the time. Her mouth seemed hard to me. She seemed hard to me. I don't know how to explain."

"Thin mouth?"

"I don't know, maybe. It was . . . mobile. What I mean is she seemed to have a lot to say. And when she wasn't talking — that I could tell — she was scowling, sneering. Her mouth kept moving. She wore earrings — hoops, I'm nearly sure, I caught the glint of them. Her hair was past her shoulders, wavy, very dark. Her sunglasses fell off when he knocked her down, but it all happened so fast. She was so angry. I had the impression of big eyes, but she was so angry, and then so shocked, and then . . ."

"How about distinguishing features," Doc continued in the same easy tone. "Scars, moles, freckles?"

"I don't remember any. Makeup," she said suddenly. "I think she wore a lot of makeup. Red lipstick. Yes! Very red, and . . . it could just have been temper, but I think too much blusher. There was a vividness to her that seemed overdone, now that I think of it. Maybe temper, maybe, or too heavy a hand with the blusher. It was so far away, even with the binoculars."

"That's all right. If you had to guess her age?"

"Oh boy. Ah, late thirties maybe. Give or take a decade," Reece added and pressed her fingers to her eyes. "Hell."

"Just go with your first impression. Is this close?"

Reece edged forward in her chair when Doc turned the pad around.

He was better than she'd assumed. It wasn't the woman she'd seen looking out at her from the pad, but the potential of her was there. "Okay. Okay," she muttered as one of the knots in her stomach unraveled. "I think her chin was a little more pointed. Just a little. And, um, her eyes not that round, a little longer maybe. Maybe."

Reece picked up her tea again, used it to soothe while Doc made adjustments. "I couldn't tell the color of her eyes, but I think they were dark. I don't think her mouth was that wide. And her eyebrows — God I hope I'm not making this up — her eyebrows were thinner, really arched. Like she'd plucked them to death. When he yanked her head off the ground by the hair, her cap came off. Did I forget that before? Her cap came off. She had a wide forehead."

"Take a breath," Brody suggested.

"What?"

"Take a breath."

"Right." When she stopped to take one, she realized how hard her heart was pounding, that her hands were starting to tremble enough to slosh the tea in her cup. "Her nails were painted. Maybe red. I forgot that, too. I can see the way they dug into the dirt while he strangled her."

"Did she scratch him?" Brody asked her.

"No. She couldn't. I don't think . . . He straddled her, and he had his knees down on her arms. She couldn't lift them to scratch at him. She didn't have a chance. Once she was down, she didn't have a chance."

"How's this?"

Reece studied the sketch. Things were missing, she thought. Things she wasn't sure she had the skill to convey or the artist the skill to invoke. The fury, the passion, the fear. But it was closer.

"Yes. Yes, it's good. I can see her in it. That's what counts, isn't it?"

"I'd say so. Let's see if we can refine it a bit. You eat one of those cookies, Reece, before Brody scarfs them all down. Dick made them. Man makes a hell of a sugar cookie."

She nibbled on a cookie while Doc asked more questions. She drank another cup of tea while she watched as he changed or finessed the shape of the woman's mouth and eyes. Thinned out the eyebrows a bit more.

"That's it." Reece set her cup down with a little rattle. "That's her. It's good, it's really close. It's what I remember she looked like. What it seemed she did. I —"

"Stop second-guessing yourself," Brody ordered. "If that's your impression of her, it's good enough."

"Not from the Fist." Doc looked up at Brody. "Doesn't look like anyone I know, not offhand."

"No. But if she passed through, someone saw her. Getting gas, supplies. We'll show it around."

"Rick can fax copies to other town authorities." Doc pursed his lips as he studied his own sketch. "Maybe Park Service, too. She doesn't look familiar to me. I've treated just about everyone in the Fist and the local vicinity over the years. Including tourists and transients, one time or another. Hell, anyone born hereabouts in the last twenty years, I'm likely the one who gave their butt its first slap. She's not one of ours."

"And if they never came through here," Reece said quietly, "we may never know who she was."

"That's what I like about you, Slim. Always thinking positive." Brody caged another cookie. "You want to take a shot at describing him for the doc?"

"I didn't *see* him. Not really. Flashes of profile. His back, his hands, but he was wearing gloves. It seemed like he had big hands, but that really could be just me projecting. Cap, sunglasses, coat."

"Any hair below the cap?" Doc asked.

"No. I don't think so. I didn't notice. She was . . . in the spotlight, you could say. She had center stage, and then when he knocked her down, I was so stunned. And still, I guess I watched her more. I couldn't stop watching her, what was happening to her."

"How about his jawline?"

"All I can think is hard. He seemed hard. But I said that about her, didn't I?" She rubbed at her eyes, tried to think. "He was very still most of the time, and I had the impression of control. She was livid and ranting, and he just stood there, hardly moved. Economical? She was all over the place, gesturing, pacing, pointing. He pushed her, but it was almost like swatting a fly. I'm projecting."

"Maybe you are, maybe you're not." Doc sketched idly. "What about build?"

"Everything about him seems big now, but I can't be sure. Taller and broader than she was, certainly. In the end, when I see him straddle her, I think he must have known exactly what he was doing. Restraining her arms that way. He could've held her down like that, worn her out until he could reason with her, then walked away. Maybe it was because of the distance, but it seemed so deliberate, so cold."

Doc turned his sketch pad around again, held it up. And Reece shuddered.

This was a full-length image, back turned, face in one-quarter profile. Because it could have been so many men, fear balled ice in Reece's belly.

"Anonymous," she commented.

"Still, you can eliminate some people right from the Fist," Doc said. "Pete, let's say. Little guy, scrawny. Or Little Joe Pierce, who's carrying around an extra hundred pounds and hypertension."

"Or Carl. He's shaped like a barrel. Wrong build." Another knot unraveled. "You're right. And I don't think he was young. I mean, say, teens or very early twenties. His carriage, his, um, body language was more mature than that. Thanks. It clears my head a little."

"Wasn't me." Brody lifted a shoulder. "Unless I channeled Superman and flew over the Snake and back."

"No." For the first time since they'd begun, Reece smiled. "It wasn't you."

"I'll make copies, post one in my office. Most everybody's through there." Doc picked up the sketch of the woman again. "I'll take copies down to the sheriff's office."

"Thanks. A lot."

"Like I said, it's a little like playing detective. Interesting change of pace for me. Brody, why don't you take this tray on back to the kitchen for me."

And the look Doc sent Brody told Reece the doctor was in again, and she was the patient. She struggled not to resent it, not after the favor he'd just done for her. But her back stiffened as Brody left the room.

"I didn't come here for a medical consult," she began.

"Maybe you should. But the fact is, I'm an old country doctor, and you're sitting in my parlor. Your eyes are tired. How are you sleeping?"

"Spotty. Some nights are better than others."

"Appetite?"

"Comes and goes. Comes more than it used to. I know my physical health is tied to my mental health. I'm not ignoring either."

"Headaches?"

"Yes," she said with a sigh. "Not as often as before, certainly not as intense. And yes, I still have anxiety attacks, but

314

not as often or as intense either. I used to have night terrors, but they've throttled down to nightmares. I still have flashbacks, phantom pain sometimes. But I'm better. I had a beer at Clancy's with Linda-gail. I haven't been able to sit in a bar and have a drink with a friend in two years. I'm thinking about sleeping with Brody. I haven't been with a man in two years.

"Every time I think about just driving out of town, I don't. I even unpacked last night, put everything away again."

Behind his glasses, his eyes sharpened. "You packed your things?"

"I . . ." She faltered a moment. "Yes. I don't remember packing, and I know that's a big X on the minus side of my mental health board, but I offset it with a big check mark by *unpacking,* and added another check mark by coming here. I'm coping. I'm functional."

"And defensive," Doc pointed out. "You don't remember packing your things?"

"No, I don't, and yes, it scared me. I put things in the wrong place once, too, and just don't remember. But I handled it. I couldn't have handled it a year ago."

"What medications are you taking?"

"Nothing."

"On doctor's recommendation?"

"Not really. I tapered off of this, tapered off of that, then stopped taking all of them

315

over six months ago. They helped when I needed them most. I know medications helped me find some sense of balance again. But I can't live my life when there are meds suppressing this or coating over that. They helped me get through the worst of it, and now I want to get through the rest myself. I want to be myself."

"Will you come to me if you decide you want medical help?"

"All right."

"Will you let me do an exam?"

"I don't —"

"A checkup, Reece. When did you last have a physical?"

Now she sighed. "A year or so ago."

"Why don't you come into my office tomorrow morning?"

"I have the breakfast shift."

"Tomorrow afternoon. Three o'clock. It'd be a favor to me."

"That's a lousy way to put it," she replied. "All right. I like your house. I like that you've kept this room the way your wife liked it. I'd like to think that one day I'll have a room and someone who'd care enough to keep it for me. I'm trying to get there." She got to her feet. "I have to go to work."

He rose as well. "Tomorrow, three o'clock." And held out a hand as if sealing a deal.

"I'll be there."

He walked her to the door as Brody strolled out from the kitchen. When they were outside, Brody headed for his car.

"I'm just going to walk," Reece told him. "I want the air, and I've got a little time before my shift."

"Fine. I'll walk up with you, and you can fix me lunch."

"You just ate two cookies."

"Your point?"

She just shook her head. "You'll have to walk back again to get your car."

"I'll walk off lunch. You do blackened chicken?"

"Can I do it, yes. But it's not on the menu."

"So charge me extra. I feel like a blackened chicken sandwich on a kaiser, with onion rings. Feeling better?"

"I guess I am. Dr. Wallace has a way of smoothing out the edges." She dipped her hands into the pocket of the hooded sweatshirt she wore against the stubborn spring chill. "He pressured me, very avuncularly, to go in for a physical tomorrow. But you probably knew he was going to do that."

"He mentioned it. He's the sort that pokes his nose in. Avuncularly. He asked me if I was sleeping with you."

"Why would he do that?"

"It's his way. You're in the Fist, you're his business. So I can tell you, if that

317

woman had spent any time here, he'd know it. Sheriff's dog's in the lake again. Rather swim than walk."

They both stopped to watch the dog paddle enthusiastically through the water, sending back a little wake that rippled through the reflection of the mountains.

"If I stay, I'm going to get a dog, and teach him to fetch a ball out of the lake like — what's her name? — Abby did with Moses there. I'll get a cabin so he can be outside when I work. My grandmother has a teacup poodle named Marceau. He travels everywhere with her."

"A teacup anything named Marceau isn't a dog."

"He certainly is, and he's sweet and adorable."

"It's a wind-up toy with a pussy name."

She snorted back a laugh. "Marceau is very smart, and very loyal."

"Does he wear cute little sweaters?"

"No. They're dapper little sweaters. And though I have great love for Marceau, I'm thinking of getting a big, sloppy dog like Moses, one that would rather swim than walk."

"If you stay."

"Yes. If I stay." And as she imagined Moses did, Reece took a running leap and dove in. "I'd like to come over to your place tomorrow night, fix you dinner and stay the night."

He walked a little farther with her, strolling by a house where a woman had planted pansies in a small circular bed in the middle of her lawn that was guarded by gnomes in pointy hats.

He wondered about people who dotted their lawns with plaster people and animals.

"Would staying the night be a euphemism for sex?"

"God, I hope so. I can't promise anything, but I hope so."

"Okay." He reached out to open the door of Joanie's. "I'll wash the sheets."

She kept her doctor's appointment and considered it another major step. She hated, *hated* the exposed sensation she had when wearing nothing but the little cotton gown.

And if she couldn't comfortably be naked in front of a doctor, how did she expect to manage it later with Brody?

In the dark, she thought as she sat on the examination table while Doc's nurse took her blood pressure. All the lights off and her eyes closed. Hopefully, his closed, too.

Drunk would also be a good thing. Lots of wine, lots of dark.

"A little high, sweetie." Willow, the nurse, was Shoshone. Her blood showed in the dense black hair she wore in one thick braid, and her deep, liquid brown eyes.

"I'm nervous. Doctors make me nervous."

Willow patted Reece's hand. "Don't you worry. Doc's a cream puff. I need to take some blood. Make a fist, and think about your happy place."

Reece barely felt the needle, and gave Willow top marks. She couldn't count the number of times she'd been stuck after the shooting. Some of the nurses had hands like angels, others like lumberjacks.

"Doc's going to be with you in just a minute."

Reece nodded, and was stunned when Willow's statement proved to be the literal truth.

Doc looked different with the white lab coat over his plaid shirt, with the stethoscope around his neck, those blinding white running shoes on his feet. Still, he gave her a wink before picking up her chart. "I'll tell you right now you need ten pounds."

"I know, but I needed fifteen a few weeks ago."

"No surgeries other than the ones for the injuries you sustained in the shooting?"

She moistened her lips. "No. I was always healthy."

"No allergies. Blood pressure could be lower, sleep pattern smoother. Your cycle's regular."

"Yes. It wasn't, after. Birth control pills helped regulate it again. I haven't had any need for them otherwise." That might be changing tonight, she thought, and wondered if her blood pressure had just spiked.

"No history of heart disease, breast cancer, diabetes in your family. You don't smoke, alcohol consumption light to moderate."

He continued to scan, then set the chart aside with a nod. "Got a good foundation."

He checked her lungs, her reflexes, had her stand to check her coordination and balance. Shone lights in her eyes, in her ears, checked her lymph glands, her tonsils.

All the while he kept up a careless conversation heavy on town gossip. "Did you hear Bebe's oldest boy and two of his cohorts got caught shoplifting candy bars from the mercantile?"

"He's under house arrest," Reece said. "Sixty days, no chance of parole. School, home, Joanie's, and two hours every afternoon doing whatever chores Mr. Drubber can find for him."

"Good for Bebe. I heard Maisy Nabb threw all Bill's clothes out the window again. Plus his MVP trophy from when he quarterbacked the high school football team."

It wasn't so bad, she realized, not really so bad to go through all this with conversation. Real conversation about people they both knew.

"Rumor is he lost the money he was supposed to be saving to buy her an engagement ring playing poker," she told him. "He claims he was only trying to win enough to get her a ring worthy of her, but she's not buying it."

"She tosses his stuff out three, four times a year. He's been saving to buy her a ring for about five years now, so that's about fifteen, twenty times his clothes have ended up on the sidewalk. Carl's grandson in Laramie won a scholarship to U of W."

"Really? I haven't heard that."

"Fast-breaking." Doc's eyes twinkled with the scoop. "Carl just heard this afternoon. He's busting buttons over it. I'm going to call Willow in, do a pap and breast exam."

Resigned, Reece put her feet in the stirrups. She stared at the ceiling, and the mobile of butterflies that circled from it, while Doc rolled his stool between her legs and Willow assisted him.

"Looks healthy," Doc commented.

"Good, because it hasn't been getting any exercise in quite a while." When she heard Willow smother a laugh, Reece just closed her eyes. She had to remember some old saying about being careful of thoughts. They become words.

When he was done, Doc patted her ankle, then stood to come to the side of the table for the breast exam. "You do your monthly self-exams?"

"Yes. No. When I remember, I do."

"In the shower, first day of your period. Make it a habit and you won't forget." His thumb brushed gently over her scar. "You had a lot of pain."

"Yes." She kept watching the butterflies, the cheerful, colorful mobile. "A lot of pain."

"You mentioned phantom pain."

"I feel it sometimes, during a nightmare or just after one. During a panic attack. I know it's not real."

"But it feels real."

"Very real."

"How often do you experience the phantom pain?"

"It's hard to say. Couple times a week, I guess. That's way down from a couple times a day."

"You can sit up now." He went back to his stool as Willow slipped quietly out. "You're not interested in continuing with therapy?"

"No."

"Or in chemical aids."

"No. I've used both, and as I told you, they helped. I need to finish this my way."

"All right. I'm going to tell you that you're a little run-down, and I don't think that comes as a surprise to you. I also suspect your blood test's going to come back borderline anemic. I want you to beef up your diet, literally. Iron-rich foods. If you don't know which foods are rich in iron, I'll have Willow print you out a list."

"I'm a chef. I know food."

"Then eat it." He wagged a finger at her for emphasis. "I also have some herbs you can use to help you sleep. In a tea you drink before bed."

Her eyebrows rose. "Holistic medicine?"

"Herbs have been used to aid in healing for centuries. I used to play chess with Willow's grandfather. He was a Shoshone shaman, and a hell of a chess player. He taught me quite a bit about natural medicine. He died last fall, at the age of ninety-eight, in his sleep."

"Pretty good recommendation."

"I'll mix the herbs for you and drop them by, with instructions, tomorrow at Joanie's."

"Not to be, ah, fussy, but I'd like a list of the herbs, too."

"Sensible. I want you back here for a follow-up in four to six weeks."

"But —"

"To check your weight, your blood, and your general well-being. If there's improvement, we'll go to three months for the next. If there's not" — he rose from his stool, put his hands on her shoulders, looked hard into her eyes — "I'm going to get tough."

"Yes, sir."

"Good girl. I hear you make a hell of a pot roast with all the trimmings. That's my fee for today, seeing as I browbeat you into the exam."

"That isn't right."

"If I don't like the pot roast, I'll bill you. Go on and get dressed."

But she sat for several minutes when he'd gone out and closed the door behind him.

14

Brody remembered to wash the sheets, but as his work-in-progress sucked him in for a straight six-hour stint, he nearly forgot to dry them.

When he surfaced from the driving rain and spring mud he'd tossed his characters into, he had a vague and nagging jones for a cigarette. He hadn't taken a long, deep drag on a Winston for three years, five months and . . . twelve days, he calculated as he caught himself reaching for the pack that wasn't there.

But a good writing session, like good sex, often teased the urge back.

So he just sat and imagined it for a while — that simple, that seductive, that deadly pleasure of sliding one of those slim white cylinders out of the red-and-white pack, digging up one of the dozens of disposable lighters he would have scattered around. Sparking the flame, taking that first easy draw.

And damn if he couldn't taste it — a little harsh, a little sweet. That, he supposed, was the blessing and the curse of a good imagination.

Nothing stopping him from going into

town right now and buying a pack. Not a damn thing. But it was a point of pride, wasn't it? He'd quit, so that was that. Same deal with the *Trib*, he reminded himself.

Once he closed the door, he didn't crack it open again.

And that, he supposed, was the blessing and the curse of being a stubborn son of a bitch.

Maybe he'd go downstairs and get some oral satisfaction from a bag of chips. Probably should make a sandwich.

It was the thought of food that reminded him Reece was due in a few hours. That made him remember the sheets in the washing machine.

"Shit."

He shoved away from the desk, headed downstairs to the utility room and the elf-sized washer and dryer. Once he had the sheets tumbling, he turned back to survey the kitchen.

The breakfast dishes were in the sink. Okay, so were last night's dinner dishes. The local paper, and the pages of his daily copy of the *Chicago Tribune* he subscribed to — old habits die hard — were spread out on the table, along with a couple of his notebooks, assorted pens and pencils, a pile of mail.

He accepted the fact he'd have to clean

it up, which was only a minor pain in the ass. And since that was offset by the guarantee of a good, hot meal and the distinct possibility of sex, it was a reasonable use of his time.

Besides, he wasn't a pig.

He pushed up the sleeves of his ratty, and favorite, sweatshirt, then took the piled dishes out of the sink. "Why do you put them in there in the first place?" he asked himself as he squirted in soap, ran hot water. "Every single damn time you do this, you have to pull them back out again."

He washed, he rinsed, he wished the cabin had a goddamn dishwasher. And he thought of Reece.

He wondered if she'd kept her appointment with Doc Wallace. He wondered what he'd see in those big dark eyes of hers when she walked in his door that evening. Ease, nerves, amusement, sorrow.

How would she look working in his kitchen, putting food together the way an artist creates. Using shapes and colors and textures and balance.

Then there would be the scents, the tastes — of what she prepared and of her. He was getting uncharacteristically wrapped up in the scents and tastes of her.

He set the dishes to drain and got to work on the table. It occurred to him he'd never really shared a meal with anyone in the cabin. Beer and pretzels maybe, if Doc or Mac or Rick dropped over.

He'd hosted a poker game a time or two when he'd been in the mood. More beer again, chips, cigars.

There'd been wine and scrambled eggs at two a.m. with the delightful Gwen from L.A. who'd come to ski and had ended up in his bed one memorable night in January.

But those casual interludes didn't have quite the same resonance as having a woman cook you a meal and share it with you in your place.

He took the papers into the utility room, to stack on the pile he hauled out for recycling weekly. Though he frowned at the bucket and mop, he gathered them up.

"See, not a pig," he muttered as he mopped the kitchen floor.

He should straighten up the bedroom, probably, in case things went that way. If they didn't go that way, at least he wouldn't have to look at the mess while he suffered through a restless night alone.

He scrubbed a hand over his face, reminding himself to shave. He hadn't bothered with it that morning.

She'd probably want candles, so he'd dig some out. Pretty sure he had something that would do, and he had to admit it was nice to sit down to dinner with a pretty woman in candlelight.

But when he caught himself wondering if it was the right time of year for tulips, he stopped short.

Absolutely not. That was crazy thinking. When a guy went out and bought a woman flowers — especially her favorite flowers — he was just asking for her to pick up serious signals. Dangerous and complicated signals.

No damn tulips.

Besides, if he bought flowers he'd have to buy something to stick them in. He just wasn't going there.

A clean kitchen would have to do it, and if she didn't like it . . .

"Wine. Damn it."

He knew without looking all he had was beer and a bottle of Jack Daniel's. Grumbling, he prepared to leave the housekeeping for a drive to town when inspiration struck.

He dug out the notepad that held phone numbers and called the liquor store.

"Hey, has Reece Gilmore been in there for wine today? Yeah? What did she — Oh, okay. Thanks. I'm good, thanks. How you doing? Uh-huh." Brody leaned a hip into the counter, knowing payment for the information that he and Reece would be dining on something that went with Chenin Blanc was a few minutes of conversation and gossip.

But he straightened back up when his informant mentioned the sheriff had been in earlier that day with a copy of Doc Wallace's sketch.

"Did you recognize the woman? No. Yeah, I saw it. No, I can't say I thought she looked anything like Penélope Cruz. No, Jeff, I really don't think Penélope Cruz was in the area and got herself murdered. Sure, if I hear anything, I'll let you know. See you later."

Brody hung up, shaking his head. People, he thought, were as much a source of entertainment as they were a source of irritation. It kept things balanced.

"Penélope Cruz," he muttered, and dumped the water from the bucket into the sink.

He remembered the sheets after he'd done a scouting expedition for candles and had come up with a couple of white tapers earmarked for power outages and a jar candle someone had given him over the holidays that he'd never used. It was called Mom's Apple Pie.

Not particularly sexy, he thought, but better than nothing.

He took it and the dry sheets upstairs to the bedroom, fully intending to straighten up. His mistake was in looking out the window for a few minutes.

A couple of sailboats skimmed along the lake with their white sails fat with wind. He recognized Carl's canoe near the north end. Probably out fishing, Brody decided. The man lived to fish and to gossip with Mac.

And there was Rick's kid with Moses. School must be done for the day. The dog took a flying leap after the ball and flushed an egret. The bird speared up, arrowed into the marsh.

Nice picture, Brody thought absently. Pretty and placid and . . .

Something in the quality of the light and shadows on the lake sucked his mind back into the book. He narrowed his eyes as Moses paddled back to shore, the ball gripped in his teeth.

But what if it wasn't a ball . . .

He left the tangle of sheets on the bed and strode back into his office. He'd just get this one partial scene down, he told himself. Thirty minutes tops, then he'd deal with the bedroom, shower, shave and put on something that didn't necessarily look as if he'd slept in it.

Two hours later, Reece set one big box of supplies on the porch of Brody's cabin, knocked briskly, then walked back to her car for a second box.

She knocked again, louder this time. The

lack of response had her frowning, and gingerly trying the door.

She knew her instinctive worry that he'd drowned in the tub, fallen down the stairs or been murdered in a home invasion was ridiculous. But that didn't make it less real.

And the house was so quiet, seemed so empty. It wasn't a place she really knew. She couldn't quite make herself step over the threshold, not until the image of him bleeding on the floor somewhere inside lodged itself with ugly clarity in her mind.

She forced herself inside, called out his name.

And when she heard the creak of floorboards overhead, she grabbed her chef's knife out of a box, gripped its handle with both hands.

He came scowling — alive and in one piece — to the top of the stairs.

"What? What time is it?"

Relief nearly sent her to her knees, but she managed to lean against the doorjamb and stay upright. "About six. I knocked, but —"

"Six? Damn it. I, ah, got hung up."

"It's okay, no problem." The pain in her chest was shifting into another kind of pressure. He looked so annoyed, so disheveled, so big and male. If she'd trusted her legs right at that moment, she might've used them to bolt up the steps and jump him.

"You want a rain check?"

"No." His frown only deepened. "How the hell do I know when it's going to rain again? I need to . . . clean up." Goddamn sheets. "You need any help first?"

"No. No. No, I'm fine. I'll just get started on dinner, if that's all right with you. It'll take about two hours, maybe a little less. So, you know, take your time."

"Good." He paused long enough to hook his thumbs in the front pockets of his jeans. "What were you going to do with the knife?"

She'd forgotten it was in her hands, and now looked down at it with a combination of puzzlement and embarrassment. "I don't really know."

"Maybe you could put it down so I don't get in the shower with the image of Norman Bates in my head."

"Sure."

She turned to set it back in the box, and when she turned again, he was gone.

She hauled in both boxes. She wanted to lock the front door — badly wanted to lock it. It wasn't her place, but didn't he realize how easily anyone could just walk in? She had, after all. How could he be upstairs, oblivious to unlocked doors? Taking a shower.

And God, *God,* she wished she had that

kind of confidence, or faith, or even plain stupidity.

Since she didn't, she locked the door. And after she'd carried her supplies to the kitchen, she locked the back door as well.

Wasn't her place, true, but she was in it. How could she concentrate on fixing a meal with unlocked doors everywhere?

Satisfied, she took out the casserole she'd prepared, measured out milk and set it on the stove to scald. She got out her brand-new knife block — she was spending too much of her paycheck on kitchen equipment. It was insane, but she couldn't seem to help herself. Waiting inside the roaster she pulled out next was a pork loin soaking inside a sealed bag of marinade she'd mixed up the night before.

Setting it aside, she put the wine in the refrigerator to keep it chilled, then did a quick inspection of the contents.

Worse even than she'd imagined. And a good thing she'd brought absolutely everything she'd need with her. He did have a couple of eggs, a stick of butter and some slices of American cheese. Pickles, milk that was already past its recommended expiration date and eight bottles of Harp. Two rapidly shriveling oranges sat like dour wallflowers on the bottom shelf. There wasn't a single leafy vegetable in sight.

Pathetic. Absolutely pathetic.

Still, as she poured the hot milk over the scalloped potatoes, she caught the scent of pine cleaner. She had to appreciate he'd troubled enough to clean up before she got there.

She slid the casserole into the oven, set the timer.

When Brody walked in thirty minutes later, she was sliding the roast in beside the casserole. The table was set with his plates and candles she'd brought with her, along with dark blue napkins, wineglasses, and a little clear bowl that held what he thought were miniature roses in sunny yellow.

There were the scents, as he'd imagined. Something succulent from the oven, something fresh from the pile of vegetables on the counter. And a combination of both the succulent and the fresh that was Reece.

When she turned, he didn't see the nerves and the sorrow in her eyes. They were deep, they were dark, they were warm.

"I thought I'd . . . Oh."

She took a step back as he strode to her, and a flicker of those nerves skipped across her face as he took her arms, lifted her to her toes.

But it was the warmth he tasted when he took her mouth, the warmth flavored very subtly by the nerves. It was, for him, irresistible.

Her arms were pinned between them, then her hands curled on his chest, gripped their way up to his shoulders. He swore he felt her melt.

He released her, stepped back and said, "Hi."

"Yeah, hi. Ah, where am I again?"

He grinned. "Where do you want to be?"

"I guess I want to be right here. I was about to do something. Oh yeah, I was going to make martinis."

"No shit?"

"Absolutely none. She moved to his refrigerator for ice to chill the two glasses she'd brought along. Then stopped. "You don't like martinis?"

"What's not to like? Jeff didn't say you'd picked up any vodka."

"Jeff?"

"Liquor Store Jeff."

"Liquor Store Jeff," she repeated with a nod. Then sighed a little as she dumped ice in the martini glasses. "What, do they post a list of my alcoholic purchases somewhere? Am I heading the line as town drunk?"

"No, Wes Pritt's undefeated in that category. I called in because I figured you'd want wine. And if you'd already picked it up, I'd save myself the trip to town."

"Well, that was efficient. I didn't think

of martinis until I was putting everything together to come by. I borrowed the glasses and shaker from Linda-gail. She got them to make Cosmos a couple years ago."

He stood back, watched her measure and shake, toss the ice, pour, add olives on long blue picks to the drinks. Then he studied the results in the glass she handed him.

"I haven't had a martini in . . . I don't know. It's not the sort of thing you order in Clancy's."

"Well then, to a touch of urban sophistication in the Fist." She touched her glass to his, waited until he'd sipped.

"Damn good martini." He sipped again, studying her over the rim. "You're something."

"Or other," she agreed. "Try this."

She lifted a small dish in which what looked like stuffed celery was arranged in some intricate geometric pattern. "What's in it?"

"State secret, but primarily smoked Gouda and sun-dried tomatoes."

He wasn't a big fan of raw celery, but figuring the vodka would kill the taste, he gave it a shot. And changed his position. "Whatever the state secret might be, it does a hell of a lot more for celery than the peanut butter my mother used to dump on it."

"I should hope so. You can sit down, enjoy." She picked up her glass for another tiny sip. "I'm going to make the salad."

He didn't sit, but he did enjoy watching her roast pine nuts. Imagine that, she was roasting pine nuts. Then he saw her putting leafy stuff in the skillet.

He had an innate suspicion of leafy stuff in the first place, much less when you put that leafy stuff in a pan on the stove. "You're cooking a salad?"

"I'm preparing a spinach and red cabbage salad, with pine nuts and a little Gorgonzola. I couldn't believe Mac ordered Gorgonzola when I just mentioned last week I wish I could get my hands on some."

"Sweet on you, remember."

"I feel very lucky to have the man who can get me Gorgonzola sweet on me. Anyway, Dr. Wallace said I need more iron. Spinach is loaded with it." She caught his expression out of the corner of her eye and swallowed a laugh. "You're a big boy. If you don't like it, you don't have to finish it."

"There's a deal. How'd it go with Doc?"

"He's thorough and he's gentle, and he's impossible to argue with." As she spoke she adjusted the heat under the skillet. "He thinks I'm a little run-down, and probably a little anemic, but otherwise pretty good.

I've had my fill of doctors, probably for a lifetime, but it wasn't as bad as I thought it would be. When I went back to the liquor store, Jeff mentioned that the sheriff had been in with the sketch."

"Yeah, I heard that, too. He mention Penélope Cruz?"

She smiled a little. "Yeah. He — the sheriff — sent a copy to Joanie's, too. No bells rang."

"Did you expect them to?"

"I don't know what I thought. I guess part of me hoped someone would look at it and say, 'Gee, that looks like Sally Jones, who lives just east of town. She's been having a rough time of it with her no-good husband.' Then we'd know, and the sheriff would go arrest the no-good husband. And it would be over."

"Neat and tidy."

"In a way." She took another minute sip of her martini. "Anyway. I finished your book. I'm glad you didn't bury Jack alive."

"He is, too."

She laughed. "I bet. I like that you didn't totally redeem him, either. He's still so flawed and funny, and poised to screw up, but I think Leah may nudge him into being the best man he can be. You let her save the day, too." She glanced back at him. "From this female reader's perspective, that was great. And it worked."

"Glad you liked it."

"Enough that I picked up another one this afternoon. *Blood Ties*." She saw the frown come into his eyes. "What?"

"It's . . . violent. Pretty graphic in a couple of scenes. It may not be something you'd enjoy."

"Because I've experienced graphic violence firsthand?"

"It might echo a little more than you'd be comfortable with."

"If it does, I'll put it down. Just like you can put down the spinach salad." She checked the oven, the skillet, picked up her martini. "We're right on schedule here. Why don't you light those candles, open the wine?"

"Sure."

"So, what hung you up today?"

"Hung me up?"

"You said, when I got here, you'd gotten hung up."

"Right." He lit the candles she'd set on the tiny table — dark blue tapers to match the napkins. "Work."

He was, she thought, so often a man not of few words but of none. At least verbally. "Do I assume in that context it means your book's going well?"

"Yeah." He found the wine in the refrigerator. Chenin Blanc, as advertised. "It was a good day."

"You're not going to talk about it."

He started to search the kitchen drawers for a corkscrew, but she handed him one she'd brought with her. "About what?"

"The book."

He considered as he opened the wine, as she added more spinach to the pan. "I was going to kill her. Maybe you remember I mentioned it, that day we were on the trail."

"Yes, I do. You said the villain was going to kill her there, push her off and into the water."

"Yeah, and he tried. He hurt her, he tormented her, he terrorized her, but he didn't manage to push her off the ridge the way he'd planned."

"She got away."

"She jumped."

Reece looked over as she began lifting the wilted greens from the pan. "She jumped."

He never talked about his work with anyone. It generally irritated him even to be asked about it. But he found he wanted to tell her, to see her reaction.

"The rain's driving, the trail's thick and heavy with mud. She's bruised and battered, her leg's bleeding. She's alone up there with him. There's no one to help her. She can't outrun him. He's stronger, he's faster. He's fucking crazy. So she jumps. I still figured she'd die. Never planned for her to make it past chapter eight. But she proved me wrong."

Saying nothing, Reece tossed the salad with the vinaigrette she'd made at home.

"She's stronger than I realized when I first met her. She has a deep and innate will to survive. She went into the water because she knew it was her only chance, and she'd rather have died trying to live than just to lie down and let him kill her. And she fought her way out of the river, even though it tried to suck her down, even though it tossed her around. She fought her way out."

"Yes," Reece agreed, "she sounds strong."

"She didn't think of it that way. She didn't think at all, she just acted. She clawed her way out. She's lost and she's hurt, she's cold, and she's still alone. But she's alive."

"Will she stay that way?"

"That'll be up to her."

Reece nodded. She arranged the salads on plates, drizzled them with cheese. "She'll want to give up. I hope she doesn't. I hope she wins. Do you . . . care about her?"

"I wouldn't spend time with her otherwise."

She set the plates on the table, then a small basket with a round of olive bread.

She poured the wine herself. "You spent time with the killer, too."

"And I care about him. Just in a different way. Sit down. I've gotten so I like the way your eyes look in candlelight."

Surprise came into them first, then that gold light as she sat. "Try the salad. You won't hurt my feelings if you don't like it."

He obliged, then frowned at her. "It's annoying. I don't like celery, particularly. I've never liked spinach. Who would? I'm not a big fan of change, either."

She smiled. "But you like my celery. You like my spinach."

"Apparently. Maybe I just like whatever you put in front of me."

"Which makes it rewarding to cook for you." She forked up some salad. "To iron in the blood."

"Have you given any more thought to putting a cookbook proposal together?"

"Actually I spent some time on that last night after my shift."

"Is that why you look tired?"

"That's not an appropriate question after you've said you like the way I look in candlelight."

"Your eyes, specifically. Doesn't mean I can't see you look tired."

He would, she supposed, always be brutally honest with her. Tough as it might be

344

on the ego, it was better than platitudes and soft lies.

"I couldn't sleep, so fiddling with the proposal gave me something to do. I was thinking of *The Simple Gourmet* as a title."

"It's okay."

"You have better?"

He continued to eat, mildly amused by the annoyance in her voice. "Let me think about it. Why couldn't you sleep?"

"How do I know? The doctor's got some sort of holistic tea he wants me to try."

"Sex is a good sedative."

"Maybe. Especially, for instance, if your partner's on the inadequate side. You can catch a quick nap during the act."

"I can promise you won't sleep through it."

She only smiled, and ate her salad.

She wouldn't trust him to carve the pork roast, which was vaguely insulting, but did so herself as she steamed asparagus. Brody decided not to complain, as the meat smelled incredible and he noted there was a serving of scalloped potatoes in his immediate future.

She drizzled hollandaise over the tender shoots, fragrant au jus over the slices of pork.

"We ought to be able to work a deal,

you and me," Brody began when he cut into the pork.

"A deal?"

"Yeah, just a minute." He sampled. "Just as I figured. So, a deal. We'll barter. Sex for food."

She lifted her brows, pursed her lips as if considering. "Interesting. However, I really think you're reaping the benefits on both sides of that deal."

"You, too. But if the sex thing doesn't work out, we can try odd jobs. Manly stuff. Painting that apartment of yours, minor plumbing, whatever. For this, you provide hot meals."

"Might work."

He tried the potatoes. "My God, you should be canonized. *The Casual Gourmet.*"

"Saint Reece, the casual gourmet?"

"No, that's your cookbook title. *The Casual Gourmet.* It's not simple, which can be construed as ordinary. It's spectacular. But you don't need to spend all day sweating over the stove to make it, or your heirloom china and sterling to eat it. Gourmet, the way people live, not just the way they entertain to impress."

She sat back. "That's a better title, and a better summary of the idea than mine. Damn it."

"I'm a professional."

"Eat your asparagus," she ordered.

"Yes, Mom. By the way? Don't even think about packing up any leftovers."

"Duly noted."

He ate, he drank, he watched her. And at some point, he simply lost the thread of the casual conversation.

"Reece?"

"Hmm."

"It's the eyes, mostly, it's the eyes. They grab me by the throat. But the rest of you? It looks really good in candlelight, too."

Unexpected, she thought. He could say the most unexpected things. So she smiled at him, and let the glow of it warm her while they ate.

15

She insisted on clearing up. He'd expected that, as she was a woman who liked to put, and to keep, things in their place. He'd have laid odds she had that tendency before the violence in Boston — where she'd probably kept a tidy house, and a tidy kitchen personally and professionally. She'd always know where the midsized mixing bowl was, and her favorite blue shirt, her car keys. Her checkbook would always be balanced.

What had happened to her had, in all likelihood, spotlighted and enhanced her organizational bent. At this point in her life, she not only wanted but *needed* things in their place. It would give her a sense of security.

For himself, most days he figured he was doing pretty well if he could find matching socks on the first pass.

Because he could see she wouldn't be satisfied otherwise, he dried off dishes, put them back in the cupboard. But he largely stayed out of her way while she stored leftovers, boxed up her equipment, scrubbed off his stove.

Nerves were coming back, and she'd

gone very quiet with them. He could prac-
tically see them popping out on her skin
like hives as she rinsed out the dishcloth,
twisted the water out of it, laid it over the
middle lip of the double sink to dry.

He supposed now that the meal was
over, and the cleanup nearly done, sex had
stumbled back into the room like an interesting and awkward guest.

He considered just grabbing her, hauling
her upstairs and into bed before she thought
about it. There was an advantage to the
technique, and he could probably have her
naked before she changed her mind. But
he rejected it, at least for the moment, in
favor of a more subtle approach.

"Want to take a walk? Down to the lake,
maybe?"

And he saw the combination of surprise
and relief on her face. "That'd be nice. I
haven't done that yet, not on this side
anyway."

"It's a clear night, so there's light
enough. But you'll need your jacket."

"Right." She stepped into the utility
room to take hers off the peg.

He moved in behind her, deliberately
reaching over her for his. She stiffened at
the light brush of bodies, sidestepped and
reached for the door.

Her nerves pumped once, like a pulse,
then seemed to evaporate into the cool air.

"It's gorgeous out." She breathed it in, soaked it in, earth and pine. "I haven't been able to talk myself into a solo walk at night. I think about it though." She pulled her jacket on as she walked. "But it's either too quiet or not quiet enough, and I come up with a dozen reasons why I should head straight up to my apartment after a dinner shift."

"Mostly towners around this time of year at night. Not much to worry about there."

"Obviously you don't know about the crazed psychopath hiding in the marsh, the serial rapist just passing through town or the kindly math teacher who, in actuality, is an ax murderer."

"I guess I missed them."

She glanced up at him as if considering, then shrugged. "One night last week I was restless and wanted a walk. I actually thought about taking my serving fork with me, in case I had to defend myself against any or all of my imaginary homicidal maniacs."

"A serving fork."

"Yeah. A knife seemed a little too over the top. But you could do some damage if you had to with a decent serving fork. But I decided against it and watched an old movie on TV instead. It's ludicrous. I'm ludicrous. Why do you want to hang around with me, Brody?"

"Maybe I find neurotic women hot."

"No, you don't." But she laughed, shook back her hair to take a look up at the sky. "My God, it's so big, so clear. I can see the Milky Way. I think that's the Milky Way. And both Dippers, which is about it for my constellation knowledge."

"Don't look at me. I just see a bunch of stars, and a white, waning moon."

"So?" Because he hadn't taken her hand, and she doubted he was the type for a lot of hand-holding, she slid her own into her jacket pockets. "Make one up. You're in the business of making things up."

Hooking his thumbs in his jeans pockets, he studied the pattern of stars. "There's the Lonely Herman — or the Fat Man Standing on One Leg. Over to the west, there's the Goddess Sally, who guards over all fry cooks."

"Sally? And here, all this time, I didn't know I had a patron goddess."

"You're no fry cook."

"Right now, I am. Besides, I want Sally for my own. Look how she shines in the water."

Stars swam in the lake, a thousand lights sparkling on the dark plate of it. And the moonlight cut a dreamy white swath over the gleam. The air was full of scent, the pine, the water, the earth and grass.

"Sometimes I miss Boston so much it's

an ache right down in the bones," she told him. "And I think I need to go back, I want to be back and find what I had there. My busy life, my busy friends. My apartment with the Chinese-red walls and sleek black dining room table."

"Chinese red?"

"I liked bold once." She'd been bold once. "Then I stand at a spot like this, and I think, even if I could bury what happened, I don't know if I could find anything there that I want or I need anymore. I'm not Chinese red anymore."

"What does it matter? You make your place where you are, and if it doesn't suit, you make it somewhere else. You use whatever colors you damn well please."

"That's exactly what I told myself when I left. I sold all my things. My sleek black dining room table, and all the rest. I told myself it had to be done. I wasn't working, and there were bills. Lots and lots of bills. But that was only part of it. I didn't want them anymore."

"Yours to sell," he pointed out. But he thought how wrenching it must have been for someone like her to push everything she had away. How painful and sad.

"Yeah. Yeah, mine to sell. And the bills got paid. And now I'm here."

She moved closer to the water's edge. "The woman in your book — the one you didn't kill after all? What's her name?"

"Madeline Bright. Maddy."

"Maddy Bright." Reece tested the name out. "I like it — friendly but strong. I hope she makes it through."

"So does she."

They stood for a moment, side by side, looking over the lake, through the night, toward the deep silhouette of the mountains.

"When we were up on the trail that day, and you were figuring out how she'd die — or how you thought she would — and I went on by, did you stay up there to make sure I got back safely?"

He kept right on looking at the Tetons. "It was a nice day. I didn't have anything else to do."

"You were heading in my direction even before you heard me running back."

"I didn't have anything else to do," he repeated, and she turned to face him.

"You were being a nice guy."

She took a chance, a big step for her. Like jumping off a cliff into a river. She lifted her hands to lay them on his face, rose up to her toes. And touched her lips to his.

"I'm afraid I'm going to screw this up. You should know that before we go back. But I'd like to go back anyway. I'd like to go back in, and go to bed with you."

"That's an excellent idea."

"I get them occasionally. Maybe you should hold my hand in case I lose my nerve and try to run."

"Sure."

She didn't lose it all, and she didn't try to run, but with every step back toward his cabin the doubts crept closer.

"Maybe we should have another glass of wine first."

"Had enough, thanks." He kept her hand in his, kept walking.

"It might be best if we talked about where this is leading."

"Right now it's leading up to my bedroom."

"Yes, but . . ." It was no use balking when he was already pulling her inside. "Um, you need to lock the door."

He turned the lock. "There."

"I really think we need to —"

She broke off, completely stunned, when he simply plucked her up and laid her over his shoulder.

"Oh, well." There were too many conflicting currents running inside her to let her decide whether being carried through the house was romantic or mortifying. "I'm not sure this is the right approach. I think if we took a few minutes to discuss . . . I'd just like to ask if you'd keep your expectations on the low side because I'm really out of practice and —"

"You're talking too much."

"It's going to get worse." She squeezed her eyes shut as he started up the stairs. "I can actually feel the babbling rising in my throat. Listen, listen, when we were outside, I could breathe, and I thought I could handle it. It's not that I don't want this, it's just I'm not sure. I don't know. God. Does the bedroom door have a lock?"

He booted it shut, then turned and locked the door. "Better?"

"I don't know. Maybe. I know I'm being an idiot, but I'm just not —"

"Knowing you're an idiot's the first step to recovery." He dropped her on her feet by the bed. "Now be quiet."

"I just think if we —"

Thoughts fizzled because he made that move on her again. Jerking her up, toward him, closing her mouth with his, with heat, with hunger. All she could do was hold on while fears and needs and reason warred inside her.

Part of her was falling apart. And part of her was falling away.

"I think I —"

"Need to be quiet," he finished and kissed her again.

"I know. Maybe you could talk. But would you turn out the lights?"

"I never turned them on."

"Oh. Oh." Now the silver moonglow and

the starshine that had been so lovely and appealing outside seemed too bright.

"Pretend I'm still holding your hand so you don't run away."

But she felt his hands run up her body, thumbs skimming not so gently over her breasts. Lovely little thrills. "How many hands do you have?"

"Enough to get the job done. You ought to look at me. Look at me, Reece. That's the way. You know the first time I saw you?"

"In the . . . in the diner." The moonlight darkened his eyes, as if the green had been swallowed up by the night. "In Joanie's."

"Yeah." He unbuttoned her shirt, lowered his head to close his teeth over her jaw until she trembled. "First time I saw you, I got that little snap in the blood. You know what I'm saying?"

"Yes. Yes. Brody, just —"

"Sometimes you act on it." He nipped his way down her throat. "Sometimes you don't, but you know when you feel it."

"If it was dark . . . It'd be better if it was dark."

He took the hand she'd lifted to cover the scar on her chest, drew it away again. "We'll test that theory sometime. You got some sexy skin here, Slim." He let his hands run up to her shoulders, sliding the shirt away as they traveled down her arms.

"All smooth and soft. A guy just wants to lap it up. No, you don't." He wrapped her hair around his hand to keep her face lifted to his. "Keep looking at me."

Cat's eyes, she thought. She was so close to them now the color seemed to have leaped back into them. A mix of green and amber, and so watchful. She didn't feel safe staring into them, not at all safe. But the fear was somehow thrilling.

Then the fingers of his free hand snapped open the hook of her bra, and her own eyes rounded.

Even as the nervous laugh tickled her throat he was devouring her again, mouth to mouth, body to body. Everything about him was hard and strong and just a little rough. Everything about him was exactly what she wanted.

Hands along her skin, learning secrets she'd forgotten she had, teeth grazing, causing delicious little lines of heat. She felt him loosen her belt before his hands slid erotically under denim to stroke flesh.

Her response came in spurts. Shy and hesitant, avid and eager. But whatever roller coaster she was on, she was dragging him right along with her, the breathless climb up, the windy flight down, and all the dangerous curves between.

She was slight and tight with that smooth, soft skin seductive in its fragility.

She fumbled at his shirt, and her breath caught, caught again and again, whenever he touched her. Wherever he touched her.

So he savored and sampled and savaged while his control teetered on a slippery edge.

Her arms tightened around him when he scooped her up, all but tossed her on the bed. Her gasp of excited shock was muffled against his mouth. In a kind of frenzy she fought to toe off her shoes, bucking her hips so he could yank the jeans down.

His mouth tore from hers to feast at her throat while her fingers dug into the muscles of his back, his shoulders. Everything in her was rising toward that heat, the threat and the promise of it.

When his mouth closed greedily over her breast, her heartbeat went to thunder. Her pulse exploded to a gallop.

His weight pinned her, his mouth claimed her. Even through the silver haze of lust, panic began to crawl. She fought it, willing her mind to shut off, to let her body rule. But in the end they both betrayed her as her lungs simply shut down.

"I can't breathe. I can't. Wait, stop."

It took him a moment to understand it was panic, not passion. He rolled aside, then gripped her shoulders to yank her up to sitting.

"You are breathing." He gave her a little

shake. "Stop gasping for air. You'll just hyperventilate."

"Okay. Okay." She knew the routine. She had to concentrate on each breath, on the physical act of inhaling slow and steady.

Mortified, she crossed her arms over her breasts as she sat in a slant of moonlight. "I'm sorry. I'm sorry. Goddamn it, I'm sick of being a freak."

"Then stop."

"You think it's so fucking easy? Oh, I'll just be normal now. You think I like sitting here naked and humiliated?"

"I don't know, do you?"

"You son of a bitch."

"There you go, sweet-talking me again." There was heat in her eyes, which he appreciated. But the shine came into them, warning of a jag. "You start crying, you're going to piss me off."

"I'm not going to cry. You asshole." She knuckled a tear away.

"Now you've done it. I'm turned on again." He pushed her hair off her shoulders. "Did I hurt you?"

"What?"

"Was I hurting you?"

"No. Jesus." She kept one arm over her breasts, covered her face with her other hand. "No. I just . . . I couldn't get my breath. I felt, I don't know, trapped under you, I guess. Just a flare of claustrophobia, performance anxiety and so on and so fucking forth."

"Oh, if that's all, I can fix it." He took her shoulders again, pulling her down to him as he lay on his back. "You can be on top."

"Brody —"

"Just look at me." He cupped a hand on the back of her head, drew her lips to his. "Take it easy," he murmured against her mouth. "Or take it any way that suits you."

"I feel clumsy."

"No, you don't." He let his hands wander, watched the flush come back into her cheeks. "You feel smooth, a little on the slight side. But not clumsy. Kiss me again."

She laid her lips on his and let go of the panic. His heart beat strong and steady against hers; his lips demanded that hers yield. The taste of him, once again, awakened all those long-denied appetites.

Still when he lifted her hips, she started to protest, to pull away. But he held her, and his eyes trapped her, until he slid inside her.

A shudder that was relief, pleasure, lust shook her. Then he began to move, and her body began to hum.

She cried out as she stumbled over the

first peak, a shock to the system, a sudden surge of sheer delight.

She moaned as she reared back. As she gave herself to it, and to him. And at last, as she took and took.

She climbed the next peak, dragging herself over as the orgasm seemed to rip right through her. She could feel him racing with her, beat for beat.

God, thank God, she thought on a sobbing breath.

When he pushed up to her, arms banding, teeth clamped on her shoulder, it was she who sent them both soaring over the last rise.

She lay replete and dazzled, and grateful. And without a clue what to say or do next. But her body felt loose. Hell, she corrected, it was limp even if her heart was still banging like a drum in a marching band. If she could muster the energy, she'd go back on her word and cry.

Tears of sheer delight.

She'd touched and been touched; she'd given and she'd taken. She'd had an orgasm — at long, long last — so hard and bright it had been like a fat fist of diamonds.

And she knew damn well she wasn't alone on that score.

"I want to say thanks. Is that stupid?"

Brody stirred himself enough to stroke a hand down her back. "Most women send me tasteful yet expensive gifts after. But I can settle for thanks, just this once."

She snorted out a laugh as she pushed herself up to look down at him. His eyes were closed, his face relaxed. The expression of pure male satisfaction on it made her want to leap out of bed and do a victory dance.

Oh yeah, she'd given as good as she got.

"I cooked dinner," she reminded him.

"Right. That counts." He opened his eyes, lazily. "How you doing, Slim?"

"Truth? I'd stopped believing I would ever feel this way again. Just something else lost, and in the big scheme . . . Hell, in the big scheme, it's a damn big loss. So really, thanks for sticking it out, and that came out completely wrong," she said when he choked with laughter. "I'll just shut up now."

"That'll be the day."

She toyed with his hair, and wanted nothing more than to nuzzle in and sleep. "I guess I should get dressed and go home."

"Why?"

"It's getting late."

"You have a curfew?"

"No, but . . . do you want me to stay?"

"I figure if you stay the night, you'll feel

obliged to cook me breakfast in the morning."

A little glow spread just under her heart. "I could probably be persuaded to cook your breakfast."

"I'm very persuasive in the morning." He tugged the spread and sheet down, then rolled her over. "Besides, it's not that late, and I'm not done with you."

"In that case, I guess I'm staying."

Later, when he slept, she lay restless and uneasy. She argued with herself, but in the end she surrendered and eased out of the bed.

She'd just check — once, just once, she told herself, and found his shirt for cover before she tiptoed out of the room. Each creak of the board underfoot had her wincing as she crept down the stairs.

She checked the front door first. See, locked, she told herself. Hadn't she locked it herself? Still, what harm did it do to check? The back door was locked, too. Of course it was. But . . .

She eased her way to the back of the house, checked the locks. For a moment she studied his kitchen chairs. She wanted to prop one under the doorknob, and had to argue with herself against it.

It wasn't as if she was alone in the house. She was with a big, strong man. No one was going to try to break in anyway, but if someone did, Brody could handle it.

She made herself turn away from the door, from the chairs, and leave the room.

"Problem?"

She didn't shriek, but it was a close call. She did stumble back, slam a hip painfully against the doorjamb. Brody came the rest of the way toward her. "Maybe you are clumsy."

"Ha. Maybe. I was just . . ." She trailed off, shrugged.

He'd heard her leave the bedroom and figured she had to pee. But the steps had creaked under her feet. Curiosity had him dragging on his jeans and going down to see what she was up to.

"All locked up?" he said casually.

"Yes. I just wanted to . . . I need to check that kind of thing before I can sleep. It's no big deal."

"Who said it was? Is that my shirt?"

"Well, yeah. I can't go walking around naked."

"Don't see why not. But since you didn't ask if you could borrow it, which is pretty damn rude, I think you'd better get your ass back upstairs and give it back to me."

"You're absolutely right." Everything inside her relaxed again. "I'm so ashamed."

"Ought to be." He took her hand, walked her back up the steps. "How would you like it if I paraded around in your clothes without permission?"

"I don't think I would. Although, it might be strangely fascinating."

"Yeah, like anything you've got would fit me. How do you want the door?"

She just stared at him, and wondered he didn't hear her heart go thud at his feet. "Closed and locked, if that's all right."

"Doesn't matter to me." He closed it, locked it. "Now give me back my damn shirt."

Dreaming woke her, a jumble of images, a quick pain. Her eyes flashed open. She wasn't in the storeroom; she wasn't bleeding. But the shadows and silhouettes of this room were unfamiliar, and had her heart skipping until she remembered.

Brody's bedroom. Brody's bed. And Brody's elbow digging like a pickax into her ribs was oddly comforting.

She was not only safe, she was damn near spectacular.

He was a stomach sleeper, she noted as she turned her head to study him. And a sprawler. During the night he'd worked her over to the edge of the bed, leaving her a stingy triangle of mattress. But that was fine. She'd gotten several solid hours of real sleep in that miserly space.

And before that, she'd gotten good use of every inch of that bed.

She eased out of what bed she had and was vaguely disappointed that he didn't reach for her. Just as well, she told herself as she gathered up her clothes. She had things to do, including fixing breakfast with the limited supplies in Brody's kitchen.

She crept out of the room and into the bath across the hall. When she pushed the lock button on the doorknob, it popped back out. After several tries she stood there, clothes bundled to her breast, staring at the knob.

How could it not lock? There was a lock on the bedroom door, but not the bathroom? That was ridiculous, that was just wrong. It *had* to lock. But no matter how she pushed or twisted, it didn't stick.

"I don't have to lock the door. Nobody broke in and murdered me last night, no one's going to break in this morning. Brody's sleeping right across the hall. Three minutes in the shower, that's all. In and out. It's all fine."

His bath was twice the size of hers, with a standard white tub and shower. Dark blue towels that didn't really go with the mottled green pattern of the countertop. But still, nothing fancy, nothing strange. She stared at the door as she backed up to turn on the taps.

She liked the smooth, sealed log walls, the floor tiles made to look like slate. He should have gone for gray towels, she thought, or tried to match the green in the countertop.

She tried to concentrate on that idea, and the simplicity of the room while she backed into the shower.

She grabbed the soap and raced her way through the multiplication tables. The soap squirted out of her jerking hand when the knock sounded on the door.

Psychos don't knock, she told herself. "Brody?"

"You expecting someone else?" He opened the door, and a moment later, tugged the shower curtain back an inch. He was buck naked. "Why do you care what eight times eight is when you're taking a shower?"

"Because singing in the shower is too ordinary for me." She tried to figure out what to do with her hands without making it obvious she was covering herself. "I'll be out in a minute."

"I think I saw all there was to see of you last night — or does water make you shy?"

"No." She made herself drop one of her arms, then push a hand at her dripping hair. But she kept her free hand lightly fisted at her chest.

Ignoring the wet and steam, Brody

reached in, tugged her hand down. And when she brought it up again, he lifted his brows and tugged it down more firmly.

He gave the scar she'd tried to hide a glance. "Close call."

"You could say that." She tried to angle her body away, but he made that impossible by tightening his grip on her hand and stepping into the tub with her.

"Are you worried about the scar because you think it makes you imperfect?"

"No. Maybe. It's just not —"

"Because you got other flaws, you know. Bony hips for one."

"Oh, really?"

"Yeah, and with your hair wet I can get a good look. I don't think your ears are quite level on your head."

"Of course they are." Instinct and insult had her reaching up to check. He moved right in, wrapping his arms around her.

"But, other than that, you're not half bad. I might as well make use of you."

He backed her up against the shower wall, and did just that.

16

Rather than a merry month, May plagued Angel's Fist with a series of wicked storms that thundered over the mountains and blew wild over the lake. But the days stretched longer with the light pulling farther and farther over the dark. Reece could all but see the snow melting along the lower ridges, while in her little valley the cottonwoods and willows began to haze with green.

Daffodils popped in cheerful yellow even when the wind and rain pelted them. She felt nearly the same. She'd been blown around and she'd been drenched. But she, too, was starting to bloom again.

And on this monumental day, she was going to venture beyond the Fist.

For most women getting a cut and style was a simple part of life. For Reece, it held all the excitement and terror of a parachute jump. And like a novice jumper, she clutched at the door.

"I can easily reschedule," she told Joanie. "If you're pressed today —"

"I didn't say I was pressed." Joanie poured pancake batter on the griddle.

"Yes, but with the weather breaking,

you'll probably be swamped at lunch. I don't mind pitching in."

"I handled this kitchen before you came along."

"Sure, sure, you did. But if you need an extra hand today —"

"I've got two of my own. And isn't Beck standing right here?"

Beck, sturdy as an oak, homely as a pot of overcooked rice, shot a grin over and kept shredding cabbage for coleslaw. "She'll work me to the bone, Reece, with you not around to stop her."

"You don't have that slaw ready by eleven sharp, she won't stop me from booting your ass, either."

"Aw now, Joanie," he said, as he always did.

"You want to be useful?" she said to Reece. "Top off Mac's coffee on your way out the door."

"All right. I'll have my cell phone if you change your mind. I'm not leaving for an hour."

She dragged her feet a little, but she grabbed the pot, moved to the counter where Mac sat waiting for his pancakes.

"You and Joanie having a round?"

"Hmm? Oh no, nothing like that." She poured the coffee. "I just stopped by. Day off."

"That so? Big plans?"

"Yes. Sort of. Linda-gail and I are going into Jackson."

"Shopping spree, huh?"

"Probably some of that." Linda-gail had certainly threatened it. "I'm getting my hair cut."

"Going all the way to Jackson for a haircut?" Fist loyalty had him frowning. "We've got the Curry Comb right here in town."

The Curry Comb was a two-chair establishment that ran to buzz cuts and poodle perms. But Reece smiled a little as she passed him the sugar bowl. "Sounds silly, doesn't it? Linda-gail says we're going to have a splurge. I really don't need to."

"Get out." Joanie delivered the pancakes with the side of elk sausage herself.

"I'm leaving." Reece picked up her purse, and the file folder she'd brought along. "I thought I'd show the sketch Doc made while I'm there. You still haven't come across anyone who recognizes her?"

As was her habit, Reece took one of the copies out, showed it to Mac again.

"Nope. Got it posted right there at the front counter at the store, in case."

"I appreciate that. Well, Jackson's a big place." Reece slipped the sketch back in the folder. "Maybe I'll have better luck there."

"Don't come whining back here if they

scalp you over there," Joanie called out. Then barked with laughter when Reece paled. "Serve you right if they did, not spending your pay here in the Fist. You be here at six sharp tomorrow morning, whatever you look like."

"Could always wear a hat," Mac suggested.

"Thanks. Thanks a lot. I'm leaving."

She sailed out, and made sure she was out of sight of the big front window before she raked a hand through her hair. She'd make Linda-gail go first, hang back, get the lay of the land. She didn't *have* to get her hair cut. It was a choice, an option.

A possibility.

But going into Jackson was a good idea, and gave her the opportunity to pass out copies of the sketch. There hadn't been a single hit on it in the Fist. Excluding Liquor Store Jeff's claim that it looked like Penélope Cruz.

If the woman had been traveling through the area, the odds were better she'd swung into a bigger, flashier place like Jackson Hole than the small, scraped knuckles of Angel's Fist.

Now, since she had a little time to spare and didn't want to spend it obsessing about her hair, she walked down to the sheriff's office.

It had been nearly a week since she'd

asked Sheriff Mardson if he'd learned anything new. Of course, she'd been spending a lot of that week working, or in Brody's bed. But thanks to the distractions, Mardson couldn't accuse her of nagging him.

When she walked in, Hank O'Brian was at Dispatch. He had a full black beard, a fondness for chicken-fried steak and a Shoshone grandmother who was a local legend for her pottery.

At the moment, Hank was drinking coffee with one hand and pecking at his keyboard with the other. He glanced over. "How you doing there, Reece?"

"Good, thanks. How's your grandmother?"

"Got herself a boyfriend. Tribal elder lost his wife a year or so back. Guy's ninety-three and sniffing around, bringing her flowers and candy. I don't know what to make of it."

"That's sweet." But since he looked pained, she added, "And she's got you to look out for her. I wonder if the sheriff's busy? I just wanted to —"

Even as she spoke, she heard the trill of laughter. Mardson walked out hand in hand with his wife.

That was sweet, too, Reece thought. The way people looked together when they *were* together. Mardson had an easy smile on his face, and Debbie was still laughing, swinging their joined hands a little as they walked.

She was a pretty, athletic-looking blonde with short tousled hair and emerald green eyes. She wore snug jeans, chestnut brown cowboy boots and a red shirt under a faded denim jacket. A pendant at the end of a sparkling gold chain hung around her neck. A shining sun, Reece noted. Pretty.

Debbie ran the outfitters On the Trail, next door to the hotel, helped arrange hiking tours with the hotel, sold fishing and hunting licenses. And was tight with Brenda. Sunday afternoons, she brought her two girls into Joanie's for ice cream.

She sent Reece a quick, friendly smile. "Hi! I thought you were heading into Jackson Hole today."

"Um, well, yeah. Later."

"I ran into Linda-gail yesterday. Big plans. Getting your hair cut? It's so pretty — but it gets in the way, I bet when you're at the grill. Still, men like long hair on a woman, don't they? Poor Rick," she said with another laugh. "I'm always having mine chopped off."

"I like it just fine." He leaned down to peck her cheek, flicked a finger at the ends of her hair. "You're my sunlight."

"Listen to him." Smiling, Debbie bumped Rick, arm against arm. "Sweet-talking. And after I came in to try to talk him into taking an hour off and taking a ride with me. Turned me down flat."

"Not all of us can play hooky. This woman gets on a horse, and an hour lasts half the day. Something I can do for you, Reece?" Rick asked her.

"I thought I'd stop by before I left, just to see if you found out anything new." She waited a beat, then pulled out one of the sketches. "On her."

"Wish I could say I had. No reports in this area of a missing person matching her description. And nobody recognizes her. Not much more I can do."

"No. Well, I know you've done what you could. Maybe I'll have some luck in Jackson. I'm going to show the sketch around while I'm there."

"I'm not going to tell you not to," Rick said slowly. "But you need to understand — and nothing against Doc — but that's a pretty rough sketch. Without more details, you're liable to run into a lot of people who'll think maybe they've seen somebody like her. You'll end up chasing a lot of wild geese."

"You're probably right." Reece put the sketch away and didn't miss the look on Debbie's face. If there was one thing Reece recognized, it was quiet pity. "I feel like I have to try at least. I'd better go. Thanks,

Sheriff. It was nice seeing you, Debbie. Bye, Hank."

She felt the heat rising up the back of her neck as she walked out. Because in addition to the pity aimed her way, she knew there was speculation mixed in with it.

Just how crazy was Reece Gilmore?

Screw it. Just screw it, she told herself as she walked back to Joanie's to get her car. She wasn't going to pretend she didn't see what she'd seen, wasn't going to stuff the sketches in some drawer and forget about it.

And she wasn't going to let it drag her down, not today.

Today she was going to town and getting her hair done.

God help her.

The sage flats were waiting to bloom. Reece thought she could almost hear them take that deep, long inhale that would burst into color on the exhale.

A trio of pelicans soared in military formation over the marsh, but it was her first sight of a coyote on its slinking lope over the flats that had her telling Linda-gail to stop the car.

Though Linda-gail called it an oversized rat, she indulged Reece.

"He looks so predatory."

"Sneaky bastards" was Linda-gail's opinion.

"Maybe, but I'd like to hear one howl like in the movies."

"I nearly forgot you're a city girl. Weather warms enough to keep the windows open at night, you can hear them sometimes."

"I'll put that on my list. Thanks for stopping for the city girl."

"No problem." Then they were zooming down the road toward Jackson Hole, with Martina McBride's powerhouse voice aptly claiming this one for the girls.

If Reece considered Angel's Fist a rough and interesting little diamond, Jackson was big and polished and faceted with its fashionable western flair and colorful neon. Shops and restaurants and galleries spread with wooden boardwalks and busy streets. And people were busy on them, heading somewhere, Reece supposed. Maybe a stop in town before visiting one of the great parks now that summer was nearly here.

Some of the people would be in town for supplies, a lunch date, a business meeting.

Thriving, she thought, alive and active it was. But beyond the structures and speed of civilization planted here, white-frosted mountains stood in dazzling splendor. They dwarfed what man had made, and shone brighter than jewels in the blaze of the sun.

It took Reece less than two minutes to understand that though the views were breath-stealing, she'd made a better choice with Angel's Fist.

Too many people here, she decided. Too much going on at once. Hotels, motels, recreation centers, winter sports, summer sports, real estate offices.

She was barely inside the town limits when she wanted out again.

"This is going to be fun!" Linda-gail swung through traffic as if it were a carnival ride. "If you're feeling a little anxious or whatever, just close your eyes."

"And miss seeing the crash?"

"I'm a terrific driver." Linda-gail proved it by threading between an SUV and a motorcycle, waving cheerily at the drivers, then zipping around a corner on a yellow light. "I think I might go red."

"I think I've already gone green. Linda —"

"Nearly there. We should do a serious splurge sometime, book the full enchilada at one of the day spas. They have *amazing* spas here. I want someone to slather me with mud and rub me with herbs and — holy shit, a parking place!"

She zoomed toward it, a heat-seeking missile in a Ford Bronco. Reece's anxiety over the crowd, the traffic, her hair, all vanished, swallowed up by the terror of certain death.

Before she could babble out a prayer, they were parked at the curb. "It's a couple more blocks, but you never know. Besides, you'll see a little of the place if we walk."

"I think I've lost all use of my lower body."

On a giggle, Linda-gail gave Reece a poke. "Come on. Let's go get us some new do's."

Reece's legs might have trembled, but they got her to the sidewalk. "How many tickets do you rack up a year? No, how many vehicles do you wrack up annually?"

On a cluck of her tongue, Linda-gail hooked her arm through Reece's. "Don't be such an old lady. Oh my God, look! Just look at that jacket!" She dragged Reece to a shop window to stare avariciously at a leather jacket in rich melted chocolate brown. "It looks so soft. Probably costs a zillion dollars. Let's go try it on. No, we'll be late. We'll try it on with our new hair."

"I don't have a zillion dollars."

"Neither do I, but it doesn't cost a thing to play with it. Snug cut like that, it'll look better on you than me, which is a pisser. Still, if I had a zillion, it'd be mine."

"I think I need to go lie down."

"You'll be fine. And if you get shaky, I've got a flask in my purse."

"You —" Reece stuttered a bit as Linda-gail pulled her along. "A flask of what?"

"Apple martinis, in case you need something to take the edge off. Or even for the hell of it. Mmmm, giddyup. Check it out."

With her head spinning, Reece turned it in the direction Linda-gail indicated and spotted the tall, lanky cowboy in boots, Levi's and Stetson.

"Slurp" was Linda-gail's opinion.

"I thought you were in love with Lo."

"Have been, am, will be. But it's like the jacket, honey. Don't cost a nickel to look. I take it you've been more than looking with Brody. Is the sex amazing?"

"I may actually need that martini if this keeps up."

"Just tell me one thing. Does his ass look as good naked as it does in jeans?"

"Yes, yes, I can tell you that it does."

"I knew it. Here we are." She got a firmer hold of Reece's arm and pulled her inside.

She didn't reach for the flask, though it was tempting, and in the time they waited for their stylists, Reece nearly balked a half a dozen times.

But she learned something.

It wasn't as bad as it had been the last time she tried. The walls didn't seem so close together, or the sounds so harsh they made her heart palpitate. And when her stylist introduced himself as Serge, she didn't burst into tears and sprint for the door.

He had the slightest Slavic accent, and a winning smile that faded into concern when he took her hand. "Baby doll, your hands are like ice. Let's get you a nice cup of herbal tea. Nan! We need a cup of chamomile. And you just come with me."

She went along like a puppy.

He had her seated at his station, swathed in a mint green cape — and his hands in her hair before her brain engaged again.

"I'm not sure I —"

"Gorgeous texture, and so thick! Very healthy. You take care of it."

"I guess I do."

"But where's the style? The flair? Look at this face, and all this hair like a curtain blocking it. What would you like today?"

"I . . . Honestly, I don't know. I didn't think I'd get this far."

"Tell me about yourself. No rings? Single?"

"Yes. Yes."

"Fancy free. And from back East somewhere."

"Boston."

"Mmm-hmm." He continued to lift her hair, let it fall, study it. "And what is it you do, my angel?"

"I cook. I'm a cook." Something inside her started to purr as his hands massaged her scalp, played with her hair. "I work with Linda-gail. Is she going to be nearby?"

"She's fine. We don't see nearly enough of her in here." And with that winning smile, he met Reece's eyes in the mirror. "Trust me?"

"I . . . Oh God. Okay. But do you have any Valium to put in that tea?"

She'd forgotten this, the indulgence of it. Hands in her hair, soothing tea, glossy magazines, the chatter of primarily female voices.

She was getting highlights, because Serge wanted her to. She probably couldn't afford highlights, but she was getting them. At some point in the process, Linda-gail trotted up, her hair slathered in product and covered with plastic.

"Vixen Red," she announced. "I'm going for it. I'm squeezing in a manicure. Want one?"

"No. No, I can't take any more."

But she actually drowsed over her copy of *Vogue* until it was time for the shampoo. And the cut.

"So now, tell me about the man in your life." Serge began to clip and snip. "You must have one."

"I guess I do." My God, she had a man in her life. "He's a writer. We're just really starting to be together."

"Lust. Excitement. Discovery."

A smile flickered over her face. "Exactly. He's smart, self-reliant and likes my cooking. He . . . well, he masks this incredible patience under pithy comments. He doesn't treat me like I'm breakable, and people were, for too long. And because he doesn't, I don't think of myself that way as much. As breakable. Oh, I forgot this."

Serge lifted the scissors when she leaned forward for the file. "I wonder if you recognize this woman."

He pocketed the scissors long enough to take the sketch and study it. "I can't say for certain, but I don't think she's been in my chair. I'd have talked her into shortening that hair — it draws down her face. Does she belong to you?"

"In a way. Maybe I could show it around, even leave a copy of it here? Someone might recognize her."

"Absolutely. Nan!"

The ever-efficient Nan zipped by, took the sketch. Reece refocused on herself long enough to blink. "Wow. That's, ah, that's a lot of hair falling off my head."

"Not to worry. Look at you! Gorgeous!" He stopped again to turn and admire the newly redheaded Linda-gail.

"I *love* it!" She spun a circle, showing off the bold red in her sassy new cut. "I'm reinvented. What do you think? What do you think?" she demanded of Reece.

"It's wonderful. It's really fabulous." The bold red turned her from pretty little blonde to hot, hip and happening. "Linda-gail, you look seriously amazing."

"I hit up the makeup samplers." She peered around Reece to admire herself in the mirror. "And I do look amazing. When we get back, I'm going to track down Lo and make him suffer." She turned, angled her head. "I love the highlights, subtle but effective. And I think I see where Serge is going here. Your eyes look bigger — as if they needed to — and your face is more out there. Kudos on the bangs, Serge. Sexy."

"Damn right, frame those gorgeous eyes. All that weight's off your shoulders, your neck. Still, nice, long layers. You'll find it easy to style yourself, I think."

Reece stared at the picture emerging in the mirror. *I almost recognize that woman,* she thought. *I almost see me again.*

When her eyes filled, Serge lowered the scissors, glanced at Linda-gail with alarm. "She doesn't like it. You're upset. You don't like it."

"No, no, I do like it. I do. It's been a long time since I looked in the mirror and saw something I did like."

Linda-gail sniffled. "You need makeup samples."

Serge patted Reece's shoulder. "You're going to make me cry in a minute. At least let me blow it out first."

She wanted to show off. She'd had the most fantastic day, and looked the part. Of course she shouldn't have let Linda-gail talk her into buying that shirt, even if it was the most delicious shade of yellow. Still, she'd given the salesclerk a copy of the sketch — as she had done in every store Linda-gail had dragged her into.

And she'd been right, the leather jacket looked better on Reece. Though it wasn't quite a zillion dollars, it might as well have been. It was just as far out of her reach.

A great haircut and a great new shirt were enough reward.

She intended to go straight home, admire herself, put the new shirt on, spruce up. Then she'd call Brody and see if he was interested in coming over for dinner.

She'd found some lovely field greens in a market in Jackson, and some nice diver-harvested scallops. And saffron, which she couldn't really afford either, but it would be nice to make a saffron and basil puree for the scallops. Then the Brie and porcini for wild rice.

While Linda-gail might have drooled over the boutiques, Reece had quivered with pleasure in the markets.

She all but danced up the steps as she carted the bags to her apartment. Humming, she unlocked the door, and was so carefree she told herself she could wait until she'd put the bags on the counter to lock it again.

"Gee, Reece, you're going to be a real girl again before you know it." She waltzed to the door, locked it. Then decided everything else could just wait until she'd taken another look at her happy self.

She did pirouettes toward the bathroom just for the pleasure of feeling her shorter, lighter hair swing.

And all the blood in her face drained, all the muscles in her body went saggy with shock as she stared at the mirror.

The sketch was taped to it so that she stared at the face of a dead woman instead of her own. On the walls, the floor, the little vanity, written over and over again with red marker, bright as blood, was the single question.

IS THIS ME?

Shivering, she sank down in the doorway and curled into a ball.

Had to be home by now, Brody thought as he drove around the lake. How long did it take to have somebody whack at her hair

386

anyway? She didn't answer the phone, and he felt ridiculous as he'd called four times in the last hour.

Goddamn it, he'd missed her. And that was even more ridiculous. He never missed anyone. Besides that, she'd only been gone a few hours. Eight and a half hours. Plenty of days went by without him seeing her for longer than that.

But on those days, he knew she was right across the lake, that he could wander over and see her if he wanted.

He hadn't yet lowered himself to trying her cell phone, like some pussy-whipped idiot who couldn't be away from a woman for a day without dialing her number. Without hearing her voice.

He'd just go to Joanie's for a while, hang out, maybe have a beer. And keep an eye out for her car. Casually.

Nobody had to know about it.

He spotted her car in its habitual place, and figured his luck was in. He'd just go on up, tell her he'd had to run into town for . . . what? For bread.

Did he have bread at home? He couldn't remember. Bread would be his story, and he'd stick to it.

He wanted to see her, to smell her. He wanted his hands on her. But she didn't have to know he'd been pacing around his cabin like a lost puppy for the last hour.

He was playing games, he realized as he parked. Making up excuses to come into town and see her.

And *that* made him feel like that pussy-whipped idiot.

Best way to offset that, in his opinion, was to be annoyed with her. Because it felt better, he had a scowl on his face as he went up her steps and banged with some impatience on her door.

"It's Brody," he called out. "Open up."

It took her so long to answer, the scowl had turned into knitted brow concern.

"Brody, sorry, I was lying down. I have a headache."

He tried the knob, found it still locked. "Open the door."

"Really, it's moving into migraine territory. I'm just going to sleep it off. I'll call you tomorrow."

He didn't like the sound of her voice. "Open the door, Reece."

"Fine, fine, fine." The lock turned, and she yanked open the door. "Do you have trouble understanding the language we speak here? I have a headache; I don't want company. I certainly don't feel like heating up the sheets."

He let it roll off him because she was pale as wax. "You're not one of those women who get weirded out if they get a bad haircut?"

"Of course I am. I, however, have a great haircut. An outstanding haircut. To get it involved a very long day and some considerable stress. Now I'm tired, and I want you to go away so I can lie down."

His gaze tracked over, passed over the bags sitting on the counter. "How long have you been back?"

"I don't know. Jesus. Maybe an hour."

Headache, his ass. He knew her well enough by now to be sure she could have severed a limb and she'd still have put her groceries away the minute she walked in the door.

"What happened?"

"God, would you back *off?* I fucked you, okay, and it was great. The angels cried buckets. We'll do it again real soon. But that doesn't mean I'm not entitled to some goddamn privacy."

"All true," he said in mild tones to contrast to her furious ones. "And I'll give you plenty of privacy as soon as you tell me what the hell's going on. What the hell did you do to your hands?"

He grabbed one, terrified for a moment it was blood smearing her fingers and palms. "What the hell? Is this ink?"

She started to weep, silently. He'd never seen anything more wrenching than the tears simply raining down her cheeks while she made no sound at all.

"For Christ's sake, Reece, what is it?"

"I can't get it off. I can't get it off, and I don't remember doing it. I don't remember, and it won't come off."

She covered her face with her smeared hands. She didn't resist when he picked her up and carried her to the bed to rock her in his arms.

17

Portions of the walls and the floor were smeared where she'd gone at them, Brody could see, with the wet towel now heaped in the tub. He imagined the towel was toast, which would upset her when she was calm enough to think about it.

She'd torn the sketch off the mirror, leaving ragged triangles of paper and tape behind, and had balled it up, tossed it in the wastebasket beside the sink.

He could visualize how it must have been for her, frantically grabbing the towel off the rod, dumping it into the sink to soak. Scrubbing, scrubbing, scrubbing while the water dripped and sloshed and her breath came out in gasps and sobs.

And still the message was clear a dozen times over.

IS THIS ME?

"I don't remember doing it."

He didn't turn to where she stood behind him, but continued to study the walls. "Where's the red marker?"

"I . . . I don't know. I must have put it back." Fogged from the headache and tears, she crossed back into the kitchen, opened a drawer.

"It's not here." On another spurt of desperation, she pawed through the drawer, then yanked open another, another.

"Stop it."

"It's not here. I must have taken it with me, thrown it away. I don't remember. Just like the other times."

His eyes sharpened, but his voice stayed exactly the same. Calm and very firm. "What other times?"

"I think I'm going to be sick."

"No, you're not."

She slammed the drawer, and her eyes, red-rimmed from weeping, burned fury. "Don't tell me what I am, what I'm not."

"You're not going to be sick," he repeated as he walked over and took her by the arm, "because you haven't told me about the other times. Let's sit down."

"I can't."

"Fine, we'll stand up. Got any brandy?"

"I don't want any brandy."

"I didn't ask you what you wanted." He began opening cupboards himself until he found a small bottle.

Under other circumstances, he'd have offended her sense of aesthetics by pouring brandy into a juice glass.

"Knock it back, Slim."

She might have been angry, might have

been in the grip of despair, but Reece knew when it was pointless to argue. She took the glass, swallowed the two fingers of brandy in one gulp. And shuddered.

"The sketch. It could be me."

"How do you figure?"

"If I imagined it . . . I've been through violence."

"Ever been strangled?"

"So it took another form." She set the glass down with a snap. "Someone tried to kill me once, and I've spent the last two years waiting for someone to try again. There's a resemblance between me and the sketch."

"In that you're both female and you both have long, dark hair. Or you did." Frowning a little, he reached out to touch the tips of her hair that fell several inches above her shoulders now. "It's not your face."

"But I didn't see her very well."

"But you did see her."

"I don't *know*."

"I do." Since he knew she wouldn't have coffee, he opened her refrigerator and was pleasantly surprised to see she'd stocked his brand of beer. He took one out, popped the top. "You saw those two people by the river."

"How can you be sure? You didn't see them."

"I saw you," he said simply. "But let's get back to that. What other things don't you remember?"

"I don't remember marking up my trail map, or unlocking my door and dragging it open in the middle of the night, putting the damn mixing bowls in the closet and my hiking boots and pack in the kitchen cupboard. Or packing my clothes in my duffel. And there are other things, little things. I need to go back."

"Back where?"

She scrubbed her hands over her face, left them there. "I'm not getting better. I need to go back in the hospital."

"Bullshit. What's this about packing your clothes?"

"I came home one night — the night I went out to Clancy's with Linda-gail, and all my things were packed up. Everything packed in my duffel. I must've done it that morning, or on one of my breaks. I don't remember. And once the flashlight I keep by the bed was in the refrigerator."

"I found my wallet there once. Weird."

She let out a sigh. "It's not the same. I don't put things in the wrong place. Ever. At least . . . not when I'm aware, not when I'm healthy. It's certainly not normal for me to take bowls out of the kitchen and move them to the shelf in the clothes closet. I don't misplace things because I can't function if I don't know exactly where everything is. And, the point is, I'm not functioning."

"More bullshit." Idly, he poked in the grocery bag. "What're all these leaves and grasses?"

"They're field greens." She rubbed at the headache drilling into her temple. "I need to go. It's what I was telling myself when I packed. I must have been telling myself that all along, back on the trail, pretending everything was on its way back to normal."

"You saw a woman murdered while you were on the trail. Not so normal. I had doubts about that at the time, but now —"

"You did?"

"Not that you saw her — them. But that she was dead. It was possible she got up, walked out of there. Marginally possible. But she's dead as Elvis."

"Are you listening to me? Did you see what I did in there?" She flung a hand toward the bathroom.

"What if you didn't?"

"Who the hell else?" she exploded. "I'm unstable, Brody, for Christ's sake. I'm hallucinating murders and writing on walls."

"What if you're not?" he repeated in the same implacable tone. "Listen, I make a pretty decent living on what-ifs. What if you saw exactly what you said you saw?"

"And what if I did? It doesn't change the rest of it."

"Changes everything. Ever see *Gaslight*?"

She stared at him. "Maybe that's why I'm attracted to you. You're as crazy as I am. What the hell does *Gaslight* have to do with me regressing to fugue states and writing all over my bathroom?"

"What if you're not the one who wrote all over the bathroom?"

Her head hurt; her stomach was raw from churning. Since she was too tired to walk to a chair, she just sat on the floor and leaned back against the refrigerator. "If you think someone is doing a Charles Boyer on me, you *are* as crazy as I am."

"Which scares you more, Reece?" He crouched down so their faces were level. "Believing you're having another breakdown, or that someone wants you to believe it?"

Everything inside her trembled. "I don't know."

"Since it's a toss-up, play along with me. What if you saw a woman murdered, an act no one else witnessed. You reported it, and word got around. What if the killer got that word — or, as we considered before, he saw you. He didn't get away clean, after all. Covered his tracks, sure, but he didn't get away clean."

"Because there was a witness," she whispered.

"Yeah. But the only witness has a history of psychological problems with their roots in violence. He can use that. Not everyone believes her anyway — new in town, a little shaky on her pins. But since she's persistent, why not give her a little push on those shaky pins."

"Well, God. Why not just shoot me in the head and get it over with?"

"Another murder, people are going to start taking you seriously."

"Posthumously."

"Sure." Still got some of that steel in there, he thought. Maybe it had a couple of dents in it, but it would hold. "But give her some of those subtle little nudges and chances are she does one of two things. She breaks down, runs naked in the street singing show tunes, or she runs and has her breakdown somewhere else. Either way, her claims as a murder witness are likely to be dismissed."

"But that's . . ."

"Crazy? No, it's not. It's very smart, and very coolheaded."

"So, instead of believing I'm a complete emotional and mental disaster area, you want me to believe a killer is stalking me, breaking into my apartment and trying to gaslight me."

He took another pull of beer again. "It's a theory."

Sometime in the last minute, as what he was saying sank in, her throat had gone desert dry. "The first option is easier. Been there, after all, done that."

"I bet it is. But you don't take the easy way."

"That's a strange thing to say to someone who's been running away from everything, including herself, for the better part of a year."

"If that's how you see it, maybe you are a little whacked."

He rose and, almost as an afterthought, held out a hand to help her to her feet. After a moment's hesitation, she took it. And she faced him.

"How do you see it?"

"I'm looking at a woman who survived. Her friends, who were next thing to family, all killed — one of them right in front of her, while she's shot and left for dead. Trapped in the dark, bleeding. Everything she knew and cherished was taken, for no rhyme, no reason, so she was left with a shattered sense of security and an endangered sense of what some would call sanity. She's standing here two years later because she's been fighting her way back, step by step, at her own time, her own pace.

"I think she's one of the strongest people I've ever met."

Her breath hitched in and out. "I guess you don't get out much."

"There you are." He smiled a little, tapped his finger on her forehead. "Right in there. Get some things together; you better stay at my place tonight."

"I can't take this in."

"You will." He poked into the grocery bag. "Would this be dinner?"

"Oh *shit!* The scallops!"

He knew she was all the way back when she leaped toward the bag and dug down. "Thank God I had them bagged with an ice pack. They're still cold. Something to be said for keeping the thermostat low."

"I like scallops."

"You haven't seen food you don't like." Then she braced her hands on the counter and just closed her eyes. "You won't let me fall apart. You just won't let me."

"I told you once before, hysterical women annoy me."

"You told me once before you were hot for neurotics."

"Yeah, I did. Not only is there a difference between hysteria and neurosis, I've decided you're not neurotic enough for me. So I'm just going to use you until something better comes along."

She rubbed her gritty eyes. "That's fair."

"When it does? You can still cook for me."

"Thanks." She dropped her hands and looked at him. "You held me while I cried. Annoying for you."

"You weren't hysterical. You were hurting. Just don't make a habit of it."

"I love you. I'm in love with you."

She heard absolutely nothing for ten full seconds. And when he did speak, she caught the faintest trace of fear mixed in with the annoyance.

"Hell. No good deed goes unpunished."

She laughed, rich and full and long. And the warmth of it soothed her raw throat, her raw nerves. "And that's why. I must be out of my mind. Don't worry about it, Brody."

She turned now, noted he was staring at her with the cautious respect a man shows a ticking bomb. "Underneath all the neuroses, I'm a sensible, contemporary woman. You're not responsible for my feelings or under obligation to reciprocate. But when you've gone through what I've been through, you learn not to take things for granted. Time, people, feelings. My therapist is the one who started me keeping a journal," she continued as she packed what she'd need. "To get my feelings, my emotions — ones I just couldn't articulate — out on paper. It's helped me do just that, and made it easier to articulate them. Like now, for instance."

"You're mixing up trust, and a misplaced sense of gratitude, and the fact we've got heat."

"My head may be screwed up, but my heart's fine. But if it scares you, I can call Linda-gail and stay with her until I figure out what to do next."

"Just get what you need," he said abruptly. "Including whatever it takes to cook this stuff."

She wasn't in love with him. But having her *think* she was worried him. Here he was, trying to help her out — which was probably his first mistake — and now she was complicating everything. Just like a woman, he thought, wrapping ribbons around everything.

They were choking him.

At least she wasn't talking about it now. Or making herself sick over what had happened in her apartment.

As he'd known it would, the act of preparing a meal settled her down. Writing could do that for him, so he understood how it worked. You got sucked into the work, and sucked out of what was bothering you.

But she was going to have to go back onto the boggy ground of what was happening. If his theory held any weight, she was in trouble.

"You want some wine?" he asked her.

"No. No, thanks. I'll stick with water." She arranged the dressed field greens, tossed with raw carrot curls, on small plates. "The rest will take a few more minutes, so we can start with this."

He figured he'd eaten more salad in a couple of weeks with her than he normally did in six months on his own.

"Joanie's going to have a fit when she sees that bathroom."

"So paint it."

Reece stabbed at her salad. "I can't paint the tiles, the floor."

"Mac's probably got some solvent or something that'll deal with it. The place isn't a frigging penthouse, Slim. Needed work anyway."

"There's a silver lining. Brody, I had lost time before. And memory lapses. Not in more than a year — or, ha ha, not that I can remember — but I experienced both."

"Doesn't mean you are now, does it? I've been around you a lot the last couple weeks. I haven't seen you go into a fugue state or sleepwalk, or redecorate the cabin walls with messages from your subconscious. I haven't seen you do anything stranger than reorganize my kitchen drawers."

"Organize," she corrected. "In order to be reorganized, they'd have had to have something at least resembling organization in the first place."

"I could find stuff. Sooner or later." Since it was there, and hell, it was pretty damn good, he ate more salad. "Has anyone at Joanie's mentioned you did anything weird?"

"Joanie thought it was weird I insisted I needed okra to make minestrone."

"Okra is the weird boy of vegetables, after all. When you had this sort of thing happen before, in Boston, were you always alone?"

She rose to put the finishing touches on the rest of the meal. "No. I always felt worse about it because it might happen anywhere, anytime. After I got out of the hospital — the first time — I stayed at my grandmother's. She took me shopping. Later, I found this hideous brown sweater in my drawer, and I asked her where it came from. I could see something was wrong by the way she looked at me, and when I pressed, she told me I'd bought it. That we'd had a conversation about it because she knew it wasn't my style. I told her, and the salesclerk, I had to have it because it was bulletproof."

She flipped the scallops with a deft flick of the wrist. "Another time, she came into my room in the middle of the night because she heard all this racket. I was nailing my windows shut. I don't remember getting the hammer or the nails. I came out of it with her holding me and crying."

"Both incidents sound like defensive measures to me. You were scared."

"Scared doesn't cover it. And there were other incidents. I had night terrors where I could hear the crashing, and the gunshots, the screaming. I'd try to break down doors. I climbed out of the window — the same one I tried to nail shut — one night during one of them. A neighbor found me standing out on the sidewalk in a nightshirt. I didn't know where I was, how I got there."

She laid a plate in front of Brody. "That's when I checked myself into the hospital. This could be a relapse."

"Which handily happens only when you're alone? I'm not buying. You work at Joanie's a good eight hours, five to six days a week. You spend time with me, with Linda-gail, around town. But you haven't had — what would you call it? — an episode except in your own apartment when no one's around. *Gaslight*."

"Are you Joseph Cotten?"

"I like a woman who knows her classic movies." He touched her hand, just a brush of fingers. "There's another in here. *Rear Window*."

"Jimmy Stewart sees a murder across the courtyard in another apartment while he's laid up with a broken leg." Thoughtfully now, she sat down with her own plate. "No one else sees, no one believes him. Not even Grace Kelly. Not his pal the cop, shoot, shoot, give me a minute —"

"Wendell Corey."

"Damn it. Or the always delightful Thelma Ritter. Nobody believes that Raymond Burr's killed his wife."

"There's no evidence to support our hero's claim. No body, no sign of struggle, no blood. And Jimmy's been acting a little strange."

"So, in your world, I'm caught up in a mix of *Gaslight* and *Rear Window*."

"Watch out for guys who look like Perry Mason and/or have a French accent."

"You're making me feel better. A couple hours ago . . ." She had to stop, press her fingers to her eyes. "I was curled up on the floor whimpering. I was all but sucking my thumb. I was back at the bottom."

"No, just slipped a few rungs. And you got up again. That's courage."

She dropped her hands. "I don't know what to do."

"Right now you should eat your scallops. They're pretty fucking terrific."

"Okay." She took a deliberate bite, and of course he was right. They were pretty fucking terrific. "I've gained three pounds."

"Three whole pounds. Where'd I put that confetti?"

"It's because I'm doing more cooking. Not just at Joanie's, but here. Like this."

"Whatever I can do."

"I'm having sex on a regular basis."

"I repeat, whatever I can do."

"I had my hair cut and styled."

"So noted."

She cocked her head. If she had to pull teeth, she'd get out the pliers. "Well, do you like it or not?"

"It's okay."

"Oh, please stop." She waved a hand. "Must you be so effusive with your compliments?"

"I'm an effusive kind of guy."

She flipped her fingers through it. "I like it. If you don't, you should just say so."

"If I didn't like it, I'd say I didn't. Or I'd say it was your business if you want to have crappy-looking hair all over your head."

"That's exactly what you'd say," she replied. "Being with you has been really good for me. I like being with you, talking to you. I like cooking for you and sleeping with you. I've felt more like . . . I won't say *who I was*, because you can never go back."

"Maybe you're not supposed to."

"No, you're not. I've felt more like who I hoped I could be since I've been with you. But we both know it would be smarter, saner, all around, for you and I to take a step back from each other."

He frowned across the table, cutting into a scallop. "Look, if this is about you thinking you're in love with me, and that's getting everything sticky —"

"It's not." She took another, very deliberate bite of scallop. "You should consider yourself lucky I'm in love with you, even if my mental health is questionable. A lot of women may find you sexually attractive, but they'd be put off by your cranky nature."

"Three-year-olds are cranky."

"Exactly. It's not about my feelings for you, it's about the situation. If I'm backsliding, I'm not a good bet for even the most casual of relationships. If you're right and it's, well, outside forces, I'm a lousier bet."

He picked up his beer, took a contemplative sip. "If you're just a wack job and I back off, it says I can't handle the rough spots. If someone's trying to make you out to be a wack job, same goes. And I miss out on figuring it all out. Plus, I'm not giving up the food and sex."

"Fair enough. But if you change your mind later on, I won't hold it against you."

She reached for the water pitcher she'd brought over, the one she used for spring water and thin slices of lemon.

He took her hand across the table, waited until her gaze shifted to his. "It's not just about food and sex. I have . . ." What, feelings? he asked himself. Feelings could mean any damn thing. "I care about what happens to you."

"I know you do."

"Good. Then we don't have to analyze and dissect it all for the next hour and a half." Her hand felt soft in his, and delicate. He laid it down, but kept his over it on the table. "We'll figure it out, Reece."

And right at that moment, with his hand warm on hers, she believed him.

When they'd eaten and put the kitchen to rights, when she was sitting with the tea she liked, he tried the next step.

"Will you be okay here alone for an hour?"

"Why?"

"I thought I'd go get Rick, and we'd take a look at your place."

"Don't." She shook her head, stared into the flames of the fire he'd built in the living room. "He doesn't believe me about what I saw on the trail. He's done what his job says he has to do, and by all accounts he's done it well. But he doesn't believe me. I went by his office this morning. I saw him, and Debbie and Hank. And when I brought out the sketch, talked about showing it around Jackson Hole, all I saw on their faces was pity."

"If someone's been breaking into your place —"

"If they have, we'd never prove it. And how would they? I had a dead bolt installed."

"Locks get picked. Or keys get copied. Where do you keep your keys?"

"In the inside pocket of my purse."

"When you're working?"

"In the inside pocket of my purse, or if I don't carry one, in my jacket pocket. Right jacket pocket because I'm right-handed, if you want specifics."

"Where are the purse, the jacket when you're working?"

"In Joanie's office. She's got a copy of the keys in her key cupboard thing on the wall in there. I don't think we're going to leap to the conclusion that I mistook Joanie for a man, she killed her lesbian lover, and is sneaking into my apartment to torment me."

"Wouldn't be hard for anyone to slip into the office, make an impression of the key, have one made."

The cup shook in her hand before she set it down. "You think it's someone from the Fist?"

"Possible. Possible it's someone who was staying in the area when this happened. And who stayed on when it got out — which it did fast — that you saw something."

"But no one's recognized the woman."

"I didn't say she was from here, or around here."

Reece sat back. "No. No, you didn't. I guess I just assumed that if she wasn't, he wasn't."

"Maybe, maybe not. Could be someone from the Fist, or who comes in with some regularity. Or someone who was camping, hunting, paddling in the area. Someone who knows how to cover his tracks, which rules out city slicker for me. Who knew you were going to be gone most of the day today?"

"Who didn't?"

"Yeah, that's how it goes. Should make a time line," he considered. "You said you keep a journal."

"That's right."

"I'll have a look through it."

"Not in this lifetime, or any other."

He started to scowl, then grinned instead. "Am I in there?"

"Of course not. Whoever heard of a woman writing about a man she's attracted to and/or their sexual exploits in her journal? That's preposterous."

"Maybe I could just read about the sexual exploits, to make sure you got all the details."

"I got them. I'll look through it, write down dates and times, if I noted them, that things happened."

"Good, but not tonight. You look wiped. Go to bed."

"I could just stretch out here for a few minutes."

"Then I'd have to cart you up when you conked out. I'm going to head up to my office, do a little work."

"Oh." Her gaze slid over to the front door. "All right, maybe . . ."

"After I check the locks. Go on up to bed, Slim."

It was silly to pretend she wasn't exhausted, so she got to her feet. "I have the breakfast shift tomorrow. I'll try not to wake you when I get up."

"Appreciate it."

"Thanks for the shoulder, Brody."

"You didn't use my shoulder."

She leaned down, laid her lips on his. "Yes, I did. A couple dozen times just tonight."

She knew he'd check the locks because he'd said he would. And even while she readied for bed, she heard his feet on the stairs. When she peeked out, the light was

411

on in his office, and she heard the light *click-clack* of his keyboard.

Knowing he was there made it possible for her to get into bed with the bedroom door open and unlocked.

Knowing he was there made it possible for her to close her eyes and sleep.

18

Brody crouched in front of Reece's apartment door with a penlight and a magnifying glass.

He felt a little ridiculous.

Though he considered being able to sleep in mornings one of the big perks of writing fiction, he'd gotten up when she had. And had ignored her claims that she could easily walk from the cabin to the diner.

Sure, he thought now, no problem at all for a woman who may or may not have a homicidal stalker focused on her strolling along by herself in the dark for a couple of miles like some idiot character in a bad slasher movie.

Besides, he'd not only gotten the first two cups of a fresh pot of coffee when he delivered her to Joanie's, he scored bacon, eggs and home fries before the place had even opened for business.

Not a bad trade-off.

Now he was squatted down, playing detective. Since he didn't have any personal experience with breaking and entering, he couldn't be absolutely certain the lock hadn't been picked or tampered with, but he couldn't see any signs of it.

He considered, again, overriding her and bringing in the sheriff. Still, he didn't think Rick could do any more than he was doing himself at this point.

Then there was the matter of trust, he thought as he sat back on his heels. She trusted him, and if he went around her on this, he'd be breaking that trust.

Claims she's in love with him — but no pressure. Women. She was just mixing up heat and . . . companionability with the *L* word. Then she was vulnerable on top of it with what she'd been through. Was still going through.

He straightened, took out the key she'd given him. Then stared at it in the palm of his hand.

Trust. What were you supposed to do?

He unlocked the door, stepped inside.

There was a scent to the air — light and subtle. Reece. He'd have recognized it anywhere now. And he found himself unreasonably angry that whoever had come into her home had walked through that same personal scent.

Light spilled through the windows now to fall on the bare floors, the saggy, second- or thirdhand furniture, the bright blue spread she'd bought for the narrow daybed.

He could only think she deserved better. He could probably help her out, slip her a few extra bucks so she could buy a rug, for God's sake, some paint.

"Sliding down a slippery rope there, Brody," he reminded himself. "Buy a woman a stupid rug, the next thing she wants is a ring."

Besides, she had the view that no amount of money could buy. Who needed rugs or a couple of decent pictures on the wall when you had the mountains painted on the sky outside your window, and the lake all but pooled at your door?

He unhooked her laptop, put it and her thumb drive into its case to take back with him. She'd need another night, at least, away from this place. She might as well have her stuff.

Idly, he opened the drawer on the little desk Joanie must have had hauled up for Reece. In it he found two sharpened pencils snapped in half, a black Magic Marker and a slim leather-bound book he recognized as the sort some people use to carry around pictures of their kids or pets. Curious, he flipped it open.

The photo of a sharp-looking older woman sitting on a bench in what looked like a nicely tended garden had thick black X's over the face. There were others. The same woman in a white shirt, black pants, holding a poodle the size of a postage stamp. A couple in long bib aprons, a group holding glasses of champagne. A man with his arms spread wide in front of a big wall oven.

Everyone had X's over their faces.

In the last, Reece was standing in a large group of people. The restaurant, Brody concluded. Maneo's. Hers was the only face in the group shot that was unmarked, and it was beaming with smiles.

Under each person, in small, neat print, was the single word: DEAD. And under Reece was written: INSANE.

Had she found this yet? he wondered. He hoped not, and slipped the book into the outside pocket of the laptop case. He'd take it out later, decide how to handle it, when he got home.

Though he hadn't intended to invade her privacy quite so deeply, Brody began to search the drawers of the squat ugly dresser.

He buried the discomfort of pawing through her underwear, reminding himself he'd already taken it off her a few times. If he could touch it when she was wearing it, it wasn't weird to touch it when it was folded in a drawer.

Okay, he admitted, it was weird.

But it didn't take long to go through the dresser; she didn't have much. The woman traveled light, he decided.

The kitchen drawers were another

matter. This was where she put the weight. It was all ruthlessly organized. No jumble. Obviously the woman didn't know the meaning of *junk drawer*. He found measuring cups, spoons, whisks — why would anyone need more than one? — and sundry kitchen tools and gadgets.

There were several whose purpose eluded him, but they, like her pots and pans in the cupboard below, were tidily stored.

He found a nested stack of bowls, casserole dishes in a couple of sizes.

Again, would anyone need more than one?

In the next cupboard he found what he recognized as a mortar and pestle, with the bowl filled to the brim with pills.

He pulled it out, set it aside.

Brody went into the bathroom. In the medicine cabinet all the bottles he'd seen before were there, lined up on the shelf. And empty.

Little booby traps, Brody thought, with another simmering surge of anger. Clever bastard.

Because they wanted to ball into fists, he shoved his hands in his pockets and studied the walls.

Neat block printing again, he noted, nothing scrawled. But with some of the words overlapping there was a sense of frantic. Certainly of madness. The detail of having some of the words travel up from the floor onto the wall, or back down again, was a good one.

Whoever did it was very deliberate, very careful, very smart.

Brody got the digital camera he'd brought along. He took pictures from every angle he could manage in the tiny room, took close-ups of the entire question, then of individual words, then of separate letters.

When he'd documented the room every way he could think of, he leaned against the jamb.

No way she could come back in here with this. He'd just go down to Mac's, see if there was something he could use to get the marker off the floor, the tub and tiles. No big deal.

He could pick up some paint while he was there. Room that size wasn't going to take more than a quart, probably. A couple of hours, tops, and that would be that.

It wasn't like he was buying her a rug or anything.

Mac asked questions, of course. Brody figured you could probably buy toilet paper in the Fist without eliciting questions, but that was about it. Anything else was going to come with a: So what're you up to?

He didn't say anything about painting at Reece's. People were bound to get the wrong idea if they found out a guy was doing household chores for a woman he was sleeping with.

In short order he — a man who considered anything domestic above brewing coffee a form of hell on earth — was back in the bathroom, on his hands and knees, scrubbing.

Reece turned the door handle gingerly. She hated that it wasn't locked. She hated the throat-closing fear that Brody was lying inside hurt, or worse.

Why was he still here? She'd expected him to drop back in downstairs with her key long before her break. But he hadn't, and his car was still outside.

And the apartment door wasn't locked.

She eased it open. "Brody?"

"Yeah. Back here."

"You're okay? I saw your car and didn't . . ." She stopped a couple of paces into the room, sniffed. "What is that? Paint?"

He stepped out of the bath with a roller in his hand, paint specks on his hands and in his hair. "It ain't the perfumes of Araby."

"You're painting the bathroom?"

"It's no big deal. You've probably got two feet of wall space all told."

"A bit more than that." Her voice was

full of emotion. "Thank you." She walked over to take a look.

He'd already done the ceiling, and all the cutting in around the tiles, had primed the walls. The color was a pale, pale blue, as if a cloud had dipped, very briefly, into the lake and absorbed a hint of its color.

None of the red letters or smears remained anywhere.

Reece just leaned against him. "I like the color."

"Not a lot to choose from if you want a quick cash-and-carry at the mercantile. Though they had a nice Pepto-Bismol pink that caught my eye."

Now she smiled, and kept leaning. "I appreciate your restraint and your illustration of good taste. I'll have to pay you back in food."

"Works for me. But if you want the rest of this place painted, you're on your own. I forgot I hate to paint."

Now she turned to him, nuzzled. "I can finish it up after my shift."

"I started, I finish." He caught himself pressing his lips to the top of her head. But it was too late to stop the gesture. Too late, he realized, for a lot of things when she tipped her head back, used those eyes on him.

"I'd rather have this done than diamonds. Just so you know."

"Good thing. I'm fresh out of diamonds." When she laid her head on his chest, sighed, he was sunk. "I didn't want you to have to see it again."

"I know. But I wonder if I could bunk at your place tonight anyway?" She nuzzled a little more. "You know how the smell of paint takes a while to fade."

"Yeah, we wouldn't want you breathing in the fumes."

She tipped her head back again, and this time lifted her mouth to his. Long and slow, and impossibly warm, almost unbearably sweet. His free hand slid up her back, curled to take a fistful of her shirt.

With a laugh she stepped back. Glowing, he thought. All the stress, the strain he'd seen in her the night before, gone.

"I'll just need a few things from here to . . . What, were you going to grind up something?"

He was still riding on the kiss, on the look on her face and only managed, "Huh?"

"You got out my mortar and pestle."

And he cursed himself for leaving it out. "Reece —"

"What've you got in here? It looks like . . ." That glow that had beamed straight out of her eyes and into him faded.

"I don't take them." Now, when she

faced him, those eyes were desolate. "I just keep them, in case, and to remind me of what I'm working to get away from. I don't want you to think I —"

"I didn't put them there."

"Then . . . Oh."

"They're booby traps, Reece." He set the roller in the tray, moved to her. "He's setting traps for you, and you can't step into them."

"What do you think he's saying with this?" She dipped her fingers into the bowl, let pills sift through them. " 'Why don't you grind these up into a nice paste, spread it on toast points and send yourself into oblivion'?"

"It doesn't matter what he's saying if you don't listen."

"It does matter." She whirled around, and instead of desolation, those gypsy eyes flashed with temper. "I can't answer if I don't listen. I can't let him know he's not going to send me back, not to the pills, not to the doctors. I'm not going back into the dark because he's a killer and a coward and a son of a bitch."

She grabbed the bowl, and even as Brody braced for her to hurl it, she upended it in the sink, then wrenched the water on. "I don't need them, I don't want them. And fuck him."

"Should've known you weren't the type

422

to throw crockery." He laid his hands on her shoulders and, with her, watched the pills melt. "He doesn't know what he's up against with you."

"I'll probably panic later when I don't have them. My security blanket."

"I imagine Doc would write you a prescription if you need the blanket."

"Yeah, I imagine he would." She blew out a breath. Down the drain, she thought. She'd sent them down the drain to prove something. "I'll just hold that in reserve, and see how I do without the blanket."

He thought of the photo book he'd tucked away, thinking to protect her. It wasn't protection she needed, he realized. It was faith. She needed someone to believe she was steady.

"There's something else. It's going to hit you a little harder than this."

"What?"

Even as she glanced around, looking for the trap, he crossed to the laptop, took out the slim little book. "He did it to upset you. Don't let him win."

She opened the book. Her hands didn't tremble this time, but her heart did. "How could he do this to them? All they went through, all they lost, and he crosses them out like they were nothing."

"They're not, to him."

"I would never have done this," she said.

"No matter how far I fell, I'd never have done this. He made a mistake doing this, because I know this wasn't me." She ran a finger over the blacked-out faces of those who'd died. "I loved them, and I'd never have tried to erase them."

She went through every page, as Brody had done, then closed the book. "Bastard. Fucking bastard. No, he won't win." She went back to the desk, laid the book down. "He won't."

He went to her, and because he did, she could turn. She could lean into him. "I can replace most of the pictures — my grandmother has copies of some of them. But the group shot was the only one I had of all of us."

"The families might have copies."

"Of course. They would." She eased back, pushed at her hair. "I can get in touch, ask for a copy. I can do that. I've got to get back down, finish my shift."

"I'll come in when I'm done." He stroked her hair. "Maybe we'll do something later. Take a drive. Or I can borrow a boat. Something."

"Something sounds good. I'm all right. I'll be fine."

Pete was back at work, and sent her a wink when she walked into the kitchen. "That teriyaki chicken san of yours is the

424

hit of the early lunch crowd. Lots going out, and not much of it coming back on the plates."

"Good."

"Went some over on your break," Joanie said from the grill.

"Sorry. I'll stay some over after my shift."

"Brody painting upstairs?"

Reece paused in the act of washing her hands. "How do you know these things?"

"Carl came in for a cup of coffee, told Linda-gail Brody was down to the mercantile and bought paint and supplies. Brody's car's still out front here. Two and two."

"Yes, he's doing me a favor."

"Better not be some crazy color."

"It's a very pale blue. It's just the bathroom. It . . . needed it."

"Likely it did." Joanie piled steak on a long bun, flipped on eggs and began to build a hoagie. "Nice having a man take on some of the chores."

"It is." After drying her hands, Reece snagged the next ticket in line.

"Don't recall Brody ever doing the same for any other woman around here. You recall him doing the same, Pete?"

"Can't say that I do."

Pete was right about the teriyaki. She had orders for two, one with onion rings, one with the black bean soup. Reece got to work.

"You both know I'm sleeping with him," she said mildly. "Men often do a few chores for women who sleep with them."

"You wouldn't be the first one he's slept with around here," Joanie put in. "But he didn't paint anyone's bathroom for the privilege."

"Maybe I'm just better in bed."

Joanie let out a hoot of laughter, dumped an order of fries on the plate with the hoagie and added a scoop of slaw. "Order up! Denny, how you doing?"

"Doing fine, Joanie." Instead of sitting, the deputy stood at the counter. "Sheriff sent me down. Wanted to see if Reece could come in for a few minutes, you could spare her."

"Hell, Denny, she's just back from break and the lunch rush is starting."

"Well." Denny pushed a hand under his uniform hat to scratch his head. "It's just . . . Can I come back there a minute?"

Looking aggrieved, Joanie waved him back.

"What's going on?" Linda-gail whispered, working her way down the counter.

"Nothing that concerns you like taking that order to a paying customer does." Joanie turned back into the kitchen. "Now why does Rick want to short me my cook at goddamn noon when I'm up to my ass here?"

"The sheriff wants me?" Reece looked over from sizzling chicken.

"He'd like it if you could come down for a couple minutes. Thing is . . . I didn't want to say much about it out there, where people are eating and all that," Denny said to Joanie. "Thing is, they found a woman's body in the marshes in Moose Ponds." His eyes looked sorrowfully into Reece's now. "Sheriff's got, um, a couple of pictures he thought you should look at. See if she's the one you said . . . I mean the one you saw up over the river."

"You go on," Joanie said briskly.

"Yes." Her voice was dull. "Yes, I should go up and . . . I'll just finish this order."

"I can finish the damn order. Pete, run on upstairs and get Brody."

"No. No. Don't bother him." Absently, Reece untied her apron. "I'll be fine. We'll just go now."

Pete waited until Reece was out of earshot. "Want me to go up and get Brody?"

"She said no. Reece knows her own mind." But there was worry on Joanie's face as she turned back to the grill.

He'd brought the radio car, so the trip was quick. It didn't give her time to settle the idea, or to obsess about it. It would all be over in a few minutes, Reece thought. She could put all this behind her — or try to.

427

"I'm going to take you right back to Rick's office." Denny gave her shoulder a hesitant pat when they were out of the car. "You want some coffee? Some water?"

"No, no, I'm fine." And she didn't think she could swallow. "Do you know how she was . . . how she died?"

"You'd better talk to the sheriff." Denny opened the door for her.

Hank looked over from Dispatch, put his hand over the mike. "Bunch of crazy tourists chasing down buffalo with an SUV, trying to get action pictures. Got a wrecked SUV now, and a pissed-off bull. Reece." He mustered up a smile for her. "Doing okay?"

"Yes."

"Denny, I'm going to need you to go on out with Lynt, haul this bunch in, tow the vehicle. Bunch of fuckheads. Beg your pardon, Reece."

"I'll just go back to Sheriff Mardson's office."

"Where are they?" she heard Denny ask as she walked away.

The door was open, and Mardson was already coming around the desk to meet her. "Thanks for coming in."

"They found someone. A woman. A body."

"Sit down now." He took her arm, gently, led her to a chair. "Kids came across her. She matches your description. I got some pictures. I'm going to tell you they're not easy pictures, but if you can look at them, tell me if you think she's the woman you saw, that would be a big help."

"Was she strangled?"

"There's some indication she might've been throttled some. You think you can look at the pictures?"

"I can look at them." She gripped her hands together in her lap to anchor herself, while he took a file off his desk.

"Take your time now."

He sat in the other visitor's chair, then held out a photo. She didn't take it; she couldn't unknot her fingers. But she looked.

Then looked away as her breath wheezed out. "She's — Oh God."

"I know it's hard. She was in the marsh for a time. Maybe a day or two. Coroner's got to determine time of death and so on."

"A day or two? But it's been weeks."

"If she walked away with him that day, was hurt but not dead, this could've happened later."

When she started to shake her head, Rick held up a hand. "Can you say, without a shadow of a doubt, she couldn't have still been alive?"

She wanted to say she could, absolutely. But how could she?

"There isn't much of a shadow in my mind."

"That's enough for now. Is this the woman you saw, Reece?"

She gripped her own fingers until they hurt, then used the pain to brace herself to look again.

The face was so bruised, so swollen, with bloodless cuts all over it, down the throat, which was raw and red. Whatever lived in the marsh had sampled her as well. She'd heard once that fish and birds often go for the eyes first. Now she knew it was true.

Her hair was dark, long. Her shoulders seemed slight.

Reece tried to superimpose her memory of the woman she'd seen over the ruined face of this one.

"I don't . . . She seems younger, and her hair . . . her hair seems shorter. I don't know."

"You were a good distance away that day, I know."

"He didn't beat her. Her face — this face — someone beat her. He only pushed her down before . . . He didn't beat her face like this."

Rick said nothing for a moment, then when Reece looked away again, he turned the photo facedown.

"It could be she wasn't dead when you ran for help. That he dragged her off, covered his trail. Might be she came around, and they patched up for a while. Traveling around the area, maybe. Had another fight a couple weeks later, and that's when the rest of it happened. A man puts his hands around a woman's throat once, he could do it again."

"The rest."

"We've got to wait for the autopsy and other evidence to be processed. I'm saying that the odds are pretty good this is the woman you saw. But if you could take another look, clearing your mind out first, it would help. She didn't have any identification with her. They've run her prints, but there's no record of them. They'll use dental, and they're running Missing Persons. But knowing if she was where you saw those two people, knowing if she was with the man you saw, that might help some, too."

Reece kept her eyes on his, level, steady. "You didn't believe me before. You didn't believe I saw what I said I did, or that anyone was even there."

"I had my doubts, I won't lie to you. That doesn't mean I didn't look into it, or that I'm not still doing just that."

"All right." And this time she held out her hand for the photograph. The shock had waned, so now there was pity as she studied the face. "I don't know. I'm sorry.

I wish I could say this is the woman I saw, but I can't. I think she was older than this, and that her hair was longer, her face narrower, but I'm not sure. If they, when they identify her, if I could see a picture of her before this was done to her, I think I could say yes or no with a lot more certainty."

"Okay." He took the photo, then laid a hand over hers and squeezed. Hers felt as if she'd stuck it into a freezer. "I know this was hard for you. You want some water?"

"No. Thanks."

"Once they get her identified, we'll have you look. I appreciate you coming down this way. I'm going to have Denny drive you back home."

"I think he had to go on a call."

"I'll take you back myself."

"I can walk." But when she got to her feet, her legs wobbled. "Or maybe not."

"I'll take you on back. You want to sit a few more minutes first?"

Reece shook her head. "If you're right. Say you're right and she was still alive that day. Why would she stay with him? Voluntarily stay with him after he tried to kill her?"

"There's no telling what people will do. Hank, I'm running Reece back home. And maybe I'm wrong," Rick added as he took his hat off the hook, opened the door. "Maybe this has nothing to do with what you saw last month. But from your description, there's a good chance of it."

"She hasn't been reported missing because she was with him, and he wouldn't report it. Or he hasn't."

"Could be."

She got in the car, let her head lean back. "I wish I knew it was the same woman. It would be a lot easier to just say yes, that's the one. Then it would be over for me; it would be finished."

"You ought to put it out of your mind now, at least for now. Let the police do their job."

"I wish I could."

When he pulled up at Joanie's, Reece glanced up and saw Brody just coming out her door.

When he saw her in the radio car, he bolted down the steps.

"What's going on? What's wrong?"

He looked so worried, and she wasn't used to seeing worry on his face. Her insides wanted to shiver. "They found a woman's body, and I went to look at the photos from . . . I don't know if it was her. Her face was too ravaged. I don't think it was the woman I saw, but —"

"She was found in the marsh, near Moose Ponds," Rick said as he got out the driver's side.

"I'm just going to sit on the steps for a

minute before I go back in. A little more air." Reece walked to the steps, sat down heavily.

"Female victim," Rick said under his breath to Brody, "Long, dark hair. Evidence she was choked. Beaten, raped. Maybe drowned. Coroner's doing the autopsy about now. Kids found her. Naked, no ID, no clothes in the area."

"Just found her?"

"Yesterday. I got word today, got the crime scene photos."

"Jesus Christ, Rick, how the hell did you expect Reece to ID a woman who's been soaking in the marsh for almost a goddamn month?"

"Day or two," Rick corrected. "If Reece saw someone that day last month, and that woman walked or was carried away from the river still breathing, this could be her. I needed to see if Reece could identify her. She handled it pretty well. She's got some guts."

"You should've called me first, let me bring her down." Brody frowned over at Reece. "You know damn well we're hooked up."

"She wanted you with her, she could've called you. What the hell's in your hair?"

"Shit." Brody raked his hands through it. "Paint. Did a little painting upstairs."

"That so?" Rick lifted his eyebrows. "I

guess you're more hooked up than I figured."

"It's just fucking paint."

Rick offered a toothy smile. "Nice, pretty blue. Back when Debbie and I *hooked up,* she had me fixing her porch, then picking up this or that at the market. Before I knew it, I was renting a tux and saying 'I do.' "

"Screw you, Rick. It's paint."

"Gotta start somewhere." He walked over to Reece, crouched so she didn't have to crane her neck to look up at him. "Are you going to be all right now?"

"Yeah. I'll be all right. Thanks for bringing me back."

"Just part of the service."

"Sheriff?" she called as he headed back to the car. "You'll let me know as soon as she's identified?"

"I will. You count on it. Take care of yourself now. You watch out if she tries to put an apron on you," he added to Brody.

"Kiss my —" But Rick was already sliding into the car and shutting the door.

As Reece pushed off the steps, Brody went back to her. "Come on, we'll get whatever else you need and take it to my place. Go for that drive or whatever."

"No, I have to go back to work."

"Joanie's not going to fire you, for Christ's sake."

"I need the work. I need the money. And I owe her an extra hour. I'll do better if I'm busy anyway. Rain check on the drive or whatever?"

"Fine." He pulled her key out of his pocket, handed it to her. "You're locked up. I'll be at home if . . . I'll be at home."

"Okay." Since he made no move, she did, and leaned in to kiss him. "Consider that a small down payment on the painting fee."

"I thought I was being paid in food."

"To start."

19

Joanie asked no questions, and had given the stern word that she didn't want to hear any aimed in Reece's direction that didn't have to do with food.

When the lunch crowd slowed, she watched Reece chop onions and celery. The girl might have had the speed and precision with a knife that a champion barrel racer had with a horse, but her mind wasn't on her work.

"Your shift's over," Joanie told her.

"I owe you time. And we're low on potato salad."

"You owed me ten minutes, already paid."

Reece shook her head, kept chopping. "I was a good thirty minutes with the sheriff."

Mortally insulted, Joanie fisted her hands on her hips. "Did I say anything about docking you for that? Christ."

"I owe you thirty minutes." Reece dumped the onions and celery into the potatoes she'd already boiled, cubed and cooled. "This would have more zing with fresh dill."

"Well, I'd have more zing with George Clooney and Harrison Ford in a threesome, but neither of us are going to get that wish. I don't hear the customers complaining, and I said your shift is over. I don't pay overtime."

"I don't want your damn overtime. I want fresh dill, and some goddamn curry and cheese that doesn't look like plastic. And if the customers don't complain, it's because their taste buds are atrophied."

"That being the case," Joanie said evenly while Pete slunk away from the sink toward the back door, "they don't give a rat's flea-bitten ass about fresh dill."

"Well, they *should*." Reece slammed the jar of dressing on the work counter. "You should. Why should everyone just make do? I'm tired of just making do."

"Then get out of my kitchen."

"Fine." Reece yanked off her apron. "Fine. I'm out." Fueled with righteous fury, she sailed into Joanie's office, grabbed her purse and headed for the door. She stopped by a booth where a trio of hikers were finishing up their lunch and pretending not to listen. "Cumin." She jabbed a finger toward a bowl of chili. "It needs cumin." And stormed out.

"Cumin, my ass," Joanie muttered, then rounded on Pete. "Get back to work. I'm not paying you to stand around looking sorrowful."

"I could go after her."

"You could be out of a job, too." Cumin, Joanie thought with a sniff, and stalked over to finish the potato salad.

Reece slammed into her car. What she should do is drive and keep on driving, she told herself. She didn't need this town, these people, this ridiculous job that made a mockery out of real cuisine. She should head out to L.A., that's what she should do. Go to L.A. and take over a kitchen in a real restaurant where people understood food was more than something you stuffed into your face.

She slammed out of the car again in front of the mercantile. She owed Joanie time, but the bitch didn't want it. She owed Brody a meal for painting, and by God, she was paying her debt.

She shoved through the door, then scowled over at the counter where Mac was ringing up a sale for Debbie Mardson.

"I need hazelnuts," she snapped out.

"Ah, can't say we have any in stock."

How the hell was she supposed to make her chicken Frangelico without hazelnuts? "Why not?"

"Don't have much call for them. Sure can order you some though."

"A lot of good that does me now." She arrowed away to the grocery section to haunt the shelves, the bins, searching for inspiration and ingredients. Ridiculous, absurd, she thought, to try to find inspiration in this backcountry nowhere.

"Oh look, a miracle," she muttered. "Sun-dried tomatoes." She tossed them into the basket, picked through the fresh tomatoes. Hothouse, she thought in disgust. Wrapped in cellophane, for God's sake. Tasteless, colorless.

Making do, that's all. And barely.

No portobellos, big surprise. No eggplant, no artichokes. No fucking fresh dill.

"Hey there, Reece."

Tossing a few obviously substandard peppers in her basket, she frowned up at Lo. "If your mother sent you down, you can go right back and tell her I'm done."

"Ma? Haven't been down there yet. Saw your car out front. Here, let me carry that for you."

"I've got it." She tugged the basket out of reach. "Or maybe you forgot I said I wouldn't sleep with you."

His mouth opened, then closed and he cleared his throat. "No, that sticks in my mind. Listen, I just came in when I saw your car because I figured you might be upset."

"Why would I be upset? Red-skinned potatoes, another miracle."

"I heard about the woman they found up near Moose Ponds. News like that doesn't stay under the lid," he added when she only stared at him. "Has to be rough on you."

"A lot rougher on her, I'd say." She headed over to pick through the packaged chicken breasts.

"I guess that's true. Can't be easy for you though. Seeing her again, even a picture of her. Having to go back in your head to the day you saw her when you were on the trail." He shifted his feet when she made no response. "But at least you know they found her."

"I don't know if it was the same woman I saw."

"Sure it was. Had to be."

"Why?"

"Just makes sense it was." He trailed her over to the counter. "Everybody's saying so."

"Everybody doesn't know jack, and I can't say the woman they found is the woman I saw just to make everyone happy."

"Well, Jesus, Reece, that's not what I —"

"Funny how it takes some kids finding a dead body to make people around here decide I wasn't making the whole thing up after all. Gee, maybe Reece isn't completely crazy, after all."

With more care than usual, Mac boxed her purchases. "Nobody thinks you're crazy, Reece."

"Sure they do. Once a nutcase, always a nutcase. That's how it goes." She pulled out her wallet and noted with resignation that with the total on the cash register, she was going to be down to her last ten dollars and change. Again.

"You shouldn't talk like that." Mac took her money, gave her back thirty-six cents. "It's insulting to yourself and the rest of us."

"Maybe. It's insulting to walk down the street, or into a room, and have people point me out as that poor woman from back East, or look at me out of the sides of their eyes as if I might start gibbering any second. Try being on the receiving end of that for a while," she suggested as she hefted the box. "See if it doesn't start pissing you off. And you can tell your mother," she said to Lo, "that she owes me for twenty-eight hours."

Reece started for the door. "Tell her I'll be in to pick up my check tomorrow."

The sound of the front door slamming shot Brody out of a tense scene between his central character and the man she has no choice but to trust.

He cursed, reached for his coffee only to discover he'd already finished the oversized mug of it. His first thought was to go down for a refill, but he heard further slamming

— cupboard doors? — and decided he'd rather stay out of the war zone and do without the caffeine.

He rubbed the stiffness out of the back of his neck, which he attributed to craning it in order to paint the bathroom ceiling. Then he closed his eyes, pushed himself back into the scene.

At some point he thought he heard either the front or back door open, but he was in the zone and continued to write until it closed on him.

Satisfied, he pushed away from his keyboard. He and Maddy had taken a hell of a ride that day, and while she still had a ways to go, right now he deserved a cold beer and a hot shower.

But the beer came first. As he headed down to get one, he rubbed a hand over his face and heard the rasp. Should probably shave, he thought idly. Letting that little bit of business go two or three days running was fine and good for a man on his own. When a woman came into the equation, it was time for regular sessions with the damn razor.

He'd shave in the shower.

Better, he'd talk Reece into the shower with him. Shave, shower, sex — then a cold beer and a hot meal.

It was, he decided, a most excellent plan. The fact that nothing was simmering on the stove was a bit of a shock. He'd gotten used to strolling into the kitchen and finding something cooking. It was another shock to realize it irritated him.

Nothing cooking, no colorful arrangement of plates and candles on the table, and the back door wide open. He forgot about shaving and stepped over to the door.

Reece was sitting on the squat back porch with a bottle of wine. From the level in the bottle, he deduced she'd been sitting there for some time.

He stepped out, sat down beside her. "Having a party?"

"Sure." She lifted her glass. "Big party. You can buy yourself a very decent bottle of wine around here, but you just try to get a goddamn sprig of fresh dill or some lousy hazelnuts."

"I complained to the mayor about that just last week."

"You wouldn't know fresh dill if I shoved it up your nose." She gulped wine, gestured sloppily toward him with the glass. "And you're from Chicago. You oughta have some standards."

"I'm so ashamed." And she was so drunk.

"I was gonna make chicken Frangelico, but hazelnuts are not to be had. So I figured I'd do pollo arrosto. Tomatoes are

444

crap, and the idea of finding Parmesan that's not dried powder in a can is a laugh."

"That's a tragedy."

"It *matters.*"

"Apparently. Come on, Slim, you're toasted. Let's go on up so you can sleep it off."

"I'm not finished being toasted."

"Your choice, your hangover." He considered it a kindness to pick up the bottle, take a slug straight from it, and save her system from dealing with at least that much of it.

"She wants to make potato salad with bottled dressing and no dill, let her. I quit."

And around to Joanie, Brody deduced. "That'll teach her."

"Go along, make do, don't make waves, just so nobody notices. No attention here, please, go about your business."

She waved her hands a little wildly, so he laid his own on the bowl of her glass to keep wine from sloshing onto him.

"I'm tired of it. I'm tired of it all. Take a job I'm so overqualified for I could do it blindfolded and one-handed, live in a dinky apartment over a diner. Wasting my time, that's all. Just wasting it."

He considered, took another slug of wine. Not just toasted, he thought. Wallowing. "You plan on bitching and moaning much longer? Because if that's all that's on the slate, I can leave you to it and get a couple more hours of work in."

"Typical. Typical man. If it's not about you, it's not worth listening to. What the hell am I doing with you, anyway?"

"Right now? You're getting drunk on my back porch, wallowing in it and annoying me."

Her eyes might have been glassy, but they still had punch when they aimed at him. "You're selfish, self-absorbed and rude. The only thing you'll miss about me when I go is having a hot meal put in front of you. So, screw you, Brody. Just screw you sideways. I'll go wallow elsewhere."

She got to her feet, swaying a little as the wine sloshed in her head as unsteadily as it did in her glass. "I should've kept driving right through this excuse for a town. I should've told you to go to hell the first time you made a move on me. I should've told Mardson that was the woman I saw. I should've just said it was and forgotten about it. So that's just what I'm going to do."

She took a few unsteady steps back toward the kitchen. "But not in that order. You first. Go to hell."

She made it into the kitchen, reached for her purse. But he was quicker. "Hey." She made a grab for it. "That's mine."

"You can have it back. Except for these." He took out her keys from the inside zipper, exactly where she'd said she kept them. Mad, sick or otherwise, he noted, she kept her tidy ways.

He pulled the car key off the ring, dropped the ring with the apartment keys on the table, then stuck the car key in his pocket. "Go wherever the hell you want, but you're not driving. You're going to have to walk."

"Fine. I'll walk to Sheriff Does-His-Job Mardson, tell him what he wants to hear, then wash my hands of it. And you, and this place."

She was halfway to the door when her stomach twisted like a wet rag between two opposing fists. Clutching it, she dashed to the bathroom.

He went in behind her. He wasn't surprised she was dog-sick. In fact he thought it was for the best, the body's way of defending itself against the overindulgent idiocy of its owner.

So he held her head, then shoved a wet cloth into her hand when it was over.

"Ready to sleep it off now?"

She stayed where she was, the cloth pressed to her face. "Could you just leave me alone?"

"Nothing I'd like better. I'll get to that

in a minute." For now, he pulled her up. She managed a weak groan when he lifted her. "If you're going to puke again, tell me."

She shook her head, closed her eyes so that her dark, damp lashes lay against her sheet-white skin. He carried her upstairs to put her on the bed. He tossed a blanket over her and, as a precaution, moved the bedroom wastebasket to the side of the bed.

"Go to sleep" was all he said before he walked out.

Alone, she curled on her side and, shivering, pulled the blanket up to her chin. She'd just wait until she was warm and steady, she promised herself, then she'd go.

But the bottom dropped out, and she fell through it into sleep.

She dreamed of riding a Ferris wheel. Color and movement, and that quick, gut-dropping circle. At first, her screams were of laughter and delight.

Whee!

But it spun faster, faster, with the music blaring louder, louder. Delight became unease.

Slow down. Please? Can you slow it down?

Faster still, faster until the screams she heard were sharp with terror. As the wheel rocked madly side to side, panic gripped her throat.

It's not safe. I want to get off. Stop the wheel! Stop it and let me off!

But the speed only picked up to a blur, and the music crashed around her. Then the wheel flew off, plunging her out of the lights and into the dark.

Her eyes flashed open. Her fingers dug into the sheets and her own breathless screams echoed in her head.

She wasn't flying through the air, she assured herself. She wasn't spinning toward certain death. Just a dream, just a panic dream. Regulating her breathing, she lay very still and tried to reorient herself.

A lamp was on beside the bed, and the light shone from the hallway. For a moment, she remembered none of it. When it flooded back, Reece wanted nothing more than to pull the blankets over her head and dive back to oblivion.

Even the flying Ferris wheel would be easier to ride out.

How could she face him? Face anyone? She wanted to find her keys, then slink out of town like a thief.

She propped herself up on an elbow, waited to see if her stomach would hold, then sat up. There was a silver insulated cup on the nightstand. Baffled, she picked it up, slid back the tab and sniffed.

Her tea. He'd made her tea, and left it

449

so it would be close and warm when she woke.

If he'd recited Keats while showering her with white roses, she couldn't have been more touched. She'd said horrible things to him, had behaved abominably. And he'd made her tea.

She sipped it, let it slide down and soothe her abused stomach. Because she could hear his keyboard now, she squeezed her eyes shut to help gather courage. A little unsteady on her feet, she got up to face the music.

He glanced up when she stepped into the doorway of his office, and only lifted that single eyebrow.

Funny, she thought, how many expressions that one move could transmit. Interest, amusement, irritation. And just now? Absolute boredom.

She'd have preferred a good, hard slap.

"Thanks for the tea." He stayed silent, waiting, and she realized she didn't have quite enough courage yet to begin. "Is it all right if I take a bath?"

"You know where the tub is."

He started to type again, though the gibberish he put on the screen would need to be deleted. She looked like a dark-eyed ghost, sounded like a penitent child. He didn't like it.

He sensed when she'd slipped away,

waited until he heard the water begin to run into the tub. Then he deleted, shut down. And went down to make her soup.

He wasn't taking care of her; he was still too pissed off to consider it. It was just what you did when someone was sick. Some soup, maybe some toast. Just bare minimum stuff.

He wondered how much of whatever poisons she'd had bottled up inside her she'd managed to reject along with the wine.

If she started spewing at him again, he was going to . . .

Nothing, he thought. It wasn't just Reece he was pissed at, he realized. He was pissed at himself. He should've expected her to blow at some point. She'd been handling herself pretty well, rocking back from each separate sucker punch. But she'd been swallowing down the fear, the rage, the hurts. Sooner or later, they'd have to spill out.

Today had been the day.

The nasty psychological warfare someone was waging against her, being asked to look at pictures of a dead woman. He didn't know dick about fresh dill, but obviously that had been one of the last straws for her.

Now she'd apologize, and he didn't want her damn apology. Now she'd very likely tell him she had to go, had to find some other shelter from her personal storm, and he didn't want her to go. He didn't want to lose her.

And that was lowering.

When she came in, her hair was damp and she smelled of his soap. He could see she'd done her best to camouflage the fact she'd been crying, and knowing she'd been up there, sitting in his tub weeping, was another punch to the heart.

"Brody, I'm so —"

"Got soup," he interrupted. "It's no pollo arrosto — whatever the hell that is — but you'll have to live with it."

"You made soup."

"My mother's recipe. Open a can, pour contents into bowl, zap in nuclear oven. It's world famous."

"It sounds delicious. Brody, I'm sorry, I'm embarrassed, I'm ashamed."

"But are you hungry?"

She pressed her fingers to her eyes while her lips trembled.

"Don't." There was the barest trace of desperation under the hard edge of his tone. "I'm at my limit on that kind of thing. You want the soup or not?"

"Yes." She dropped her hands. "Yes, I want the soup. Aren't you having any?"

"I had a sandwich while you were lying upstairs in a drunken stupor."

The sound she made was trapped between a laugh and a sob. "I didn't mean what I said to you."

"Just shut up and eat."

"Please, let me say this."

With a shrug, he put the bowl of soup on the table, saw her blink in surprise when he put a plate of buttered toast beside it.

"I didn't mean it. You are rude, but it works for me. You're not selfish, or what selfishness you have seems awfully healthy from where I stand. I don't want you to go to hell."

"That one may not be your choice."

"I can't remember if I said anything else I should apologize for, being drunk at the time. If you want me out, I'll go."

"If I was going to kick you out, why did I spend all this time and trouble making you my mother's famous soup?"

She stepped to him, wrapped her arms around him, pressed her face into his chest. "I fell apart."

"No, you didn't." He couldn't help himself, just couldn't stop himself from lowering his head and pressing his lips to the top of her head. "You had a drunken tantrum."

"Several tantrums, and only the last one was alcohol-driven."

"Sounds like interesting dinner conversation." He steered her to a chair, then poured himself coffee before sitting down across from her.

She spooned up soup and confessed all.

"I blasted everyone. Fortunately, it's a small population so there weren't many who came in range. But my spree's left me without a job, very likely without an apartment. If he wasn't so thick-skinned, I'd guess it would have left me without a lover."

"Do you want them back? The job, the apartment?"

"I don't know." She broke off a corner of a piece of toast, crumbled it onto the plate. "I could take today as a sign — which I'm big on — that it's time to go."

"Where?"

"Yeah, that's a question. I could prostrate myself in front of Joanie and swear a blood oath never to mention fresh herbs again."

"Or you could go back into work tomorrow and fire up the grill, or whatever it is you do back there."

She looked up, confusion in her tired eyes. "Just like that?"

"It wouldn't be the first shouting match to play out in Joanie's. What do you want, Reece?"

"To push rewind, I guess. But since I can't, to deal with the consequences." This time when she broke off a corner of toast, she ate it. "I'll talk to Joanie tomorrow, see where I go from there."

"That's not to the point. Do you want to go or do you want to stay?"

She stood, took her bowl to the sink to rinse it out. "I like what I see everywhere I look when I walk around town. I like having people wave as they drive by, or stop to talk when I'm walking. I like hearing Linda-gail laugh when she's taking orders, and the way Pete sings when he washes dishes."

She turned, leaned back against the sink. "The air feels good on my skin, and any day the flats are going to bloom. But there are other places with beautiful views and friendly people. The trouble with them is they're not here. The trouble with them is you're not in them. So I want to stay."

He rose and went to her, and in a gesture more tender than she'd ever expected from him, brushed the hair back from her face. "That's what I want, too. I want you to stay."

When he kissed her, gently, very gently, her arms slid up to wind around his neck. "If you wouldn't mind — I know you've already gone to a lot of trouble on my behalf today — but if you wouldn't mind, maybe you could show me what you want."

Now she rubbed her lips against his. "If you wouldn't mind."

Together, they circled their way out of the room, lips brushing, bodies warming.

"Indulge me," she told him.

"That was my plan."

"No." She chuckled against his throat. "Indulge me and say it again. Just say you want me to stay."

"Women always want a man to grovel." He found her mouth again, turned her toward the living room. "I want you to stay."

Oh yes, she thought, better than Keats. And held him close when he lowered her to the couch.

The fire he'd lit as he did most nights had gone to simmering red embers. That's what she felt inside her, felt from him, the warmth and the simmer instead of the flash of leaping flames.

She could bask in it, stroking his hair, his skin, letting her mouth surrender to his. Tonight she could be soothed by his hands and know the quiet glow of contentment. He'd made her tea and soup, and he wanted her to stay.

Love washed over her in slow, swamping waves.

As she reached for him, as she offered, he wanted more than to take. He wanted most to comfort her, to smooth out all her troubles. Then to lift her from them. No one else had ever reached that tenderness inside him, no one else had ever coaxed it out until it drenched him.

He could give her that, that tenderness. And every soft sigh she offered back only enhanced his own pleasure.

As he undressed her, his fingers, his lips, brushed and stroked over newly exposed skin. The scent of his soap on her aroused a possessiveness in him. His. To touch, to taste, to hold. Her fingers feathered over his face, into his hair as her body arched to give. And give.

The strength of him, the muscles, the big hands, the tough build now so gentle thrilled her. That he could touch her with such care and patience, that his lips could meet hers, again and again, with such sweetness left her dazzled.

Everything inside her went loose and liquid, and still he gave her more.

The blood began to pulse under her skin; the first beats of urgency. As if he heard it, he took her up, let that coiled need spring loose. And as she drifted down again, she made a sound like a woman who'd just tasted something rich and honeyed.

Her heavy eyes opened, dreamed into his.

He fell into them, into the dark magic of them. His heart fell with him, tumbling,

tumbling free. He couldn't stop it, couldn't catch it, or himself.

He slipped into her, watched her start the rise again.

"Don't close your eyes." He covered her mouth with his, still watching while they moved together.

Rhythm quickened; breath shortened. His body began its final rush while she raced with him. He gripped her hands and saw those eyes he couldn't resist blur as she fisted tight around him. As she said his name.

His own vision dimmed as she pulled him with her.

They lay together, wrapped together, as the night ticked away and the embers died. When he felt her begin to drift off, he simply reached up to pull the throw on the back of the couch over them.

She cuddled in, murmured something. Then slept.

Beside her he closed his eyes and smiled into the dark. She hadn't asked him to check the locks, he thought, but had slipped into sleep without fear.

Lo had his hand up Linda-gail's shirt and a condom in his pocket. The part of his brain that still remained above his belt buckle flashed back to when they'd been sixteen and the situation had been remarkably similar.

Only this time they were in her little house instead of the old Ford pickup his mother had helped him buy. There was a bedroom close by, though the couch would do just fine.

Her pretty breast — which he hadn't gotten a look at since that summer so long ago — was soft and warm in his hand. Her mouth, and he'd never forgotten her mouth, was just as hot and sweet as spiced candy.

And God, she smelled good.

She was so miraculously curvy. Fuller than she'd been at sixteen, but in all the right places. And if at first he'd been baffled, even a little annoyed that she'd gone off and dyed her hair, he was currently finding it damn sexy. Almost like having his hands on a stranger.

But when that hand slid down to the button of her jeans, hers clamped over it. She said, as she'd said at sixteen, "Uh-uh."

"Oh now, honey." He spread his fingers up over her belly, felt it tremble as he nibbled his way down her throat. "I just want —"

"Can't always get what you want, Lo." Her voice wasn't steady, but she kept her hand firm over his. "And you're not getting it tonight."

"You know I want you. God almighty, I always have. You want me, too." His lips made a lazy journey back to hers. "Why do you want to tease me this way, sweetheart?"

"Don't call me sweetheart unless you mean it. And this isn't a tease." It took a lot of willpower to push away from him, but she did just that. When she did, she could see the surprise on his face, and the first hints of anger. "It's not going to be like that between you and me."

"Like what?"

"You won't be banging me, then moving on."

"Well, for Christ's sake, Linda-gail." Sincere confusion rippled over his face. "You're the one who said I should come over."

"To talk about Reece."

"Now that's bull and you know it. You didn't scream for help when I kissed you."

"I liked when you kissed me. I like it just fine. I always did, Lo."

"Then what's the problem?"

"We're not kids anymore, and I'm not looking for a couple of nights of wrestling. If you are, you might as well go find one of the women you know who're happy with just that." Fussily, she smoothed her half-buttoned shirt. "I've got higher standards."

"Higher standards?" The hints of anger coalesced. "That's a hell of a thing to say to me. You got me over here just to stir me up, then flick me off. Got names for women like that."

Her chin lifted, very slowly, until their eyes met. Hers shot hot bullets. "You think that, you'd better get out. Right now."

"I'm going." He shoved to his feet. "What the hell do you want?"

"When you figure it out, you can come back." She got up, picked up his hat, tossed it to him. "But you leave here and go hunt up one of those women and I hear about it, you won't get in the door again."

"So I can't have you, or anybody else until you say different?"

"No, Lo, you can't have me or anybody else until you know the difference. One thing you do know is the way out."

Twisted with unreleased lust and frustration, Linda-gail strolled back to her bedroom and shut the door. With a bang.

For a moment Lo only stared after her. What in the damn depths of hell had just happened? He could still taste her, his palm was still warm from her breast. And she walked off, slammed the damn door?

Furious, he stormed out. Women like her, he thought, women who used a man, ordered a man around, played games, should be made to pay a price for it.

He slammed into his truck, sent one dark look back toward the house with the yellow shutters. She thought she knew him, thought she had him pegged.

She was dead wrong.

20

It wasn't hard to walk into Joanie's. What did she have to lose? In any case, she'd learned in therapy how important it was to face and resolve problems, and to take responsibility.

Embarrassment was a small price to pay for mental health, Reece told herself. And accepting the embarrassment might get her job back.

Groveling wasn't out of the question.

Added to it, her daily horoscope had advised her to shoulder burdens. If she did so, she would find they didn't weigh as much as expected.

That was a good sign.

Still, she went in the back way, and ten minutes before opening. There was no point in spreading her embarrassment around to customers chowing down on steak and eggs if it wasn't absolutely necessary.

Joanie, feet planted in their practical shoes, was mixing up an enormous bowl of batter. The air smelled of coffee and warm biscuits.

"You're late," Joanie snapped. "Unless you got a note from Doc, don't think I won't dock you for it."

"But —"

"I don't want excuses, I want reliability — and I want onions, chili peppers and tomatoes prepped for huevos rancheros. Stow your things and get to work."

"All right." More chastened than she would have been had Joanie showed her the door, Reece scooted into the office, left her purse and jacket. Back in the kitchen, she grabbed an apron. "I want to apologize for yesterday."

"Apologize while you work. I don't pay you to talk."

Reece set herself up at the work counter. "I'm sorry I was such a bitchy pain in the ass yesterday. I had no right to insult you, even though the addition of fresh herbs and other basic ingredients would improve the breadth of your menu."

Out of the corner of her eye, Reece saw Joanie's brows shoot up, and her lips twitch. "That covers it."

"All right."

"Wasn't any damn dill set you off."

"No. It was something handy to throw at you, metaphorically speaking."

"I had to deal with a dead body once."

"What? I'm sorry?"

"Rented one of my cabins to this fella from Atlanta, Georgia. Rented to him the year before, and the one before that. Used to come for two weeks in the summer with his family. That'd be, oh, ten years back.

But this time, he came by himself. Seems the wife was divorcing him. Go on, get some sausage started. Lynt'll be in first thing this morning, and he likes sausage with his eggs."

Obediently, Reece got the tub of loose sausage from the refrigerator and began to make patties.

"So, when this Georgia boy doesn't come back into town to turn in the cabin keys, I have to haul my ass out there. Anyway, I used to do the cleaning of the rental places myself back then. I went out there with my cleaning kit. His car's still there, so I banged on the door. Irritated, because he was supposed to be out by ten sharp. I had another tenant coming in that day at three. He doesn't answer, so . . ."

She paused to pick up her mug of coffee, took a drink. "In I go. I expect I'm going to find him sleeping off a toot in bed. Guy who worked the liquor store back in those days, name of Frank, told me how the good old boy from Georgia bought himself two fifths of Wild Turkey the one time he came into town.

"Instead I found what was left of him on the floor in front of the fire. I guess he drove from Georgia to Wyoming with a shotgun in his trunk for a reason. The reason being to blow his own head off."

"Oh my God."

"Did a good job of it. Blood and brains every damn where. Blew himself right out of the chair he'd been sitting in."

"That's horrible. It must've been horrible for you to find him."

"It wasn't a stroll on an island beach. After the cops did what cops do in such cases, I went back in. Had to clean the place, didn't I?"

"Yourself?"

"Damn right myself. I scrubbed and I scrubbed, and I bitched and I cursed. Look what that son of a bitch did to my place. Bastard drove thousands of miles to shoot his stupid head off in my place. I poured out buckets stained with blood and God knows and I threw out what had been a perfectly good rug that'd cost me fifty dollars. And I chewed the head off anybody who offered to help me. I skinned the hide of my William when he came out to try."

"I see," Reece replied. And she did.

"Had to be mad, didn't I? Had to rant and rage and slap at my boy for wanting to help me out. Because if I didn't, I'd never be able to stand it."

Joanie walked over to the sink, dumped out the coffee that had gone cold. "Don't rent that particular cabin to outsiders anymore. Just to locals who want to use it for a hunting or fishing trip or the like."

She poured herself more coffee. "So I've got some understanding of what was in your gut yesterday. True enough you didn't know that, but you damn sure should know me better by this time."

"Joanie —"

"If you needed to take off after going down to Rick's office — if you needed to *go* off — it's stupid, and it's goddamn insulting for you to think I'd've given you any grief over it. Or I'd give you any about it now."

"You're absolutely right. I should've known better." She slid her gaze to where Joanie popped breakfast biscuits out of the oven. "I slapped at you and Brody the hardest, because you're the closest. The two people I trust most."

"That's some compliment."

"Did Lo come in, after I saw him at the mercantile?"

"He did. Linda-gail, open her up! But since I don't take orders from you, you'll get your check on payday like everyone else."

"I, ah, swiped at him, too, and at Mr. Drubber."

"Grown men ought to be able to handle a woman's temper from time to time."

A snort from Linda-gail had Joanie looking over her shoulder.

"Some men never grow up. They're

spoiled little boys all their lives. Only way you'd've hurt Lo's feelings, Reece, is if you'd swiped at his balls. That's what runs the show for him."

"He may be an ass, Linda-gail," Joanie said mildly, "but he's still mine."

Though she colored up a little, Linda-gail shrugged. "Can't help how I feel about it. But if you're worried, Reece, he told me he could see you were awful upset. He didn't hold anything you said against you."

The door opened with a jingle. "Hey, Doc, hey, Mr. D." Linda-gail grabbed the coffeepot. "You're bright and early this morning."

Reece hunched her shoulders, but she got out the eggs and bacon she expected to be cooking up shortly.

"I don't reckon Mac'll hold anything against you, either." In a move that took Reece completely by surprise, Joanie gave her a couple of light pats on the back. "You want to use your break later, you can use my office, call my produce supplier. I'll give you a fifty-dollar budget — not a cent more — to order some of the damn fancy-pants herbs and such you're always whining for."

"I can do a lot with fifty." To start, Reece thought, and in her head she was pumping her fist in the air.

"Better damn sight," Joanie muttered.

468

★ ★ ★

In the booth, Doc cut into his short stack. Wasn't his day for pancakes, but it was hard to deny himself after Mac had asked for this little breakfast meeting. And if he had a second cup of real coffee instead of switching to decaf, it wasn't such a big deal in the larger scheme.

"Now, Mac, you know I can't discuss Reece's medical business. It's privileged."

"I'm not asking you to. I'm just asking what you think. I'm telling you, that girl's in trouble. You didn't see her yesterday." Mac gestured with his fork before scooping into his huevos rancheros. "I did."

"Heard enough about it."

"I wasn't sure she'd still be here." Mac angled his head so he could see back into the kitchen. "In fact, I figured she'd be long gone by now."

"I guess she has more reason to stay than go."

"I don't know, Doc." Concern deepened the creases in Mac's brow, tightened his voice. "The way she was storming around my place. Mad, sure, but she just didn't look well. I told you I was worried enough I went on down to check on her after I closed up. And her place was locked up tight as a vault, her car gone. Figured she'd lit out."

He dug for more eggs. "Wanted to talk

469

to you about it. You could've bowled me over when I saw her back there in the kitchen this morning. Some relieved by it, I guess. I hated thinking she was out driving off somewhere in the state she was in."

"People get in states, Mac." Doc waved a hand at Mac's stubborn frown. "Some more than others. Plain to see she had a rough time yesterday."

"That's the other thing." Mac glanced over to make sure Linda-gail wasn't on her way back to top off their coffee. Though the juke was silent — no music until ten o'clock was Joanie's hard-and-fast rule — there was enough buzz of conversation and clatter to cover his voice.

"First off, seems to me Rick should've known better than to have her come in alone to look at those pictures. Chrissake, Doc, most women couldn't have handled that sort of thing, much less one who's had the kind of time Reece has. He should've had you there."

"Well now, Mac, I don't know why Rick would've thought to call me. I'm a family doctor, not a psychiatrist."

"Should've had you there," Mac said, setting his jaw. "And second, from what she said in my place, she's saying it wasn't the woman she saw. Now, Doc, it damn near has to be, doesn't it? This isn't New York City or whatnot. We don't get people murdered right and left in these parts."

"I don't know what you're getting at."

"I'm wondering if, in the circumstances of all this, she just doesn't want it to be the same woman. Maybe she's hanging on to it too hard."

Doc smiled thinly. "Who's playing shrink now?"

"Working behind the counter for a couple decades is as good as being a shrink. Not everybody believed that girl when she said she'd seen that woman attacked," Mac added with another wag of his fork. "I did. Just like I believe that same poor woman ended up dead in that marsh. Reece can't handle it, that's what I think."

"May be."

"Well, you're the doctor. Help her out."

"Don't you two look all serious and secretive." Linda-gail tipped coffee from the pot into their mugs. "Sitting here with your heads together."

"Man talk," Doc said with a wink.

"Sex, sports or horses?"

Doc only grinned and forked up more pancakes.

"How's Reece doing today?" Mac asked Linda-gail.

"Better than yesterday, I'd say." She glanced over her shoulder. "Either of you hear if the sheriff's got word on that woman's identity?"

"Haven't heard anything today, but it's early yet. Terrible thing," Doc added.

"Scary, too, thinking we might have somebody around here killing women. Moose Ponds's a good way from the Fist, but still."

"Women?" Mac frowned.

"If it's not the one Reece saw, then it's two different women. And okay, sure, Moose Ponds is all the way up by Jenny Lake, but maybe the same person did both of them. Like a serial killer or something."

"Oh now, Linda-gail." Mac shook his head. "You're watching too much TV."

"They wouldn't make so many TV shows about killing if people didn't go around killing, would they? And you know what else?" She lowered her voice now. "If Reece hadn't been up on the trail, just at the right time, nobody'd know anything about that woman. Could be this killer's done it before. I can tell you, I'll be sticking close to home until they catch him."

"Now hell, that's another problem." Mac scratched at his head as Linda-gail walked away. "Before you know it, people in the Fist'll be looking cross-eyed at each other, wondering if we got some psycho serial killer in our midst. Or some damn reporter'll write about it that way, and the tourists'll bypass us, and we'll lose the summer season. Some hothead will have one too many down at Clancy's and start a fight over it."

Doc frowned thoughtfully. "On that one, at least, you may have a point."

Since he still had an hour before office hours, Doc went up to the sheriff's office before heading home. Denny sent him a sunny smile. "How you doing, Doc?"

"Can't complain. Your ma have any trouble with that ankle?"

"No. She's up and around just fine."

"You tell her I don't want her doing any jigs just yet. That was a nasty sprain. Your boss around?"

"Not yet. He's got till ten, unless something hits. Sheriff's been putting in a lot of late hours lately. Guess you heard about the body they found."

"I did. Any word on who she is?"

"Nothing's come in this morning yet. Sure is a hell of a thing. Son of a bitch must've kept her alive a couple weeks. God knows what he did to her all that time."

"That's assuming she's the same one Reece saw."

"Well, sure." Denny looked perplexed. "Who else could it be? Sheriff thinks it is."

"Mind if I take a look at the photos?"

"I dunno, Doc. The sheriff —"

"I've seen dead bodies in my time,

Denny. Could be I'd recognize her. Maybe I treated her at some time or another. And it's my sketch Rick's using to determine she's one and the same."

"Yeah, I guess. Hank," he added as the dispatcher walked in.

"Anything brewing but bad coffee around here? Hiya, Doc."

"Hank. How're the knees?"

"Ah, not too bad."

"They'd be better if you took off twenty-five pounds. Not going to do that eating those doughnuts you've got in that sack."

"Man's got to keep his energy up in a job like this."

"Sugar high's not energy." Doc adjusted his glasses as Denny came out of Rick's office with the file.

Opening it, Doc pursed his lips in what looked like a combination of interest and pity. "Looks like man and nature were both unkind to this girl."

"Got the shit beat out of her, that's for sure. Was raped," Denny added with a grim nod toward the photos. "Sheriff didn't show Reece all the crime-scene pictures. Didn't want to upset her more than he had to. See there? How her wrists and ankles are all raw and bruised? Had her tied up."

"Yeah, I see."

"Hauled her away from the river. Truck,

camper, RV, something. Kept her tied up and did what he wanted with her until he was finished. Dumped her in the marsh after. You recognize her, Doc?"

"No. I can't say I do. Sorry, Denny, wish I could be more help. I'd better go see to my patients. Hank, you go easy on those damn doughnuts."

"Aw, Doc."

He did some thinking on his walk home. About his conversation with Mac, about the photographs he'd studied. He thought about the town, and how long it had been his. How he liked to think he kept his finger on the pulse of it and his ear tuned to its heartbeat.

He let himself in the front door he hadn't locked in two decades. Instead of going back to his office, he walked to the living room phone. Willow would deal with any early patients or walk-ins, he thought.

He made his call, then popped a cherry Life Savers to take the coffee off his breath before he saw his first patient of the day.

A little after twelve, Brody was pacing around Doc's living room. Doc's instructions had been to come by at noon and make himself at home. Interrupting the middle of his day, Brody thought, when the book was not just moving but actually racing.

If he'd wanted a break in the middle of the day — which he damn well didn't — he'd have preferred to take that time at Joanie's. Have some lunch, see Reece.

At least he assumed he'd see Reece. She hadn't called to say she was still out of a job, and her car was parked in its usual place. Still, he'd like to see for himself.

Not that he was looking after her, he assured himself. Just checking, that's all.

If the doc hadn't been so damn cryptic on the phone, Brody figured his curiosity wouldn't have been piqued. And he'd be at his keyboard.

His female lead was pushing him through the story. Almost dragging him through it, snapping at him to keep up, for God's sake. And to think he'd originally conceived her as a victim. A couple scenes onstage, a terrible death, then gone.

Well, she hadn't taken that lying down.

He wanted to get back to her. But since he was across the lake anyway, he'd get back to Maddy after he stopped off to grab a bite and see Reece. He probably should suggest to Reece that she stay at his place again tonight.

He should probably let that alone, he corrected. Let her go back to her own apartment before things got messy and she was, unofficially, living with him.

He'd been careful to avoid that stepping-stone to lifetime commitment with other women. No need to stumble over it now.

He wandered to the window, wandered away again. Wandered to a bookshelf, scanned titles. As always, he was a little jolted to see one of his own books, his own name emblazoned on the spine.

After skimming a finger down that spine, he wandered some more.

The photographs scattered around the room caught his attention. Idly he picked one up, one of Doc and the woman who'd been his wife for aeons, it seemed to Brody. Outdoorsy shot, camping gear, Doc holding up a string of fish while the wife grinned.

They looked nice together, Brody decided. Happy. Though if his gauge of the ages was on, they'd been married a couple decades when the picture was snapped.

He picked up another, family shot. The whole brood. Then a young Mr. and Mrs. Doc holding a toddler. Various graduation pictures, wedding pictures, grandparent pictures.

The life and times, Brody thought, of a man and his family.

What was that like?

He didn't have anything against marriage, Brody mused as he kept pacing. It worked for some people. Obviously it had worked for Doc Wallace. It had worked, and was still working, for Brody's own parents.

It was just so . . . absolute, he decided. This is it, for the rest of your natural life. Just this one person unless you want to go through the hellish combat of divorce.

What if you changed your mind, or things just went wrong? Which they did, half the time.

Even if you didn't, and they didn't, there was all that adjusting and making room and compromising. A man couldn't just do what he wanted when he wanted.

What if he wanted to move back to Chicago, for instance? Or hell, Madagascar? Not that he did, but what if? There was no pulling up stakes on a whim when you were married.

You weren't just a man anymore, you were a couple. Then maybe you were a father, and now — wham — you're a family. And there was no turning back. No editing it out and going in a different direction in the storyline.

He probably wasn't in love with her anyway, any more than she was with him. It was just . . . involvement. Involvement was different, and the levels and intensity of it came and went.

He turned when Doc came in.

"Sorry, ran over on the last couple of patients. Appreciate you coming, Brody."

"Why did you want to see me?"

"Come on back to the kitchen. I'll rustle us up a little lunch while we talk. Won't be what you're used to lately," he added as they started back. "But it'll fill the hole."

"I'm not fussy."

"I heard about what went on with Reece yesterday."

"Have you talked to her?"

"Not today." Doc got out some turkey, one of the hothouse tomatoes Reece disparaged, a half head of iceberg and a jar of sweet pickles. "I did talk with Mac. He's worried about her." He took a partial loaf of whole wheat out of his bread bin. "I wondered if you were."

"Why?"

"Trying to get the full picture. I can't tell you anything she told me as a patient. You may feel you can't tell me anything she discussed with you as a . . . friend. But if you feel otherwise, I wanted to ask if she's told you anything you find troubling."

"She told you she came back to her apartment one night and found all her clothes packed up?" Brody nodded when Doc glanced over from slicing the tomato. "That she didn't remember packing. I don't think she did the packing."

"Who else could have?"

"The same person who wrote all over her bathroom with a red marker and dumped out all her pills, moved her stuff around. And other similar tricks."

Doc set down the knife. "Brody, if Reece is having memory lapses and episodes, she needs to be treated."

"I don't think she is. I think someone's screwing around with her."

"And you perpetuating her delusions only deepens them."

"They're not delusions if they're real. Why does she only have these memory lapses and episodes when she's alone?"

"I'm not qualified to —"

"Why did they start *after* she saw a woman murdered?"

Doc blew air out of his nose, then went back to building the sandwiches. "We can't know, absolutely, there weren't other episodes before that. But if they began at that time, there could be a couple of reasons. One, what she saw triggered the symptoms."

Doc put the sandwiches on plates, added two pickles and a small handful of potato chips each. Then poured two glasses of milk.

"I've been spending a lot of time with her. I haven't seen any symptoms. Not like you mean."

"But you have seen something."

"I don't like the position you're putting me in."

"I don't like the position she may be in," Doc countered.

"Okay, here's what I've seen. I've seen a woman fighting her way back from the abyss. Who trembles in her sleep most nights, but who gets up every day and does whatever needs to be done next. I see a survivor who gets through on spine, on heart and humor, who's trying to rebuild a life someone else shattered."

"Sit down and eat," Doc suggested. "Does she know you're in love with her?"

Brody's stomach jerked but he sat. And, picking up the sandwich, bit in. "I didn't say I was in love with her."

"Subtext, Brody. Being a writer you'd know about subtext."

"I care about her and what happens to her." He could hear the defensiveness — and was that a little fear? — in his voice. "Let's leave it at that."

"All right. If I'm reading you correctly, you're thinking, or at least considering, that these things happening to Reece are being done by someone who wants to hurt her." With a thoughtful frown Doc picked up his milk. "The only individual who could, as far as we know, be motivated to hurt her would be the man she claims to have seen strangle the woman she claims to have seen."

"Did see."

"I agree, but it's still unproven." With that same frown in his eyes, Doc drank. "But if she did, and if you're right . . . Have you gone to the sheriff with this?"

"Rick's just going to conclude she's a nutcase. Whatever credibility she has about what she witnessed will go right down the tubes."

"Without all the facts, he can't do his job."

"For now, I can look out for her. He can concentrate on finding out who was dumped in Moose Ponds, and who was killed by the Snake. I told you this in confidence."

"All right, all right." Doc held up a hand for peace. "Don't upset your digestion. I went by the sheriff's office, had Denny show me the pictures."

"And?"

"I can only go by the description Reece gave me, and the sketch she approved. I can't be sure one way or the other. Is it possible it's the woman she saw? It is."

"What about the time lag? It's been weeks since Reece saw it happen."

"That troubled me, as I imagine it troubled the authorities. There were ligature marks on her wrists and ankles. She may very well have been held all this time. But it doesn't explain to me, and this is very troubling, why there was no sign these people were there, where Reece saw them. Why did this man throttle a woman violently enough for Reece to believe she was dead, then take that woman away, erasing his trail so that Rick, a man who knows tracking, found nothing?"

"Because he saw her."

"Saw her?"

"Maybe not enough to recognize her, but he saw someone up on the ridge. Or he saw the things she left up there when she ran back and found me. He knew someone saw what went on."

"Is that possible?" Doc asked. "From that distance?"

"Reece had field glasses. Who's to say he didn't? That after he killed the woman, he scoped out the area. Just another way of covering tracks, isn't it?"

"I can't argue. But it's a lot of supposition, Brody."

"Suppose this. Whether or not this body they found is the same woman, the man Reece saw had to know someone witnessed what happened there. There's just no reason to erase the tracks otherwise. Take the body, sure. Can't leave it there where a floater or paddler, a hiker may spot it. Take it away, wait for dark, bury it or dispose of it by other means. But cover all tracks? Not unless he knew he'd been seen."

"Yes, of course," Doc agreed. "And if he knew he'd been seen, he'd only have to wait a short time, keep his ear to the ground, to find out who."

"And since, someone's been screwing with her, trying to make her think she's losing her grip. I'm not going to let them get away with it."

"I'd like to talk with her some more. I made a point of telling Mac this morning that I wasn't a shrink. But I do have some training, some experience."

"That'd be up to her."

Doc nodded. "A lot of this is. That's a lot of weight for someone with her background to carry. She trusts you?"

"Yeah, she does."

"Weight for you, too. Tell her we spoke," Doc decided after a moment. "Don't breach the trust. But I'd like you to keep me in the loop. How's the sandwich?"

"It's pretty good. But you're no cordon bleu chef."

He went back to the river. There was no sign of what had happened there, and he was sure of that. He'd been careful. He was a careful man.

It should never have happened, of course. Would never have happened if he'd had a choice. Everything that he'd done since was because she'd *left* him no choice.

He could still hear her voice if he let himself. Screaming at him, threatening him.

Threatening him, as if she'd had the right.

Her death had been her own doing. He understood that, and felt no guilt over it. Others wouldn't understand, so he did what needed to be done to protect himself.

None of that would have been necessary if it hadn't been for the caprice of time and place.

How could he have known someone would be on the trail, would have looked in that direction at that time, with field glasses? Even a careful man couldn't anticipate every quirk of fate.

Reece Gilmore.

She should have been easy to handle, too. So easy to discredit, even to herself. But she wouldn't let it go, wouldn't crack and turn it loose.

Still, there was a way to fix it all. There was always a way to put things right. There was too much at stake to allow some refugee from a padded room to ruin things for him. If he had to turn the pressure up, he'd turn it up.

Look at this place, he thought, drinking in the river, the hills, the trees. All so perfect, so pristine and private. It was his place, all he wanted. Everything he had was bound to it, rooted in its soul, fed by its waters, guarded by its mountains.

Whatever needed to be done to protect and preserve what he had, he'd do.

It was Reece Gilmore who would have to go.

One way or the other.

HOME

I was well; I would be better;
I am here.

— ANONYMOUS

21

Since she didn't have to be at work until two, Reece considered just futzing around Brody's cabin, doing some light housekeeping, maybe some laundry. She could easily keep out of his way while he wrote, and put together tomorrow's soup of the day for Joanie.

She was already dressed and making the bed when he got out of the shower. "Anything special you want for breakfast? I don't have to be in until this afternoon, so your wish can be my command. Gastronomically."

"No. I'm just going to have some cereal."

"Oh. All right." She smoothed the spread and thought idly that a few throw pillows in primary colors would liven it up. "I'm going to put together some Italian wedding soup for Joanie. You can have some at lunch, see if it passes the test. I can make a casserole or something easy to heat up for your supper since I'm working the dinner shift. Oh, and I thought I might toss in some laundry while I'm at it. Is there anything you want washed?"

Wedding soup? Was that some subliminal message? And now she was, what, going to wash his shorts? Christ.

"Let's just back up."

She gave him a puzzled smile. "Okay."

"I don't need you to start planning breakfast, lunch, dinner or a damn midnight snack every damn morning."

The smile dropped into a blink of surprise. "Well . . ."

"And you're not here to do laundry and make beds and casseroles."

"No," she said slowly, "but since I am here, I'd like to be useful."

"I don't want you fussing around the place." There it was again, that same defensive tone he'd heard in his voice at the doc's the day before. It irritated him. "I can handle my own chores. I've been handling them for years."

"I'm sure you have, and exactly as you please. Obviously I've misunderstood something. I thought you wanted me to cook."

"That's different."

"Different than, say, tossing our laundry in together. That being somehow symbolic of a level of relationship you don't want. That's completely stupid."

Maybe. "I don't need you to do the laundry or leave me a damn casserole or any of this stuff. You're not my mother."

"Absolutely not." She stepped back to the bed, yanked the spread down, tugged out the sheets. "There, all better."

"Now who's stupid?"

"Oh, trust me, you still win the prize. Do you really think because I'm in love with you I'm trying to trap you into something by washing your damn dirty socks and making chicken and dumplings? You're an idiot, Brody, and you think entirely too much of your own worth. I'll just leave you to bask in the delusion of your own reflected glory."

She strode toward the doorway. "Not your mother, my ass! She doesn't even *cook!*"

He frowned at the bed, rubbed irritably at the tension lodged in the base of his neck. "Sure, that went well," he muttered. And winced as the door downstairs slammed hard enough to rattle his teeth.

Reece grabbed only what was closest at hand, then shoved it into her car. She'd worry about the rest of her things — not that there was much — later.

She'd get the ingredients she needed for the soup from Joanie's and from her own pantry. She'd get some change and haul her laundry — and *only* her laundry — to the crappy machines in the hotel's basement. It wasn't as if she hadn't done it before.

Or maybe she'd just say screw it all and take a drive, see if the flats were blooming.

She aimed the car toward town, frowning

at the way it handled. "What now, what now?" she muttered as the steering dragged. She gave the wheel one bad-tempered smack. Then, resigned, she detoured to Lynt's.

The garage doors were up with an aging compact up on the lift. Lynt came out from under it, a rangy forty in a chambray shirt with the sleeves rolled up to expose tough sinews. There was an oil-stained rag sticking out of his back pocket, a similarly stained gimme cap on his head and a chaw tucked into his cheek.

He pursed his lips, tipped back the bill of his cap as Reece stepped out of the car.

"Got yourself some trouble?"

"Seems like it." When she realized her teeth were clenched, she deliberately relaxed them. "The steering's funny, dragging."

"Not surprised, seeing as you got your two back tires next to flat."

"Flat?" She turned to look. "Damn it. They were fine yesterday."

"Could be you drove over something." He crouched down to take a look at the right rear tire. "Probably got a slow leak. See what I can do."

"I have a spare in the trunk." God, was she going to have to replace two tires?

"I'll get to it as soon as I finish these brake pads. You need a lift somewhere?"

"No. No. I could use the walk." She got

her laptop out of the backseat, then took her house keys off the keychain and stuffed them in her pocket. "If I have to get new tires, how much do you think?"

"Let's just worry about that when we have to worry about it." He took her car key. "I'll give you a call."

"Thanks." She hitched her purse on one shoulder, her laptop on the other.

It was a nice day for a walk, and she reminded herself of that in an attempt to chase depression away. She had a job and she had a roof over her head. And if she was in love with a jackass, she'd just have to start working on getting over it.

If she needed new tires, she'd walk until she could afford the damn rubber.

She didn't *have* to have a car right this minute. She didn't *have* to have a lover. She didn't have to have anything but herself. That had been the whole point of leaving Boston, leaving everything. She'd proved she could function, she could heal, she could build a new life.

And if Brody thought she was trying to drag him into that life with her, he was not only a jackass, he was a conceited one.

She needed some time by herself anyway to catch up on her journal. To get serious about writing that cookbook. Not that she was going to pass that through Brody now. Insulting son of a bitch. But she wanted to organize the recipes, take a more focused stab at writing an introduction to them.

Something like . . . *You don't have to be an expert chef to cook gourmet meals. Not when you have an expert guiding you.*

"And that sounds pompous and patronizing." *Tired of trying to come up with a new answer to "What's for dinner?" Desperate to find something exciting and fresh for that Sunday brunch? Panicked that the chair of that fund-raiser assigned you to make the canapés?*

"A little lame," Reece said aloud, "but you have to start somewhere."

"Hey! Hey!"

Reece jerked to a stop and saw Lindagail kneeling in her tiny front yard with marigolds and pansies tucked into a black plastic flat beside her.

"Too busy talking to yourself to talk to me?"

"Was I? I was going over something in my head. Too often it runs out of my mouth. They're so pretty. Your flowers."

"Should've put the pansies in before." She tipped the straw cowboy hat back on her head. "They don't mind the cold. But with one thing and another. What are you doing over this way?"

"Flat tire, or tires. I had to take the car to Lynt."

"Bummer. You're out early. I figured you'd be hanging at Brody's today."

"Clearly, he didn't. All I did was make the bed and offer to toss some of his laundry in with mine. You'd think I pulled a shotgun out of one pocket and a minister out of the other."

"Men suck. I booted Lo out the other night. He got surly when I wouldn't let him into my pants."

"Men suck."

"So, the hell with them. Want to plant some pansies and curse Y chromosomes?"

"I really would, but I have things I need to do this morning."

"Then we'll go to Clancy's after work tonight, drink a few beers and karaoke all the down-with-men songs on the menu."

Who needed a jackass when you had a girlfriend? "I can get behind that. I'll see you at work."

There, Reece thought as she walked toward home, she could add something else to her list of haves. She had Linda-gail Case.

Then there was the lake, she thought as her direction angled toward it. So blue and beautiful with the greening willows dipping down like dancers, the tender buds of cottonwood leaves unfurling.

On impulse she crossed to the water instead of continuing home. She set her bags down, pulled off her shoes and socks. She rolled up her pant legs. Sitting on the bank, she dangled her feet in the water.

Freezing! But she didn't give a damn. She was sitting with her feet in the blue waters of Angel Lake and her eyes on the towering rise of the Tetons. In a little while she'd be making soup, writing a cookbook, sorting laundry. And what could be more normal? She'd have to scramble around to get everything done so she wouldn't be late for work. And that was normal, too.

So for now, she'd just soak it all up.

She lay back so her eyes were on the sky now, blue as the lake with harmless white clouds drifting. The sun beamed down, but instead of digging her sunglasses out of her purse, she flung her arm over her eyes. And just listened.

To the lap of the water, the happy splash of it as she kicked her feet. Birdsong sounded so cheerful, so carefree. She heard a dog bark, the rumble of a car passing. Everything in her relaxed.

The sudden boom had her choking back most of a scream, jerking up so fast she nearly slid into the water. She managed to catch herself, crawl free, but only after she'd soaked one pant leg to the knee.

"Carl's truck. It's Carl's truck," she reminded herself as she huddled on the grass. She could see it, rumbling and rattling its way toward the mercantile. Pushing to her hands and knees, she stayed where she was, catching her breath.

And flushed when she saw Debbie Mardson standing outside On the Trail, watching her. "Yeah, it's the crazy woman," Reece said between her teeth as she forced herself to smile and wave. "Just taking a dip in a freezing lake with all her clothes on. No big deal."

Now that the moment was spoiled, she grabbed her bags, her shoes, and walked, wet and barefoot, home.

Didn't matter what the damn near-perfect-in-every-way Debbie Mardson thought, Reece assured herself. Or what anyone thought. She was entitled to sit and dangle her feet in the lake. She was entitled to jump like a rabbit at that damn shotgun blast of Carl's truck.

She stripped off her wet pants, put on dry ones. Just like she was entitled to do her laundry. She gathered it up, along with her detergent and some of the thin supply of singles she had left.

Start the wash, she thought, come back and start the soup. Go back and switch the wash to the dryer. Come back and work on the cookbook. She carried her little laundry basket out, started the walk to the hotel.

Because she had to pass On the Trail,

she kept her eyes trained forward and prayed, just this once, Debbie wouldn't spot her. She didn't run past the window, but she did significantly increase her pace, slowing only when she reached the hotel.

"Hi, Brenda. Wash day. Can I get some change?"

"Sure, no problem." Brenda smiled widely and lifted her eyebrows. "Need some shoes while you're at it?"

"Sorry?"

"You're not wearing your shoes, Reece."

"Oh. Oh *God*." Reece looked down at her bare feet. She flushed, but when she looked back up at Brenda there was just enough of a smirk on the desk clerk's face to turn embarrassment to temper. "I guess they slipped my mind. You know how slippery my mind is. Quarters, please." She slapped the bills on the counter.

Brenda counted them out. "Watch where you step now."

"I'll do that." Because the elevator wasn't an option for her, Reece took the stairs down. She hated the damn hotel basement. Hated it. If Brody hadn't been such a dick, she could've used his machines, could've avoided all this stupidity and bother.

"Seven times one is seven," she began as she wound her way past the maintenance area. "Seven times two is fourteen."

She made it through the sevens, into the eights, then rushed out of the laundry area as the machine hummed.

She slowed to a normal pace as she stepped back into the lobby, sent Brenda an easy wave. She wasn't quite as lucky on her way back by the outfitter store.

"Reece." Debbie slipped out the door. "You okay?"

"Sure, fine. How are you?"

"It's a little cool yet for bare feet."

"You think? I'm just toughening mine up. I hope to be the first woman to walk barefoot along the Continental Divide. Lifelong dream of mine. See you."

Go ahead, spread that one around, Reece thought as she hiked back home.

She put it all out of her mind by starting her stock, making meatballs for the soup. She actually debated leaving her shoes off, to give the gossips more to talk about, but decided it was too silly and self-defeating. She zipped back to the hotel, braved Brenda and the basement again to transfer her clothes from washer to dryer.

Only one more trip, she reminded herself, dashing back home again. And plenty of time to draft the introduction to the cookbook while her clothes tumbled dry.

After setting up her laptop, she warmed up her writing muscles with an update to her journal.

Pissed at Brody. Make up a bed and he thinks I'm shopping for wedding rings. Is that the way the male mind really works? If so, they need serious therapy as a species.

I suppose, when it comes down to it, I've just worn out my welcome there. He's done more than anyone could expect where I'm concerned. So I'll try to be grateful as well as pissed, and stay out of his way.

The dick.

Meanwhile, I've cemented my status as the town loony by having a perfectly justified absentminded moment and going shoeless to the hotel to do laundry. I'm trying not to care about it. I'm making soup, and I only checked the locks on the door once.

Damn it, twice.

I may have to buy two new tires. God, that's so depressing. What would once have been a minor irritation is a huge problem under my current circumstances. I don't have the money. It's as simple as that. I guess I'll be walking for the next few weeks.

Maybe a miracle will happen and I'll actually write and sell this cookbook. I could use an infusion of cash, just as a buffer against whatever wolf might show up at the door.

Linda-gail's planting pansies. We're going to Clancy's after work tonight to trash men. I think it's just what I need.

Satisfied, Reece opened a fresh document and began to toy with different styles and approaches for an introduction.

When her kitchen timer went off, signaling her clothes were finished, she backed up, shut down and headed out one more time.

She'd just dump everything in the basket and get the hell out of that spooky basement, she decided. Fold them at home. She could leave the soup on low simmer while she worked at Joanie's, and run up on her breaks to check on it.

She hoped they were busy tonight. Busy was just what she needed.

She zipped through the lobby, spared any conversation since Brenda wasn't at the front desk. Reece could just hear the murmur of her voice from the back.

Small favors, she thought. Something else to be grateful for.

Reece tried the twelve times tables this time — a tough one — as she hurried downstairs and through to the laundry area.

She pulled open the dryer door and found nothing.

"Well, that's . . ." She opened the other

dryer, thinking she'd mixed up which one she used. But it was empty.

"That's ridiculous. No one would come down here and steal my clothes."

And why was her basket on top of the washer instead of on the little folding table where she knew, she *knew* she'd left it? Gingerly, she picked it up, then slowly opened the washer's lid.

Her clothes were there, wet and spun.

"I put them in the dryer." She dug an unsteady hand in her pocket, found only the single coin she had left after plugging change into the machines. "I put them in the dryer. This is my third trip. My third. I didn't leave them in the washer."

She tugged them out, furiously pulling wet clothes free to heave them into the basket. A Magic Marker fell with a rattle to the floor.

A red marker. Her red marker. Shaking now, Reece tossed it in the basket, with the clothes she now saw were spotted and stained with the red.

Someone had done this to her, someone who wanted her to think she was losing it.

Someone who could be down there, watching her.

Her breath wheezed out as her head swiveled right and left. She bit off a moan, grabbed the basket and ran. The sudden clang of a pipe had her jumping, choking out a half scream. The slap and echo of her own shoes on the cement floor sent her heart shoving up to the base of her throat.

This time she didn't stop running when she reached the lobby but sprinted to the desk. Back at her post, a surprised Brenda gaped at her.

"Somebody's down there. Somebody went down there."

"What? Who? Are you okay?"

"My clothes. They put my clothes in the washing machine."

"But . . . Reece, you put them in the machine." Brenda spoke slowly, as to a slow-witted child. "Remember? You went down to wash clothes."

"After! I put them in the dryer, but they were back in the washer. You saw me come back to put them in the dryer."

"Well . . . sure, I saw you come back, go down. Maybe you forgot to put them in. You know, like you forgot your shoes before. I'm always doing things like that," Brenda added, without the smirk now. "Just, you know, getting distracted and forgetting —"

"I didn't forget. I put them in. Look." She dug out the single quarter. "That's all I have left because I used the rest to wash *and* dry my damn clothes. Who went down there?"

"Look, just calm down. I didn't see anyone go down but you."

"Maybe you went down."

"Jesus, Reece." Genuine shock blew across Brenda's face. "Why would I do something like that? You need to get ahold of yourself. If you need more quarters, I can —"

"I don't need anything."

Rage and panic pounded through her, shortened her breath as she rushed out and jogged down the street with her basket of wet clothes.

Get home, was all she could think. Get inside. Lock the door.

At the beep of a horn, she stumbled, and whirled around, lifting the basket like a shield. She watched her own car slide into its habitual place near her steps. Lynt got out.

"Didn't mean to startle you."

She managed a nod. Why was he watching her that way, like she was some alien species? Why did people look at her that way?

"Ah, tires look fine. They were just low. Real low. I put air in them for you."

"Oh. Thanks. Thank you."

"And, ah, since I was at it, I was going to check your spare for you. But . . ."

She moistened her stiff lips. "Is there something wrong with the spare?"

"The thing is . . ." He pulled on the brim of his hat, shifted his feet. "It's kind of buried in there."

"I don't know what you mean." She made herself set the basket on the steps, cross over. "I don't have anything but emergency gear in there."

When he hesitated, she took the key from him, popped the trunk.

The smell came first. Garbage just going over. The trunk was full of it — eggshells, coffee grounds, wet, stained papers, empty cans. As if someone had dumped a full can of waste into it.

"I wasn't sure what you wanted me to do."

"I didn't do this." She took a step back, then another. "I didn't do this. Did you?"

That same sudden shock that had run across Brenda's face ran across Lynt's. " 'Course not, Reece. I found it like this."

"Somebody *did* this. I didn't do this. Someone's doing this to me. Someone —"

"I don't like shouting outside my place." Joanie came out the back, down the side of the building. "What's going on here? Well, for chrissake, what's all this?" She wrinkled her nose as she peered into the trunk.

"I didn't do this," Reece began.

"Well, I sure as hell didn't. Went to get her spare," Lynt said. "Found this. She's

got some crazy idea I dumped all this garbage in here."

"She's just upset. Shit, Lynt, wouldn't
you be if you had this happen? Kids,"
Joanie said mildly. "Bunch of asinine kids
most likely. Lynt, I got some cans around
back, some rubber gloves in the backroom.
Give me a hand cleaning this out."

"I'll do it." The words jerked out of
Reece's raw throat. "I'm sorry, Lynt. I just
don't understand —"

"Go upstairs," Joanie ordered Reece.
"Go on. Lynt and Pete can deal with this.
I'll be up in a minute. Don't argue with
me," she added when Reece started to protest.

"I'm sorry." Tired now, Reece dragged
up the basket. "I'm sorry. I'll get your
money."

"No charge." Lynt waved it away. "It
was nothing but air."

Joanie gave Lynt's arm a pat as Reece
went up the steps. "Go on back, will you,
tell Pete to give you a hand with this. Got
your next meal on the house."

"How'd kids get the trunk open, Joanie?
I can tell you it hasn't been forced."

"God knows how kids do anything. Or
why," she said before Lynt could voice the
question. "But the fact is that trunk's full
of stink and garbage. You and Pete take
care of that."

When Joanie went inside the apartment, Reece was sitting on the side of the daybed, the basket of wet laundry at her feet.

"Soup smells good." Joanie stepped over, frowned at the basket. "Those clothes'll mildew you don't at least hang them up. Why didn't you use the dryer?"

"I thought I did. I know I did. But they were in the washer."

"What the hell's all over them?"

"Ink. Red ink. Someone put my red marker in the machine with them."

Joanie puffed up her cheeks. She went over, got a saucer out of Reece's cupboard. She lit up a cigarette when she came back, sat on the bed beside Reece.

"I'm going to have a cigarette, and you're going to tell me what's going on."

"I don't know what's going on. But I know I put those clothes in the dryer, I put in the money, I pressed the button. But they were in the washer, wet, when I went back for them. I know I didn't put that garbage in the trunk of my car, but it's there. I didn't write all over the bathroom."

"My bathroom?" Joanie popped up, went to have a look. "I don't see anything written in here."

"Brody painted over it. I didn't put my hiking boots in the kitchen cupboard or my

507

flashlight in the refrigerator. I didn't do those things, but they happened all the same."

"Look at me. Look me in the face here." When Reece did, Joanie studied her face, her eyes. "Have you been taking drugs? Doctor-prescribed or otherwise?"

"No, nothing but the herb tea Doc made up for me. And Tylenol. But all my security blanket meds ended up poured into my mortar."

"Why would anyone do that? Or any of the rest?"

"To make me think I'm crazy. To make me crazy, which doesn't take much of a push. Because I saw what I saw, but it's easy to dismiss a crazy woman."

"They found a body —"

"Wasn't her," Reece interrupted, and her voice began to rise and pitch. "Wasn't the same. It wasn't her, and —"

"Stop that." Joanie's voice snapped out like a slap. "I'm not talking to you unless you calm down."

"You try it, you try to be calm when someone's doing things to you. You stay rational when you just don't know what might happen next. Or when. My clothes are ruined. I barely had enough left till payday to wash them; now they're ruined."

"You can run a tab at Mac's, or I'll give

you an advance if you need to replace some things."

"That's not the point."

"Nope. But it's better than a stick in the eye. How long has this been going on?"

"Little things since . . . almost since I got back from seeing that woman killed. I don't know what to do."

"You ought to be talking to the sheriff."

"Why?" Reece dragged her hands through her hair, just fisted them in it. "You think that pile of garbage in my trunk has fingerprints on it?"

"All the same, Reece."

"Yes." On a sigh, she lowered her hands to scrub them over her face. "Yes, I'll tell the sheriff."

"Fine. For right now, you'd better go through those clothes, see what you can salvage and hang them up to dry. You need a new shirt or underwear, you can get it at Mac's on your break. You've got about five minutes before your shift."

Joanie stubbed out the cigarette. She rose and dug a twenty out of her pocket. "For painting the bathroom."

"I didn't. Brody did."

"Then give it to Brody, you want to be a dumbass."

Pride warred with practicality, and practicality had more muscle. "Thanks."

"Brody knows about all this?"

"Yes, except for what happened today, yes."

"Do you want to call him before you come down to work?"

"No. I seem to be getting in his way."

Joanie snorted. "Men have their uses, but unless you're under one having an orgasm, it's hard to see what else they've got to offer. Pull yourself together and come on down. Prime rib's the special tonight."

Reece stirred herself, poked at the basket with her foot. "Prime rib of what?"

"Buffalo," Joanie said with a thin smile. "Maybe you got a way to fancy that up."

"As a matter of fact . . ."

"Then get your ass down there and do it. I've only got two hands."

Brody considered tossing a frozen pizza in the oven and thought of chicken and dumplings.

She'd done that on purpose, he decided. Thrown that at him so he wouldn't be able to think of anything but her — of it, he corrected.

He'd just wanted her to back up. Isn't that exactly what he'd said? But she overreacted, as women always did.

A man was entitled to a little breathing room in his own house, wasn't he? A little solitude without a woman fussing all around him.

He was entitled to frozen pizza if he wanted it. It just so happened he didn't. He wanted a good, hot meal. And he knew where to get one.

He'd eaten at Angel Food before she came along, Brody thought as he went out to his car. He wasn't headed there because she was there. That was just circumstance. And if she wanted to keep her nose up in the air, that was her business. All he wanted was a decent meal at a reasonable price.

But when he pulled up at Joanie's, Joanie herself came out.

"I was just coming over to see you," she said.

"About what? Reece is —"

"Yeah, Reece is." And in that instant concern, she saw what she'd expected. The guy was gone. "Take a walk with me. I got ten minutes."

She told him quickly, overriding his interruptions, rolling over his temper. "Said she'd call the sheriff, but she hasn't. Not yet. Handles herself once she gets her balance back. That was a nasty bit of business, that garbage in her trunk. I don't like nasty."

"It's all been nasty. I need to talk to her now."

"She can have ten, if she wants to take it. Go around to the back. I don't want the two of you spitting at each other over my counter."

He did as Joanie suggested, then brushed right by Pete and took Reece's arm. "Outside."

"I'm busy."

"It'll wait." He hauled her straight out the door.

"Just a damn minute. I'm working. Nobody comes in and pulls on you when *you're* working. If you have something to say to me, you can say it when I've finished."

"Why the hell didn't you call me when all this crap happened today?"

"As usual, word travels," she said sourly. "And I didn't feel like calling you. If you're here to ride to the rescue, keep right on riding. I don't need a hero. I need to do my job."

"I'll wait until you're finished and drive you back. We'll go see Rick in the morning."

"I don't want anyone waiting for me, and when I'm finished I have plans."

"What plans?"

"Ones that don't concern you. I don't need you to go to the sheriff with me. I don't need a babysitter or a white knight or pity any more than you need me to make your bed and do your laundry. And it's not time for my break."

When she turned toward the door, he took her arm, pulled her around again. "Goddamn it, Reece." He sighed, gave up. "Goddamn it," he said quietly now. "Come home."

She stared at him, then she shut her eyes. "That was a sneaky punch." And it took her breath away. "I think we both better take a little time thinking about that. I think we'd both better be sure just what that means, and if it's what we both want. Maybe we'll talk tomorrow."

"I'll sleep in my office, or down on the couch."

"I'm not coming to your place so you can protect me. If it turns out it's more than that, we'll see what happens. You'd better figure it out before we talk again."

She left him, baffled and edgy, to go back to the grill.

22

One beer, Reece thought. If a woman couldn't afford to buy herself one beer, what was the point of holding down a job, and working at it so that the small of her back quietly wept at the end of a long day?

Clancy's was hopping with locals mixing and mingling with the tourists who'd sprinkled into the area to fish or float, to hike or horseback ride. The long, tall Reuben had the mike and was doing a soulful version of Keith Urban's "You'll Think of Me." A group of cowboys had flirted a couple of town girls into a game of pool, so the balls cracked amid a thin sexual haze. Two couples from back East were hoisting drinks and snapping pictures of themselves against the backdrop of elk and sheep's heads.

At the bar, his boot propped on the rail, Lo brooded into his bottle of Big Horn.

"He looks like he's suffering."

At Reece's comment, Linda-gail shrugged. "Not enough. This time around, he's going to have to come my way, hat in hand. I can wait." She popped one of the pretzels out of the black plastic bowl on the table, crunched down hard. "I've been hung up on that stupid cowboy most of my life, and I've given him enough time, enough space to finish riding the damn range."

"Nice metaphor," Reece told her.

But Linda-gail wasn't in the mood to take a compliment. "I figured Lo carried around more wild oats than most, so fine, let him sow them, get all that business out of his system. Man like him, women are always going to jump when he crooks a finger."

Reece raised a hand. "I didn't."

"Yeah, but you're crazy."

"True. I guess that explains it."

"But I'm ready to start building the rest of my life now." With her eyes narrowed at Lo's back, Linda-gail crunched another pretzel. "He either catches up, or he doesn't."

Reece considered it. "Men are assholes."

"Oh well, 'course they are. But I just don't like women in the same way. So I'm going to need one to get things going."

"What sort of things?"

Propping her elbow on the table, Linda-gail rested her chin in her palm. "I want to buy my house from Joanie. She'd sell it to me if I asked her to. And when she's ready to take a step back, I want to manage Angel Food."

Unsurprised, Reece nodded. "You'd be good at it."

"You're damn right I would. And I want a pair of silver candlesticks to put on the dining room table. Nice ones that I can pass down to a daughter. I want a daughter, especially, but I'd like it best if I could have one of each. A boy and a girl. I want a man who'll work beside me for that, and who looks at me like I'm the reason. I want to hear him scrape his boots outside the door at night when supper's cooking. And every once in a while, just now and then, I want him to bring me flowers when he comes home."

"That's nice."

"And I want him to be a damn conquistador in bed, and make me deaf, dumb and blind on a fairly regular basis."

"Excellent goals, every one. Lo's up for that?"

"The sex part, I'm pretty sure of, though I've only had the previews and not the whole show." She grinned, a little fiercely, as she popped another pretzel. "The rest? He's got the potential. But if he wants to waste it, I can't stop him. Want another beer?"

"No, I'm fine."

Linda-gail signaled for one as the two women from back East took over the stage with an energetic version of "I Feel Like a Woman." "What about you? What are your excellent goals?"

"They used to be to run the best kitchen in the best restaurant in Boston. To be listed as one of the top ten — better, in the top five — chefs in the country. I had the idea for marriage and children somewhere in the back of my mind. I thought there would be plenty of time for that. Eventually. Then after I was hurt, I just wanted to get through the moment. Then the next hour, then the next day."

"Nobody knows what that's like unless they've been there," Linda-gail said after a moment. "But I think it's the smartest thing to do. You have to get through to go on."

"Now I want my place. To do a good day's work, and be able to have a drink with a friend."

"And Brody?"

"I can't imagine not wanting him. He came back into the kitchen tonight, dragged me out the back."

"What? What?" Linda-gail set down her fresh beer so quickly, foam sloshed over the rim to dribble down the sides. "How did I miss this? What happened?"

"He wanted me to go back home with him."

"And you're here nursing a beer and listening to bad — and I do mean bad right at this particular moment — karaoke because?"

Reece's jaw set. "I'm not going back until I know he wants me. Not that he wants to protect me. I'm going to get a dog," she said with a scowl.

"I'm lost."

"If I only want protection, I'll get a damn dog. I want a lover on equal terms. And if I'm going to be in that cabin with him, I don't want to feel like a guest. He's never even offered to give me a drawer in his dresser."

Pouting now, Linda-gail propped her chin back on her hand. "Men suck."

"They do, entirely. I'm so pissed off that I'm in love with him."

With a mournful look, Linda-gail tapped her glass to Reece's. "Right there with you."

Then she glanced toward the bar and noted that Lo was telling his troubles to one of the waitresses. One of the women she *knew* he'd bounced on at one time or another.

"Let's dance."

Reece blinked. "What?"

"Let's go over, see if a couple of those fly-fishing types want to take a turn on the dance floor."

The dance floor consisted of a stingy strip of wood in front of the stage. And the fly-fishing types were rowdy and half-lit. "I don't think so."

"Well, I'm going over and pick me one out of the pack." She shoved back. She dug in her purse first, pulled out a tube of lipstick. She painted her lips perfectly — a bold, kick-ass red — without the benefit of a mirror. "How do I look."

"A little dangerous just now. You ought to —"

"That's perfect." Shaking her hair back, Linda-gail glided over, making sure she moved into Lo's line of sight. Then she braced her palms on the table where the three men sat, leaned over.

Reece couldn't hear what was being said. She didn't have to. The men were grinning; Lo looked murderous.

Just a bad idea, Reece thought. Those kind of games were always a bad idea. But Linda-gail was sauntering hand in hand with one of the men while his companions whistled and cheered. She led him to the strip of floor, put her hands on his shoulders. And led with her hips.

At the table, the two left behind whooped. One of them shouted: "Go for it, Chuck!"

And Chuck planted his hands on Linda-gail's ass.

Even with the distance, even through the blue haze of smoke, Reece saw Lo's knuckles go white on the long neck of his beer.

Seriously bad idea, Reece decided. Her conclusion was confirmed when Lo slapped the bottle back on the bar and strode onto the dance floor.

She could hear bits. "It's my ass, you jerk," from Linda-gail. "Mind your own business, buddy," from Chuck.

The two women who'd moved from Shania Twain to a slurred version of "Stand by Your Man" stopped singing and watched in bleary fascination.

Chuck shoved Lo; Lo shoved Chuck. Linda-gail put her full hundred and twenty pounds into it and shoved them both.

Any hopes that would be the end of it shattered when Reece saw Chuck's friends push up from the table.

The small herd of cowboys playing pool stepped forward. Lo was, after all, one of their own.

She was going to be in the middle of a bar fight, Reece thought with full amazement. About to be caught in a melee in a karaoke bar in Wyoming.

Unless she managed to grab Linda-gail and run.

She glanced around quickly to check the direction and distance to the exit.

And saw, moving through the noisy, surged-to-its-feet crowd, a man wearing an orange hunter's cap.

Her breath hitched and tore. She lurched

up, knocking her half-full beer to the floor, where the glass shattered with a sound like a gunshot. She stumbled, shoving into one of the cowboys as she tried to get clear, and sent him bumping hard into one of the fishermen.

Fists flew. Onstage, the women screamed and clutched at each other. Bodies thudded against, or in some cases actually leaped onto, table and bar. Glassware, bottles crashed and shattered, wood splintered. She swore she heard someone yell "Yee haw!" before an elbow caught her along the cheekbone and sent her sprawling onto the floor and into spilled beer.

Reeking of beer and smoke, holding an ice pack to her throbbing cheek, Reece sat in the sheriff's office. If she'd been more humiliated in her life, her brain wouldn't allow the previous incident to surface.

"Last thing I expected from you was to pull you in here out of a bar fight."

"It wasn't in my plans for the evening. It just happened. And I wasn't fighting."

"You pushed Jud Horst into one Robert Gavin, inciting the incident. You threw your beer."

"No, I didn't! I knocked my beer over when I tried to get up from the table, and I slipped into Jud. It was an accident."

"You were drinking," Rick continued.

"A half a beer. For God's sake. I was in a bar, of course I was drinking. So was everyone else. And I wasn't drunk. I panicked, okay. Fine. I panicked. I saw . . ."

"You saw?"

"I saw a man in an orange hat in the back of the crowd."

Rick's weary, annoyed expression sharpened. "You saw the man you previously saw by the river?"

"I don't know. I couldn't see that well. It all happened so fast. I got up. I wanted to get away. I wanted to see him better."

"Which was it?"

"Both," she snapped. "I was scared. I knocked the beer over. I slipped. That's all."

He let out a windy sigh. He'd been pulled out of bed by a screaming call from one of Clancy's waitresses. He'd barely closed his eyes when he had to get up and dressed again, and go down to clean up the mess in the bar.

Now he had property damage, bodily injuries, possible civil and criminal charges to wade through.

"Min Hobalt claims you struck her. I got another statement here that says you shoved over a table, causing a beer mug to land on the foot of a Ms. Lee Shanks from San Diego. I've got a tourist with a broken toe."

"I didn't hit anyone." Had she? "Not on purpose. I was trying to get clear. I got jabbed in the face, I was seeing stars. I was scared. I *fell* into a table, which is a hell of a lot different than shoving one over. *I* got hit in the face," she continued. "*I've* got bruises over most of my body."

He puffed out a breath. "Who swung first?"

"I don't know. The guy they called Chuck gave Lo a little shove; Lo gave him one back. Then I saw . . . I saw the hat."

"You saw the hat."

"I know how ridiculous that sounds. And yes, yes, I know a lot of men around here wear those damn hats. But I was jumpy because I could see a fight coming, then I saw the hat, and I freaked out a little. Big surprise."

"Clancy said he was moving in to break it up when that glass hit the floor. Says it was like the bell going off in the boxing ring. And when that cowboy bumped the tourist, that's all it took."

"So it's my fault," Reece said evenly. "Fine. Charge me with inciting a riot, or whatever you want. Just give me some goddamn aspirin before you lock the cell."

"Nobody's going to lock you up. Chrissake." Rick rubbed his face, pinched the bridge of his nose. "The thing is, you've got a habit of stirring things up.

You had some trouble down at the hotel laundry today?"

"I . . ." Of course he knew about it. Brenda was tight as spandex with Debbie, the sheriff's wife. Reece imagined she'd been the hot topic of conversation around the Mardson dinner table that night.

"That was different. Someone played a joke on me. I didn't think it was funny." While he waited, brows lifted, for her to explain, Reece contemplated the wisdom of telling him the truth.

And the truth, she decided, would sound, at the moment, like nonsense. "It was nothing. It doesn't matter. Do you interrogate everyone who has words with the hotel's desk clerk, or is it just me?"

His face hardened. "I've got a job to do, Reece. You don't have to like how I do it. Now I've got to sort through this mess. I may need to talk to you again tomorrow."

"Then I'm free to go?"

"You are. You want Doc to look at that cheek?"

"No." She got to her feet. "I didn't start what happened tonight, and I didn't finish it. I just got caught in it." She turned for the door.

"You've got a habit of getting caught in things. And, Reece, if you jump and swing every time you see orange, we're going to have a problem."

She just kept going. She wanted to go home where she could burn off her anger and humiliation in private.

But first, she noted, she'd have to get through Brody.

Since he was sitting in one of the visitors' chairs in the outer office, legs stretched out, eyes half closed, she tried to simply go around him.

"Hold on there, Slim." He got lazily to his feet. "Let's have a look at that face."

"Nothing to see."

He got to the door first, closed his hand around the handle, then just leaned on it. "You smell like the barroom floor."

"I spent some time on it tonight. Will you excuse me?"

He opened the door, then curled his fingers around her arm the minute they were outside. "Let's not go through the ridiculous routine about you walking home alone. It's late, I'm driving."

Since most of her body ached, including the knee she must have fallen on during the scuffle, she didn't bother to argue. "Fine. What are you doing here?"

"Linda-gail called me in case you needed somebody to post bail." He pulled open the passenger-side door. "You sure keep life interesting."

"I didn't *do* anything."

"You stick with that."

She stewed until he'd skirted the hood and climbed behind the wheel. "You think this is funny?"

"It has several of the classic elements necessary for farce. Yeah, I think it's funny. The only other woman I've ever had to spring from the cops was a stripper I knew back in Chicago who beaned a guy with a beer bottle when he got a little overenthusiastic during a lap dance at a bachelor's party. She was a lot more grateful than you."

"Linda-gail's the one who called you, not me." Reece folded her arms, and wished desperately for ice and aspirin. "And it's her fault anyway. None of this would've happened if she hadn't gotten a wild hair to make Lo jealous."

"Why'd she do that?"

"Because she's in love with him."

"She's in love with Lo, so she incited a bar fight. Makes perfect sense." In the Bizarro World women lived in. "Okay, Slim, your place or mine?"

"Mine. You can drop me off and consider your Good Samaritan duties at an end."

He started to drive, tapping his fingers against the steering wheel. "Do you want to know why I got out of bed and came to get you when Linda-gail called?"

Reece closed her eyes. "Because you

have a need to play savior for strippers and lunatics."

"Maybe. Maybe I care about you."

"Maybe you do. Let me know when you decide."

"Damn it, you know I care about you. Why else would I have been lying awake in bed cursing you when your partner in crime called?"

"I couldn't say."

"I think about you. It gets in my way." Resentment rippled in his voice. "You get in my way."

"As this is the second time you've popped up in front of me tonight, I'd say you're getting in my way." She stirred enough to shift in her seat when he pulled up behind her car. "You wanted me out of your house. I left. You wanted me to back up, back off, I did. Your whim changes, Brody, that's not my problem."

"Hard-ass," he retaliated. "I felt squeezed this morning. You start off with Italian wedding soup, for God's sake."

"What's wrong with Italian wedding soup? It was one of my specialties when . . . Oh, you idiot. Wedding? You shudder in fear of the word?"

He very nearly squirmed. "Nobody's shuddering."

"I'm going to make soup and you get it

into your pinhead that I'm picking out the china? Jerk."

She started to yank the door handle, but he leaned over her, clamped his hand on hers. He preferred being pissed off to squirming. "Making the bed, offering to do my laundry. What do I want for breakfast."

She put her free hand on his chest, shoved. "I slept in the bed, so I made it. You let me stay at your place when I needed a sanctuary, and I was doing laundry anyway. I thought I could pay you back a little by doing some of the house-work. I like to cook for you. I like to cook period. That's all it was."

"You said you loved me."

"I did. I didn't ask you to love me back. I didn't write off for my subscription to *Brides* magazine. I never even asked you to clean out a drawer so I had somewhere to put my things. I never asked you for anything but companionship."

It was hell being absolutely wrong. "Okay, so I overreacted —"

"So you said before. I'm tired, Brody. If you want to hash this through, it'll have to be some other time. I want to go to bed."

"Wait. Damn it." He sat back, raking his fingers through his hair, his expression both pained and frustrated. "I was out of line this morning. I'm sorry."

She said nothing for a moment. "Ow. I

bet that hurt you as much as my face hurts me."

"Maybe more. Don't make me repeat it."

"Once does the job." She touched his arm, then reached for the door again.

"Will you wait? Jesus. Listen."

At the ensuing silence, she studied his face. "I'm listening."

"Okay. Before you said you didn't want me to take care of you. That's fine. The thought of wanting to take care of you is scaring the hell out of me. But I want to be with you. There's no one else I want to be with. Can we get back to that?"

She pushed open her door, then stopped. Looked at him. Life was so terrifyingly short. Who knew that better than she did? "That's all I was looking for. Do you want to come up?"

"Yeah." He waited while she walked around the car, then held his hand out for hers. "Come here a minute." Leaning down, he brushed his lips gently over her bruised cheek. "Ouch."

"You can say that again. You ought to know I'm not going to be very good company. All I want is a hot bath, a bottle of aspirin and a soft bed."

"You don't have a soft bed."

"I'll compensate." She unlocked the door. "I feel like I've been in a soccer match. As the ball."

As she opened the door, he pulled her back, shifted his body in front of hers.

"What's that sound?" she demanded. "Do you hear? It sounds like water running."

"Stay right here."

Of course she couldn't, and eased in behind him when he stepped in, started across the room. "In the bathroom," she whispered. "The door's closed. I never close the door because I need to be able to see inside the room when I come in. There's water running. Oh God, it's flooded; it's coming under the door."

He shoved the door open so more water sloshed out. Inside, the tub overflowed as the water running from the faucet poured into it. The few things she'd deemed usable after the incident in the laundry floated like flotsam.

"I didn't leave it on. I didn't even turn it on. I just ran up here . . ."

Saying nothing, he sloshed through the floor to wrench the faucet off. Shoving up a sleeve, Brody reached down and pulled the plug.

"I hung those things over the shower rod before I went down to work. After work, I ran up here to change my shoes. That's all I did before I went out with Linda-gail."

"I'm not saying different."

"The floor's going to be ruined. I have

to get something to . . . Oh God, Joanie's. Downstairs. It'll have leaked through the floor and down into the diner."

"Go call her. Tell her she needs to come over here, bring the keys for the diner."

She came with the keys, and a Shop-Vac. Her eyes grim, she pushed the vac at Reece. "Go up, suck up that water. When you're done, bring it down here."

"Joanie, I'm so sorry —"

"Just be quiet and do what I told you."

Joanie unlocked the door, stepped in, flipped on the lights.

Water dripped and streamed through the ceiling of the north corner. The drywall had buckled under the weight and split like bad fruit. Below it two booths were soaked.

"Son of a bitching bastard."

"She's not responsible," Brody began, but Joanie only jabbed a finger toward him, her eyes on the damage.

"I'm going to need some fans in here, dry things out. Some plastic to put up over that fucking hole in the fucking ceiling before the fucking health inspector shuts me down because of it. You want to be helpful, go back there and drag out that big standing fan I've got in the storeroom. Then you can go back to my place. I got a roll of plastic out in my shed. A staple gun."

Brody glanced at the ceiling. "Stepladder."

"That, too. Son of a bitching bastard."

Reece wept as she worked. It wasn't only herself being hurt now, but the woman whose only crimes had been giving her a job, renting her an apartment, standing up for her.

Now it was all a mess. Ruined floor, ruined ceiling and God only knew what else was ruined.

She emptied the tank of the vacuum, started it again.

She glanced up miserably when Joanie came through the door.

"All crying's going to do is make more water to suck up."

Reece knuckled tears away. "How bad is it?"

"Bad enough. Fixable."

"I'll pay —"

"I got insurance, don't I? Sons of bitches ought to shell out a claim after they skin me for premiums every blessed month."

Reece stared at the floor as she worked. "I know how this looks, and you couldn't possibly be in the mood for excuses. But I didn't leave the water on in the tub. I didn't even —"

"I know damn well you didn't."

Reece jerked her head up. "You do?"

"You never forget a goddamn thing.

Didn't I just have to use my key to open that stupid door? You said somebody's been screwing with you. Now they're screwing with me. And I am *pissed.* But the point is now we fix what has to be fixed, then we figure out the rest." She planted her hands on her hips. "That floor's going to have to come up. You got a problem staying over at Brody's?"

"No."

"Then finish up in here, pack up your things. I'm going to get a couple of boys working on this first thing in the morning." She kicked the desk, then took her first good look at Reece's face. "Where'd you get that cheek?"

"There was a sort of fight at Clancy's."

"Oh, Christ on a crutch. If it's not one thing, it's two. Get a bag of frozen peas out of the freezer below before you leave."

"It's just until I can move back in over the diner."

It was after three when Reece stowed the last of her things in the back of Brody's car.

"Uh–huh."

"Just a few days." Burned out, sick at seeing the damage down at Joanie's, Reece climbed into the car. "I won't offer to do your laundry. I'm not having a lot of luck in that area anyway."

"Okay."

533

"She believed me. I didn't even have to try to explain."

"Joanie's a smart woman. She sees through most bullshit."

"Whoever this is, he didn't have to do this to her. He didn't have to bring her into it." She looked out the window as he drove, at the dark surface of the lake. Her life felt like that tonight. Too dark to see what lay under it.

"If she blamed you for it, she'd have fired you, kicked you out. Odds were you'd leave town. Knocking your paycheck and living quarters out from under you. It's a smart move."

"I'm glad I'm not being stalked by a dummy. Following that logic, which I agree with, you'd be the next on his list. I'm not exactly anyone's good luck charm, Brody."

"I don't believe in luck." He pulled up at his cabin.

From the back of the car he took the hefty box of her kitchen tools, slid the strap of her laptop case over his shoulder. He left the second box and the duffel for her.

Inside, he set the box on the floor. "I'm not putting this stuff away." He took the other box from her, set it down. "Go on up and take a shower."

"I think a bath." She managed a smile,

sniffed the back of her own hand. "Pretty bad."

"Not if you like stale beer and smoke." He took the frozen peas out of the lighter box, tossed them to her. "Use this."

She went up, ran the tub hot. Sinking into it, she pressed the cold bag on her throbbing cheek. Then scooted straight up when Brody walked in.

"Aspirin," he said. He set the bottle, a glass of water on the lip of the tub, then walked out.

When she came out wearing a baggy gray T-shirt with red stains and a pair of loose flannel pants, he was standing by the window. He turned, cocked his head.

"Nice outfit."

"I don't have a lot left."

"Well. You can put what you do have left in there." He jerked a thumb at his dresser. "I cleaned out a couple drawers."

"Oh."

"It's not a marriage proposal."

"Check. I'll, ah, do it tomorrow. I'm really tired. I'm sorry, Brody, but did you —"

"Yes. The doors are locked."

"Okay." She slipped into bed and sighed at the sheer relief it gave her.

Moments later, the lights switched off, the mattress dipped. Then his body was warm against hers, and his arm draped around her waist.

She took his hand. She fell asleep with her fingers linked with his, too exhausted to dream.

23

Brody drove Reece to Joanie's at six sharp. The lights were on in the diner, a hard shine against the dark. A pickup truck sat at the curb along with a vile green dumpster, top up, already half loaded with drywall and debris.

The sight of it had Reece's shoulders going tight as she walked by. "How much do you think this is going to cost?"

"I haven't got a clue." Brody shrugged. "My manliness doesn't extend into this area."

Insurance was all well and good, Reece thought. But what about the deductible? She walked inside to see Joanie, hands on hips, frowning up at a curtain of plastic. She wore the work boots Reece had seen in the mudroom the first time they baked together, rough brown trousers and a tan western-style shirt with one of the breast pockets bulging a bit with what was, surely, her always handy pack of Marlboro Lights.

Behind the plastic, Reece could see a couple of men on stepladders.

The place smelled of coffee and wet. The big fan continued to whirl, chilling the air.

"You're not on until eleven today," Joanie said without looking around.

"I'm working off my part of this. Argue," Reece added, "and I'll just quit, move to Jackson Hole and get a job there. You'll not only be shy a couple of booths but a cook."

Joanie stayed just as she was. "These boys've been at this an hour already. Go on back and rustle them up a couple of cattleman's breakfasts."

"How do they want their eggs?"

"Fry 'em. Sunny side."

Brody stepped up to Joanie as Reece headed back. "Did you get any sleep?"

"I can sleep when I'm dead. Are you just here to chauffeur her around and send her smoldering looks, or are you apt to be useful?"

"I can multitask."

"Then go on in there, see what Reuben and Joe can use you for. We'll have customers coming in before long. Reece, make that three cattleman's."

Reece served them herself, at the counter, as Joanie had Bebe hauling in tables to make up for lost seating. The regular early birds were already dribbling in, and the always sleepy morning guy shuffled in the back door to wash dishes.

No one complained about the inconvenience or the mess, but it held as top topic of conversation throughout the morning. When speculative looks were sent her way, Reece told herself it was no less than she could expect. But they ate her food, clattered dishes, and at ten sharp someone had the juke going over the noise of hammer and saw.

She had the day's soup in the kettle and was making salsa when Linda-gail slipped back. "What an awful mess. You must be so mad at me."

"I was." Reece chopped and considered trying out a little bruschetta on the lunch crowd. "Then I looked at the big picture and decided it wasn't your fault. Well, not completely your fault."

"Really? I feel like such an ass."

"You were an ass." She paused long enough to grab a bottle of water. "But that was only one element that contributed to the general mayhem."

"Oh, Reece honey. Your poor face."

"Don't remind me." But since she had, Reece held the cold bottle against her bruised cheek for a moment. "Does it look terrible?"

"Of course it doesn't. You couldn't."

"That bad, huh? Between the riot at Clancy's and the mess here, people are going to have something to talk about for a week."

"It's not your fault."

"No." Apparently her days of wallowing in guilt were over. Cheers. "It's really not."

"Does anybody know how it happened? I mean, who'd do something so stupid and mean?" Linda-gail looked around, watched Brody and Reuben carrying in some drywall. "The bright side is, I heard Joanie say she might as well paint the whole damn place as slap some just on the ceiling. We could use some freshening up."

"Crappy way to redecorate."

Linda-gail rubbed a hand up and down Reece's back. "I'm just so sorry about everything."

"It's okay."

"Lo isn't speaking to me."

"He will. But maybe you should do the talking first. When there's something you want, something you need, life's too short to play games with it."

"Maybe. Reece, I want you to know that if you need to, you can stay at my place as long as you want."

"Thanks." She glanced over her shoulder. "He gave me two drawers."

Linda-gail's eyes went wide and bright. "Oh, Reece!" She wrapped her arms around Reece's waist and rocked side to side. "That is just awesome."

"It's drawers, Linda-gail. But yeah, it's a nice step."

"Linda-gail Case, I don't believe I'm paying you to dance." Joanie walked in, gave the soup a stir. "Rick's out front, Reece, wants to talk to you soon as you can. You can use my office if you want privacy."

"I guess that's best." But then she turned, saw the people lingering over coffee at the counter, at tables. "No, I think we'll have this conversation out front. People'll just talk about me more if we go behind closed doors."

With a light of approval in her eyes, Joanie nodded. "Good for you."

Reece left her apron on, took the water with her. Rick was loitering by the counter, and straightened when she came out. "Reece. Why don't we go sit in the back?"

"Out here's fine. Table five's empty. Linda-gail," Reece called without taking her eyes from Rick's. "Would you bring the sheriff some coffee? Table five."

She led the way, sat. "Is Min pressing charges?"

"No." He took out his notebook. "Talked to her again this morning, and she allows as you didn't so much hit her as get pushed into her. And on some rethinking, witnesses agree you didn't push over a table, but fell on one when other people scrambled to get away or join in the brawl. Before we move on from that, the consensus, you could say, is that the business at Clancy's was a result of a series of lame-brain actions by a number of people."

"Me included."

"Well." He smiled, just a little around the edges. "You do seem to draw . . . responses. Now." He paused, looked toward the plastic and the noise of drywall being hammered in place. "Why don't you tell me about this one?"

"After I left your office, Brody drove me back here. We went upstairs. I heard water running, and when we went in, the bathroom door was closed. Water leaking under it. Someone had turned the water on in the tub, plugged it up. It flooded."

"Someone?"

She'd prepared for this, and kept her gaze level. Kept her voice clear and firm. "It wasn't me. I wasn't there. You know I wasn't there because you know I was at Clancy's, then at your office."

"I know you were at Clancy's a couple hours, at my office a couple hours. From what I've been told, what I can see, the water was running for some time. Hard to pin down just how long."

"I didn't turn the water on. After my shift, I went upstairs to change my shoes and . . ."

"And?"

Check the locks, the windows. "Nothing.

I changed my shoes, and I went back down to meet Linda-gail. I couldn't have been upstairs for more than three minutes."

"Did you go in the bathroom?"

"Yes, I used the bathroom, and I checked the clothes I had hanging on the shower rod to see how well they were drying. That's it. I had no reason to turn the water on."

"The clothes you took to the laundry at the hotel earlier?"

Okay, she thought. All right. "Yes. And, yes, someone took the clothes I'd washed and put in the dryer *out* of the dryer and put them back in the washer. I'd taken them down there, put them in to wash, went home, came back, put them in the dryer, came home again. And when I went back to get them, they were in the washer."

He glanced up as Linda-gail brought his coffee, and a poached egg on toast for Reece. "Joanie says you're to eat that, Reece. Can I get you something else, Sheriff?"

"No, just the coffee, thanks."

"Linda-gail can tell you I wasn't upstairs more than a couple minutes before we went to Clancy's."

"Sure." The confirmation came after only a whisper of hesitation. "She was up and down, two shakes."

"You didn't go up with her?" Rick asked.

"Well, no. I just went in the bathroom here, fixed up my makeup and fiddled with my hair a little. Reece was right here waiting for me when I came out. Couldn't have been but a few minutes. Somebody played a stupid trick, a mean one. That's what happened."

"Why would I turn the water on?" Reece demanded. "I was going out."

"I'm not saying you did. And I'm not saying if you did you turned it on to cause any of this." He pulled at his ear. "Sometimes, when you've got a lot on your mind, you forget. Pot on the stove, phone off the hook. It's natural enough."

"It wouldn't be natural to run a bath when you had no intention of taking one, then walk out and leave the water on. And that's not what I did."

" 'Course you didn't." Linda-gail laid a hand on Reece's shoulder, rubbed. And Reece wondered if there was a hint of doubt along with the comfort of the gesture.

"Someone's been in my apartment," Reece said. "This isn't the first time."

Rick leveled his gaze at Reece. "First I'm hearing about it. Thanks, Linda-gail. I'll let you know if we need anything else."

"All right. Reece, you eat now. You haven't had anything all day, and if that plate comes back untouched, Joanie's going to be mad."

"It started right after I saw the murder," Reece began. She told him: the guidebook, the door, the bathroom, finding her things packed, the boots and the bowls. The pills, the photograph album. She forced herself to eat a little, hoping the action would somehow give her statements more validity.

He took notes, asked questions. His voice was flat and cool.

"Why didn't you report these incidents before?"

"Because I knew you'd think just what you're thinking now. That I either did them or I imagined them."

"You don't have a window into my head, Reece." There was a quality in his voice that warned her his patience was at a low ebb. "Have you noticed anyone loitering around?"

"Half the town loiters here at some point."

"Who has access to your key?"

"I keep it with me. There's a spare in Joanie's office."

"Brody have one?"

"No, no, Brody doesn't have one."

"You had trouble, had words with anyone in town?"

"Not until I clocked Min at Clancy's last night."

He gave her that faint smile again. "I think we can rule her out."

"He must have seen me."

"Who?"

"The man, by the river. The one I saw strangle that woman."

Rick drew a breath, sat back. "Saw you, at that distance? The distance you gave in your statement?"

"Not me. I mean he must have seen there was someone on the trail. It wouldn't take any effort to find out it was me, not after the whole town knew about it. So he's trying to discredit me as a witness."

Rick closed his book.

"What are you going to do?" Reece demanded.

"I'm going to do my job. I'm going to look into it. Next time something happens, you need to tell me about it. I can't help you if I don't know you've got trouble."

"All right. Have they identified the woman? The body?"

"Haven't matched dental records yet. She's still a Jane Doe. Have you thought about it? Can you confirm she's the woman you saw?"

"I can't. She's not."

"Well then." He pushed to his feet. "You got a place to stay while these repairs are going on?"

"I'm at Brody's."

"I'll be in touch."

Reece rose, cleared the table herself. Back in the kitchen Joanie scowled at the half-eaten egg. "Something wrong with my cooking?"

"No. He doesn't believe me."

"Doesn't matter if he does or he doesn't, he'll do what he's paid to do. I want some of those cluckers barbecued for the lunch special. You're behind."

"I'll get right on it."

"And make up some potato salad. You got your famous fresh dill in the cooler. Use it."

Reece was ending the first of a double shift when Rick tracked down Doc Wallace. In strong, even strokes, Doc rowed his boat to its mooring on the lake. Rick grabbed the line, secured it. "You got a fishing license?"

"You see any damn fish? You hear the one about the game warden come across this woman in a boat, reading a book. Asks her if she has a fishing license. She says she's not fishing, she's reading a book." Doc climbed nimbly out of his boat. "Game warden says 'You got the equipment for fishing in there, so I'm going to have to write you a citation.' She says, 'You do that, I'm going to have to bring sexual molestation charges against you.'"

Rick waited patiently while Doc took off his prescription sunglasses, polished them on the tail of his shirt. "Well, the warden says with some outrage, 'Lady, I never sexually molested you.' And she says, 'But you got the equipment for it.' "

Rick's laugh was quick and easy. "Pretty good. Nothing biting today?"

"Not a damn thing on my line." Doc laid his rod over his shoulder. "Pretty day not to catch fish though."

"It is that. You got a few minutes?"

"Got more than a few. It's my day off. Could use a walk after sitting in that boat the last couple hours."

They fell into step, slowly following the curve of the lake. "Reece Gilmore's been to see you, I hear. Medically."

"You know I can't talk about that kind of thing, Rick."

"Not asking you to. We're going to be talking in the hypothetical area of things."

"That's a shaky line."

"It shakes too much, you can step off."

"Fair enough."

"You heard about what happened at Joanie's place."

"Water damage."

"I got a statement from Reece. Says she never turned the water on in the tub. Says someone's been getting into her apartment, doing things in there. Says someone took her laundry out of the dryer and put it back into the washer down in the hotel basement while she wasn't there. Now maybe somebody around here's taking a dislike to her. Though she's a likeable enough woman, if you ask me."

"There are some people who take a dislike to the likeable."

"True enough. Yesterday she all but falls in the lake. Then she's running down the street in her bare feet. She's climbing down Brenda's throat about somebody going down to the laundry, messing with her clothes. Last night she's in a brawl at Clancy's."

"Oh now, Rick, I heard all about that foolishness. Linda-gail flaunting some tourist in Lo's face to get his goat. And she got it."

"My point is, Reece was involved." The sun glinted off Rick's dark glasses as he turned his head to look at Doc. Behind them, boats sailed across the water, through the mirrored mountains. "We haven't had this much trouble in town all at once, not before she came around."

"You think she's causing all this. Why would she?"

Rick held up a hand as they walked. "I'm asking, hypothetically, if you had a patient with a history of emotional and mental problems, if that patient could likely function well enough for the most part. And have, well, what you might call delusions, or hell, just plain forgetfulness."

"Hell, Rick, you could have just plain forgetfulness, and you could toss in a few delusions now and then."

"This is more than forgetting where you left your keys. Could this be in her head, Doc?"

"Hypothetically, it could. But could's not is, Rick. There's no crime if she's been forgetful. But there's a crime if someone's doing this to that girl."

"I'm going to keep an eye on it. On her."

Doc nodded, and they walked a little more in companionable silence.

"Well, I guess I'll go on up to the hotel, take a look down in the laundry," Rick said.

He detoured by Reece's apartment first. The door was wide open, and rock pumped out along with the sound of hammer on chisel.

Inside, Brody was on his knees in the bathroom, painfully from the looks of it, chipping up the ancient linoleum.

"Not your usual line of work," Rick called out.

"Change of pace." Brody sat back on his heels. "An ugly, sweaty, knuckle-scraping change of pace. It got dumped on me when it was discovered I have no latent carpentry talents."

Rick hunkered down. "Subflooring's trashed."

"So I'm told."

"You should've come to me with these incidents with Reece before this, Brody."

"Her choice. Understandable. I can look at your face and see you're not leaning toward believing her."

"I'm not leaning any particular way. Hard to investigate if I don't know, don't see for myself. You painted over what was done in here before."

"Took pictures first. I'll get you copies."

"That's a start. None of these incidents happened at your place, or while you were with her?"

"Not so far." He went back to chipping. "Listen, even objectively it's hard for me to buy her leaving the water on in here. She checks the stove every time she leaves the kitchen. Checks the lights, the locks. A person with a mile-wide anal streak doesn't forget she's running a bath. And she doesn't run one when she's got someone waiting for her downstairs."

"I can't see any signs of that lock being tampered with, or forced entry."

"He's got a key. I'm going to see the locks're changed."

"You do that. I'm going to head down to

the hotel, take a look in the laundry area. You want to come along?"

"And leave this fascinating hobby?" Brody dropped the tools. "Bet your ass."

Brody could imagine how Reece felt as she carted her basket through the basement. There was light, harsh light that cast shadows in corners. The furnace hummed, the water heaters clanged, all hollow, echoing sounds as you walked over the raw cement floor to the worn vinyl of the cramped laundry.

Two washers, two dryers, commercial grade. A dispenser that sold laundry soap and fabric softener in miniature packages at inflated prices.

There was a narrow jalousie window high above the machines, rolled closed, that let fitful light through frosted glass.

"Guest elevators don't come down to this level," Rick began. "Got an outside entrance, too, back by the maintenance room. Couple windows. Not hard for somebody to get down here without anyone noticing. Still. How'd they know she was down here doing wash?"

"She walked back and forth on the street. Easy to know if you're keeping tabs on her."

Rick studied the lay. "Let me ask you something, Brody. If someone wishes harm

552

on her, why haven't they harmed her? She's got it in her head the man she says she saw by the river's doing this."

"I put it in her head."

As if suddenly tired, Rick leaned back against a washing machine. "Now why the hell did you go and do that?"

"It makes sense to me. Play on her weaknesses, scare her, make her doubt herself. Make sure everyone else doubts her, too. It's smart, and in its way, it's clean. Doesn't mean he won't harm her."

And that, Brody thought, was why she wasn't going anywhere alone. "It seems to me it's escalating," he continued. "She wasn't isolated this time. Joanie got hit, too. Because it's not working. Reece is sticking."

"Brody, did you ever forget you left laundry wet in the washing machine?"

"Sure. But I'm not Reece."

Rick shook his head. "I'll go up, talk to Brenda."

Brenda was at the desk using her professional welcome voice on the phone. "We'll be expecting you on July tenth. I'll make those reservations for you, and send you a confirmation. It's absolutely my pleasure. Bye, Mr. Franklin."

She hung up. "Just booked the second of our two suites for a week in July. We're going to be full up for the summer if this keeps up. How you doing?"

"Well enough," Rick told her. "You saw Reece in and out of here yesterday?"

"I sure did. I told Deb —"

"You can tell me now. She came in to do laundry."

"Had her basket. No shoes." Brenda rolled her eyes. "Got change for the machines. Zipped right down. Was out again in, I don't know, ten minutes at most. Had her shoes on when she came back, about a half hour later. Down and up, same as before. I didn't see her come in the last time. Must've been in the back, but she came up like a wild woman, let me tell you. Spitting mad. Claimed somebody was down there."

"Did you see anyone else go down?"

"Not a soul. She said somebody'd put her dry clothes back in the wash. Now who'd do that?"

"But you weren't at the desk the whole time?" Brody said, then glanced at Rick. "Sorry."

"Not necessary. You said you were in the back last time she came in. Were you back there long?"

"Well, I can't say how long, exactly. Ten, fifteen minutes maybe. But most times when I'm back there I hear the door."

"Most times," Brody pressed.

"If I get caught on the phone back there or whatnot, I might not hear unless somebody hits the bell on the desk." Her tone turned defensive. "That's what it's for."

"Anyone been in here asking about Reece?"

"Well no, Rick, why would they? Listen, I like her. She's a nice woman. But she was acting damn strange yesterday. Never seen anybody so het up about some wet clothes. And I didn't tell you how she told Debbie she was training for some sort of marathon or whatever, and that's why she was running down here barefooted? Now, that's just crazy."

"All right, Brenda. Appreciate the time."

When they walked back outside, Brody turned to Rick. "Did Brenda get her sense of humor surgically removed recently?"

"Oh now, Brody, she's all right, you know that. With all the hoopla's been going on, and Reece at the center of a lot of it, you can't expect everybody to understand how it is."

"Do you understand how it is?"

"Trying to. Why don't you drop those pictures you took of the bathroom off to me when you get the chance? And since you're a writer, maybe you could write me up your version of the events and incidents. Get me dates and times best as you can."

Brody's jaw relaxed again. "Yeah, I can do that. It's a little more my line than hanging drywall."

"Be specific," Rick added as they walked. "If it's something Reece just told you happened, make sure that's how you put it. Something you saw yourself, put that."

"Okay."

Outside On the Trail, Rick paused for a moment. He could see Debbie inside, but she had customers. As was his habit, he tapped his knuckles on the glass, sent her a quick salute when she glanced over.

"Starting to busy up around here," Rick commented as they continued down the sidewalk. "Ah . . . You got a serious thing happening? You two?"

"We've got a thing happening."

"Be best if you try not to let that color your statement. When you've got feelings for a woman, it tends to shade things some."

"She's not crazy, Rick. Hell, she doesn't even hit eccentric in some areas."

"And in others?"

"Sure, she rings the bell. Who doesn't? People around here used to think I was strange because I write about murder, I don't fish, don't shoot mammals and I can't name the top ten songs on the country music chart."

Rick smiled his little smile. "Brody, people still think you're strange."

24

Linda-gail wasn't quite sure what to do. As far as she could remember, she'd never screwed up so completely with a man before — and there'd never been a man who'd mattered as much as Lo.

Which was probably why she'd screwed up.

He wasn't answering her calls. She wanted to be pissed off at him for it, but instead just felt a little scared, a little sad. And a whole lot confused.

She'd planned it all out, spent hours and days and nights calculating just how to bring Lo to heel, when the time was right. When it suited her, she admitted. But damn it, if a man had ever needed to be brought to heel, it was Lo.

She'd given him plenty of time, plenty of room. It was time for both of them to settle down. Together.

As she drove out toward the ranch, with the sage flats ripening to bloom around her, she was determined to tell him just that. Fish or cut bait.

And if he opted to cut bait, she didn't know what the hell she was going to do.

She wished she could have talked to

Reece before taking this step. Reece had experience, city smarts and style. But Reece had plenty of problems of her own, and was probably a little bit irritated since she'd gotten sucked into a bar fight.

She had to brake for a moment as a bull buffalo stood in the middle of the road as if he owned it. With a sharp blast of her horn, she got him moving over to the flats through the grasses.

God, what had she been thinking, sashaying up with that stupid guy right in front of Lo's face? Make him a little jealous, make him see what he was missing. It seemed like the thing to do at the time. The problem was it had worked too well.

How could she have known they'd start swinging?

Men. She sniffed on the thought, scowling at the wildflowers, the herd of pronghorns that snacked on them, and working up a new head of mad.

She'd only been dancing, for heaven's sake.

She tapped her fingers on the wheel in time with Kenny Chesney. What she ought to do was turn right around, go back to town and let Lo stew in his own bile for a few more days. Possibly forever. What she ought to do was keep on going, track that brainless cowboy down and give him a piece of her mind for causing a ruckus over nothing.

So she drove, pushing her little car up to eighty on the flats, letting the wind fly through her open windows while Chesney wondered who you'd be today.

She slowed as she approached the big open gate with its wrought-iron *K* wrapped in a circle. No point in mowing down some tourist who wanted a taste of western life just because her love life was in the dumpster.

She passed a corral where a foal nursed from his mama, the bunkhouse with its faded logs and wide front porch built to look as if it had stood, frozen in time, for a couple of centuries. She happened to know that, among other things, the kitchen inside boasted a microwave and a Mr. Coffee.

The main house was log as well, and sprawled in every direction. Guests could stay in one of the second-floor rooms and one suite, or bunk in one of the one- or two-bedroom cabins tucked into the pretty pines. They could ride, rope, take overnight campouts, hike with a guide, float, fish, do a white-water trip.

They could pretend to be cowboys for a few days, and take home the bumps and blisters that went with the fantasy. Or they could just sit in a rocker on one of the big porches and contemplate the view.

At night they might belly up to the bar in the lodge and talk about their adventures before they slid into a feather bed, under a cozy duvet no cowboy had ever found at the end of the trail.

She turned at the fork of the dirt road toward the stables. Her contact, Marian, who worked in the kitchen there, had given her the intel that Lo would be on grooming detail that evening.

She parked, flipped down the vanity mirror to check, then finger-fluffed her windblown hair. As she got out of the car, the cowboy giving a riding lesson tapped a finger on the brim of his hat in salute.

"Hey there, Harley." She fixed a bright smile on her face. Nothing wrong here, she thought. Just dropping by to pass the time.

And kick Lo's stupid ass.

She swung into the stable, into the strong smell of horses and hay, the sweet scent of grain and leather. She shot a smile toward LaDonna, one of the women who guided trail rides.

"Linda-gail, how ya doing?" LaDonna raised an eyebrow. News traveled, especially when it involved fists and fury. She nodded toward the rear of the stables. "Lo's back in the tack room. Pretty pissy, too."

"Good. I'm feeling the same."

Linda-gail marched back, turned the

quick corner and, stiffening her spine, walked into the tack room.

He had Toby Keith on the CD player and his hat tipped back on his head as he worked saddle soap into leather. His jeans were faded and snug, riding low on his hips. His denim shirt was rolled up to the elbows. The toe of his scuffed left boot tapped the time.

His handsome face looked sulky and ridiculously handsome despite, maybe because of, the puffy bottom lip and the bruising around his eye.

The sight of him made Linda-gail's heart melt, drowning the leading edge of her temper.

"Lo."

His head came up. Sulky went to scowl. "What do you want? I'm working."

"I can see that. I'm not stopping you." She'd be big about it, Linda-gail decided, take the high road. "I'm sorry about your eye."

He kept his gaze on hers for one long, humming moment, then shifted it back to the saddle, got back to work.

"I am sorry," she said. "Still, it's not like it's the first time you've ever had a fist in the eye. I was just dancing."

He rubbed leather, kept his silence. And Linda-gail felt a tickle of anxiety bubble under her melted heart. "That's it? You're not even going to speak to me? You're the one who got all het up just because I was dancing with somebody. How many times have I been in Clancy's when you've been dancing with somebody?"

"That's different."

"That's the stupidest thing I ever heard. What's different about it?"

"Just is."

"Just is," she repeated, scathingly. "I dance with somebody and it's okay for you to start a brawl. But you can dance and whatever with anyone you like and I'm not supposed to think anything of it."

"Doesn't mean anything."

"So you say." She poked a finger in the air at him. "And I say I can dance with whoever I want and you've got no right to cause trouble."

"Fine. You can bet I won't from here on. So if that's it —"

"Don't you dismiss me, William Butler. Why'd you start that fight?"

"I didn't. He did."

"You got in his face."

"He had his hands on your ass!" Lo threw down his rag and surged to his feet. "You let him paw you, in public."

"He was not pawing me. And I wouldn't have let him put his hands on my ass if you weren't being such a dick."

"Me?"

"Damn right." This time, she jabbed her finger into his chest. "You've always been a dick because that's what you use for a brain. I've waited long enough for you to grow the hell up and be a man."

Danger shot into his eyes. "I am a man." He grabbed her arm and yanked her forward. "And I'm the only man who's going to put his hands on you. Got that?"

"What gives you the right?" Tears started in her eyes even as her pulse bumped. "What gives you the right?"

"I'm taking the right. Next time you let some other guy handle you, he's going to have more than a bloody nose."

"What do you care who handles me?" she shouted. "What do you care? If you can't say it, say it to my face and mean it, right here and now, I'm walking away. I'm walking, Lo."

"You're not going anywhere."

"Then say it." Tears tracked down her cheeks. "Look at me and say it, and I'll know if you mean it."

"I'm so damn mad at you, Linda-gail."

"I know you mean that."

"I love you. Is that what you need to hear? I love you. Probably always have."

"Yeah, that's what I need to hear. Hurt a little, didn't it?"

"Some."

"Scares you a little, too."

His hands had gentled on her, stroked up and down her arms. "Maybe more than a little."

"That's how I know you mean it. That's how I know," she murmured, laying a hand over his bruised cheek. "I've been waiting my whole life to hear it from you."

"I never could get over you." He pulled her close, sent his abused lip throbbing by pressing it to hers. "I wanted to. I tried to. A lot."

"A hell of a lot. Here." She took his hands, pushed them around until they cupped her ass. "No other guy puts his hands where yours are, and you don't put them on any other woman. Is that a deal?"

"That's a deal."

"You think you can get the rest of the night off?"

His smile spread, slow. "I reckon I can arrange it."

"And come on home with me?"

"I could do that."

"And get me all stirred up, and naked, make love with me till sunrise?"

"Only till sunrise?"

"This time," she said and kissed him again.

He was good. Linda-gail imagined he would be — and she'd been imagining since she was old enough to understand what men and women did together in the dark. But he was better than even her active imagination had reached. Strong hands that found all the right places, a hot mouth with an endless appetite. A long, lean, tireless body.

He had her twice before her fevered brain could cool long enough to think, Hallelujah.

Naked, loose, skin slick with sweat, she sprawled crossways on the bed. "Where in God's name did you learn all that?"

"I've been studying on it for some time." He spoke lazily, eyes closed, his head resting on her belly. "So I could perfect the matter before I got to you."

"Good job." She reached down to toy with his hair. "You have to marry me now, Lo."

"I have to . . ." His head came up. "What?"

She stayed as she was, the same cat-drenched-in-cream look on her face. "Had to make absolutely sure we got on good in bed. You don't have good sex, you're not going to have a good marriage, to my way of thinking anyway. So now that we know, we're going to get married."

She shifted her gaze to his. Shock, she thought, but that she'd expected. "I'm not another one of your women, Lo. I'm the only woman from here on out. If all you want is what we just had, you say so. No hard feelings. But I can promise you, you won't get me here again."

He pushed up until he was sitting, and she could hear him taking several long, steadying breaths. "You want to get married?"

"I do. I'm a traditional woman, Lo, at the bottom of it. I want a home and a family, a man who loves me. I've loved you as long as I can remember. And I waited. I'm done with the waiting. If you don't want me enough, don't love me enough to start a life with me, I need to know it."

For a time he said nothing, only stared over her head. She wondered if he saw the door and himself on his hasty way out of it.

"I'm twenty-eight years old," he began.

"You think that makes you too young to settle down and —"

"Just be quiet, will you, and let someone else talk for a change."

"Fine." She'd be calm, she told herself as she sat up, tugged at the sheets to cover herself. She wouldn't make a scene.

"I'm twenty-eight years old," he repeated. "I got a good job, and I'm good at the job I do. I got money put by. Not a lot, but my pockets aren't empty. I've got a strong back and I'm pretty good with my hands. You could do worse."

He looked back at her now. "Why don't you marry me, Linda-gail?"

She caught her breath, let it out again. "Why don't I?"

Later, she rustled up some scrambled eggs they could wolf down in bed.

"My ma's going to faint dead away."

Linda-gail shook her head. "You under-estimate her. She loves you so much."

"I guess I know she does."

"She loves me, too." Linda-gail scooped up some eggs from the plate they shared. "How come you didn't come in, help out with the repairs?"

"She said she didn't need me. Had enough people crowding in. She didn't even want to talk about it. You know how she is."

"She was shook, more than she let on. Who'd do that to her, Lo?"

He paused. "I heard it was an accident. Reece flooded the bathroom upstairs."

"No such thing. Somebody broke into Reece's, turned the water on. She wasn't even there."

"But . . . Well, for Christ's sake, how come that didn't get back to me?"

"Maybe because you were sulking in the tack room." Her lips curved as she slipped the fork between them. "Somebody's been playing tricks, nasty ones, on Reece."

"What are you talking about?"

She told him, at least what she knew, what she'd heard, and what she concluded from it.

"It's a little scary when you think about it. Somebody's poking at her, and she doesn't know who. And if it's the guy she saw kill that woman —"

"How can it be?" Lo interrupted. "That was weeks ago. He's long gone by now."

"Not if he's from around here."

"Well, goddamn, Linda-gail." He raked his free hand though his disheveled, sun-streaked hair. "It can't be anyone from the Fist. We know everybody. Don't you think we'd know if we had some killer standing at the counter of the mercantile with us, or having coffee at my ma's place?"

"People don't always know. What do they always say when they find out their next-door neighbor is a psycho or something? 'Oh, he was so quiet, so nice. Kept to himself and never bothered anyone.' "

"Nobody keeps to themselves so much around here," Lo pointed out.

"Same difference. You never know until you know. I just wish there was something I could do to help her."

"Seems to me you have. You gave her a friend."

Linda-gail's smile bloomed again, warm

this time, and full. "You're smarter than some people think."

"Yeah, well, I like to keep a low profile."

Tim McGraw was crooning on the juke, with one of the carpenters Joanie had dragooned in an off-key duet while Reece juggled orders in the lunch rush. She could block out the music — the best way to stay sane — and most of the background clatter: a baby crying, a couple men arguing baseball.

It was almost normal, as long as she didn't think beyond the moment. Elk burger, rare, white bean soup, meatloaf sandwich, chicken sub. Slice, dice, scoop, man the grill.

She could do it in her sleep. Maybe she was, and maybe that was a good way to block out the fact that Brenda's brother Dean was massacring McGraw while he hammered behind the plastic curtain.

It was all routine, the heat, the sizzle, the smoke. Routine was good. There was nothing wrong with clinging to routine between crises.

She plated the meatloaf san, the burger, their sides, and turned. "Orders up."

And saw Debbie Mardson sliding onto a stool at the counter.

Debbie pursed her lips, touched her own glowing cheek and said, "You poor thing."

"Probably looks worse than it is."

"I hope so. I saw Min Hobalt. She said you pack a hell of a punch."

"I didn't —"

"She was joking." Debbie held up both hands for peace. "She's taking it okay, now that she's calmed down. She told me her fifteen-year-old boy thinks she's pretty cool now that she's been in a bar fight."

"Glad I could help raise her status."

"Soup smells good. Maybe I could get a cup of that and a side salad." She glanced around, conspiratorially. "Your dressing," she said in a stage whisper.

"Sure." It was, Reece supposed, a kind of olive branch. She could be gracious enough to accept it. "Coming right up."

She made out the ticket herself, put it in line.

Twenty minutes later when the rush had settled, Debbie was still there.

"Boy, I thought getting dinner on the table most nights was a challenge. How do you keep it all straight?"

"It gets to be routine."

"Feeding three kids and a man is more routine than I can handle some days. Can you take a break? Buy you a cup of coffee?"

"I don't drink coffee." Which sounded petty and rude, Reece decided. "But I can take a break."

She grabbed a bottle of water before she came out to sit at the counter. If nothing else, it felt good to get off her feet. Maybe she felt wilted and sweaty beside Debbie's white linen shirt and pretty pink cardigan, but she was off her feet.

"The soup was amazing. I don't suppose you'd part with the recipe?"

"I'm thinking about parting with a lot of them."

"Really?"

"Maybe doing a cookbook."

"Really?" Debbie angled on her stool, swinging it a bit so her rose quartz bangles danced. "That's so interesting. We'd have two famous writers in the Fist. We just won't know how to act around here. Seems like you and Brody have an awful lot in common."

Reece sipped her water. "You think?"

"Well, you're both from back East, and creative. No wonder you two hooked up so fast."

"Did we?"

"A lot of women around here had their eye on him, but he didn't do a lot of eyeing back. Until you. Men outnumber the women in this part of the world, so a woman can afford to be picky." Debbie beamed a smile. "Nice pick."

"I wasn't looking for a man."

"Isn't that always the way? Go out

hunting for a buck, and you don't see so much as a track. Take an easy morning walk, and one jumps right out at you."

"Hmmm. You hunt?"

"Sure. I like being outdoors as much as I can. Anyway, you look good together — you and Brody. It seemed, at first, you were just passing through. We get a lot of that. The way things are now, I guess you're settling in."

"I like it here. Bar fights notwithstanding."

"It's a good town. A little sparse on culture maybe, but it's a nice solid base. If you know what I mean. People look after each other." She inclined her head toward the plastic tarp. "Like that. You have trouble, you can count on your neighbors lending a hand." She added a wry smile. " 'Course, everybody mostly knows your business, but it's a trade-off. Something like that happened in the city, Joanie'd probably have to shut down for a week."

"Lucky break."

"I'm sorry." She patted a hand on Reece's arm. "You probably don't want to think about it. I just meant you shouldn't feel bad about it. It's all getting fixed right up. Be the better for it, too, when it's done."

"I didn't turn the water on upstairs," Reece said flatly. "Still, I do feel bad that whoever's messing with me took it out on

Joanie. She's been good to me, from the minute I walked in the door."

"She's got a bigger heart than she lets on. Listen, I didn't mean to make it sound like you did something to cause her trouble. I was just saying it's all going to work out fine. And the other day, I hope you don't think I thought anything about you heading out to do your laundry without your shoes on. Sometimes I've got so much on my mind I'd forget my head if it wasn't attached. God knows you've got a lot on your mind."

She gave Reece's arm another friendly pat. "You should try aromatherapy. When I'm stressed, nothing smooths me out like lavender oil."

"I'll put that on the list. The next time a murderer breaks into my apartment and floods it, I'll smooth myself out with lavender oil. Good tip."

"Well, for God's sake —"

"No offense." Reece pushed off the stool. "I appreciate the attempt. I've got to get back to work." She hesitated, then decided to finish it out. "Debbie, you're a nice woman, and you've got really nice kids. Sticking with the theme, it was nice of you to take the time to be friendly. But you don't know, you really can't know, what's on my mind. You've never been there."

She stewed about it for the rest of her shift, and was still stewing when she left the diner. Since Brody had insisted on driving her in that morning — and that was going to stop — she didn't have her car.

Didn't matter, she thought. She could use the walk to cool herself down. It was warm enough to leave her jacket un-buttoned, breezy enough to smell the water, the woods and the grass that was beginning to green.

She missed the green, the lushness of it on lawns and in parks. The stately old trees, the zipping traffic. The anonymity of a busy, thriving city.

What was she doing here, flipping elk burgers, defending herself to Wyoming's version of a soccer mom, worrying about the death of a woman she didn't even know?

She had twelve dead people, ones she'd known and loved, on her heart already. Wasn't that enough?

She couldn't change it. She couldn't help. Living her life was her only responsi-bility now. And it was more than enough to handle.

She walked with her head down, her hands stuffed in her pockets. And wished she knew where the hell she was going.

When the car slowed beside her, Reece

didn't register it. The light tap of the horn made her jump.

"Want a ride, little girl? I've got candy."

Reece scowled at Brody through the open window. "What are you doing?"

"Driving around looking for hot women to pick up. You're close enough. Get in."

"I don't want you breaking up your day to drive me back and forth to work."

"Good, because I didn't. Break up my day." He unhooked his seat belt to lean over and open the passenger door himself. "Get in. You can snarl just as well in here as out there."

"I'm not snarling." But she got in. "I'm serious, Brody, you have your own work, your own routine."

"I like changing my routine. In fact, getting my ass out of bed early enough to drive you in had me at the keyboard earlier than usual. I had a damn good day there, and now I feel like driving. Buckle up, Slim."

"Had a good day? Kudos. Mine sucked."

"No, really? I never would have guessed, not with that black cloud rumbling over your head."

"I've been bombarded with country music all day; the sheriff thinks I'm a scatterbrain at best, but he'll look into all my strange and wild allegations; his wife came in to pry into my personal life in the guise of a friendly pep talk. My feet hurt, and it'll be a miracle if I don't catch Pete's cold. I'm the town cuckoo who's been advised by the seriously pretty, annoyingly perfect Debbie Mardson to lower my stress with lavender oil. Oh, and I snatched you away from all the female hopefuls in the Fist because we're both from big cities and creative."

"I thought it was my sexual endurance."

In an irritable move, she yanked her sunglasses out of her bag, shoved them on. "We didn't get into that area, but it could be next up for discussion."

"Well, when it's on the table, don't forget to mention you've never had better. No, not just better, more inventive."

She shifted on her seat. "You really did have a good day."

"A fucking excellent day. And it ain't over yet."

He drove out of the Fist. He wanted the flats, the bloom of them. The quiet and the space. He figured it was a major shift in place that he didn't want all that alone. He wanted her with him.

He was surprised by his own sentiment when he stopped where they'd had their first kiss.

She stared out the window, saying nothing. Still silent, she reached out, touched her hand to his before climbing out.

She stood where the world was a carpet of color guarded by the silver and blue peaks of the Tetons, gilded by the sun that sat low in the west.

Pinks and blues, vibrant reds and purples, sunny yellows spiked and spread among the soft green of sage. And where the flats blurred into marsh was a dreamy green ribbon of cottonwood and willow.

"I've never seen anything like it."

"Worth seeing?" he asked.

"Oh yeah. Is that larkspur?"

"Yeah, and stonecrop, harebells, a lot of Indian paintbrush. Ah . . ." He began to gesture. "You got your pussytoes, bitterbrush. The intense red trumpet is scarlet gilia."

"How do you know the names of the wildflowers?" She angled her head toward him. "A man with your sexual endurance isn't usually into flowers."

"Research. I killed a man in that marsh today."

"Handy."

"See that bird? Green-tailed towhee."

She felt a giggle tickling her throat. "Are you making that up?"

"Nope. Pretty sure that's a meadowlark you hear singing." He took a blanket out of the back of the car, tossed it to her. "Why don't you spread that out."

"Why do we need a blanket, if I may ask?"

"That tone indicates your mind's in the gutter. I like it. However, the blanket's to sit on, while we drink the wine I've got in the cooler. Got about an hour before the sun sets. It's a good spot to drink wine and watch the sun set."

"Brody?"

He hefted out the cooler, glanced her way. "Yeah?"

"We need to go over your fucking excellent day point by point, so you can have more of them."

She spread out the blanket, sat on it, then lifted her brows when she saw he had not only wine but cheese and bread and fat purple grapes.

Every irritation, every annoyance, every worry that had dogged her heels slipped away, one by one. "Well, just let me say: Wow. I didn't expect to end my day with a picnic."

"You won't. You're going to end it having sweaty sex with me. This is a prelude."

"So far, I like it." She took the wine, stared out over the sea of color, the tender leaves, to the majesty of mountain. "How could I have thought I missed the green?"

"The green what?"

She only laughed, and popped a grape into her mouth. "I was so pissed off. She was only trying to be nice — for the most part. Debbie Mardson. I'd been trying to squeeze myself into routine, ignore the hammering, the reminder of what happened. Then she pulled me out of it — come on, sit down, take a break, have a conversation. She thinks we look good together."

"That's a given. You're beautiful, without being traditionally so. And I'm a damn good-looking bastard."

She slanted her gaze at him. "What's this about not traditionally beautiful?"

"Not milkmaid creamy, not sultry and exotic, not all-American. You mix it up. It's fairly compelling."

They ate bread and cheese, drank wine, and watched the sun slide behind the mountains until their edges went from silver to fire red.

"This is better than lavender oil," she told him. She leaned forward until she found his lips with hers, then let herself slide into the kiss as silkily as the sun was sliding behind the mountain. "Thanks."

He cupped a hand behind her neck, pulled her a little closer, took the kiss a little deeper. "You're welcome."

25

She had three glasses of wine, which may have accounted for her feeling giddy. Giddy enough that the moment they got out of the car in front of Brody's cabin, she boosted herself onto his back and began gnawing on his ear.

He'd had only one glass of wine, so it was probably the sudden attack on his senses that had him dropping his keys.

She laughed when he bent down, with her still wrapped around him, to scoop them up again.

"Mmm. Strong man."

"Skinny woman."

"Used to be skinnier." Her hands got busy, had his shirt nearly unbuttoned before he managed to open the front door.

"Take me to bed." She got her fingers on the button of his jeans.

He nearly stumbled on the steps when she clamped her teeth on the back of his neck.

"You're going to have to cut that out," he said breathlessly, "in two or three hours."

He made it to the bed, then flipped her over his shoulder. She flew with a squeal, landed with the whooshing laugh. Then he was on her, popping buttons as he pulled her shirt open. Trapping her arms as he yanked the shirt down so that it stretched behind her back, over her wrists like a rope. Even as she gasped, his mouth was taking hers with a hot, heady possession that flooded her with helpless excitement.

"Oh God. I can't —"

"You started it." He pulled the straps of her bra down her shoulders, tugging until he'd freed her breasts and could feast on them.

Senses careening, she writhed under him, shuddered. Then moaned when he released her jeans to slide his hand under the denim. On her first choked cry he caught her nipple between his teeth, nibbling there until her hips began to pump against his hand. Until he felt her gather, until he felt her give.

"Scream all you want," he whispered, clamping his hands on hers, imprisoning her as his tongue and teeth grazed down her. "Nobody's going to hear but me."

She did scream as he did things to her with that tongue, those teeth, those lips. And the sound of it shocked her, the wildness of it.

She couldn't stop him. The fingers of her trapped hands dug into the bed as if to keep them both anchored to it. Her breath caught in her throat, burst out on another cry that sobbed out utter pleasure. For the first time in more than two years, being completely helpless brought thrills instead of fear.

If this was a Ferris wheel gone mad, this time she was eager for the ride. Faster. Spinning. Breaking free to fly.

Sensations racked her, soft then sharp, tantalizing then torturous. He dragged her up, yanked the shirt away. Then she was rolling with him over the bed, crazed to touch, to taste, to have.

She groaned when he pulled her arms over her head, arched to press heat to heat. And he wrapped her fingers around the rungs of the headboard. "Better hold on," he told her.

Then plunged.

It was an earthquake, a dangerous tumult of exhilaration and power and speed. Battered by the force, she held on, half afraid she'd fly into pieces even as she matched him stroke for desperate stroke.

Then she let go, wrapped her arms around him so they could fly together.

Everything went limp, her mind, her body. Her arms slid weakly away. His weight was on her but felt insubstantial, as if they'd somehow melted together. The only thing real was the pounding of his heart against hers.

She drifted there, with his thundering heart the center of her world.

When he shifted, she tried to reach out and stop him. But he rolled onto his back, then linked his fingers with hers. And she let her spinning head fall to his shoulder.

From the shadows of the trees, he watched the house. Watched the bedroom window where the light from the three-quarter moon was just strong enough to give him silhouettes, shadows, the sense of movement behind the glass.

It was too early for sleep, he knew. Never too early for sex. He could wait them out. Patience was an essential tool of success, and survival.

He had several options, several plans. Plans and options were other important tools. He would adjust them to suit whatever opportunity presented itself.

She hadn't spooked as easily as he'd assumed she would. In truth, as he'd hoped she would. So he'd adjusted. Instead of running, she appeared to be heeling in. He could work with that, too.

He might have preferred it otherwise, but his life was full of preferences, and many only half realized. But the ones he had realized he damn well meant to keep intact.

When the bedroom light came on, he continued to watch.

He saw Reece through the window. Naked, she gave a long stretch that transmitted sexual satisfaction.

His blood didn't warm at the sight, nor did his loins tighten. After all, he wasn't a Peeping Tom. In any case, she wasn't the type that appealed to him as a man. Too skinny, too complicated. He barely saw her as a woman.

She was an obstacle. Even a kind of project. He enjoyed projects.

He saw her laugh, watched her mouth move as she shrugged into a shirt. Obviously Brody's, as it was miles too big for her.

He watched her cross to the door, stop and say something over her shoulder.

So he adjusted his plans to opportunity.

"Water first," Reece repeated. "I'm about to die of thirst."

"The shower has water, so I'm told."

"I'm not getting into the shower with you — that's another path to perdition, and I need to hydrate. I can throw something simple together while you get yours."

"As in food?"

"I didn't figure bread and cheese would hold you, even with sweaty sex tossed in. I'll do a quick stir-fry."

His satisfied expression shifted instantly to scowl. "You said food, not vegetables."

"You'll like it."

Loose and limber from sex, Reece all but floated out of the room. An easy meal, she thought — slice up a couple of the chicken breasts she'd frozen in marinade. Sautéed with garlic, onion, broccoli, carrots, cauliflower. Served over rice with some of her ginger sauce.

Couldn't miss.

She wished she had some water chestnuts, but what could you do.

She rubbed her throat, imagined she could drink a gallon of water. Hardly a wonder since they'd gone at each other like animals. Fabulous.

Most likely she'd find bruises in some very interesting places — but then, so would he. The idea made her stop and do a little happy dance. Then rolling up the sleeves of Brody's shirt, she walked toward the kitchen.

She switched on the light and went for the water first. Standing with one hand braced on the refrigerator, she gulped it down straight from the bottle like a camel refueling at a desert oasis.

When she lowered it, a faint tapping had her glancing toward the window over the sink.

She saw the shape of him. Shoulders covered in a black coat, head covered with an orange cap. Sunglasses black as the night hiding most of his face.

On a hitching gasp, she stumbled back as the bottle dropped out of her hand. The plastic thudded on the floor, and water glugged out on the tiles, over her bare feet.

There was a scream in her, trapped by shock and terror and disbelief, clawing madly at her throat.

Then the image was gone. She stood frozen in place, trying to gather her breath, her senses.

And saw the doorknob move right, move left.

Now she screamed, leaping forward to grab the chef's knife from the block on the counter. She kept screaming, gripping the knife with both hands even as she backed up.

When the door flew open, she ran.

Brody had his head under the spray when he heard the door slam open. Idly, he pulled back the curtain, then stared at Reece. She held a big knife in her hands and had her back pressed to the door.

"What the hell?"

"He's in the house. He's in the house. In the back door, in the kitchen."

Moving fast, Brody shut off the water, grabbed a towel. "Stay here."

"He's in the house."

With one snap, Brody wrapped the towel around his waist. "Give me the knife, Reece."

"I saw him."

"Okay. Give me the knife." He had to pry it out of her hands. "Get behind me," he said, already rethinking having her lock herself in the bathroom. "We're going to the bedroom first, where there's a phone. When I'm sure it's clear, you're going to lock yourself in. You're going to call nine-one-one. Understand me?"

"Yes. Don't go." Gripping his arm, she darted glances at the door. "Stay in there with me. Don't go down there. Don't go down."

"You'll be fine."

"You. You."

He shook his head, nudged her behind him. He shifted the knife to combat grip, shoved the door open quickly. He saw nothing to the right, nothing to the left. Heard nothing but Reece's labored breathing.

"Did he come after you?" Brody demanded.

"No. I don't know. No. He was just there, and I grabbed the knife and ran."

"Stay close."

He moved to the bedroom, calculated the odds, then shut and locked the door first.

He searched under the bed, in the closet — the only two places he deemed conceivable for anyone to hide. Satisfied, he set down the knife to grab his jeans, yanked them on. "Call the cops, Reece."

"Please don't go out there. He could have a gun. He could . . . Please don't leave me behind."

He turned to her briefly, stifling his own need to move. "I'm not leaving you behind. I'll be back in a few minutes."

He left the knife where it was, took his baseball bat out of the closet. "Lock the door behind me. Make the call."

He didn't like leaving her, not when she was afraid, when he couldn't be sure she'd keep her head. But a man had to defend what was his.

Probably long gone by now, Brody thought as he checked his office. Probably. Still, it was his job to make certain, to secure the house, to make it safe.

To keep her safe.

He moved to the bathroom next. An intruder could have slipped in to hide when they went into the bedroom. Keeping the bat cocked on his shoulder, he took a quick scan. He felt foolish even as his stomach jittered.

Assured the second level was clear, he started down the stairs.

Alone, Reece stared at the door. She leaped onto the bed, crawling over it to the phone.

"Nine-one-one. What's the nature of your emergency?"

"Help. We need help. He's here."

"What kind of — Reece? Is this Reece Gilmore? It's Hank. What's going on? Are you hurt?"

"Brody's. Brody's cabin. He killed her. He's here. Hurry."

"Stay on the line. I want you to stay on the line. I'm sending someone. Just hang on."

A crash from downstairs had her choking out a scream, dropping the phone. Gunfire? Was that gunfire? Was it real or in her head?

Breath sobbing, she clawed across the bed and picked up the knife.

She hadn't locked the door. But if she locked it, Brody would be trapped on one side, she on the other. He could be hurt. He could die while she did nothing.

Ginny had died while she did nothing.

She got to her feet. It was like standing in syrup. Like pushing through that thick goo that clogged the ears, the nose, the eyes. And as she approached the door, through the dull buzzing in her head, she heard footsteps on the stairs.

They'd find her this time, and this time they'd know she wasn't dead. They'd know, and they'd finish it.

"Reece. It's okay. It's Brody. Unlock the door."

"Brody." She said his name first as if

testing the sound of it. Then on a gasp of relief that was like pain, she yanked open the door and stared at him. Swayed.

"It's okay," he repeated, and reached down to take the knife out of her hand. "He's gone."

Dots flashed in front of her eyes, black and white. Even as the edges went red, he propelled her into a chair, shoved her head between her knees.

"Cut it out. You cut it out and breathe. Now."

His voice sliced through the dizziness, the queasiness, chipped away at the pressing weight on her chest. "I thought . . . I heard . . ."

"I slipped. There was water on the kitchen floor. Knocked over a chair. Keep breathing."

"You're not shot. Not shot."

"Do I look like I'm shot?"

Slowly, she lifted her head. "I wasn't sure what was real, where I was."

"You're right here and so am I. He's gone."

"Did you see him?"

"No. Cowardly bastard took off. That's what you need to remember." He took her face firmly in his hands. "He's a coward."

He heard the sirens but kept his eyes on hers. "There's the cavalry. Get some clothes on."

Dressed, she came down to find the back door open, with the floodlights on. She could hear the mutter of voices. Seeking solace in order, she started coffee, then mopped up the wet floor.

She brewed tea for herself, and had cups, milk and sugar on the table when Brody came in with Denny.

"Coffee, Deputy?"

"Wouldn't mind it. You up to giving a statement, Reece?"

"Yes. It's coffee regular, isn't it?"

"Sorry?"

"Milk, two sugars."

"Yeah." Denny pulled on his earlobe. "You got a mind for details. Okay if we sit?" He took a seat at the table, took out his pad. "Can you tell me what happened?"

"I came downstairs. I was thirsty, and I was going to make dinner. Brody was in the shower."

She poured the coffee, glanced at Denny's face. From the light flush on it, she assumed Brody had told him what they'd been doing beforehand, or he'd certainly inferred it.

"I got a bottle of water from the fridge," she continued, set his coffee and Brody's on the table before turning for her tea. "I heard something, like a tapping, at the window. When I looked over, I saw him."

591

"What did you see, exactly?"

"A man. Black coat, orange hat, sunglasses." She sat, stared into her tea.

"Can you describe him?"

"It was dark," she said carefully. "And the kitchen light reflected on the glass. I didn't see him clearly. Then he was gone. I saw the knob on the back door move. I heard it turn. I grabbed a knife from the block by the stove. The door opened, and he was standing there. Just standing there. I ran upstairs."

"Height? Weight? Coloring?"

She squeezed her eyes shut. He'd seemed huge to her, impossibly huge. How could she see through the haze of her own fear? "White, clean-shaven. I'm not sure. It was quick, it was dark, and I was so scared."

"Did he say anything?"

"No." She jumped at the sound of a car pulling up.

"That's probably the sheriff," Denny said. "Hank contacted him after me. I'll just go on out, fill him in."

She sat with her hands in her lap when Denny went out. "It's pitiful, isn't it? He was standing right there, but I can't tell you what he looked like. Not really."

"It was dark," Brody said. "I imagine he stood back far enough to be in the shadows. You had the glare of the light in your eyes. And you were scared. What did I tell you he was, Reece?"

"A coward." She lifted her head. "And he knows just how to play me. They won't believe me, Brody. I'm an hysterical woman, with delusions. You and Denny, you didn't find anything outside. No handy clue."

"No. He's careful."

"But you believe me." She took a breath. "When I was upstairs alone, I thought I heard gunshots. I got everything tangled up."

"Give yourself a fucking break, Reece. You snapped back."

"He had to have watched us. Standing somewhere outside, watching the house, watching us." She saw Brody's face tighten. "You didn't think I'd click onto that?"

"I hoped you wouldn't."

"I'm not going to freak because he's seen me naked or knows we had sex. That's small change."

"Okay then." He glanced over, signaled at the knock on the back door. Rick came in, removed his hat.

"Evening. Heard you had some trouble."

"A little breaking and entering and harassment," Brody told him.

"Maybe I could get a cup of that coffee. I asked Denny to take another look around." He paused while Reece poured another cup. "Reece, why don't you show me where you were standing when you saw someone — at the window, is that right?"

"At first. I was here." She moved to the refrigerator, placed a hand on the door. "I heard a sound and looked over. He was outside the window."

"Kitchen light glares some on the window glass, doesn't it? You go any closer?"

"I . . . no. Not then. I saw the doorknob turn. He stepped back from the window, then I saw the doorknob turn. I grabbed a knife." She moved forward, mimed taking one from the block. "And I . . . I think I stepped back, I think I kept stepping back. I was scared."

"Bet you were."

"Then the door opened, and he was standing just outside."

"You were about where you are now?"

"I . . . I'm not sure. No closer. Maybe back another step or two. I just turned and ran."

"Uh-huh. Best thing you could've done. You were in the shower?" he asked Brody.

"That's right."

"How about the door there? Locked? Unlocked?"

"It was locked. I locked up before I went out to pick up Reece."

"Okay." Rick opened the back door again, squatted to examine the lock, the jamb. "Was he wearing gloves?"

"He —" Reece forced her mind back. "Yes. I think so. Black gloves, like he wore when he strangled that woman."

"Any other details about him?"

"I'm sorry."

Rick straightened. "Well, let's take it back some. You were home here, Brody, until what time?"

"I left about six-thirty, quarter to seven, I'd say."

"Went and picked Reece up at Joanie's, came back here."

"No, we drove out to the flats." Brody had a sudden, unexpected yen for a cigarette. Quashed it.

"Blooming out there. Nice night for it. So you took a drive."

"Few miles out," Brody confirmed. "Had some wine and cheese, watched the sunset. Got back here about eight-thirty, maybe. Might've been more like nine. We went straight up to the bedroom. After, Reece came down here for some water and I went to shower."

"About what time?"

"Wasn't watching the clock. But I wasn't in the shower more than a couple minutes when she came running in. I took her back into the bedroom, got my pants, my ball bat, told her to call nine-one-one."

Rick glanced over when Denny came in, shook his head. "Okay then. I'd say you've had all the excitement you're going to have for tonight. I can swing by tomorrow, see what I see in the light of day. You go on back, Denny, file the report. Brody, why don't you walk me out?"

"All right." He looked at Reece. "I'll be back in a minute."

They went out the front. Rick took a look up at the star-flooded sky, hooked his thumbs in his pockets. "Hell of a night. The kind you only get standing in the Fist. Going to be summer before we know it. We're already getting crowded with tourists, summer people. Won't have that sky all to ourselves much longer."

"You didn't ask me to walk you out so we could stargaze."

"No. I'm going to lay this out for you, Brody." He shifted so they were facing. "First, there's no sign that door was forced. You said, for certain, it was locked."

"He picked the lock, had a dupe key. He's done it before."

"Christ." With obvious frustration, Rick rubbed his hand over his face. "And he managed that at just the narrow window when she's downstairs alone and you're in the shower? This guy have superpowers, too?"

"He had to be watching the house."

"For what? To play bogeyman? If he was going to do anything, he'd have done it when he had her alone. If he existed."

"Just wait one damn minute."

"No, you wait one damn minute. I'm a tolerant man, Brody. A man wears a badge and a gun, he better have a store of tolerance. I'm open-minded, but I'm not stupid. You've got a woman with a history of emotional disorder, who's been drinking, who just rolls out of bed and claims she sees the same man she claimed to see kill some unknown woman — that *only* she's seen. And this happens at the exact moment there's no one to verify it.

"There's no sign anyone's been at that cabin, or lurking around it. Just like there was no sign anyone was killed by the river, no sign anyone broke into her apartment over Joanie's, or messed with her laundry at the hotel. You're sleeping with her, so you want to believe her. Nothing's so alluring as a damsel in distress."

Temper leaped. "What bullshit. Fucking bullshit. Since you've got that badge, you've got a responsibility to protect and serve."

"I've got a responsibility to protect and serve this town, these people. You go ahead and be as pissed as you want," he said with a nod. "You go right on, but I've done about all I can for Reece Gilmore. Those tourists and summer people are coming in, and I can't waste time and manpower I need to keep order around here chasing her demons. I'm sorry for her, God knows. She's a nice woman who caught a big, bad break. She's going to have to get over it and settle down. Do yourself a favor, talk her into getting some treatment."

"I thought better of you, Rick."

"At this point, Brody," Rick said wearily as he pulled open the door of his truck, "I can say right back at you." He climbed in, slammed the door. "You care about that woman, get her some help." He started the engine. "She needs it."

When Brody stomped back in Reece was at the stove. Rice in a covered pot, chicken and garlic sautéing in a skillet.

"Fuck him," Brody muttered and pulled a beer out of the refrigerator.

"Thanks. Thanks for taking my side." She shook the pan, flipping chunks of chicken. "I didn't have to hear the conversation to know his part of it. He doesn't believe me, and this last incident colors all the rest. I've wasted his time, disturbed the routine, moved up from town cuckoo to town nuisance. And when you come right down to it, you can't blame him."

"Why the hell not?"

"Everything points to me making it up, or just being crazy." She added the vegetables she'd already chopped and sliced to the pan, dashed in some white wine, gave the skillet another shake. "Just as it points to you sticking with me because we're sleeping together."

"Is that what you think?"

"I know you believe me, and knowing that is a lifeline."

He took a long, slow sip of beer. "Want to pack it up? Try New Mexico maybe? The thing about both of our professions is we can do them anywhere we damn well please."

Her eyes stung, but she kept stirring and shaking. "You know what? You could have fallen on your knees, holding an eye-gouging diamond, a puppy and a fifty-pound box of Belgian chocolate, professed your undying love and devotion, then recited Shelley. It wouldn't have meant more."

"Good, because I don't know any Shelley offhand."

"And it's tempting," she continued. "But I know better than anyone that you can run away, even walk away, and it doesn't change the bottom line. I liked seeing the flowers bloom out there, liked knowing they can. If they can root out here, so can I."

She took the bowl in which she'd

whisked up her sauce, poured it over the contents of the pan. "This'll be ready in a couple minutes. Why don't you get the plates?"

26

Reece sat in Doc Wallace's examination room, grateful she didn't have to strip down for the follow-up. She felt sluggish, the way she did when she'd overindulged at a party.

Sleeping pill, she thought. Just an over-the-counter deal Brody had urged on her. Not that he'd had to do much urging, she recalled.

Though it kept the curtain closed on the nightmares, she felt heavy-headed and dull this morning. It was worth the trade-off — this one time. She didn't want to go back to them, to the sleeping pills, the anti-depressants, antianxiety.

She wasn't depressed. She was being stalked.

The door opened. Doc strolled in, carrying a chart, wearing a smile.

"Congratulations. You've gained six pounds. That's real progress, young lady. Four more, and I'll stop hounding you."

His smile faded as he came around the table and got a look at her face. "Or maybe not. Last time I had you in here you looked pale and worn out. You still do."

"I had a bad night. A horrible night. I

ended up taking a sleeping pill — non-prescription type. Even that left me washed out."

"Anxiety?" He took her chin, turning her head to study the yellowing bruise on her cheek. "Nightmares?"

"I took the pill to avoid anxiety and nightmares. I saw the killer last night."

Doc pursed his lips, and his eyes were sharp on her face when he slid onto his stool. "Why don't you tell me about it."

She ran it through, every detail. "You don't have to believe me, or say you do," she finished. "It's been a crappy few days, so I look pale and worn out."

"This tender?" he asked as he gently pressed the bruise.

"A little. It doesn't bother me."

"How long have you been taking the sleeping pills?"

"Last night was the first one in nearly a year."

"Have you started back taking anything else since you were here last?"

"No."

"Any other symptoms?"

"Like forgetfulness, seeing things that aren't there? No."

"Let me play devil's advocate for a minute. Is it possible that this man you saw could represent your fear? You didn't see the face of the man who shot you. Not clearly. Or the trauma you experienced wiped that face out of your memory."

"I don't think I saw him," she said quietly. "It was like snapping a finger. The door slamming open, me starting to turn. I saw the gun . . . and then . . . well, then he used it."

"I understand." Briefly, gently, he laid a hand on hers. "You never, from what I understand, saw the other men who killed your friends?"

"No, I never saw any of them." Only heard them, she thought. Only heard them laughing.

"Have you considered that the figure at the window last night, potentially the man you saw by the river, is a manifestation of the fear and helplessness you experienced during the attack and after it?"

Inside her belly something twisted. Disappointment, she realized. Simple disappointment that he didn't believe her after all. "You've been reading psych books."

"I admit I have. Giving your fear mass and shape doesn't make you crazy, Reece. It could be a way of bringing it out so you can see it, experience it, resolve it."

"I wish it were. But I know a woman died by his hands. I know he's watching me and doing what he can to break my nerve and undermine my credibility." She smiled a little. "It's not paranoia if they're really after you."

Doc sighed.

"I know what paranoia feels like. How it tastes in the throat. I'm not paranoid. I'm not manifesting my fear. I'm living it."

"Another possibility. Just hear me out. The first time you saw this man, and the violence, you'd just encountered Brody on the trail. The other incidents increased as your relationship with Brody developed. The more serious you've become, the more serious, or personal, the incidents. Is it possible your sense of survivor's guilt is putting up obstacles to your happiness?"

"So I'm making myself crazy to sabotage my relationship with Brody? No. Damn it, I've *been* crazy. I know what it feels like, and this isn't it."

"All right then, all right." He patted her hand. "We — how was it said? — eliminate the probable and whatever's left, however improbable, must be the truth. We're going to draw a little blood, see how you're doing."

Reece went back to Joanie's for the second half of a split shift. Mac Drubber and Carl were plowing through pork barbecue subs. Mac held up a hand to stop her as he chewed and swallowed. "Ah, I got in some fresh Parmesan. Kind comes in a chunk."

"You did?"

"Thought you might want it. It's a little dear."

"I'll come by later and get it. Thank you, Mr. Drubber." On impulse, she leaned down, kissed the top of his head. "Thanks. I don't deserve it."

"Oh, now." A little pink rode along his cheekbones. "You got a mind for something we don't stock as a rule, you just let me know what it might be. No problem getting it in for you."

"I will. Thanks."

And first chance she got, Reece decided, she was going to make something special, something superb, and invite him over to Brody's for dinner.

She walked into the kitchen in time to see Linda-gail slam a tub of dirty dishes next to Pete.

"Uh-oh."

"Trouble in paradise," Pete said out of the corner of his mouth.

"Don't you mutter around me," Linda-gail snapped, whirling so her hair swirled out like a short red cape. "I'm not deaf."

"Going to be unemployed you keep slamming things around."

Linda-gail rounded on Joanie. "I wouldn't be slamming things around if your son wasn't a liar and a cheat."

Her expression remained placid as Joanie continued to grill steak and onions. "My boy may be a lot of things not so complimentary, but I've never known him to be either of those. Mind yourself, Linda-gail."

"Did he or did he not tell me he had to stay at the ranch last night helping out with a colicky mare? And was that or was that not a big, fat lie as Reuben was in here fifteen minutes ago asking me how I enjoyed the movie Lo took me to last night?"

"Could be Reuben was mistaken. Could be a lot of things."

Linda-gail lifted her chin. "You're his ma, and you've got to stand by him. But I won't tolerate being lied to or cheated on."

"Can't blame you for that, and you take it up with him whenever you like. As long as it's not when I'm paying you to wait tables."

"He said he loved me, Joanie." This time her voice cracked, just a little — and had Joanie's lips going tight. "He said he was ready to build a life with me."

"Then I expect you'll have to have a conversation with him right soon. But now, you're going to get out there and do your job. You've got customers."

"You're right, and I've wasted enough of my time on him. Men are no damn good for anything." She stalked out, leaving Joanie sighing.

"If that boy's messed this up, he's a bigger jackass than I ever gave him credit for."

While Joanie looked worried, Reece felt a tightly clenched fist knead in her belly. Where had Lo been last night and why had he lied about it?

"And are you going to stand there daydreaming," Joanie demanded, "or take over this grill? I've got office work waiting, and I've got to pay for all this damn paint."

"Sorry." Reece grabbed an apron, headed to the sink to wash her hands. "The new paint looks good. Cheerful."

"New and cheerful costs."

There'd been a three-man crew painting after closing, Reece recalled, and the daffodil yellow with red trim perked up the diner considerably. But what had those men been doing at nine the night before?

"So, when did the painting start, exactly?"

"Eleven. And you'd think that Reuben would be too tired to flap his lips in here today after working till three in the morning."

Casually now, Reece warned herself. Very casual. Just making conversation. "Is that when they came in, eleven?"

"Didn't I just say so? Reuben and Joe and Brenda."

"Brenda? Hotel Brenda? I thought her brother was on the crew."

"Dean had something else to do, so she said. She's better at the cutting in anyhow."

Reece began to cook, and as she cooked she tried to imagine Reuben or Lo, Dean or Joe behind sunglasses and an orange hat, outside Brody's kitchen window.

After work, Reece snagged a ride home with Pete.

"I appreciate you taking me to Brody's."

"Not far, no problem."

"Pete, what do you suppose Lo was up to last night?"

"Some woman's skirt. Never can think without thinking with his dick — beg pardon."

"I guess if that's so, he must've had more than his share of trouble with women."

"Usually sweet-talks them out of kicking his balls into his throat — beg pardon again. But he won't have an easy time sweet-talking our Linda-gail. She's a tough nut."

"You're right about that. Now take Reuben, for instance." Casually again, Reece reminded herself. "You don't see him with women, at least not right and left."

"He gets around. He's just got the sense

to be discreet." Pete slanted his gaze over to Reece, gave a quick, gap-toothed grin. "Had himself a red-hot fling last winter with a snow bunny. A married one."

"Really?"

"Kept it pretty quiet, but it ain't easy slipping in and out of a woman's hotel room without somebody noticing. That Brenda's got a nose for that sort of thing. Even if, as I heard, he came in through the basement entrance."

"The hotel basement," she murmured.

"Then word got out altogether when they had a hell of a row one night. Her yelling and throwing things. Beaned him with some sort of perfume bottle, it seems. He ended up hightailing it out of there, face all scratched up, boots in his hand."

"What did she look like?"

"What?"

"The snow bunny, the woman. I guess I'm just curious."

"Good-looking brunette, as I recall. About ten years older than Reuben's what I heard, too. Called him up at the ranch off and on for weeks after, crying, yelling, spitting. Reuben, he confessed to me one night over a few beers how the experience put him clean off married women."

"That would do it." They were already turning toward Brody's. "I guess Brenda's brother, Dean, had a hot date last night."

"Or a poker game." Pete clucked his tongue. "I tell you a fact, that boy's got ten dollars in his pocket, he's going to stake himself to Texas Hold 'Em with it. That's why he's broke more often than not, and shining up Brenda for a loan. Gambling's bad as heroin you don't know how to handle it."

He stopped his truck in front of the cabin. "Heard you had some doings out here last night."

"I guess everyone's heard by now."

"Don't you let it get you down, Reece."

Curious, she turned to him. "How come you don't think I'm crazy?"

"Hell, who says you're not?" He smiled. "Everybody is, to some extent or other. But you say somebody was prowling around out here, I figure there was."

"Thanks." She opened the door, shifted to smile at him as she got out. "Thanks, Pete."

"Nothing to it."

There was to her. Maybe the cops didn't believe her, but Pete did. And Brody, Lindagail, Joanie. Doc Wallace suspected she was manifesting, but he was trying to look out for her. Mac Drubber probably thought she needed a few screws tightened, but he'd bought Parmesan because she wanted it.

She had a lot of people on her side. And another angle to pursue.

She found Brody on the back porch, drinking a Coke and reading a paperback.

He glanced up, and as he was obviously pleased with what he saw, a smile flitted at the corners of his mouth. "How'd it go today?"

"From bad to better. Doc's happy I've gained some weight, and proposed the possibility that my orange-hatted man is a manifestation of my fears and survivor's guilt — but is willing to be open-minded, if I am. Mr. Drubber ordered me some fresh Parm, and Pete gave me a thumbnail rundown on the romantic lives of a couple of guys in town."

"Been busy."

"And then some. Lo lied to Linda-gail about his whereabouts last night."

"He's been known to play it pretty loose with the ladies." Brody laid the book aside. "You think Lo's a killer?"

"He'd be the last I'd have picked. Damn it, I like him, and my friend's in love with him. But isn't it, traditionally, the least likely who's the one? Isn't that how it works?"

"In fiction, and only in good fiction if it makes sense. Lo bangs the ladies, Slim, but he doesn't choke them to death."

"And if one threatened him in some way, pushed him until he snapped?" She crouched by Brody's chair. "Reuben had a hot affair with a violent ending with a married woman last winter."

"From Lothario to the Singing Cowboy?"

"It should be possible to find out where he was last night. He didn't start painting at Joanie's until eleven. And Brenda's brother didn't show at all."

"So you've decided on your suspect list because you're not sure where these three guys were last night — at the time in question."

"I have to start somewhere. Fighting back. Substantiate where they were, take them off the list. Can't substantiate, keep them on."

"And, what, work your way through every man in the Fist?"

"If necessary. I can cross some off. Hank — the bushy beard and his build is huge. I'd never have missed that. Pete, because he's too little. We talked about this before, right after, but never really focused on it."

"No, I guess we didn't."

"So, anyone over, say, sixty-five, under twenty. This wasn't an old man or a kid. Anyone with a beard or mustache, considerably over or under average height and weight. I know he might not be in the Fist —"

"Yeah, I think he is."

"Why?"

"You didn't hear a car last night. How'd

he get away from the cabin without one?"

"Walked?"

"Maybe had a car far enough away not to be noticed. But, if this is someone from outside, he'd have to be in and around enough to get your routine, to know when you're out of your place, at work, here. Somebody would notice and, however innocently, comment. Comments get around."

"They do," Reece agreed. "They really do."

"And nobody's stayed at the hotel for more than a week since April. No single men for more than two. Some of the cabins have rented, but again not for long and all to families or groups. Could be a family man or part of a group, but it doesn't play as well for me."

"You've done some research."

"One of my things. Could be camping," Brody continued, "but he'd have to come in for supplies. Even if he went somewhere else for them, he'd have to come in to get a handle on your routine, to do what he's done. If he came in more than once, he gets noticed. So, going with that reasoning, he's one of us."

"Brody, I don't want to call the police in again unless it's . . . let's be dramatic. Unless it's life or death."

"Just you and me, Slim."

613

"I like you and me."

"Funny. So do I."

She decided to offset the stir-fry of the night before with a manly meal of pork chops, mashed potatoes, green beans and biscuits. While the potatoes cooked and the chops marinated, she sat down at the kitchen table with her laptop.

The list came first, every male in Angel's Fist she could think of who fit her very wide profile.

Along with the names, she keyed in the basics she knew of them.

William (Lo) Butler, late twenties. Lived in Angel's Fist most of his life. Knows the area well, understands tracking, hiking, camping, etc. (Could the couple by the river have come there on horseback?) Cowboy type, womanizer. Drives a pickup. Easy access to Joanie's office — and keys. Violent streak when riled, as demonstrated at Clancy's.

It seemed so cold, she thought as she read. And unfair perhaps not to note that he seemed so sweet-natured, loved his mother and had considerable charm.

She continued with Reuben.

Early to mid-thirties, she supposed. *Em-*

ployed at Circle K Guest Ranch. Knows area well, as above. Good with his hands. Pickup — with gun rack. Is in town at least once a week. Likes to sing at Clancy's. Previous affair with married woman (possibly victim).

She blew out a breath. She knew he liked his meat rare, his potatoes fried and his pie à la mode. That didn't say much for her purposes.

She continued on, listing names, information, then stopped with a twinge of guilt as she thought of Doc Wallace. He was hitting toward the top of her age barrier. But he was healthy, even robust. He hiked, fished and was welcome everywhere. And wouldn't a man who healed know how to kill?

Then there was Mac Drubber, Dean, Liquor Store Jeff, the stalwart sheriff, accommodating Lynt. And more besides. The idea of listing them all, men she knew, some she considered friends, made her feel a little ill.

She made herself finish, copied to a thumb drive. When she had put the laptop away, she soothed her nerves and guilt with cooking.

Across the lake, Lo knocked on Lindagail's door. He had a single pink rose in his hand and lust in his belly.

When the door opened, he held out the rose and said, "Hey, baby."

Linda-gail ignored the rose and fisted a hand on her hip. "What do you want?"

"You." He made a grab for her with his free hand, but she stepped back and gave the door a boot that nearly slammed it into his face.

He caught it on the shoulder, butted it open again. "What's the problem. Jesus, Linda-gail."

"I don't take flowers from liars. So you can just turn around and get your boots walking."

"What the hell are you talking about?" This time he kicked the door when she swung it. "Cut that out. I put in fourteen hours today so I could get tonight off and see you."

"Is that so? Seems unfair when you had to work extra last night, too. With a colicky horse." She saw his wince, and her eyes narrowed. "You lying son of a bitch. You may have been rolling in the hay, but it wasn't with any damn horse."

"It wasn't like that. Just hold on."

"How could you lie to me like that?" She swung on her heel, stomped away. "I told you I wouldn't be one of the herd for you, Lo."

"You're not. You couldn't be. Hell, you never were. Let's just sit down a minute."

"I don't want you sitting down in my house. I gave you what you wanted. Now it's done."

"Don't say that. Linda-gail. Honey. It's not anything like what you think."

"Then what is it, Lo? You didn't lie to me?"

He shoved back his hat. "Well, yeah, I did, but —"

"Get out."

He tossed the rose, then his hat, aside. "I'm not leaving like this. Yeah, I lied to you about last night, but I had a good reason to."

"Oh? And what's her name?"

The frustration, the hint of embarrassment hardened on his face into cold anger. "I don't cheat. Never have, not with women, not with cards, not with anything. If I'm ready to move on, then I break it off first. I don't two-time anyone. Why would I start with you when you're the one who matters?"

"I don't know." Her eyes filled. "I wish I did."

"I wasn't with another woman, Linda-gail. I swear it."

"And I'm just supposed to take your word on that, when you've already lied to me?"

"You got a point. But I've got one, too. If you love me, you need to trust me on this one thing."

"Trust gets earned, William." Furious with them, she dashed the tears away. "Tell me where you were."

"I can't. Not yet. Don't turn away. Don't, honey. I had something I needed to do. It wasn't another woman."

"Then why won't you tell me?"

"I will, if you just wait till Saturday night."

"What's Saturday night got to do with it?"

"I can't tell you that, either, or not all of it. But it's all part of the whole thing. Give me until Saturday night. I want a Saturday night date with you."

She finally gave up, sat down. "You want a date with me after you lied and won't tell me why?"

"That's right. Trust me on this one thing. I'm banking it'll be worth it to you." He crouched down now, brushed a tear from her cheek. "I swear on my life, Linda-gail, it wasn't another woman."

She sniffled. "You rob a bank?"

And he smiled, slow and utterly charming. "No, not exactly. Do you love me?"

"It seems I do, though it's awfully inconvenient and annoying right this minute."

"I love you, too. It's getting so I like saying it."

She took his face so she could study it

closely. "You've got till Saturday night, and God help me, Lo, I believe you when you say it wasn't another woman. I don't see how you'd hurt me that way. So don't make a fool out of me."

"I couldn't if I tried." He took her wrists, then leaned in to touch his lips to hers. "I wouldn't if I could."

"I was going to make a pizza," she announced. "I like pizza when I'm feeling sad and mad. I guess I like it however I'm feeling. You can share my pizza, Lo, but you're not sharing my bed. If I have to wait for Saturday night for the truth, you'll have to wait until then for sex."

"I guess that's fair. Painful, but fair." He got to his feet, reached out a hand for hers. "You got a beer to go with the pie?"

He was coming, through the dark, through the wind. Her boots rang on the hard-packed trail. Could he hear them? She heard nothing but the wind and the river, but she knew he was coming, moving steadily behind her like a shadow, slipping closer and closer. Soon his breath would be on the back of her neck; soon his hand would curl around her throat.

She'd lost all sense of direction. How had she gotten here? Her only choice was ahead, up and up so that her legs wept with the effort.

The slice of moon showed her the curve of the trail, the rock face, the dangerous and hypnotic gleam of the river below. It showed her the way, but the way held no escape. And it would guide him to her.

She chanced a look behind her, saw nothing but sky and canyon. Relief came with a choked sob. She'd gotten away, somehow. If she could just keep going, keep running, she'd find her way back. She'd be safe again.

But when she turned, stumbling forward, he was there. In front of her now, impossible. Blocking her path. Still she couldn't see his face, couldn't know him.

"Who are you?" She screamed it out in a voice that blew across the wind. "Who the hell are you?"

As he came toward her, the fingers of his gloved hands curling, uncurling, she made her choice. She jumped.

The wind slapped her. Back into the kitchen at Maneo's. A spin to the door, another faceless man, this one in a hooded jacket. The blast of a gun. Pain exploded — the impact of the bullet, the impact of the water.

The river closed over her, the pantry door shut.

And there was no light, there was no air. No life.

She woke with Brody gripping her arms.

"Snap out of it," he ordered. "Right now."

"I jumped."

"What you did was fall out of bed."

"I died."

Her skin was slicked with sweat, and his own heart was still skipping several beats. "You look pretty lively to me. Bad dream, that's all. You were putting up a hell of a fight."

"I . . . what?"

"Kicking, clawing. Come on. Up."

"Wait. Just wait." She needed to orient herself. The dream was brutally clear, every detail. Until she hit the water, or fell into the pantry. "I was running," she said slowly. "And he was there. I jumped. Into the river. But then, it got mixed up. Or it blended. I was falling into the river, I was falling into the pantry at Maneo's. But I didn't just sink." She pressed a hand to his chest, felt the warmth against her cold skin. "I didn't just give up."

"No. I'd say you were fighting your way to the surface. You were trying to swim."

"Okay. Okay. Good for me. About damn time."

27

Getting up early every day changed Brody's perspective. He saw more sunrises, and some of them were worth the trouble of prying his eyes open. He got more work done, which was going to make his agent and his editor happy. It gave him more time to poke around his cabin, and consider the possibility of change.

The location was good, and while he'd toyed on and off with the possibility of buying instead of renting, maybe he should get more serious about becoming a home owner.

Investment value, equity.

Mortgage, maintenance.

Well, you had to take the bad with the good.

And if he owned the place, he could expand his office, maybe add on a deck. Better view of the lake from up there, especially in the summer when the leaves thickened up. In summer, he could barely catch a glint of the water from the first-floor windows.

A deck would be a nice place, he mused, to sit in the morning and have coffee, gear up for the day.

He stood at the window of his office now, with coffee, picturing the change. It could be good.

One chair or two? he asked himself as he imagined the deck. If keeping the cabin was a big step, keeping the woman was a giant leap over a chasm.

He'd always enjoyed women, for their brains as well as their bodies. But if anyone had told him he'd one day want a very specific woman around all the time, he'd have reeled off a long list of reasons why such a possibility wasn't for him.

Now, with Reece, he couldn't think of one item for the list.

Having her around started his day early, that was true. And he'd gotten into the habit, once he'd quit the *Trib*, of rolling out of bed whenever he damn well felt like it. But there was always coffee, really good coffee he didn't have to make himself. And food. Hard to overstate the advantages of getting up to food and coffee every morning.

And her voice. The smell of her. The way she *arranged* things. Ingredients for a meal, her clothes, the pillows on the bed. He'd found himself ridiculously charmed by the way she folded the bathroom towels over the rung.

That was a little sick. Probably.

But what man could resist the way those

amazing eyes of her stayed a little blurry for the first half hour in the morning?

She was a more compelling reason to get out of bed every morning than the most spectacular sunrise.

She was troubled, complicated and would probably never shake off all her phobias and neuroses. But that's what made her Reece, made her interesting. What sucked him in. There was nothing, absolutely nothing run-of-the-mill about Reece Gilmore.

"Two chairs," he decided. "It's going to have to be two chairs."

Turning away from the window, he went to his desk. He picked up the thumb drive she'd given him. When he booted up, he saw there were two documents on the drive. One headed CB, the other LIST.

"Cookbook thing," he mumbled, and wondered if she meant for him to have it, or had slipped up. Well, either way, he had it now.

He opened that first, started reading the text she had headed as INTRO.

The in-laws are coming into town unexpectedly — tomorrow . . . It's the third date, and you're making her dinner. And hoping to follow it up with breakfast in bed . . . It's your turn to host your book club . . . Your perfect

*sister invited herself and her fiancé —
the doctor — to dinner . . . Your son
volunteered you to make cupcakes for
the entire class . . .*

Don't panic.

*No matter how busy you are, how
overwhelmed, how inexperienced you
might be in the kitchen, it's going to
be fine. In fact, it's going to be spectacular. I'm going to walk you through
it, every step.*

*From the sumptuous to the casual,
from tailgate parties to elegant dining
and everything in between, you're the
chef.*

*All right, I'm the chef. But you're
about to become a Casual Gourmet.*

"Not bad," he decided, reading on.
She'd woven in little bits about time,
equipment, lifestyles. Kept it all light, a
little frothy. Accessible.

After the introduction, she'd included a
basic summary of the tone of the book she
was proposing, then half a dozen recipes.
The instructions — with bits of pep talk —
were clear enough that he thought it might
not be completely impossible for him to
follow one through himself.

Topping each were stars, running from
one to four. Degree of difficulty, he noted.
Smart. In parentheses, she'd made a note

suggesting the asterisks might be chefs' hats.

"Clever girl, aren't you, Slim?"

He considered for a moment, then composed a quick e-mail to his agent. And attached Reece's file.

He closed it, opened her list.

Oh yeah, she was clever, he thought again. Her little sketches of the men were insightful and on target. Maybe it surprised him to find names like Mac Drubber and Doc Wallace, but she was thorough. And he enjoyed reading comments about Mac such as *mildly flirtatious, likes to gossip.*

He'd have to ask Reece what she'd have put after his name if she'd included him on her list.

He edited in some of his own comments, observations. She couldn't have known, for instance, that Deputy Denny had gotten his heart broken by a girl who'd worked as a maid at the hotel, had strung him along for six months, then blown out of town with a biker the previous autumn.

He saved the updated file, copied both it and the cookbook data to his machine.

When he'd finished, it was still shy of eight in the morning.

Nothing left to do but go to work.

He broke at eleven, went down to the kitchen to switch coffee for Coke and added a handful of pretzels. He was munching down on the first of them when his phone rang. He scowled, as he always did when the phone rang, then lightened up when the caller ID readout showed his agent.

"Hi, Lyd. It's going good," he told her when she asked about the book. He looked at the cursor on his screen. Today it was his friend. Other days, it might be the enemy. Then he smiled when she asked if he had time to talk about the proposal from his friend. "Yeah, I got a few minutes. What did you think?"

When he hung up, he scratched around through his piles of notes for the copy he'd made of Reece's schedule. He found it between a gun magazine — research — and a printout on the plasma TV he was thinking of buying.

He looked at the clock, back at the cursor. And decided he wasn't going to feel guilty for knocking off early.

He wandered into Joanie's just as Reece was stripping off her apron. He leaned on the counter. She had her hair bundled up, and the heat from the grill had her face flushed. She looked soft, he thought.

"You eat anything you cooked today?" he asked her.

"Not exactly."

"Pack something up."

"Pack something up? What's this? Another picnic?"

"No. It's lunch. Hey, Bebe, how's it going?"

"I'm pregnant."

"Ah . . . congratulations?"

"Easy for you to say. You don't have morning sickness. The fun never ends." But she smiled, eased her feet by leaning on the counter across from him. "Jim's hoping for a girl this time. I wouldn't mind. How come you never ask me to pack something up, Brody?"

"Because Jim would kick my ass. Am I supposed to ask when you're due and stuff like that?"

"You're a guy. You're supposed to look flustered and a little afraid. And you're doing a good job. In November, around Thanksgiving. By then, I'll look like I've swallowed an entire Butterball anyway. When's your next book coming out?"

"A couple months sooner, and much less painfully."

At the call of order up, Bebe rolled her eyes. "Well, back to the thrill and excitement of food service."

"Lunch." Reece held up a large bag as she came out of the kitchen. "You can be among the first to sample our new and experimental paninis."

"Paninis. At Joanie's."

"*Et tu,* Brody? You'd think I was cooking snails and calf brains — which I can do, and deliciously."

"I'll take the panini." He led her outside, taking her elbow and steering her across the street as she glanced around for his car.

"Where are we going?"

"To the lake."

"Oh. Nice idea. It's a pretty day for lunch by the lake."

"We're not having lunch by the lake. We're having lunch on the lake." He nodded toward a canoe. "In that."

She stood where she was and eyed the boat, a little dubiously. "We're going to sit in a canoe and eat paninis?"

"I picked the spot, you picked the food. It's Doc's boat. He said we could borrow it for a few hours today. We're going to do a little paddling."

"Hmmm."

She liked boats. That is, she liked boats with motors, or boats with sails. But Reece had no idea how she felt about boats with paddles. "I bet that water's still pretty cold."

"You bet right, so let's stay on it, not in it. Get in the boat, Reece."

"Getting in the boat." She stepped aboard, balanced herself and walked to the rear bench.

"Turn around the other way," Brody told her.

"Oh."

He got in, handed her a paddle, then took the front bench. Using his paddle, he launched them from shore. "Just do what I do, only on the opposite side of the canoe."

"You've done this before, right? What I mean to say is this wouldn't be the maiden voyage for both of us, would it?"

"I've done it before. I haven't bought a boat yet because I waver between a canoe and a kayak, and it feels stupid to have both. Besides, there's always one to borrow without storage and maintenance hassles. You just buy the owner a six-pack or a bottle, and you're good."

"Always an angle." She had to put her shoulder into the paddle. "Water's harder than it looks."

Her muscles were already warming, and as she watched Brody paddle like a hawk watches a rabbit, she thought she had his rhythm. She could admit she liked the sensation of gliding; the boat just seemed to skim over the water. But gliding took work, and she could already feel it in her shoulders, her biceps.

Time to start weight resistance again, she told herself.

"Where are we going?" she called out to him.

"Nowhere."

"There again?" She laughed, shook back the hair that had blown loose in the breeze.

And the mountains caught her like a fist.

"Oh God. Oh my God."

In the front of the boat, Brody smiled. He heard the awe, the reverence in her voice. "A kick in the head, aren't they?" He secured his paddle, turned to face her, then took her paddle from her still hands, secured it.

"It's different from here. It's all different somehow. They look . . ."

"They look?"

"Like gods. Silver and shining with thin crowns of white, dark belts of green. Bigger somehow, and more powerful."

They rose, rose and spread, silver blue against the purer blue of the sky. The snow that clung to the higher peaks was as white as the clouds that drifted over them. And on the water, they mirrored. On the water, she felt as if she were inside them.

An egret soared up, skimmed the lake, glided like a ghost into the marsh on its north end.

There were other boats. A little Sunfish with a yellow sail fluttered in the center of the lake; a kayaker worked on his skills. She recognized Carl fishing out of a canoe, and a couple who must have been tourists streamed out of one of the braided channels and slid onto the plate of the lake.

She felt weightless and small, and punch-drunk.

"Why don't you do this every day?" she wondered.

"I usually do it more once June hits, but I've been busy. Last summer, Mac talked me into going on a three-day trip on the river. Him, me, Carl, Rick. I went along because I figured it would be good research. Floated along the Snake, camped, fried fish Carl caught like they were eager to jump in the boat for him. Drank cowboy coffee. Told a lot of lies about women."

"You had fun."

"Had a hell of a time. We could do that, take a couple of days once you get the hang of paddling and try one of the easy channels."

"Easy might have to be the key word, but I think I'd like that."

"Good. I read your list."

"Oh." It was like a cloud over the sun. Still, it had to be discussed, she thought, explored. She opened the bag of sandwiches. "What did you think?"

"Pretty thorough. I added some bits. A little discreet poking around, we should be able to eliminate some. I already found out Reuben, Joe, Lynt and Dean were in a poker game in Clancy's back room. Seven to after ten for Reuben and Joe, when they knocked off to head to Joanie's. Dean,

Lynt, Stan Urick, who's not on your list since he's seventy and built like a twig, and Harley — who's not due to the thicket he calls a beard — were in it until after one in the morning. Nobody left for more than the time it takes to piss. Dean lost eighty bucks."

"Well, three down."

"My agent liked your cookbook proposal."

"What? *What?*"

Brody took a bite of the panini. "Damn good sandwich," he said with his mouth full of it. Then swallowed. "Needs to talk to you directly though."

"But it's not ready."

"Then why'd you give it to me?"

"I just . . . I thought, if you felt like it, had the time, you could glance over it. That's all. Give me an opinion, or I don't know. Pointers."

"I thought it was good, so I asked my agent for her opinion. Being a bright individual, she agrees with me."

"Because you're her client or because it's good?"

"First, she's got bigger clients than me, a lot bigger. I'm a little fish in her pond. But ask her yourself. Anyway, she liked the way you structured it, but it needs to be formalized into a proposal. She called the intro 'fun and breezy.' Claimed she was going to try out one of the recipes to-night to see how it translates. She actually cooks, but she's also going to give one of the simpler ones to her assistant, who doesn't."

"Like an audition."

"She's a busy woman, and wouldn't take on a client unless she believes she can sell. You probably want to talk to her to-morrow, after the audition."

"I'm nervous."

"Sure. Lydia won't bullshit you." He pulled out the take-away fountain Coke she'd packed with the sandwiches. "She copped to who you were."

"I'm sorry?"

"She's smart, savvy, and she keeps up with current events." Brody eschewed even the idea of a straw and simply pulled off the plastic cap and drank. "Has a memory like a herd of elephants. She asked me if you were the Reece Gilmore from Boston who survived the Maneo Massacre a couple years ago. I didn't lie to her."

Her appetite took a steep dive. "No, of course you didn't. What difference does it make to her?"

"It may make one to you. If you sell, if you publish, she won't be the only one to put it together. You've been flying under the radar for a while now, Slim. You'll be back on it if you try for this. Reporters, questions. You'll have to decide if you're up for it."

" 'Mass-murder survivor, former mental patient writes gourmet cookbook.' I get it. Shit."

"Something to think about."

"I guess it is." She looked around, the water, the mountains, the marsh. Willows dipped their feathery green leaves into the water. Across the lake, a silver fish wiggled madly on the end of Carl's line.

It was so beautiful, so peaceful — and there was no place to hide. "She may not represent it anyway. And even if she does," Reece considered, "she may not be able to sell it." She looked back at Brody. "It's a lot of big steps."

"Smaller ones get you to the same place, but they take a hell of a lot longer. So figure out where you want to go, and how long you want to take to get there." He took another bite of his sandwich. "Why'd you put paninis on Joanie's menu today?"

"Because they're good, fun, fast. Add a little variety."

"Another reason" — he gestured with the sandwich — "you're creative. You can't stifle it. You like to feed people, but you like to do it your own way, or at least add a dash of yourself to the process. If you keep working there, you're going to be compelled to put yourself into it, little by little."

She shifted on the bench, uncomfortable because she knew he was right. Knew she was already doing just that. "I'm not trying to take over."

"No. But you're not just trying to fit in anymore. The Fist's never going to be Jackson Hole."

Confused now, Reece shook her head. "Okay."

"But it's going to grow. Look again," he suggested, and gestured to the mountains. "People want that. The view, the air, the lake, the trees. Some want it for a weekend, or a couple of weeks on vacation. Some want it for good, or for a second home where they can boat or ski or ride horses. The more crowded the cities and the burbs get, the more people want a place that isn't for their alternative time. The thing about people is, they always need to eat."

She uncapped the bottle of water she'd brought along for herself. "Is this a convoluted way of suggesting I open a restaurant here?"

"No. First, you'd seriously piss Joanie off. Second, you don't want to run a restaurant. You want to run a kitchen. Do you know who happens to be the biggest entrepreneur in Angel's Fist?"

"Not offhand, no."

"Joanie Parks."

"Come on. I know she owns a couple of places."

"Angel Food, half the hotel, my cabin and three others, four houses, just in the Fist, and a chunk of acreage in and outside it. She owns the building that holds Teton Gallery and Just Gifts."

"You're kidding. She squawks if I want to spend a few cents extra on arugula."

"Which is why she owns a big handful of the town. She's frugal."

"I've come to love and admire her, but come on. She's cheap."

He grinned as he lifted his take-away cup again. "Is that any way to talk about your business partner?"

"How does she go from my boss to my partner?"

"When you propose to her that she open a Casual Gourmet on the opposite side of town from the diner. A small, intimate restaurant, with upscale yet accessible dining."

"She'd never . . . She might. Small, intimate for that special night out or that fancy ladies' lunch. Hmmm. Hmmm. Lunch and dinner service only. Revolving menu. Hmmm."

The third *hmmm* had Brody fighting back a smile. Her brain was already caught up in the idea. Her nerve, he imagined, would catch up quickly enough.

"Of course, it depends on where you want to go."

"And how long I want to take to get there. You're a sneaky bastard, Brody, putting that seed in my head. I won't be able to get it out."

"Gives you a lot to think about. Are you going to eat the other half of that sandwich?"

Grinning, she passed it over, and the cell phone in her pocket rang. "Nobody calls me," Reece began as she dug it out. "I wonder why I carry it most of the time. Hello?"

"Reece Gilmore?"

"Yes."

"It's Serge. I made you beautiful in Jackson."

"Oh, yes. Serge. Um, how are you?"

"Absolutely fine, and hoping you and Linda-gail will come back to visit me."

Instinctively, Reece lifted a hand to her breeze-tousled hair. She could use a trim, no question. But she also needed to pay her car insurance. "I'll have to talk to her about that."

"Meanwhile, I called about the picture you left with me. The flyer?"

"The sketch? You recognized her?"

"I didn't, no. But I just hired a new shampoo girl who thinks she does. Do you want me to give her your number?"

"Wait." Her eyes rounded as she stared at Brody. "Is she there now? The new girl?"

"Not at the moment. She's not starting until Monday. But I have her information. You want it?"

"Yes. Wait!" She dug into her purse for a pad, a pen. "Okay."

"Marlie Matthews," Serge began.

She wrote it down, name, address, phone number, while the canoe drifted lazily on the lake. "Thank you, Serge, thanks so much. As soon as I can possibly manage it, Linda-gail and I are coming in for the works."

"Looking forward to it."

She clicked the phone closed. "Someone recognized the sketch."

"I got that much. Better get your paddle. We'll have to secure the boat before we go to Jackson Hole."

28

Marlie Matthews lived on the ground floor of a two-level wood box of furnished apartments off Highway 89. There'd been an attempt to give it a bit of style, with fake stucco walls forming a little cement courtyard gated with wrought iron. Inside it, there were a few faded mesh chairs, a couple metal tables that still had the white gleam of fresh paint. It looked clean and, though the tiny parking lot was still pocked with potholes from the winter, decently maintained.

In the courtyard, a towheaded boy of about four was riding a red tricycle in wide, determined circles. Through an open window on the second floor came a baby's long, furious wails.

The minute they started across the courtyard, a woman stepped through the sliding glass doors of a lower unit. "Help you?"

She was small, wiry, with a short, sleek cap of dark hair liberally streaked with bronze. She gripped a rag mop, eyeing them as though she was prepared to beat them off with it if she didn't like their response.

"I hope so." Because she knew what it was like to be wary of strangers, Reece tried an easy, open smile. "We're looking for Marlie Matthews."

The woman signaled to the little boy. All it took was a crook of her finger to have him aiming his little bike in her direction. "What for?"

"She may know someone we're looking for. Serge from the Hair Corral called me. I'm Reece, Reece Gilmore. This is Brody."

Apparently the mention of her new boss was password enough. "Oh, well, I'm Marlie."

Upstairs, the baby stopped crying, and someone began to sing in crooning Spanish. "My neighbor just had a baby," Marlie added when Reece automatically glanced up toward the singing. "I guess you can come in for a minute. Rory, you stay where I can see you."

"Mom, can I have a juice box? Can I?"

"Sure, you go get one. But if you go back outside, you stay right where I can see you."

The boy dashed inside, with the adults following. He went directly to the refrigerator in the kitchen, sectioned off from the living room by a counter. "You all want something?" Marlie asked. "A cold drink maybe?"

"Thanks. We're fine."

The place was whistle clean and smelled of the lemony cleaner in Marlie's mop pail. Though it was on the sparse side with its two-seater sofa and single chair, there had been attempts to make it homey with a red glass vase of yellow fabric daisies on the counter, a potted peace plant on a table situated so it could bask in some light through the sliders.

A corner of the living room had been fashioned into a play area with a little white table and red chair. On the wall, a corkboard was covered with a child's drawings; on the floor, a clear plastic tub held toys.

Obviously more interested in the strangers than his trike, Rory carried his juice box up to Brody.

"I have a race car and a fire engine," he announced.

"Is that so? Which is faster?"

With a grin, Rory went to retrieve them.

"You can go ahead and sit down," Marlie told them.

"Mind if I sit over here?" Brody wandered over to the toy box, sat on the floor with the boy. Together, in male unity, they investigated the contents.

"I left a sketch at the salon a few weeks ago," Reece began while Marlie kept an eye on her son. "Serge said you thought you might have recognized her."

"Maybe. I can't say for certain sure. It's just that when I saw the drawing sitting on the counter, I thought — guess I said — 'What's Deena's picture doing in here?' "

"Deena?"

"Deena Black."

"A friend of yours?" Brody said it casually while he ran the fire truck along the floor with Rory's race car.

"Not exactly. She used to live upstairs where Lupe does now. The new baby?"

"Used to?" Brody repeated.

"Yeah, she left. A month or so ago."

"Moved out?" Reece asked.

"Sort of." As if satisfied Brody wasn't going to grab Rory and run off with him, Marlie perched on the edge of the couch. "She left some stuff, took her clothes and like that, but left some kitchen stuff, magazines, that kind of thing. Said she didn't want it, just junk anyhow."

"She told you that?"

"Me? No." Marlie thinned her lips. "We weren't actually on what you'd call speaking terms by that time. But she left a note for the super. He lives next door. Said she was moving on to better. She always said she would. So she took her clothes, got on her bike and blew."

"Bike?" Brody repeated.

"She drove a Harley. Fit her, I guess, 'cause she brought a lot of biker types home while she lived here." She glanced over to make sure Rory wasn't paying attention. "Worked in a titty bar," she said under her breath. "Place called the Rendezvous. Deena used to tell me, when we were still talking, that I'd make more money there than at Smiling Jack's Grill. I waitress there. But I didn't want to work at that kind of place, and I can't be out until God knows serving beer, half naked, when I've got Rory."

"She lived alone?" Reece prodded.

"Yeah, but she'd bring company home pretty regular. Sorry if she's a friend of yours, but that's the way it was. She had *company* most every night up until about six, eight months ago."

"What changed?"

"Pretty sure there was a man — a particular one. I heard them up there once a week or so. Then she'd light out for a day, sometimes two. Told me she had a fish on the line — that's how she talks. He bought her stuff, she said. New leather jacket, a necklace, lingerie. Then, I don't know, I guess they had a falling-out."

"Why do you think that?"

"Well, she came roaring in here early one morning. I was getting Rory in the car to take him to preschool. She was steaming. Cursing a streak. I told her to take it down, that my boy was in the car.

She said how he was going to grow up to be a bastard like the rest of them.

"Can you beat that?" Marlie demanded, obviously still insulted by it. "Saying that about that sweet boy and right to my face?"

"No, I can't. She must have been angry about something."

"I don't care what she was mad about, she had no cause to talk about my Rory that way. Set me off. We had a round right out there in the parking lot, but I backed off first. I had my kid, plus I heard she once smashed a guy in the face with a beer bottle at the bar. She isn't the type I want to mess with."

"Can't blame you." Reece thought of how Deena had slapped her killer, how she'd leaped at him.

"*She* didn't back off," Marlie continued. "Got right up in my face. She said how nobody pushes her around. Nobody screws with her. And he — must've been the guy she was seeing — was going to pay. When she was done with him, she'd be moving on to better."

Marlie shrugged. "That's the gist of it anyway. She stomped away, and I got in the car. I was pretty steamed."

"Is that the last time you saw her?" Brody asked.

"No, I guess I saw her around a couple

more times. Avoided her, to tell the truth. Heard her bike a few times."

"Would you remember the last time you heard it?" Reece asked her.

"I sure would because last time it was the middle of the damn night. Woke me up. It would've been the next day the super told me she lit out. Put the keys in an envelope and split. He said he was putting the rest of her things in storage for a while." She shrugged again. "Maybe he did, maybe he didn't. None of my business. I'm glad she's gone. Lupe and her husband are a lot better neighbors. Serge said I can schedule working at the salon when Rory's in preschool, but Lupe's watching Rory evenings when I work at the grill. I'd never have trusted Deena with my kid."

Suddenly Marlie frowned. "Are you cops or something? She in trouble?"

"We're not cops," Reece replied and glanced at Brody. "But I think there may have been trouble. Do you know if the super's home?"

"He mostly is."

He was. Jacob Mecklanburg was a tall, lean seventy with a dapper white mustache. His apartment, a mirror image of Marlie's in design, was crammed with books.

"Deena Black. High maintenance," he said with a shake of his head. "Always complaining. Paid the rent on time — or nearly. Not a happy woman, the sort that likes to blame everything and everyone else for the fact her life isn't what she imagined it would be."

"Is this Deena?"

Reece took a copy of the sketch from her purse.

Mecklanburg changed his glasses for a pair in his pocket, pursed his lips as he studied the sketch. "Strong resemblance. I'd say it was her, or a close relation. Why are you looking for her?"

"She's missing," Brody said before Reece could speak. "Would you still have the note she left you?"

Mecklanburg considered a moment, studying Brody's face, then Reece's. "I like to keep everything in a file. Wouldn't want her coming back to me, saying I'd rented the place out from under her. I don't see any harm in letting you look at it."

He moved over to the far end of one of his bookshelves, pulled up a rolling stool and sat to go through a lateral file cabinet.

"Nice collection," Brody said easily. "The books."

"I can imagine living without food. I cannot imagine living without books. I taught high school English for thirty-five years. When I retired, I wanted a job where I'd have plenty of time to read, but not enough I'd turn into a hermit. This provides that balance. I'm fairly handy with small repairs, and once you've dealt with teenagers for a few decades, handling tenants is no strain. Deena was one of the more difficult. She didn't want to be here."

"Here?"

"In a small, inexpensive apartment on the edge of the action. And while she paid the rent, she didn't want to. She offered me, at various times, quite an expansive menu of sexual favors in lieu of rent." He smiled a little as he pulled out a folder. "We'll just say she wasn't quite my type."

He took the top sheet out of the folder, handed it to Brody.

Screw all of you and this dump. I'm moving on to better. Keep the junk upstairs or burn it. I don't give a flying fuck. DB

"Succinct," Brody commented. "This looks like it was written on a computer. Did she have one?"

Mecklanburg frowned. "Now that you mention it, I don't believe she did. But there are any number of Internet cafés and accesses in town."

"Seems odd," Reece put in, "that she'd take the bother to tell you to get screwed. Why not just leave?"

"Well, she did like to bitch and to brag."

"She was seeing someone the last several months."

"I believe so. But she stopped . . . entertaining here, oh, sometime before the holidays last year."

"Did you ever see him, the man she was involved with?"

"I may have. Once. Most of her 'companions' didn't bother to be discreet. We have laundry facilities downstairs. One of the tenants had reported the washer was acting up. I went down to take a look, see if I could fiddle with it or needed to call a repairman. I was just coming up when he — her friend — was leaving. It was a Monday afternoon. I know as, at that time, all the tenants worked on Mondays."

"A Monday," Reece prompted. "Around the holidays."

"Yes, just after New Year's, I believe. I remember we'd gotten several inches of snow overnight, and I had to go out and shovel first thing. Generally I do any maintenance necessary in the morning or between four and six, barring emergencies. I like to read during lunch, then take a nap. But I'd forgotten about the machine that morning and needed to get to it."

Brushing a finger over his mustache, Mecklanburg paused a moment, pursed his lips in thought. "I'd have to say he was surprised to see me — or be seen. He turned, angled himself away and quickened his pace. And he wasn't parked in the lot. I was curious enough to hurry into my apartment and look out the window. He turned away from the lot."

"Maybe he lives in town," Reece supposed.

"Or parked elsewhere. But I do know that from that point on, Deena went out to meet him. If indeed that's who she was meeting. As far as I know, he never came around here again."

"He didn't want to be seen. Wouldn't you say that?"

"Seems that way," Brody agreed. "Which says married, or in a sensitive position."

"Like a politician? A minister?"

"That'd be two."

At his car, she turned around to study the building again. "It's not a dump. It's basic, but it's clean and tended. But not good enough for Deena Black. She wanted more. Bigger, better, shinier."

"And thought she'd hooked one who'd give it to her. Fish on the line," Brody repeated when Reece frowned at him.

"So either he wasn't providing her as she wanted him to, or he broke it off. I'd say he broke it off — this maybe married, maybe public figure. But, Brody, if he was afraid to be recognized here, what does that do to the theory that he's from Angel's Fist? That he's been stalking me on the home ground."

"Doesn't change it." He pulled open her door, walked around to the driver's side. "Someone who does business in Jackson Hole, for instance. Or could be recognized by someone here who does business in the Fist. Or it was just a guilt reaction."

Like Reece, he stood and leaned on the open door for a moment. "But he didn't kill her because she objected to being dumped. That happens it's annoying, potentially inconvenient, but it's still basically: 'Too bad, sister. We're done. Deal.'"

"Men really are bastards."

"Your breed gets to call it off, too."

"Yeah, but we're usually: 'I'm sorry. It's not you, it's me.'"

He made a dismissive noise as they climbed in. "Rather be stabbed in the eye with a fork than hear that one. But the point is, she had something. She threatened something. He'll pay, that's what she told Marlie. I'd say he didn't want to pay."

"So he killed her, disposed of the body, covered his tracks. Came back here in the middle of the night, on her bike. He'd already written the note."

"He's the one with a computer or with

access to one," Brody agreed. "Which narrows it down not a single bit."

Still, as a puzzle she could see it coming together. They had a name, a lifestyle and, unless they were forcing in the wrong pieces, a motive.

"Took her clothes," Reece added. "A woman doesn't leave her clothes, her personal things behind. So he took them. Easy enough to get rid of. Left the dishes and so forth — too cumbersome. Did the note to cover his ass, too. Just to tie up the ends. Nobody would look for her because everyone would think she'd just pulled stakes."

"He didn't count on you. Not only seeing what you did, but caring enough to stick with it until you found her."

"Deena Black." Reece closed her eyes a moment. "I guess we've got a name now. What's next?"

"Next? We go to a titty bar."

Reece didn't know what she was expecting. A lot of leather and chains, hard looks, hard music.

In reality, there was as much denim as leather, and the looks were disinterested. Still, the music was harsh, gritty rock that pumped out over the stage, where a woman with an explosion of purple hair wore nothing but a red G-string and platform heels.

Smoke curled blue in the light over a stage-side table where a couple of hefty guys with generously tattooed arms watched the show and sucked down bottled beer.

There were a lot of tables — small, one- and two-seaters — most of them facing the stage. Only a few were occupied.

Since it seemed the thing to do, Reece sat at the bar and said nothing while Brody ordered them Coors on draft.

The bartender had a russet-colored mustache that hung to either side of his chin. And a head as bald as a peeled melon.

Brody shifted back to the bar to pick up his beer. "Seen Deena lately?" he asked the bartender.

The man swiped at spilled foam with his rag. "Nope."

"Quit?"

"Musta. Stopped showing up."

"When?"

"While back. Whatsit to ya?"

"She's my sister." Reece sent out a big smile. "Well, half sister. Same mother, different fathers. We're on our way to Vegas, and I thought we could hook up with Deena for a day or two."

She glanced briefly at Brody and noted he'd simply lifted that single eyebrow in an expression she recognized as surprised amusement.

"We went by her place," Reece con-

653

tinued, "and they said she moved out last month, but this is where she worked. Haven't heard from her in a while. Just wanted to say hey, you know?"

"Can't help you."

"Oh well." Reece picked up the beer, frowned at it. "It's not like we're tight or anything. I just figured since we were so close and all we'd touch base with her. Maybe somebody knows where she went."

"Didn't tell me. Left me short a dancer."

"Typical." Reece shrugged, set down her beer without drinking. She wasn't at all convinced it was the sort of place that worried about health inspections. "I guess we wasted our time," she said to Brody. "Maybe she took off with that guy she said she was seeing."

There was a snort from the waitress as she dumped a tray of glasses, bottles and ashtrays. "Not likely."

"Sorry?"

"Had a bust-up. Big, bad one. Pissed her off. You remember, Coon?"

The bartender only shrugged. "Pissed off half the time, you ask me."

"I guess that's typical, too." Reece rolled her eyes for effect. "But she made out like this one was serious. What the hell was his name?"

"Never told me," the waitress replied.

"Just called him Trout. He was her fish on the line, get it?"

"Yeah, I get it."

"Two beers and bumps, Coon. Bud and the house whiskey."

Reece bided her time as the waitress gathered the order, clipped over to the table nearest the stage. When she came back with another tray of empties, Reece tried a smile.

"Couldn't have been that serious then."

"Huh?"

"Deena and this guy, this Trout. Guess it wasn't much of anything."

"Got to be, you ask me. Her side, anyway."

"Really?" Reece shrugged, took a very small sip of beer. "That's not typical. Deena liked to bag 'em, but she wasn't into tagging 'em."

With a grin, the waitress leaned over the bar, pulled a pack of Virginia Slims from behind it. "Good one. Coon, I'm taking a break."

"I'm Reece." She offered a smile again. "Maybe Deena mentioned me."

"No, not that I remember. Didn't even know she had a sister. I'm Jade."

"Nice to meet you. So, Deena was hooked on some guy, huh?"

"Well, she stopped picking marks to take back home with her." She pulled a matchbook out of the pocket of her abbreviated shorts, struck flame. "Sorry, her being your sister, but that's how she was."

"That's not news. I guess that's why I was surprised she talked differently about this guy."

"Said he had some class." Jade tipped her head back as she blew out smoke. "Don't see how, since she met him in here."

"Oh." Now Reece struggled to keep her voice casual. "You saw him then."

"Might've. Can't say. Wasn't a regular, 'cause she'da pointed him out when he came back. Did buy her stuff though. Showed off this necklace he coughed up. Said it was eighteen-karat gold. Probably bullshit, but it was nice. Had a moon on it. Like a little white plate, I guess. Said it was like mother-of-pearl, and that the sparkles in the chain were real diamonds."

"Diamonds? No shit."

"Probably was shit, but she said how they were. She took to wearing it all the time, even during her act. Said there was more where that came from. Trout called her his dark side of the moon, she said. Whatever that means."

"Maybe this Trout knows where she is." Reece glanced at Brody as if for agreement.

He decided to keep drinking his beer and act like a man who couldn't care less either way.

"Do you think someone else who works here might know him? Maybe one of the other dancers?"

"Deena wasn't one to share, if you get me. Brag, sure, but she was keeping this one close. Wasn't a biker."

"Oh?"

"She said it was time she got one who had a straight job and knew more about life than what he saw on the back of a Hog. Anyway, they busted up, like I said. Then she took off. Greener pastures, I expect."

"I guess you're right."

Brody didn't speak until they were back in his car. "Here's a whole new side to you, Slim. You can sit in a titty bar and lie with absolute believability."

"It just seemed the most direct route. Saying something like 'I saw Deena Black murdered a few weeks ago, but hardly anyone believes me,' just didn't ring. I don't know if it did any good though."

"Sure it did. All information points to her disappearance, which coordinates with what you saw by the river. She was involved with a man who obviously didn't want her tossing his name around, and didn't want to be seen with her. Regardless, he was in deep enough to spend money on her. Jewelry's major points with your species, right?"

"It certainly is."

"So he sprang for a bauble, which tells me she was more than a lay, at least for a while. They broke up, and she didn't want to leave it that way. She pushed, he pushed back — and pushed back too hard."

"She may have been serious about him, but she didn't love him."

"You thought she did?"

"I don't know what I thought," Reece said, "but now I know. A woman doesn't talk about a man the way she did him, doesn't call him Trout if she has any real feelings. She was just after what she was after."

He waited a moment. "Does that change your stand on going on with this?"

"No. Bitch or not, she didn't deserve to die that way. I think . . ." Abruptly she pulled up short, grabbed his arm. "Is that Lo? Is that Lo's truck, Brody?"

He looked around as she gestured, just in time to see the back of a black pickup turn a corner. "I don't know. Didn't see enough of it."

"I think it was Lo." Had he seen them? she wondered. If he had, why hadn't he beeped, waved? Stopped. "Why would he be in Jackson?"

"A lot of people come to Jackson for a lot of reasons. It doesn't mean he followed us, Slim. It'd be a hell of a trick tailing us on the stretch of road from the Fist."

"Maybe."

"Are you sure it was him?"

"No. Not absolutely." And there was nothing she could do about it, either way. "So, what now?"

"Once we get back to the Fist I use my innate reporter's skills to find out more about Deena Black. First, we'll browse around some of the local jewelry stores. We may find out where he bought the necklace."

"Oh, that's a good one. A little mother-of-pearl moon on a gold chain, possibly with diamonds. How many jewelry stores are in Jackson?"

"I'm afraid we're going to find out."

Too many, was Brody's opinion after the first hour, especially when you added in the craft and specialty stores that carried jewelry. He'd never understood the need for people to hang metal and stone all over their bodies, but since they'd been doing so since the dawn of time, he didn't expect the activity to go out of fashion.

He was, however, relieved that the back-of-his-mind fear that Reece would surrender to the need to *browse* wasn't realized. She didn't succumb to the temptation that he believed plagued her breed to *just try this on.* A woman who could stay focused on a task when having her senses blasted with glitter and shine was, in his opinion, a hell of a woman.

Now and then he'd see her gaze track offerings, but she stayed on point. He respected that. Particularly when he noticed other men suffering in silence while their women cooed and drooled and hummed over baubles and bits.

His respect and pleasure was such that he stopped along their walking route, pulled her up against him and kissed her enthusiastically.

"Nice. Why?"

"Because you're a sensible, straightforward woman."

"Okay. Why?"

"This business would take twice as long, at least, if you were the type who had to stop and make girl noises at every shop window or display. Taking long enough anyway, but this way we're moving along."

"True." She slipped her hand into his as they headed for the next shop. "I also try to be an honest woman, so I should tell you the only reason I'm not stopping and making what you condescendingly term 'girl noises' is because I can't afford to buy anything. And I'm out of the habit. But it doesn't mean I wouldn't if I could, or that I haven't noticed particularly appealing items. Like the black two-and-a-half-inch ankle boots — I think they were crocodile — two shops back, and the tourmaline earrings on white gold hoops in the last shop. Or —"

"You *were* browsing."

"In my limited fashion."

"My illusions are shattered."

"Better to know the truth now." She gave his hand a friendly squeeze. "Anyway, at this point I'd rather have a set of Sitram than tourmaline."

"Sitram?"

"Cookware."

"You've got pots."

"Yeah, that's just what I've got. What I don't have is heavy-gauge stainless with a thermic copper core base. If I actually sell the cookbook, Sitram's first on my list. Did you buy anything wonderful when you sold your first book?"

"New laptop, loaded."

"There you are. Tools are tools. This place looks like a good possibility. Upscale," Reece continued, scanning the window display. "The real deal. If Deena was telling it straight about the eighteen karats and the diamonds, this could be the place."

It was, Brody noted on entering, a bit more rarefied than most of the shops they'd visited. A woman with luxuriant auburn hair and a smart leather jacket sat at a table studying some sparklers on black velvet while she sipped from a thimble-sized cup. The man who sat across from her spoke in hushed, somewhat reverent tones.

Another woman in stylish red came out from behind a counter with a winning smile. "Good afternoon, and welcome to Delvechio's. Is there anything you'd like me to show you?"

"Actually, we're looking for a specific piece," Reece began. "A necklace. A moon symbol pendant in mother-of-pearl. Diamonds spaced along the chain."

"We had something along those lines a few months ago. Lovely piece. While we don't have anything quite like that now, it may be possible to design something similar for you."

"You sold it?"

"I don't believe I sold it personally, but it was sold."

"You'd have a record of the purchase?"

The winning smile shifted down several notches. "Perhaps you'd like to speak with Mr. Delvechio personally. He's with a client now." She gestured toward the customer. "If you'd like to wait and speak with him about a design, you're welcome to do so. Would you like some coffee, tea, espresso?"

Before they could answer, the redhead

rose. With a light laugh she leaned over and gave Delvechio — a distinguished type with pewter hair and horn-rims — a peck on both cheeks.

"They're perfect, as always, Marco. You knew I couldn't resist."

"I only had to see them to think of you. Would you like them sent?"

"Absolutely not. I have to take them with me."

"Melony will take care of it for you. Enjoy."

"I certainly will."

The clerk in red hurried over to scoop up the sparkles on black velvet. Delvechio turned to Reece and Brody. "A mother-of-pearl moon pendant on a gold chain, with diamond accents?"

"Yes," Reece said, impressed he'd followed their conversation as well as his own. "Exactly."

"Very specific."

"A woman named Deena Black had one. She's missing. Since she said it was a gift, we'd like to find the person who bought it for her. He may have information."

"I see," he said in the same polite tone. "Are you with the police?"

"No, we're interested parties. All we want to know is who bought that necklace."

"We had several pieces last year designed

with moons, stars, suns, planets. Our Universe of Gems theme. They sold quite well for the holidays. I'm afraid I wouldn't be able to give you client information, not unless you're with the police and in possession of a warrant. Even if you were and did, it would take time as all of those pieces were sold in the previous inventory year. And some certainly sold for cash, and there would be no client information in any case."

"How about when it was sold, and for how much?"

Delvechio raised his eyebrows at Brody's question. "I couldn't say when, with absolute certainty."

"Best guess? Don't need a warrant for a guess on when and how much."

"No. We ran that theme, with those pieces, from October of last year through January. A piece as you describe would have been priced at around three thousand."

"Whoever gave it to her knows what happened to her," Reece insisted.

"If that's so, you should contact the police. I can't tell you any more under the circumstances. If you'll excuse me."

He left them to go into the back and closed the door firmly. After a moment's pause, he went to his computer, called up data. He nodded at the name and the transaction.

His memory was excellent, and no less honed than his client loyalty.

Picking up the phone, he made a call.

29

"Three thousand isn't chump change," Brody commented on the drive back.

Reece continued to frown out the window. The shadows were long as the sun eased toward the far west with the mountains holding on to every drop of that fading light. "A man even goes into a store like that, he's decided on an important gift. And as you said, a man doesn't buy an important gift for someone when it's just sex."

"So, they were serious."

Reece shifted around to him. "He wouldn't be seen with her, snuck around. How serious is that? I think *obsessed* or *infatuated* are better words. She was using him, he was using her."

"Okay."

"From what we know about Deena, she was a topless dancer at a dive, dissatisfied, bitchy. She brought a variety of men home, drove a motorcycle and wasn't above exchanging sexual favors for rent. And maybe not for cash, either."

"Figuring she charged some of those men."

"Seems likely. But this guy's different.

He wants an exclusive, and she gives it to him. Maybe she wanted it, too, or maybe she saw it as an investment. If Delvechio was telling it straight — as much as he *would* tell — this was probably a Christmas gift. A man doesn't buy an important piece of jewelry as a Christmas present for someone he's just banging. Especially one who'd have probably been impressed with a fifty-dollar pair of earrings."

"You women are hard on each other," Brody commented after a minute.

"She wasn't an innocent, nor by any accounts so far a particularly nice woman. She didn't deserve to be strangled for it, but she wasn't a passive participant, either. I'm just saying this man was involved. He was infatuated. He was seeing her on the side, or certainly the sly, but she mattered. At least for a while."

She turned back. "So who on the list could spend three thousand dollars on a secret sex partner without it being noticed?"

"I'd say any one of them. Some live alone, and their bank balance is their own concern. Guys who don't live alone often have a nice stash tucked away, just like women do."

"Even a nice stash trickles away after a while. Maybe that was part of the problem."

"She wanted more."

"Isn't it likely? 'Why don't you take me anywhere nice? I'm tired of living in this dump. When can we go on a trip' and variations of the same. They'd been seeing each other for months. She'd want more."

"And infatuation trickles away," Brody decided, "just like cash."

"Dark side of the moon," Reece murmured. "It wants to click in my head with something. Did I see the necklace when he strangled her? I can't remember, not quite. But there's something."

"In fiction land we could go to the cops with all this and they'd get a warrant, get the name. Unfortunately, in this world there's the pesky problem of probable cause."

"There's positive cause," Reece argued. "Deena's dead, and whoever bought her that necklace is the killer."

"No proof she's dead. Or even missing. Just gone and considerate enough to turn in the keys to her apartment. Even if we got lucky and nailed down who bought the necklace, it's still no proof. No absolute proof he gave it to her. Certainly none that he killed her."

Logically, he was right, but Reece was growing weary of logic. "Then what the hell are we doing, Brody?"

"Gathering information. And we have more today than we did yesterday."

"It's not enough. For weeks, months, after the murders in Boston, the investigators would tell me they were looking, they were compiling information. But there was never an arrest, never a trial, never a conviction. I had to walk away. I had to. But how many times can you walk away?"

"No one's walking, Reece. We'll figure out a way to get the name from the jeweler. Or we'll find somebody else who knows something else. But no one's walking."

She said nothing for the next mile. "I could have used you in Boston. I could've used that bullheadedness."

"It's called tenacity."

"A rose by any other name." She laid a hand over his. "Listen, if your infatuation trickles out, let me down easy, will you?"

"Sure. No problem."

It made her smile as they zoomed across the blooming flats toward Angel's Fist.

His hand shook as he closed his cell phone. How had they gotten so close? An inch away from him. How could he have covered his trail so carefully, and still they followed it to Deena?

They knew her name.

He'd done everything — *everything* — that could be done to protect himself, to shield that part of himself.

A temporary madness, that's all Deena

had been. And when he'd regained his senses, he'd done his best to act honorably.

When honor hadn't worked, he'd done what was necessary.

All a man could do was what was necessary.

He would do so now. For the good of the whole. To preserve what deserved preserving.

They weren't part of the Fist. Strangers really, changing what should remain constant. They'd have to be removed, as Deena had been.

He had to restore the balance.

The Saturday crowd kept Reece busy while she left what she knew, didn't know, wanted to know simmering in the back of her mind.

She imagined, even now, Brody was picking his way through the Internet, gathering information on Deena Black. But knowing where and when she was born, where she went to school, if she had a criminal record wouldn't point the way to her killer. Not in Reece's mind.

Met him at the bar, most likely, she decided. He picked her up, or she picked him. Either way, they started an affair. Or a business arrangement.

A man didn't want his friends and neighbors to know he was paying a woman to have sex with him — it was embarrassing.

First, he traveled out of his own sphere to frequent topless bars and engage hookers. Basic preservation of reputation.

But he'd gotten involved, maybe even believed himself in love for the short term. Enough so that he bought her expensive gifts. Made promises? Reece wondered.

Older men often fell for younger, inappropriate women. She tried to imagine Doc Wallace or Mac Drubber with a woman like Deena Black. Reece wondered what it said about her, about them, that it was all too easy to do so.

Just as someone young, still impressionable like Denny, might fall — or someone used to getting his own way with women, like Lo.

Maybe they should bypass Sheriff Mardson — as for all she knew, really, he could be a stone killer — and dump all they knew or suspected in the lap of the Jackson police.

It couldn't be any less productive than doing nothing. And she couldn't keep living with these people, cooking for them and wondering if one was a killer.

"Talking to yourself again."

She jumped a little, then glanced over at Linda-gail. "Probably."

"Well, when you finish your conversation

and it's time for your break, can you take a look at something?"

"Sure, what?"

"This dress I ordered online. It just came in. I ran and picked it up at the post office on my break. God, I hope it fits. I just want your opinion."

"All right, as soon as I —"

"If the two of you are going to stand in my kitchen talking fashion, you might as well take your break now." Joanie moved in, took over the grill. "Make it quick."

"Thanks, Joanie." Linda-gail grabbed Reece's arm and pulled her out of the kitchen, into Joanie's office.

"I paid more than I should have," she said as she hustled Reece inside. "But I just loved it." She snagged it from where she'd hung it on the back of Joanie's office door, then held it up against her. "What do you think?"

It was short and strapless in a tender, spring leaf green. Reece imagined when Linda-gail filled it, it would be a knockout.

"It's great. Sexy and still fresh. Should be fabulous with your hair, too."

"Really? Thank God. Now if it doesn't fit, I'll kill myself."

"Or try something radical like exchanging it for the right size."

"No time. I need it for tonight. Special Saturday night date with Lo. His term —

and he said to wear something wow." She turned and angled in front of the mirror again. "This is pretty wow."

There was a quick jump in Reece's belly. "Where are you going?"

"He won't say. Really secretive about it. I wish I could've gotten back to Jackson for a touch-up, but I had to color my hair myself. It's not too bad, is it?"

"No, it's fine. It's good. Linda-gail —"

"It's an ultimatum night." She fluffed one hand at her hair as she did a three-quarters pose for the mirror. "He's got to explain — and make it good — about why he lied to me the other night about where he was. He knows it's on the line."

"Linda-gail, don't go."

"What? What are you talking about?"

"Just wait. Don't go off with him anywhere until you know what's going on."

"I'm going off with him to find out what's going on." With care, she hung the dress on the door again, smoothed its skirt. "He swore it wasn't another woman, and I believe him. If I want this to work I have to give him a chance to explain things."

"What if . . . what if he was involved with someone? Before. Seriously involved."

"Lo? Serious?" She huffed out a laugh. "Not a chance."

"How could you know, really? How could you be sure?"

"Because Lo's been on my radar since we were fifteen. He hasn't been serious about anyone ever." Her pretty face went tight with determination. "Not the way he is with me, and the way he's going to stay. What's gotten into you? I thought you liked him."

"I do. But he wasn't honest with you."

"That's right, and now he's going to be. I'm either going to like what he has to say tonight, or I won't. I'll either take him or leave him. But I'm damn well going to look fantastic either way."

"Just . . . call me. On my cell. Call me when you get where you're going, and after he explains."

"Jesus, Reece."

"Just do me that favor. I'll be wondering and worrying if you don't. Just do me that favor, Linda-gail. Please."

"Okay, fine. But I'm going to feel pretty stupid."

Better stupid, Reece thought, then hurt and alone.

At his computer, Brody was making some progress. He knew Deena Black was born in Oklahoma in August 1974, had a high school diploma and some slaps for soliciting, one for disturbing the peace, two for assault. The second assault had earned her three months in county.

Her credit rating was in the toilet. Not that this would be a major concern to her now, if it ever had been.

He'd managed to backtrack her to her last two places of employment and residences. She didn't receive glowing references from her employers — a strip club in Albuquerque and a biker bar in Oklahoma City — and her last landlord was still bitter about the two months' rent she'd skipped on.

He found one marriage and divorce — both involving one Titus, Paul J., currently doing the second side of a dime in Folsom for assault with a deadly. A quick search on Titus showed Brody this was not the man's first trip courtesy of the state.

"Weren't what we'd call a sterling citizen, were you, Deena?"

Still, she'd been a looker in her way. He had an ID photo of her now, on screen, and could admit there was something compellingly sexy about her.

"The bad girl," he said aloud. "Who knows it, and likes it that way. And lets you know you'll like it, too."

According to the data he found, she still had family in Oklahoma. A mother, a scant seventeen years older than Deena. There was always the possibility Deena had kept in touch, and that she'd told her mother what she hadn't — apparently — told anyone else. The name of the man she was involved with.

So how to play it? An old friend of Deena's trying to catch up? Chatty, friendly. A Wyoming cop trying to track down information on known associates? Tough, brisk.

Odds were he wasn't going to find out a damn thing anyway.

He decided it was time to take a short break and let his head clear before he tried contacting Deena's mother.

Before he could get up, his phone rang.

The familiar voice had him relaxing back again. The unusual but interesting request had him considering.

Ten minutes later, Brody was walking out of the house, then driving out of town.

He glanced at Angel Food as he passed. If this panned out, he hoped to have a resolution for Reece in a couple hours.

Everything started now. And now there would be no going back — no regrets, no mistakes. It was risky, and the timing would have to be perfect. But it could be done. Had to be done.

The cabin was the right place for this first step. Quiet and secluded, with the cover of the woods, the marsh. No one would come there looking for them. Just as no one had ever come there looking for Deena.

676

When it was done, he'd have hours to make certain it was all done properly. He'd cover all the tracks, as always. And he'd put things right again. Back again. The way they should be.

"All right, Lo, I want to know where we're going."

"That's for me to know."

Linda-gail folded her arms and tried a narrow stare, but he didn't crack.

It wasn't the way to Jackson Hole. She'd secretly hoped he was taking her to a fancy dinner somewhere especially nice. Where she could show off her new dress.

But he hadn't gone that way. In fact —

"If you think for one minute I'm going to sit around some campfire in this dress, you're crazier than I ever gave you credit for."

"We're not going camping. And that dress sure is a killer." He shot her a quick, heated look. "I hope whatever you got on under it's just as lethal."

"You're not going to see what's under it, this keeps up."

"Wanna bet?" He gave her a smug grin, made the next turn.

She saw where he was going now, and went to silent fume. "You might as well turn this truck around and take me right back home."

"If you still feel that way in ten minutes, I will."

He pulled up at the cabin with all the plans and preparations circling in his head. Nerves threatened, but he steeled himself against them.

He'd come too far to back down now.

Since Linda-gail didn't budge, he got out, came around and opened her door. It was probably the way it should have been anyway, he decided, since she was wearing that sexy dress and he was duded up in his best suit.

"Just come on inside, honey, don't be stubborn." He eased and cajoled her as he might a fractious mare. "Otherwise, I'm just going to cart you in anyway."

"Fine. I'm going to call Reece and ask her to come out and get me as soon as she can."

"I don't think you're going to be calling anybody," Lo muttered, and pulled her toward the cabin. "We weren't supposed to get here this soon, but you were all fired up to leave. I wanted it to be heading toward dusk when we got here."

"Well, it's not."

She stalked inside, fully intending to pull out her phone and call Reece. Then she was too stunned to do anything but stare.

For the third time in ten minutes, Reece checked her watch. Why didn't Linda-gail call? Why hadn't she been able to convince her not to go with Lo tonight?

Five more minutes, she vowed. And she was calling Linda-gail. No matter how crazy it sounded, Reece was going to demand to know her whereabouts. And she'd make sure Lo understood she knew.

"Looking at the time isn't going to make it go any faster. You're on till ten regardless." Joanie ladled up stew from the pot. "And don't even think about asking to leave early. I'm already a waitress short."

"I'm not leaving early. It's just Linda-gail said she'd call me, and she hasn't."

"I expect she's too busy to think about calling you. She wheedled the night off, didn't she? Saturday night, too. Her and my boy ganging up on me. Couple of lamebrains, that's what. Everything's sunshine, roses and moonbeams from where they're standing. Well, in here, it's burgers, stew and fried steak, so get that order up."

"What? What did you say?"

"I said get that order up."

"Sunshine and moonbeams. I remember. Oh, oh, God! I remember. I'll be back in a minute."

Arms akimbo, jaw up, Joanie planted her feet. "Girl, you're not leaving that grill until I say."

"Two minutes."

"In two minutes that burger's going to be burnt. Get that order up."

"Goddamn it." But Reece rushed to get the order up.

There was a table in front of the fireplace in the cabin. On the table was a white cloth, on the cloth a blue vase filled with pink roses. There were candles and pretty dishes. Most astonishing, beside the table was a stand holding a silver bucket. In the bucket rested a bottle of champagne.

And when Lo picked up a remote and pressed play, Wynonna Judd sang a ballad, very softly.

"What is all this?" a confused Linda-gail asked.

"It's a Saturday night date." Eager now to play his part, Lo slipped off the shawl she wore around her shoulders. Laying it aside, he hurried around the room lighting candles. "I thought it would be a little darker, but that's okay."

"That's okay," she repeated, dazed. "Lo, it's just so pretty."

The mounted head of a bighorn sheep didn't detract. The lamp with a bear climbing a tree forming its pole only made it all sweeter somehow.

And though it was heading toward June and warm enough, Lo crouched in front of the fire to light kindling already laid.

"Does your ma know about this?"

"Sure. She doesn't rent this one out much since . . . you know that guy shot himself here." He stopped, winced. "That doesn't put you off, does it?"

"What? No. No."

"Good. Still, I had to ask her if we could use the place — and to fix up something I could just heat up for dinner. She wasn't too happy about it; in fact, she's a little pissed off at both of us. But I figure that'll change when we tell her the reason why."

"The reason why what?"

He rose from the hearth, turned and grinned at her. "Gonna get to that. Right now, what do you think about me opening that champagne?"

And my, didn't he look handsome? she thought. All that pretty sun-streaked hair, that nice, lean body all done up in a gray suit. "I think that'd be just fine."

She wandered over to the table, brushed her fingertips over the velvety petals of a rosebud. "You bought me pink rosebuds once before."

"For your sixteenth birthday. Been some time between deliveries, I guess."

"I guess. I guess we needed it. You set this all up?"

"Wasn't that much. The trick was to do it on the QT." He gave her a wink as he started on the champagne. "I wanted it special, and if you try to do anything special around here and it gets out, everybody knows. Had to go clean into Jackson for those roses. Figured if I had Mac order them in, he'd just have to know why and be speculating with everybody who came into the mercantile on it. One person I know in the Fist can keep a secret, it's Ma. So she's the only one who knows we're here. I nearly told her the rest, but . . ."

"The rest?"

When the cork popped, he let out a little whoop of delight. "Sounds good, doesn't it? Fancy."

"What rest?"

"She, ah . . . You got a few things back in the bedroom. In case you wanted to stay over."

"You went into my house, into my *things?*"

"No. Ma did. Don't get riled already. Here." He handed her a glass. "It's for just in case. Should we have a toast or something? How about to surprises, and lots of them?"

Her eyes were narrowed, but she tapped her glass to his. She wasn't going to miss out on having a glass of champagne. "This is all beautiful, Lo, that's the truth, and it's sweet as can be. But we have issues to deal with, you and me, and I'm not going to be distracted by flowers and champagne."

"Didn't figure you would, but maybe we could relax, have some dinner, then —"

"Lo, I need to know why you lied to me. I gave you till tonight, and I'll be honest first and say I really want to sit at that pretty table, drinking champagne and having you serve me dinner. I want to be here with you and think about how nice it is to have someone go to all this trouble for me. But I can't. Not till I know."

"I had this planned out different, but okay." In truth, he didn't think his nerves would stay in check all through dinner. "You have to come in the bedroom."

"I'm not going in that bedroom with you."

"I'm not going to try to get you naked. Christ's sake, Linda-gail, give me some credit, will you? Just come on in for a minute."

"This better be good," she grumbled, and set the champagne down before she walked to the bedroom door with him.

There were more candles he'd yet to light, and more flowers on the dresser. A single rose lay on the pillow. She'd never in her life been on the receiving end of anything so romantic. The center of her heart yearned so that she had to harden its rim to keep it from spilling right out at his feet.

"It's pretty and it's romantic. And it won't work, Lo."

"That's your special rose. You need to take your rose there. The one on the bed. Please," he said when she didn't move. "Do that one thing."

On a windy sigh, she crossed over, snatched up the rose. "There, are you . . ." As she turned, the ribbon tied to the stem swung, and what was looped through it banged gently into her forearm. It shot sparks and light.

"Oh my God."

"Now maybe you'll be quiet for a minute." Smug, he drew the ring off the ribbon. "I went out to buy this the evening I said I was working. I wanted to keep it to myself, that's all. I go telling any of the boys I'm hunting up an engagement ring, they're going to rib me about it until I have to punch somebody in the face. So I lied to you because I didn't want you to know what I was up to. I wanted to give it to you, to ask you when it was special. Like this."

Her heart was actually fluttering. This, she realized, was what they meant when they said it was like your heart grew wings. "You lied so you could go out and buy this?"

"That's right."

"And when I found out you lied, you wouldn't tell me."

"I didn't want us yelling at each other when I gave it to you. Before, after, that's fine, but not during."

"You did this, all this, for me."

"About time I got started. You like it? The ring?"

She hadn't really looked at it. The *idea* of it, of all of it, was so huge. But she looked now at the sparkle of the diamond in a gold band. As simple, she thought, as traditional as a plate of warm apple pie. And absolutely perfect.

"I like it. I love it, I do. But there's a problem."

"What? What now?"

She looked up, smiled. "You haven't asked me yet. Not officially."

"You're going to have to marry me, Linda-gail, and save me from wasting my life on wild women. You do that," he continued when she choked out a laugh, "I'll work hard to make you happy."

"I'll do that." She held out her hand for the ring, "and I'll make you happy right back."

The minute the ring was on her finger, she jumped into his arms. "This is the best Saturday night date in recorded history."

When his mouth met hers, she thought she heard a car on the road outside. But she was too busy to care.

★ ★ ★

Back in town, Reece flew down the street. She still wore her apron, and it flapped around her legs as she ran. People stopped strolling to stare at her or to scramble back before she could plow through them. She burst through the door of On the Trail.

"The necklace."

Debbie turned from showing a couple of customers a selection of backpacks. "Reece." Her gaze registered surprise, followed by faintly amused annoyance. "I'll be right with you."

"You have a necklace."

"Excuse me," Debbie said to the customers, "just one minute."

With her business smile in place, Debbie crossed over, took Reece's arm in a firm grip. "I'm busy here, Reece."

"A symbol of the sun on a gold chain."

"What the hell are you talking about?" Debbie demanded in a whisper.

"I'm crazy, remember. Indulge me or I'll probably make a scene. I saw you wearing that necklace."

"And so what?"

"A sun," Reece repeated. "It came from Delvechio's in Jackson."

"Very good, you win today's trivia contest. Now go away."

Instead, Reece turned into Debbie, all

but nose to nose. "Who gave it to you?"

"Rick did, of course. Last Christmas. What is *wrong* with you?"

"You're his sunlight," Reece murmured. "I heard him say that. That's the opposite of the dark side of the moon."

Debbie backed up a step. "You really are crazy. I want you out."

"Where is he? Where's the sheriff?"

"Let go of my arm."

"Where?"

"In Moose, he has a meeting tonight. But in about two seconds I'm calling the office and having Denny come down here and haul you out."

"Call whoever you want. Where was he the night we had the break-in at Brody's cabin?"

"What break-in?" Debbie said with a sneer. "Or do you mean the night you imagined, again, somebody was there?"

"Where was he, Debbie?"

"At home."

"I don't think so."

"I've lost about all patience with you. I'm telling you he was home, right out in his workshop. And he'd have more time to relax out there if it wasn't for people like you dragging him away on false alarms and stupidity. I had to go out there myself and get him when Hank called."

"Oh? No phone in the workshop?"

"He had the music on, and the saw . . ." Debbie drew herself up. "I've had about enough of this nonsense. I have customers, and I want to finish my work and get home to my kids for popcorn and movie night. Some of us have normal lives."

And some of us just believe we do, Reece thought. Sympathy welled up inside her. Debbie was going to have that belief shattered very soon. "I'm sorry. I'm really sorry."

"You will be," Debbie replied as Reece turned for the door.

Reece pulled her cell phone out of her pocket as she hurried back toward the diner. Then cursed when Brody's answering machine picked up on the fourth ring. "Damn it. Call me back, soon as you can. I'm going to try your cell."

But that, too, switched to voice mail.

Frustrated as she knew he could walk ten feet in any direction from his cabin and lose his service, she jammed the phone back in her pocket.

It was all right, she told herself. Rick was in Moose, and even if Debbie called him when she got home to complain about crazy Reece Gilmore, he couldn't be back for a couple hours. Probably more.

It would give her time to sort it all out in her head. So when she dumped it all on Brody, it would be with organized thinking.

That was best. It was going to be difficult enough to tell him his friend was a killer.

Brody spotted Lo's truck when he passed Joanie's cabin. Had Reece seen it in Jackson when they were there? He hated the fact that his first thought was that he knew the location of one of the suspects. All he could hope was in the next hour, he'd know who Reece had seen by the river. And it would be over for her.

He wanted it over for her.

He thought about buying her some tulips. Probably something he should do. Maybe take her away for a couple days until the bulk of the dust settled. She'd have to give statements, answer questions. Be the center of attention, at least for a while.

Rough on her, but she'd get through it.

And once she had, they'd have to get started on some pretty serious business of their own. He was buying that damn cabin from Joanie, and building on that new office, that deck.

And Reece Gilmore was staying put. With him.

He could bribe her with a set of those fancy pots. The Sitram.

These stay in my kitchen, Slim, and so do you. The idea of it made him smile. She'd appreciate that. She'd get that.

He turned onto the quiet, secluded drive, winding among the pines, and parked in front of the cabin.

Rick came out on the porch, his face sober, his eyes grave. He walked down the steps as Brody got out of the car. "Thanks for coming, Brody. Let's go on inside."

30

About the time Reece was trying Brody's cell, he was walking into the kitchen at the Mardson cabin.

"Got coffee fresh," Rick told him, and poured out a mug for Brody.

"Thanks. State cops aren't here yet?"

"On their way. Might as well go in and sit down."

"You said you didn't want to get into details over the phone."

"Complicated business. Touchy business." Rick stirred in the sugar and cream Brody took in his coffee, then rubbed the back of his neck. "I hardly know where to start, what to think."

He led the way to the living room, sat in the wingback chair as Brody settled on the rusty red-and-gray checks of the sofa. "I appreciate you coming out here like this, so we can keep this quiet for now."

"No problem. I should tell you that we're pretty confident we've identified the victim. Deena Black, out of Jackson."

Leaning forward in his chair, Rick narrowed his eyes. "How'd you come by that?"

"So," Brody murmured as he drank his

coffee, "we were right. We followed a tip, on the sketch, tracked her name down in Jackson."

"Lowering to have to admit a couple of civilians got there about the same time I did." Rick shook his head, laid his hands on his knees. "First off, I'm going to say I owe Reece a big apology. I never did believe her, not really. Not in the gut where it counts. Maybe I didn't follow through as much as I should have because I didn't. I've got to take the weight of that."

"But you believe her now."

Rick sat back. "I do. I did think she might've seen something when I got that wire alert on the Jane Doe. But she wouldn't identify her, and . . ."

"Was it Deena Black?"

"No, turns out it was a runaway from Tucson. They got the two men who picked her up, hitching for Christ's sake. Did that to her. That's something anyway."

"So, Reece was right about that, too."

"I'd say she was right about a lot of things. Took me out at the knees when the state boys got in touch with me. I talked to them about what Reece said she saw, Brody. I did that. Checked with Missing Persons. But . . . well, I didn't push through like I should have."

"And now?"

"Well . . ." Rick looked off. "Lot I should've done, could've done, would've done. I asked you to come out here and talk about this, Brody, because I felt you should know first. You stuck by Reece through this. A lot of us didn't."

"She knew what she saw." His vision blurred briefly.

"Yeah, she did." Rick rose, walked to the window. "Couldn't shake her off it. Damn shame."

"She ought to be here, too." Brody took another swallow of coffee to reach for the buzz. Fatigue was falling over him like a fog.

"She will be."

"Give me some details before . . ." Was that his voice, slurred like a drunk's? When the room spun, he tried to push to his feet. A quick spurt of knowledge had him stumbling toward Rick. "Son of a bitch."

"Nothing else I can do." When Brody fell, Rick looked down at him with sincere regret. "Not a damn thing I can do but this."

Reece called Brody's home phone and his cell half a dozen times each. It was getting dark now. She wanted to hear his voice, wanted to tell him what she knew.

She knew.

And knowing, she just couldn't slice

more baked chicken or make another mountain of mashed potatoes.

"I have to go, Joanie."

"This here's what we call the dinner rush. You're what we call the cook."

"I can't reach Brody. It's important."

"And I've had about enough of romance inconveniencing me."

"This isn't about romance." This time she took off her apron. "I'm sorry. I'm really sorry. I have to find him."

"This place doesn't have a revolving door. You go out it, you keep going."

"I have to." She bolted out with Joanie's curses racing behind her. The sun was already behind the peaks; the lake had gone gray with twilight.

She cursed herself because Brody's insistence she not drive herself to and from work alone now meant she had to hike to the cabin. She did the first mile at a steady jog, searching through the gloom for the light he should switch on at dusk.

He went out for some beer, she told herself. Or for a drive to clear his head. Or he was in the shower, or taking a walk.

He was fine, wherever he was. Just fine.

She was panicking over nothing.

But who did you call when you knew the top cop in town was a killer?

She'd call the state police, that's what she'd do. As soon as she'd talked to Brody.

Sunshine and the dark side of the moon. Rick Mardson had bought both those necklaces, one for his wife, one for his lover. He'd been the one having an affair with Deena Black, sneaking around, taking precautions so no one would see him with her.

And he killed her. It had to be.

He could have slipped in and out of the apartment over Joanie's easier than anyone else. Wasn't everyone used to seeing the sheriff strolling around town? He'd know how to get keys, get duplicates. Or to hide the fact that he'd broken in.

To cover his trail.

She slowed, catching her breath, struggling against another spurt of panic. Something plopped in the waters of the lake, rustled in the long grass beside it. And she ran again with her heart stumbling in her chest.

She had to get inside, lock the doors.

Find Brody.

Her breath snagged when she saw the shadows by the lake, then she forced back the scream when she saw the trio of elk taking their evening drink.

She veered away from them, raced by the willows, the cottonwoods and finally hit the hardpack of Brody's short drive.

His car wasn't parked beside hers. And the cabin was dark.

She fumbled out the key he'd given her,

then had to stand with her head pressed against the door. It was harder, so much harder, to enter the dark than to leave it behind.

"Six times one is six," she began, fighting the key into the lock. "Six times two is twelve." Stepped in, slapped her hand on the wall for the switch.

"Six times three is eighteen." Breathe in, breathe out. "Six times four is twenty-four."

She locked the door behind her, then leaned back against it until the worse weight of anxiety eased.

"Not here. But he'll be back in just a minute. Maybe he left a note. Except he never leaves notes. It's not his way. But maybe this time."

The kitchen first, she decided. She'd check the kitchen first. She turned on lights as she went, chasing the dark away. There were dregs of coffee in the pot, an open bag of pretzels on the counter.

She checked the pot; found it cold. She looked in the refrigerator, saw he had a supply of beer, of Cokes.

"So he went out for something else, that's all. And he's probably going to swing by and pick me up on the way back. I'm stupid. Just stupid."

She grabbed the kitchen phone to try his cell again.

And heard a car pull up.

"Oh God, thank God." After slamming down the phone, she ran out of the kitchen to the front door. "Brody." She yanked the door open, and there was his big, burly SUV. "Brody?" she called again, nearly moaned in frustration. "Where the hell did you go that fast? I need to talk to you."

At the sound behind her, she whirled in relief. She saw the blur of a fist, felt a burst of pain, then was back in the dark.

When she came to, her jaw ached like a bad tooth. On a moan, she tried to lift a hand to it and found her arms pinned behind her.

"Only tapped you," Rick said. "Didn't give me any pleasure to hit you. Quickest way, that's all."

She struggled, a mad moment of wild panic and denial.

"You're cuffed," he said calmly, and continued to look straight ahead as he drove. "Padded your wrists good. Shouldn't hurt, and it'll keep any marks off your skin, most likely. That'd be best. You'll have a bruise on your jaw there, but, well, there'd have been a struggle so that's all right."

"Where's Brody? Where are you taking me?"

"You wanted to talk to Brody. I'm taking you to Brody."

"Is he . . ."

"He's all right. I kept a supply of those sleeping pills of yours. Gave him enough of them to put him out for a couple hours. Maybe three. Plenty of time. He's a friend of mine, Reece. It didn't have to be this way."

"People think I'm crazy." Even knowing it was useless, she strained her wrists against the handcuffs. "But *you* have to be if you think you can just cuff me, kidnap me and drive me out of town this way."

"In Brody's car. In the dark. Anybody saw us go by, they'd see a couple of people in Brody's car. You and Brody. That's what they'd see, 'cause that's what they'd expect to. That's the way it'll work. I'm going to make this simple as I can, quick as I can. It's the best I can do."

"You killed Deena Black."

"Did what I had to, not what I wanted. Same as now." He looked over, met her eyes. "I tried other ways. Tried everything I knew. She wouldn't back off. Neither would you."

He trained his gaze straight ahead again, and made the turn toward his cabin. "I want you to be quiet, and to do what I tell you. You want to yell and scream and kick, you go ahead. It won't make any difference. But the more you do, the more I'll hurt Brody. Is that what you want?"

"No."

"Then you do what I say, and it'll be easier all around." He stopped the car, got out and came around for her. "I can hurt you, too, if I have to," he warned her. "It's your choice."

"I want to see Brody."

"All right then." Rick took her arm, quick-stepped her to the cabin.

He gave her a light shove inside before locking the door, turning on the light.

Brody was tied to a kitchen chair, his chin slumped on his chest. On a muffled cry, Reece stumbled toward him to fall on her knees beside the chair. "Brody. Oh God, Brody."

"He's not dead. A little drugged is all." Rick checked his watch. "Should be coming out of it soon enough. When he does, we're taking a hike, and we're getting this done."

"Done?" She shoved herself around, and hated that she was on her knees in front of him. "Do you think because you got away with killing once, you can kill both of us and no one will know? It won't work, not this time."

"Murder/suicide's what it'll be. That's how it's going to look. You talked him into driving out this way, hiking down to where you said you saw the killing. You drugged him. Got his thermos right over there." He nodded to the end table by the couch.

"Coffee in it's spiked with pills from one of your bottles. Bottle's going to be in your pocket when we find you."

"Why would I hurt Brody? Why would anyone believe I'd hurt Brody?"

"You snapped, that's what you did. You snapped, drugged him so he wouldn't see it coming. You shot him, then you shot yourself. You took the gun Joanie keeps in her desk drawer to do it. Your prints'll be on the gun, gunshot residue on your hand when it's done. That's the physical evidence, and your behavior gives it plausibility."

"That's bullshit. It's just bullshit. I've already called the state police and told them about Deena Black."

"No, you didn't. I'm going to take those cuffs off you. If you try to run, I'll hurt you. And I'll put a bullet in Brody where he sits. You want that?"

"No. I won't run. Do you think I'd just leave him?"

He rose, a patient, cautious man. Taking out his key, he uncuffed her. "You sit right there." He touched the gun in his holster as warning. "I don't want any trouble. And I don't want any bruises or signs on your wrists showing some M.E. you've been restrained. Rub the circulation back into them. Do it now."

Her arms ached like a fever, and trembled with it as she rubbed her wrists. "I said we called and reported to the state police."

"You'd've done that, Brody would've said so when he came out here. Told him I found out information on the killing from the state police myself. Asked him to come out here and meet me, and them, to get the details before we made an arrest."

Going to the table, he picked up the plastic cup of water and the pill he'd set out. "Want you to take this."

"No."

"It's one of yours, said it was for anxiety. Might help a little, and I want them to find drugs in your system. You're going to take it, Reece, or I'm going to force it down your throat."

She took the glass, the pill.

Satisfied, he sat, rested his hands on his knees. "We'll give that a few minutes to work for you, then we'll get started. I'm sorry it's come to this, that's the truth. Brody's been a friend of mine, and I've got nothing against you. But I've got to protect my family."

"Were you protecting them when you screwed Deena Black?"

His face tightened, but he nodded. "I made a mistake. A human mistake. I love my wife, my kids. Nothing's more important. But there are needs, that's all. Two,

701

three times a year I took care of those needs. None of it ever touched my family. I'd say I was a better husband, better daddy, better man for taking care of them."

He believed it, Reece realized. How many people deluded themselves into believing cheating was somehow honorable?

"You took care of them with Deena."

"One night. It was supposed to be just one night. What difference could it make to anyone but me? Just sex, that's all. Things a man needs but doesn't want his wife doing. One night out of so many others. But I couldn't stop. Something about her got into me. Like a sickness. I couldn't leave her alone, and for a while I thought, I guess I thought it was love. And that I could have them both."

"The dark and the light," Reece said.

"That's right." He smiled with terrible sadness. "I gave Deena all I could. She kept wanting more. The kind of more I couldn't give. She wanted me to leave Debbie, leave my kids behind. I was never going to do that, never going to lose my wife and kids. We had a fight, terrible fight, and I woke up. You could say I woke up from a long, dark dream. I broke it off then and there."

"But she wouldn't let it stay broken off." Wake up, Brody, she thought desperately.

Wake up and tell me what to do.

"She kept calling me. She wanted money, ten thousand or she'd tell my wife. I didn't have that kind of money, and I told her. She said I'd better find it if I wanted to keep my happy home. How you feeling? Calmer?"

"I saw you, by the river. I saw you kill her."

"I was just going to reason with her. I told her to come here. I used to bring her here, here to the cabin when I was in that long, dark dream. But when she came, I couldn't talk to her here, not here, not again. Maybe you should have two of those pills."

"You took her down to the river."

"Wanted to walk, that's all. Never planned it. We just walked, we kept walking until we came to the river. I told her maybe I could scrape together a couple thousand, stake her, if she left Wyoming. Even when I said it I knew it wouldn't work. Once you pay, you never stop. Said she wasn't settling for crumbs. Wanted the whole cake. I could take it out of the money we had for the kids. I don't know why I told her we've put by money for our kids, for their college. She wanted it. Not ten now, she said, but twenty-five. Twenty-five or I'd end up with nothing. No wife, no kids, no reputation.

"I called her a whore, because that's what she was, what she'd always been. And she came at me. And when I pushed her down and told her it was done, she came at me again, screaming.

"You saw how it was."

"Yes, I saw how it was."

"She was going to ruin me, she swore it. No matter what I paid now, she was taking it all. She was going to tell Debbie every dirty little thing we'd ever done together. I couldn't even hear her anymore. It was like wasps buzzing in my head. But she was on the ground, under me, and my hands were around her throat. I kept squeezing, squeezing, until the buzzing stopped."

"You didn't have any choice." Reece's voice was absolutely calm. "She pushed you to it. She attacked you, threatened you. You had to protect yourself, your family."

"I did. Yes, I did. She wasn't even real. She was only a dream."

"I understand. My God, she was literally holding a gun to your head. You haven't done anything wrong yet, Rick. You haven't hurt anyone who didn't deserve it, done anything that wasn't absolutely necessary. If I'd understood all this before, I'd have let it go."

"But you didn't let it go. No matter what I did. All I wanted was for you to leave town. Just go away and get on with your life so I could get on with mine."

"I know that now. I'm on your side now. You can just let me and Brody go, and this all disappears."

"I wish I could, Reece. That's the God's truth. But you can't change what is. You've just got to work with it, and protect what you have. Guess one of those pills was enough, after all. Now, I want you to move away from him. It's time I woke him up."

"If you do this, you don't deserve your wife and your children."

"Once it's done, they'll never have to know." He crossed to her, grabbed her by the back of the shirt and dragged her away from Brody.

As he turned back, Brody pumped his legs, rising up, chair and all. He swung his body hard into Rick's and sent them both sprawling.

"Run!" Brody shouted. "Run now."

She ran, terrified and blind with it, following the order as if a switch had been flicked inside her. Spitting out the pill she'd cheeked, she yanked open the front door. She heard the crash, the curses, the crack of wood as she flew outside.

And she ran with a scream shrieking in her head when she heard the gunshot.

"Did you hear that?" Linda-gail pushed up on her elbow in bed. "I heard a shot."

"I heard the angels sing."

She laughed and poked Lo in the side. "That, too. But I heard somebody shooting."

"Now who'd think you'd ever hear somebody shooting in the backwoods of Wyoming?" He pulled her back down, digging his hands into her ribs to make her laugh.

"No tickling or I'll . . . Did you hear *that?* Is that someone shouting?"

"I don't hear anything but my own heart begging yours for a little more sugar. Now come on, honey, let's —"

This time it was Lo who broke off at the crash outside the cabin. "Stay right here."

He leaped up and, buck naked, strode out of the bedroom.

When Reece burst in, he could only cross his hands over his privates and say, "Well, Jesus Christ!"

"He's got Brody. He's got Brody. He's going to kill him."

"What, what? What?"

"Help. You have to help."

"Reece?" Linda-gail fought to wrap a sheet around herself as she came out. "What in the world's going on?"

No time, Reece thought. Brody could already be bleeding, dying. As she'd been once. She spotted the rifle in a display case. "Is that loaded?"

"That's my granddaddy's Henry rifle.

Just a damn minute," Lo began, but Reece rushed to the case. She gave the lid a jerk, found it locked. She spun, grabbed the bear pole lamp and shattered the glass.

"Chrissake, chrissake, my ma's going to kill us both." Even as Lo made a dash for her, Reece yanked the rifle out, whirled around with it.

Lo stopped dead in his tracks. "Honey? You want to be careful where you point that thing."

"Call for help. Call the state police!"

Leaving them both gaping behind her, Reece streaked for the door.

Reece prayed Lo's reaction meant the rifle was loaded. That if it was, she could figure out how to work it. She prayed harder still that she wouldn't have to.

But it wasn't fear, that familiar burn in her throat; it wasn't panic, with its sharp, fluttering wings in her belly. It was rage she felt, the hot, bubbling gush of it pumping through her blood.

She wouldn't lie helpless this time, not this time, while someone she loved was taken from her. Not this time, not ever again.

She heard Rick shouting her name, and forced back the tears that wanted to blur her eyes. Brody hadn't stopped him.

So she stopped, closed her eyes and ordered herself to think. She couldn't go running back to the cabin. He'd hear her, see her. And he would end it. He might very well end up killing Lo and Linda-gail as well.

Circle around, she decided. She could do that. He'd think she was still running, or just hiding. He wouldn't expect her to come back to fight.

"No place for you to go, Reece," Rick shouted. "No place I can't find you. This is my land here, my world. I can track you as easy as I can walk down the street in the Fist. You want me to finish Brody here and now? Is that what you want? Want me to put a bullet in his head while you're hiding like you did back in Boston? Think you can live through that one again?"

In front of the cabin, Rick dragged a bleeding Brody to his knees. And pressed the gun to his temple. "Call her back here."

"No." Brody's heart squeezed as the barrel pressed hard against his temple. "Think about it, Rick. Is that what you'd do if it was your woman's life on the line? You killed to protect someone you love. Wouldn't you die for her?"

"You've known her a couple of months, and you want to tell me you'd die here for her?"

"It only takes a minute. When you know, you know. She's it for me. So pull the trigger if that's what you have to do. But it's ruined for you now. That's your service revolver you're holding, not Joanie's gun. How are you going to explain Reece shooting me with your service weapon?"

"Adjust. I'll adjust. I'll make it work. You call her back. Now."

"You hear me, Reece?" Brody shouted. "If you hear me you keep running."

When Rick kicked him down, he landed on the arm where a bullet was lodged. It screamed.

"I've got no choice," he said to Brody, but now his face was pale and ran with sweat. "I'm sorry."

He lifted the gun.

Struggling not to shake, Reece brought the rifle to her shoulder. She sucked in a breath, held it. And pulled the trigger.

It sounded like a bomb. It felt like one had exploded in her hands as the recoil slammed into her. She fell back, fell down. And because she landed flat on her back, the shot from Mardson's revolver flew over her head.

Still she scrambled up. When she did, she saw Brody and Rick struggling on the ground, the gun gripped in each of their hands.

"Stop it." She rushed forward. "Stop it. Stop it." Pressed the barrel of the rifle to Rick's head. "Stop it."

"Hold on, Slim," Brody panted out. He shifted to get a better grip on the gun. Rick rolled into Reece, knocking her down as he yanked it clear. As he turned it toward his own temple, Brody plowed his fist into Rick's face.

"It won't be that easy," he told him, and crawled over to retrieve the gun that had fallen out of Rick's hands. "Point that thing somewhere else," Brody told her.

She sat where she was a moment, the rifle still clutched in her hands. "I ran."

"Yeah, you did. Smart."

"But I didn't run away."

Because he was tired, hurt and queasy, Brody simply sat beside her. "No, you didn't run away."

Lo and Linda-gail, the first in only jeans, the other in a trailing sheet, rushed over. "What in the name of Christ is going on?" Lo demanded. "Jesus, Brody. Jesus! You shot?"

"Yeah." Brody pressed a hand to his arm, studied the palm that came away wet and red before he looked up at Reece. "Something else we've got in common now."

Between them, Rick lay as he was, and he covered his face with his hands and wept.

At dawn, Reece helped Brody out of the car. "You could've stayed in the hospital for the day. A couple of days."

"I could've spent a couple hours banging a bedpan over my head. I didn't relish either experience. Plus, did you see that nurse they sicced on me? She had a face like a bulldog. Scary."

"Then you're going to do what you're told. You can have the bed or the sofa."

"Where will you be?"

"In the kitchen. You're not having coffee."

"Slim, I may just be off coffee for life."

Her lips trembled, but she firmed them against a sob. "I'm making you some tea, and some soft scrambled eggs. Bed or couch?"

"I want to sit in the kitchen and watch you cook for me. It'll take my mind off my pain."

"You wouldn't have pain if you'd take the drugs."

"I think I'm off drugs for life, too. Felt like swimming through glue back there at Rick's cabin. I could hear the two of you talking, but couldn't compute the words, not at first. All I could do was play possum and hope for a chance to take him down."

"While you were tied to a chair and dopey with pills, he might've killed you."

"He might've killed both of us. Would have," Brody corrected, "but you didn't run like a rabbit when you had the chance." He let out a long breath when she eased him into a chair at the kitchen table. "Hell of a night. Reece?" he said when she kept her back turned and said nothing.

"At first," she began, "when I first ran out, that's all it was. Fight or flight, and boy, it was flight all the way. Run and hide. But . . . it changed. I don't even know when. And it became run and find something so you can fight. I guess I scared a couple of decades off Lo and Linda-gail."

"Something to tell their grandchildren about."

"Yeah." She put on water for tea, got out a skillet.

"You figured it out before I did. I'm the mystery writer but the cook figured it out first. I walked right into it."

He'd never forget, never, swimming through the drugs and hearing her voice. He'd never forget that marrow-deep terror. "My walking into it might've gotten you killed."

"No, he might have gotten me killed. You walked into it, Brody, because he was your friend."

"He was."

She got out the butter, sliced off a hunk for the skillet. "I don't know what'll happen to Debbie and those kids. How will they get through this? Nothing will ever be the same for them."

"Nothing was the way they thought it was before this. Better to know, isn't it?"

"Maybe. That's a thought for another day." She broke eggs, began to whisk them with a little fresh dill and pepper. "He really believed all he was saying. That he was protecting them, doing what he had to do. That Deena left him no choice. He thinks he's a good man."

"Part of him is. And part of him split off, took what he should never have touched. It cost him, Slim. It cost Deena Black."

"He killed her. Buried her body, covered his tracks, hid the motorcycle until he could use it to go back to her apartment and get her things — cover those tracks, too. He did all that, kept absolutely calm, even when we called him and reported what I saw happen."

"If he'd managed to scare you off, or make you doubt yourself, he'd have gotten away with it."

"If you hadn't believed me, that's probably what would have happened. I think, getting through this, it's pulled me back from an edge I kept sliding toward." She scooped his eggs onto a plate, set it in front of him. Then touched his face.

"I'd have gone over it without you, Brody. I'd have gone over it if he'd killed you. So" — she bent down, touched her lips to his — "thanks for staying alive. Eat your eggs."

She turned to finish making his tea.

"There was an edge for me, too. Do you get that?"

"Yes."

"One question. Why don't you push?"

"Push what?"

"Me. You're in love with me — do I still have that right?"

"You do."

"We've just been through a near-death experience together; you probably heard me say something about being ready to die for you. But you don't push."

"I don't want what I have to push out of you, so this is fine." She set his tea on the table, then frowned at the knock on the front door. "Already," she stated. "I imagine we're going to have a lot of visitors, a lot of questions, a lot of people wanting to know exactly what went on."

"No big deal. No, I need to get that," he said and grabbed her hand before she could turn from the table. "I'm expecting something."

"You're supposed to rest."

"I can walk to my own damn door. And drink that prissy tea yourself. I'll wash down the eggs with a Coke."

She shook her head as he walked out, but decided to indulge him. Taking down a glass, she filled it with ice, took out a Coke. After pouring it out, she picked up the tea he didn't want.

She paused with it halfway to her lips as he came back into the kitchen. Carrying a load of tulips in the cradle of his good arm.

"You never said what color, so I got all of them."

"Wow."

"Favorite flower, right?"

"It is. Where'd they come from?"

"I called Joanie. If you really need something, Joanie's your girl. You want them or not?"

"I certainly do." Her smile was luminous as she took them, as she buried her face in them. "They're so pretty and simple and sweet. Like a rainbow after a really bad storm."

"Hell of a storm, Slim. I'd say you deserve a rainbow."

"We both do." She lifted her head to grin at him. "So, are you asking me to go steady?"

When he said nothing, nothing at all, her heart began a slow, steady thud.

"I'm going to be buying the cabin," he told her.

"You are?"

"As soon as I talk Joanie into it. But I can be very persuasive. I'm going to add on to it some. Bigger office, deck. I see two chairs on that deck. I see tulips outside — spring, right?"

"They would be."

"You can cook at the diner, go into business and run your own kitchen. You can write cookbooks. Whatever suits you. But you're going to have to stay, and sooner or later, we're going to make it legal."

"Are we?"

"You love me or not?"

"Yes. Yes, I do."

"I love you right back. How about that?"

With two quick whooshes, her breath came in and out. "How about that?"

He curled a hand around the back of her neck, bringing her toward him, taking her lips with his as the tulips glowed between them. "I'm where I want to be. Are you?"

"Exactly where." Everything inside her settled when she tipped her head back, looked into his eyes. "Exactly where I want to be."

"So. Want to sit on the deck with me one of these days," he asked her, "look out at the lake, see the mountains swimming in it?"

"I really do, Brody." She pressed her cheek to his. "I really do."

"We're going to make that happen, you and me." Now he drew back. "For right now, why don't you do something about those flowers? Then get another fork. We ought to share these eggs."

So the morning bloomed bright with hints of summer that would stretch through to fall. And they sat at the kitchen table, a vase of rainbow tulips on the counter, eating scrambled eggs that had gone cold.

We hope you have enjoyed this Large Print book. Other Thorndike, Wheeler or Chivers Press Large Print books are available at your library or directly from the publishers.

For more information about current and upcoming titles, please call or write, without obligation, to:

Publisher
Thorndike Press
295 Kennedy Memorial Drive
Waterville, ME   04901
Tel. (800) 223-1244

Or visit our Web site at:
www.gale.com/thorndike
www.gale.com/wheeler

OR

Chivers Large Print
published by BBC Audiobooks Ltd
St James House, The Square
Lower Bristol Road
Bath BA2 3BH
England
Tel. +44(0) 800 136919
email: bbcaudiobooks@bbc.co.uk
www.bbcaudiobooks.co.uk

All our Large Print titles are designed for easy reading, and all our books are made to last.